ATOM BOMB BABY

BRANDON GILLESPIE

A Revenant Creative Studio Book <https://revenant.studio>

Hardback ISBN: 978-0-9987499-2-1
Paperback ISBN: 978-0-9987499-3-8
Ebook ISBN: 978-0-9987499-4-5

January 2026 (1.8.0)

Author
Brandon Gillespie

Development Editors
Casey Fenich, Christina Crosland

Line and Copy Editors
Amy Guan, Colin Murcray

Cover
Brandon Gillespie, Margaret Faro

Interior Art
Brandon Gillespie, Margaret Faro

Alpha and Beta Readers
Derrick Boudwin, Lindsey Duncan, Cidney Edgington.
And those from the online discussion forums: Bella, D&D Kittey,
Isa505, Lampofshadez, Malcontent, Mister 5x5, PyroFingers,
Scratchy, SteveJ, Tache, Vulpes-Inculta, Warthog-Rex, Xeongt.

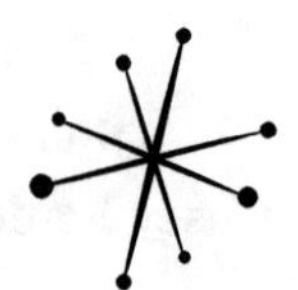

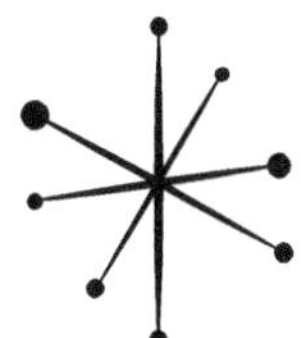

Riders of the Stars

There is another dimension beyond our own—a reflection of the familiar, subtly altered. A realm where the golden age of the atom takes center stage, and the stars themselves serve as the canvas for humanity's boldest dreams. Riders of the Stars recounts tales not of our earthly past, nor our future, but of a universe both recognizable and markedly different.

Unveiling a new setting entails a delicate balance in revealing just enough information without burdening the narrative with excess details. For those seeking deeper insights, explore the website: https://**Riders Of The Stars**.com

Furthermore, each chapter's heading corresponds to actual song titles, providing additional layers of connection to the events within, either through the song's lyrics, or simply the title itself— the appendix also includes more on these musical references.

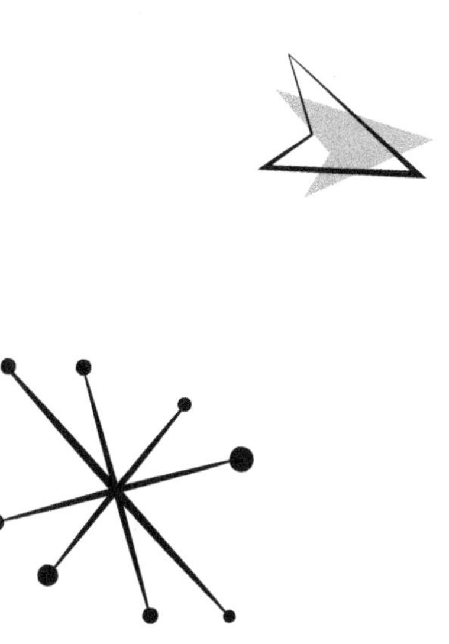

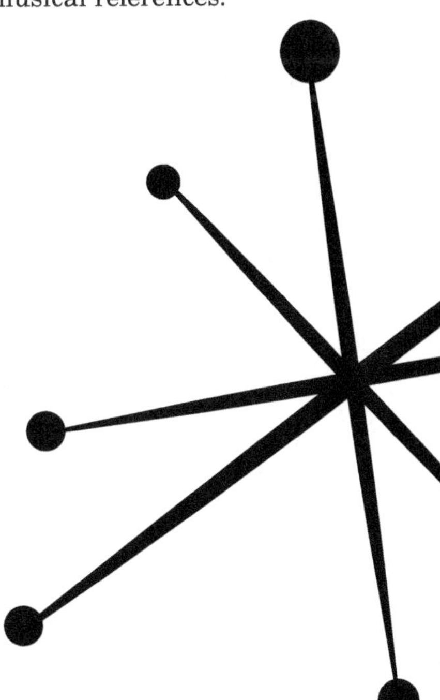

Pistol Packin' Mama

A she collapsed, gasping for breath, and rolled onto her back. A cold numbness seeped from the granite cliffside into her burning muscles. Above, tree branches quaked in an unseen breeze, a quiet counterpoint to the dread she felt after her mad dash through the forest. She had nowhere else to run.

Her gaze locked on the ringed moon Aetheron riding high in the sky, which stirred a melancholy ache. It was her favorite of Arcadia's two moons, and she had dreamed of journeying to it aboard a rocketship someday. But those dreams now lay shattered—with the fall of civilization, such hopes were out of reach.

Lying near the cliff's edge, Ashe exhaled. Her eyes closed, her fingers relaxing to release the rifle—her constant companion for so long—while confronting the thoughts that plagued her: *Should I give up? The world ended twenty-five years ago. Everyone left is walking dead; we just don't know it yet.*

Almost a year ago, Ashe and the residents of Fenclave, an underground shelter, were forced to leave their sanctuary. They scattered, with each family choosing a different path, scavenging through the ruins of the past.

It wasn't long before a void-terror found Ashe's family. The attack was swift, and afterward, she was left alone to navigate the perilous surface of Arcadia, engulfed in grief and remorse, with little choice but to persevere in the mutated, horror-infested wasteland.

Straining to hear any sign of pursuit, her lips traced a thin line as relief washed over her—the silence indicated a momentary reprieve.

A smoldering anger built in her chest as her attention turned back to her lost backpack, which held all she had left.

In her mission to locate the raider warlord known as "Warthog," Ashe had sought directions from a wandering band of raiders, and this ill-fated decision had quickly descended into a skirmish.

After a year immersed in the grim realities of humanity's descent, Ashe knew well that raiders had many sins woven into the fabric of their savage existence. When they suggested capturing her for "their amusement," she had instantly realized her mistake. While she'd moved quickly, so had they, and she lost her pack amidst the struggle to escape. Even then, she managed to break free, leading to a frantic sprint through the forest with her assailants in pursuit, where she stumbled into a horde of gaunt, zombified humans known as growlers.

Quick thinking and nimble footwork allowed her to slip through their midst untouched, leaving the raiders to grapple with the growlers—a plan that, to her relief, appeared to have succeeded.

With her pulse calming, Ashe confronted the true fear that had halted her flight, and it wasn't the raiders or even the growlers. Having spent her formative years in the underground shelter Fenclave—a place devoid of expansive vistas and towering summits—she loathed to admit it, but she had a fear of heights.

Groaning, she inched on her belly to the cliff's edge and peered down, squinting against the gusting wind that brought tears to her eyes. Through the trees, a cabin emerged midway down the slope, perched on a ledge overlooking the densely forested Fen. A fragile hope blossomed in Ashe—secluded meant potentially undiscovered supplies and safety. Not as safe as Fenclave, but it was something.

"Damn Commissioner," she growled, reflecting on her simple life in Fenclave. At least there, everything didn't try to eat you. Plus, it had regulated temperature, food at the ready, and the companionship of friends—a stark contrast to the harsh reality aboveground.

Feral screams echoed from the forest behind her, and she groaned, forcing herself to look down at the cabin again.

"It's not that far down, is it?" she muttered, her heart racing, being this close to the cliff's edge.

She didn't know what was worse: descending the treacherous and unnervingly exposed cliff face or confronting the horrifying growlers. Formerly human, the growlers had transformed due to the void storms, which were a side-effect of the Kraal's arrival and the ensuing nuclear cleansing. A fundamental question remained unanswered: were they alive or reanimated corpses? Ashe felt it didn't matter; they had become feral, mindless killers, and to her, that's all that mattered.

Regaining control of her breathing, Ashe sat up, deliberately averting her gaze from the cliffside. Her fingers threaded through sweaty, cropped red hair, each movement exuding quiet confidence. A glint of frustration smoldered in her steel-blue eyes as she considered the situation.

I could just let them devour me, I suppose.

But that would probably hurt.

With a sigh, she grabbed her gun and swiftly checked the chamber.

Out of ammo.

Pulling a string from around her neck, Ashe contemplated the bullet tied to its end. Even with the growler's wails coming closer, she took a moment to debate her options. This particular round, earmarked for the Commissioner who exiled everybody from Fenclave, might be able to help against the growlers, but was it enough?

A branch snapped in the distance, helping to make her decision.

Eyes closed, Ashe bolstered her courage before turning around and sliding backward on her belly over the cliff's edge. The wind howled, tugging at her clothes and whipping strands of hair across her face while she clung to the rock face with white knuckles. Her feet dangled freely over the abyss below, and her senses surged, heightening the resinous aroma of the evergreen trees and the musky scent of moss.

Worrying she might slip, she swung her legs until one foot finally found a toehold. Teeth clenched, her limbs trembled as she paused, struggling to control the terror that threatened to overcome her.

Knowing she had to press on, Ashe forced herself to envision the drop as only a few feet, even though it seemed like hundreds. She'd honed this skill over the last year—willfully reshaping her perception of reality. It allowed her to face challenges that might otherwise break her.

The growlers' calls intensified, and Ashe caught a glimpse of them running toward her through the trees.

Despite their imminent arrival, she concentrated on staying calm and moving with care as she tested each hand and foothold while inching her way down the sheer rock face—enough to evade the growlers before they arrived. Loose gravel cascaded around her as they shuffled at the cliff's edge, their faces twisted and charred.

One of them, a young man in a red baseball cap, noticed her descent and snarled through cracked lips, "Escape!" while futilely swiping at her in mindless frustration.

The rough surface scraped against her palms as she continued downward, and she muttered, "They won't follow me, right?"

Though time seemed to stretch endlessly as she continued, to her relief, the growlers didn't follow, and, despite lacking climbing gear, her descent went surprisingly well. Finally, her feet touched solid ground. She slumped against the rock wall, allowing her nerves to settle, and the oppressive bleakness that had gripped her earlier began to fade.

Once recovered and keeping to the shadows, Ashe cautiously approached the cabin she'd spotted from the ridge. As she drew near, the song "Atom Bomb Baby" crackled through the air from an old radio inside. Her brow tightened—so much for her hopes of finding an abandoned stash of supplies.

Her stomach growled, reminding her she'd missed lunch. Ashe clenched her jaw, hoping there was something edible inside— and that the cabin's owner either wasn't home or at least wasn't hostile.

She pulled a hood over her face and, with a subtle tap on her thigh, activated the chameleon effect of her body suit—a rare find from an abandoned AstroTec lab up north. Drawing upon every skill she had learned since leaving Fenclave, she crept closer while staying in the expanding shadows cast by the setting sun.

The log cabin, an A-frame with an upper floor, looked to be in decent shape. It sat secluded among the trees, nestled midway along a steep incline. A rusty old truck rested nearby, complete with the rounded, flaring fenders that were a signature of the pre-arrival world that was no more.

An automated turret chirped a warning, and Ashe froze, grumbling, "Of course they have robotic defenses." Her chameleon suit was great at hiding her from people, but not turrets with infrared sensors.

I am shadow incarnate, she reassured herself. *I have stealthy mojo. I've snuck past a whole squad of Wardens. Which, unfortunately, doesn't matter, thanks to the turret. I suppose I could just run for it...If I run fast, it can't get a lock on me...I think.*

It'll work, won't it?

Her stomach groaned again, and she mumbled, "Sorry, Miss Sneaky Pants. Looks like we'll be running for it today."

Ashe dashed toward the building at a calculated angle. The turret unleashed a staccato barrage, and bullets peppered the ground behind her, close enough that she could feel the sting of ricochet from their strikes. Putting on a desperate burst, she rounded the side of the building.

A second turret on the cabin's wall swiveled to face her.

Noticing a basement door left partially ajar, Ashe lunged through the opening while the turret traced her steps with a lethal spray of bullets.

"Too close," she muttered as the automated guns wound down.

Leaving the door cracked open for light, Ashe paused to let her eyes adjust to the gloomy basement.

Even with the soft whine of a tired old reactor running in the corner and the radio's scratchy melody above, she could still discern the buzzing drone of flies from upstairs. Nevertheless, she waited, listening intently for any alarm at her intrusion.

After a few tense heartbeats, the pervasive odor of decay convinced Ashe that nobody would object to her presence. Climbing the staircase to the main floor, she turned off the radio and traced the source of the stench—a deceased man in a bedroom, likely the victim of a vicious bout of void worms.

She winced at the macabre scene and mumbled, "Poor guy."

If she was going to stay, Ashe needed to address the body. But first, a swift search led her to a switch that disabled the turrets, and she made a mental note to reactivate them later.

Gagging at the malodor, she bundled the cabin's prior owner up in his old blanket, carefully avoiding the glowing, purplish worms crawling through his remains. Moving the fetid bundle out to the trees, she ensured it was far enough to deter predators or void-created terrors and returned to inspect the cabin.

Despite its run-down appearance, a panoramic window pane in the east wall remained unbroken, framing a captivating view overlooking the forested hills of the Fen. After a brief circuit of the cabin's rooms, she found herself pleased with the overall condition and started to consider the idea of making it her new pad.

Ashe took pride in her ability to unearth the most obscure items in pre-arrival ruins, and she eagerly dove into searching the place for food. But, to her dismay, all she could uncover were old clothes, dried toothpaste, and dusty books.

Undeterred, she started over, this time with more deliberate care, and her efforts paid off when she discovered a hidden stash of supplies concealed behind a bookshelf in the loft. A smug grin tugged at her lips as she pushed the shelf aside.

Her eyes lit up as she noticed a package of Frosted Sugar Bombs cereal, and she immediately snatched it up. Munching on her sugary treat while ferrying the rest of the supplies to the kitchen, she began a dialogue with herself.

"Is this a *cornucopia*? Oh, hey! Did you hear that Mister Emmet? I remembered vocabulary from your class. Fat lot of good that will do me now, thanks to you, Mrs. Commissioner."

Unearthing a box of ammunition in the back of the stash, she set everything else aside and reloaded her rifle, finishing by taking the Commissioner's bullet from the string around her neck and renewing her vow.

"There will come a time we meet, and I'll make everything right. It's your fault that Mom, Dad, and—" Her voice broke.

She paused, taking a slow, deep breath and willing the anger to pass. After a few moments, she turned back to her task. Repetitive actions like sorting the stash into organized piles helped bring her a sense of calm. Confident that the automated turrets would warn her of any danger, she lost herself in the focused rhythm of the work.

Ashe hadn't even realized how late it had become until she noticed deep shadows slowly enveloping the room. She flicked on her AstroCom's lamp and sought the cabin lights. A smile touched the corners of her lips as she recalled receiving the device on her eighth birthday.

Despite its weight and awkwardness, with three pieces wrapped around her wrist on a canvas strap, the device held immense value to her. Its capabilities ranged from helping her navigate the badlands to analyzing substances and all sorts of other things in between. Yet, her greatest joy came from the songs her parents had loaded into it. At the time, she had enjoyed sharing the tunes with her best friend, Talia, to the point where the constant music had prompted her parents to insist she use headphones to curb the noise.

Twisting the cable extending from the AstroCom to the headphones around her neck, a touch of melancholy settled in as she remembered her last birthday at Fenclave, and she counted the months, wondering, *When did I turn sixteen? It feels like a decade since we left, not a year.*

Ashe and her family were among the fortunate few who had lived in Fenclave, a nuclear fallout bunker established by the government before "the arrival." As medical doctors, her parents had gained early entry to set things up. Then the Kraal came, followed by "the cleansing," after which it was too late for anyone else.

At least, that's what she was told.

Ever since their expulsion, she had begun questioning the Commissioner's story.

Thinking of her birthday brought to mind her father declaring Ashe as his favorite daughter, and she smiled. "Admittedly, Dad, I'm your only daughter."

Despite this positive note, her mind invariably circled back to the Commissioner—an unhealthy obsession she just couldn't shake.

We could have stayed there. She didn't have to send everybody out to clean up the world. I don't think anything was wrong with the water system either. Everything was fine.

Ashe sighed in frustration as her thoughts spiraled, reminding herself that she now had this amazing cabin to make her own. Locating the light switch, she flicked it on, illuminating the open common area thanks to the ever-running domestic reactor in the basement.

A growing sense of satisfaction accompanied her survey of the room. Deciding a pick-me-up might help, she donned her headphones and dialed into the AstroCom's entertainment library. With "Pistol Packin' Mama" playing, she started inventorying the rest of the cabin and couldn't help but bob along to the tune.

"That's right, Miss Sneaky Pants, the dulcet tones of some dead guy can put a hop in your step long after civilization has ended. Besides, I am a pistol-packin' mama. Well, an Arbiter combat rifle-packin' mama, but that's a mouthful."

Caught up in the moment, Ashe strutted in time with the music while she began an internal dramatized monologue about her survival skills—notably her sneaky mojo, a point of pride for her.

A sudden, thunderous clap reverberated through the hills, shaking the floor and rattling the furniture. The unexpected clamor startled Ashe, and she might have let out a yelp in surprise if anyone had been there to witness her uncool reaction. With adrenaline rushing through her stealthy veins, she silenced the music and lurched toward the Arbiter.

Unfortunately, her stealthy mojo didn't prevent her from tripping over a wire stretched across the room, and the lights went out.

"Fuuuuu—!" she bit back a curse, resisting the urge to let it loose despite the pain shooting through her bruised knee, and reflexively glanced around. Even a year later, her mother's shadow kept her in check. Her mom had often praised her cultured demeanor, straight posture, and high-society voice, but those accolades were from a different time.

After the pain subsided, Ashe growled in a sulky voice, "I know, Mom!"

Feeling around in the darkness for her rifle, she located the Arbiter in a brief flash of violet lightning. Creeping to the door, she cautiously eased it open and peered through the gap.

The impending void storm cast everything in a surreal, purple-tinted gloom, causing her pulse to quicken—growlers were more active during a void storm. These other-worldly tempests had emerged after the Union of Stars military nuked all the worlds in their fight against the extra-cosmic Kraal invaders.

Now, all that remained of the military were the Wardens, and Ashe always tried to give them a wide berth. They had very dogmatic thinking—notably, that superior force was necessary to maintain civil order, and they still defended their use of nukes twenty-five years before, despite the devastating effects on all the planets.

The storms were the icing on the Wardens' cake. They came without warning and left behind ruined creatures: desiccated, voracious shadows of people, like the growlers, and void-mutated aberrations, such as the Deathmarks.

Even the thought of the Deathmarks sent a spike of terror through Ashe. The thought of those unspeakable horrors haunted the edges of her mind, teasing at raw memories etched with pain from the day she lost her family.

Clenching her teeth for focus, she peered through the Arbiter's scope, sweeping the nearby terrain as she mentally ran through how to fortify the cabin before the storm hit. The front door had a bar she could drop in place; all the windows had shutters she could lock down. And the turrets—

Her thoughts lurched to a stop, her gut clenched, and a sinking uneasiness crawled up her spine.

Amidst her efforts to organize and catalog the cabin, she had forgotten to reactivate the turrets, let alone close the basement door.

The reactor's whine cut out, plunging the cabin into dark silence, interrupted only by a rumble from the approaching void storm.

"We're coming," came a hiss from below and her pulse spiked —the growlers were inside.

The instinctual, primal side of her howled demands to run, but she knew heading outside in a void storm was a death sentence.

The stair creaked, and she flung the front door wide open, sparing a glance for the coming storm before pivoting around to face growlers shambling up from the shadows of the basement.

With a pull of the trigger, bullets sprayed in an angry chatter. Many shots missed, but enough landed, dropping the first two growlers at the top of the stairs. More followed. Through clenched teeth, she snarled, "How many of you are there?!"

One of them, wearing a tattered business suit, lurched over the two writhing on the floor and darted toward her while hissing through withered lips, "Run!"

The single word sent a chill down her spine. Growlers often unleashed random exclamations while attacking—unnerving cries that often came as eerie warnings. She'd learned to ignore them, yet occasionally, a haunting realization resurfaced: Some believed that the remnants of the person the growler had once been still lingered within, and their disjointed utterances served as desperate warnings to those they preyed upon—a feeble attempt to communicate in a state where they had no control over their actions.

Her next trigger stroke sent a burst of bullets across the growler's chest to his shoulder, knocking him down, but more emerged from below, and she backed out the door, resigning herself to the void storm.

It's either death by a growler now or turning into a growler later. I'll take the latter for ten points, thank you.

Ashe turned and leaped from the steps to the ground in a single motion, knowing the growlers followed. On the horizon, an ominous wall of churning clouds rolled toward her, lit from within by an extra-cosmic purple radiance and occasional flickers of energy. She knew not to study it too closely because if she did, inexplicable things beyond rational comprehension would begin to manifest, such as tentacles and unblinking eyes.

Two shapes appeared before her, illuminated by a flash of violet lightning and accompanied by the ominous clicking from the Geiger counter in her AstroCom.

Instinctively, she raised the Arbiter and pulled the trigger, her mind trailing behind her muscle memory as she slowly realized these two didn't resemble withered growlers. At the last moment, she shifted her aim, even as bullets sprayed. One of them cried out in pain, and the other barked, "Don't shoot!"

Distrust warred within her as the pursuing growlers' shrieked warnings. The larger man darted past like a flickering shadow in the gloom while the other fired a pistol at the growlers.

She turned, holding her Arbiter at the ready.

The taller man faced three growlers, slashing with a fierce, bladed gauntlet. Two more approached, and she sighted in on one, hesitated, then fired but missed—fear of hitting him threw off her aim.

Taking a deep breath, she fired again, landing a shot in the growler's chest. It shuddered and collapsed to the ground.

She and the two strangers dispatched the remaining growlers and paused, scanning the area for new dangers before their gazes fixed on each other. Meeting strangers in the badlands was often dangerous, a fact Ashe had once again learned earlier that day.

Extra-cosmic violet lightning flashed, and the wind picked up.

The taller, darker man wore a top hat, his features obscured in the gloom. Behind him, the other held his shoulder with care, which sparked a twinge of guilt in Ashe as she realized she had, indeed, landed an errant shot.

The moment passed in a single heartbeat, and, wired with adrenaline, Ashe darted to the cabin, reaching the porch before the wounded one called, "Don't run! We're friendly! We come in peace!"

She paused and lowered her voice as best she could to be more intimidating. "Then you can go in peace, too! Or come closer and be in pieces! Now make like a tree and leave!"

The void storm flickered overhead, and the Geiger counter clicked again, this time matching the patter of rain.

The wounded man took a few steps toward the cabin. "My friend, Rainwood, said we should find shelter. Then, would you believe it, we saw your cabin!"

She growled, "If you come any closer, I shoot!"

"Well…that wouldn't be very nice."

He continued to approach, closing the gap.

Ashe backed into the cabin, keeping her Arbiter trained on him. "I've killed hundreds," she declared confidently, racking a new round, hoping he could hear it.

The ejected bullet rolled away.

He took a few more steps, keeping his hands high.

Even in the gloom of the coming void storm, she noted his features and realized he was near her age. He gave her a gentle smile. His dark, wavy hair curled around to frame his eyes just right. And the way he stood with a little shrug of his shoulders. A rogue part of her—the part that still seemed to think she was back at a safer time in Fenclave—had an irresponsible thought: *He is kinda cute.*

Ashe hollered in frustration at herself as much as at him. "Stop coming closer!"

With measured steps, he had already made it to the stairs, his presence encroaching on her comfort zone, leaving her uneasy. Ashe didn't want to be near people and had spent months avoiding human contact.

Despite this desire, she had made the mistake of befriending the folks in Mosstown, followed by a boast that she could resolve their problem with the raider leader, Warthog. One moment of weakness, and look where that had led her.

Furrowing her brow, Ashe gave him that dead look she figured scary killers had while reassuring herself, *I can be intimidating. I look like a raider. He has to see my raider attire and war paint.*

Yet, he didn't seem to notice as he mounted the first step of the porch.

Just behind him, the tall man arrived, his features dark as the night. Ashe snapped the gun to the new target. He spoke in a low, husky voice, "Go on inside, son. She ain't gonna shoot us."

A boiling fury welled up in Ashe, and she racked the chamber again, hoping it would intimidate him.

With frightening efficiency, he caught the ejected bullet mid-air and walked past her, his eyes darting around the interior. His scarred face showed stories of hard-fought survival, and his white-peppered hair indicated somebody predating the arrival of the Kraal twenty-five years ago.

Considering the imminent storm, Ashe suppressed a dramatic sigh and declared, "Fine, come in. But stay over there, where I can keep an eye on both of you."

Crazy He Calls Me

Backing into the cabin, Ashe lowered her rifle yet still held it ready. The tall, dark man walked in and scanned a flashlight across the remains of the growlers near the stairs. He briefly met her gaze and then effortlessly hoisted the first one in a rescue hold, carrying it outside.

The other guy bounced into the cabin, sporting a broad smile, and declared, "Awesome sauce!" He wore a ragged AstroTec jacket over a tattered purple shirt adorned with the AstroTec logo.

Pushing dark, wet, curly locks of hair out of his almond-shaped eyes, he introduced himself, "So that gloomy fellow is Rainwood, and I'm Moonbeam. What's your name?"

"...Ashe," she answered hesitantly.

Internally, she couldn't help but think of her real name, Ashley. But no, that girl was left behind in Fenclave. Only a burned-out husk wandered the badlands—the ashes of who she once was.

She knew they wouldn't even recognize the dark irony.

Rainwood returned, sent a glance their way, and added, "Boy, check the basement. Looks like they came in from below." Moonbeam raised his arm to give Rainwood a thumbs up but winced and grabbed his shoulder.

She sighed and asked, "How bad is it?"

"I reckon it's fine," he answered, "but it does smart some. And I can feel it bleeding."

Thunder rumbled, and the storm crashed down with unrestrained fury.

Switching on the AstroCom's lamp, Ashe gestured with her Arbiter towards a vinyl-padded kitchen chair, directing, "Take your jacket off. Let me see."

As Moonbeam settled into the seat, Rainwood growled and strode down the stairs, muttering, "Someone should check the blasted basement door."

Blood had soaked down Moonbeam's arm, and she reluctantly set her Arbiter on the white-and-cyan mica table, complete with aluminum trim. Helping him was the least she could do, considering she shot him.

The wire across the cabin floor shook as Rainwood tugged on it from below. Soon after, the reactor emitted a familiar whine, and the lights flickered on. Ashe made a beeline to the switch and reengaged the turrets, feeling relieved when she heard the chirps declaring their active status.

Moonbeam rolled his shirt sleeve up, exposing his bicep. Ashe hesitated, contending with hormones and internal emotions that, by her reckoning, were entirely inappropriate given the state of the world outside. Even then, she couldn't deny that he seemed well fit.

Pinching her lips, Ashe assumed the professional demeanor she'd witnessed countless times from her parents in their roles as medical professionals and probed at the wound before commenting, "You're lucky. Just a graze. Doesn't even need stitches."

Locating bandages, Ashe cleaned and wrapped Moonbeam's wound while Rainwood cleared the growlers, tossing them from the porch—they would have to move them again after the storm cleared. He then shook the rain from his trench coat before hanging it on a hook and working his way around the cabin, closing the steel shutters on all the windows.

Ashe retrieved her Arbiter, pointing it at the couch on the far wood-paneled wall, "Sit there. I suppose you two can stay. At least till the storm is over."

Smiling innocently, Moonbeam stood up and opened his arms to embrace her in a friendly hug while he said, "Thank you, Ashe!"

Her first instinct was to punch him in the throat and run, but she managed to keep her fists in check. She still backed away quickly, which caused him to stop with confused surprise.

Rainwood interjected, "Boy, you have no sense in that head."

Moonbeam seemed disappointed, then shrugged, scanned the room, and began buzzing around with the enthusiasm of a child fueled by too many Pop-a-Colas, touching and prodding at everything in sight. Each action set Ashe's nerves on edge. The audacity of his casual comfort within her newfound sanctuary stoked the flames of frustration within her. This was her new pad. How dare he, in such a nonchalant manner, invade the sacred space she had already claimed as her own, even if only a few hours before?

He picked up a box of mashed potato flakes, which she had sorted alphabetically with other food items on the countertop, and declared, "Wow, this is a great place you have. Nice and dry, too."

Ashe stared at the water dripping from the ceiling, then took the box away from him and put it back in its proper place between the cans of imitation crab and pork-n-beans.

Trying not to grind her teeth, something deep inside her began to dislike him. *No, he doesn't have a nice smile—it's infuriating. How could anybody be so happy in this destroyed world? We are all living corpses, just walking out the last of our lives.*

Accept it.

She watched drops from the leaky roof hit his head, and sarcasm lined her response. "You must be kidding."

He froze and looked at her with wide eyes. "I am? Gee, I didn't realize I was kidding. Oh, hey, you have a Pop-a-Cola bottle collection!" He wandered to the corner to look at the display shelf.

Rainwood unbuckled his fierce-looking bladed gauntlet and set it on a side table. She'd heard about people who fought with these, preferring to engage in close-quarters combat. From what she knew, the twelve-inch blades along the top of the gauntlet were keenly effective if wielded properly—but it took some finesse to learn how to use them well.

The old man then eased himself into a reclining lounge chair with a suppressed groan—not the couch she had pointed at.

Ashe ground her teeth, suppressing a rising tide of frustration as the situation spiraled out of control. Threads of anxiety wove through her, and she grappled with their tightening grip.

Moonbeam stared at the guns Ashe had sorted on the floor by size and stopping power—gifts from the prior owner. "You know, it's bad for these to be on the ground. You should have them on a rack. On the wall, maybe." He glanced around the room as if expecting a gun rack to appear on the wall.

What's the deal with this guy? Ashe wondered, then forced herself to calm down, wrestling to rein in her emotions while taking a deep breath. *No. I can be civilized. Cultured, even. Not everybody is out to get me.*

With that thought, her shoulders sagged, and the will to fight drained away. She adjusted her grip on the Arbiter and asked Rainwood, "How did you know I wouldn't shoot you?"

He grumbled like an ancient bear, "You may dress like a raider, kid, but a raider would've plugged us before we could even say hello. And why bother cocking a gun twice? That was just for show."

"Well, maybe I *will* shoot you next time. One can't be too careful in the badlands, you know?"

He nodded, a tiny smile teasing at the corner of his mouth as he responded, "True."

An awkward silence filled the room. Ashe wasn't sure how to have a casual conversation anymore—a year spent evading people had eroded her social skills. She was great at conversing with herself, but that wasn't the same. Those internal dialogues were typically stimulating and agreeable...except when not, and then things just got ugly. It's not like she could banish herself to the couch in anger.

Chewing on a fingernail, Ashe debated whether she could trust the two men or if she should insist they leave. The prospect of staying awake all night in worry lingered in the back of her mind. Rolling thunder shook the foundations, reminding her she couldn't simply put them out. Her hopes of having the cabin as her own began to sink, and she fretted that if they stuck around, she couldn't claim it as her pad. She was a solo wanderer, not a team member—best that way for all involved.

While her thoughts continued bouncing back and forth, Moonbeam wandered downstairs, upstairs, and through all the rooms. His footsteps occasionally echoed through the cabin during lulls in the storm as he whistled a tune to himself.

Unsure what to do, Ashe nervously started packing food into a backpack she'd found in the loft, glad to have something to keep herself busy so she didn't have to talk. As a contingency plan, she always liked having a bag with critical supplies ready.

A few minutes later, Moonbeam returned, still sporting that smile, and broke the silence with a question. "While you two were conversating, did Rainwood mention we're hunting treasure? And we're lost!"

Rainwood's lips made a flat line. "Would you quit saying that!"

"Oh...right, yeah, sorry Daegom—we're not lost. But we are hunting treasure," Moonbeam said, retrieving a loosely bound book from his backpack and holding it up like it explained everything.

Rainwood grimaced, speaking slowly for emphasis, "Stop telling folks we're hunting treasure."

Moonbeam cocked his head. "But we *are* hunting treasure? We aren't lost now. We're here at Ashe's cool digs. We even have a treasure map. But it talks about places we can't find. We just arrived a few weeks ago and don't know anything about this planet!"

"You aren't from Arcadia?" she asked.

Moonbeam grinned and started explaining with excitement, "Nope! Rainwood got us a ride on a freighter that used a Star Ranger's jumpship. I'm from the planet Miratori—not that it's much different from Arcadia, from what I can tell. It also has void storms, and everybody is trying to survive—and the freighter dropped us off at some big empty spaceport back east, by a ruined city called Saratoga, I think—and we walked through a bunch of badlands until we came to the Fen, but we can't figure anything out here—"

"Boy, I've told you, and told you, you need to stop sharing so much," interrupted Rainwood. "All you need to say is, 'We're not from around here.'"

Moonbeam raised an eyebrow. "But people like to know about each other! If you say that, they just ask, 'Where are you from?' I'm simply skipping to the good parts!"

Rainwood gasped with exasperation, "It's not about them! It's about keeping your own hide safe. Truth be told, I don't know how you've managed to survive this long."

Ashe had become distracted by their comfortable banter. Something about them made her feel safe in a way she hadn't felt for some time, which scared her. She knew she should stay on edge. But they had given her no reason for alarm. The opposite, if anything.

A flicker of interest grew within her as she realized they probably didn't know about the horrors of the Commissioner. The Fenclave residents' banishment was common knowledge in the area, and Ashe had done her best to further elaborate on the mistakes of the Commissioner whenever the opportunity presented itself. Yet, the prevailing response from the locals remained dismissive—they usually felt she was lucky to have had even a few years in the enclave instead of on the harsh surface.

Despite wanting to avoid people, Ashe yearned to vent about the hard times created by the Commissioner. While her thoughts tumbled about, the desire to tell them overcame her, and she abruptly blurted, "The Fen is dangerous!"

They looked at her with baited curiosity, and Moonbeam opened his mouth to respond, but Ashe needed to get it out and dove in, "I don't know how it is elsewhere, but here we have lots of horrible creatures, like growlers, skulks, star vines, and even things much worse, like Deathmarks. We all had to leave Fenclave, which made no sense because it was perfectly safe. You should leave, and not just the Fen, try to find another rocketship off-world —"

Rainwood listened patiently, a smile teasing at his lips until he cut her off mid-sentence with a question. "If it's as awful as you say, why haven't you packed up and left?"

She froze, not wanting to voice her hope that she could sneak back into the safety of Fenclave. That she could fix things, and everything would get back to how it was. Even though she knew that would never happen.

"Well...some of us are here trying to, uhh, to make it safe again," she said awkwardly, feeling a twinge of guilt. While she had witnessed fellow Fenclave survivors striving to make life better—encouraging people to create towns and trying to make communal farms, in truth, she wasn't part of that effort.

Rainwood glanced at the shuttered windows. As if on queue, a flash of violet lightning from the void storm illuminated his features, followed by a curdling wave of extra-cosmic unease that often came from the void storms. He lifted an eyebrow and stated flatly, "Safe."

The bleakness of his statement hit her like a splash of cold water. Her motivation spiraled downward like it did when she pondered why she bothered trying to survive alone in such a destroyed world.

The Kraal changed everything. Nobody knew why they had arrived, but they had appeared across the galaxy from another dimension out of time and space and fed upon the essence of living creatures—most notably being attracted to large gatherings of people. Within months, they had killed 98% of the interstellar population. Between that and the Wardens' "cleansing," everything collapsed, leaving those few survivors to pick over the ruins of their lost civilization—an intergalactic wasteland, with communication and interplanetary travel controlled by only a handful of power groups, like the Wardens and Star Rangers.

While hopelessness teased at Ashe, she resumed stuffing things into the backpack, telling herself, *These two are walking dead, just like me. Really, is any world safe? Even if I could take a rocketship, where would I go? Another blasted world?*

Moonbeam stood in the middle of the room, fidgeting from foot to foot while considering Ashe's shifting demeanor.

After a moment, her thoughts settled, and she returned to what he'd mentioned—a treasure map. She'd heard of others looking for treasure, vaults, and archives—troves of ancient technology, food, and supplies—but she'd never heard of anybody having a map.

With focused intent, Ashe stuffed another can of food into her new pack and then shifted her gaze to the book Moonbeam still held. Its pages were loosely bound, with notes protruding from the sides.

Placing hands on her hips, she said, "Okay, fine. Tell me more. Where did you get a treasure map?"

Rainwood pinned her with an icy stare, and she realized what a cold-hearted killer's gaze actually looked like. Ashe suddenly wished she hadn't asked the question, and a desire to reconsider many of her life choices came over her.

It was that good of a stare.

Of course, she tried to remember every part of it, tucking it away for future reference.

Moonbeam sent a sideways glance at Rainwood, and Ashe could detect a thread of trepidation and confusion in his voice. "It… isn't a treasure map?" Then, after a moment of determined thought, he confidently clarified, "It isn't a treasure map. It's a map that guides us to a place of…hidden things which have great value."

Rainwood put his head in his hands with a deep sigh.

Moonbeam casually leaned against a cabinet, looking very smug. He opened the book, explaining, "It's supposed to lead to the greatest treasure there ever was. But the Fen…it's different. All the trees are tangled up, roads are washed out, and the land has moved. But, now—"

He paused, deep in thought, while scrutinizing the book, unaware that he held it upside down. After a moment, he nodded with a clever surety. "We are currently…unable to find our way."

"So…you're lost," Ashe clarified, wondering at his clumsy symphony of self-assuredness.

"Yes!" He answered confidently, then, noticing the book was upside down, quickly turned it around, his aplomb only increasing.

Ashe resisted the urge to smile or laugh, which demanded some effort. She needed to stay on topic. It seemed as if the guy was deliberately trying to divert her anger, which, upon reflection, only fueled her frustration.

With her emotions properly realigned, she glanced at Rainwood, trying to find the right words to articulate the profound bleakness that had enveloped her world. "This place is terrible. Is Miratori really as bad as this? I don't know about elsewhere, but here in the Fen, things will kill you in an instant, and there are also the Star vines, which did a number on things, from what I can tell—"

Then, Ashe's pride took the reins, and her tongue, which had already landed her in trouble by boasting that she could take care of Warthog, continued. "Although, for somebody like me who's walked every corner, it's not a big deal."

Moonbeam grinned, a mischievous glint shining in his eyes as he asked, "Well, if you're such a cool cat, you know how to get around the Fen, right?"

A sense of dread struck her as she realized she, once again, had let her mouth run too much.

3.

Straighten Up and Fly Right

The rocketship's hull blazed with fiery intensity as it reentered the atmosphere nose up. The engines thundered to life, altering the vessel's trajectory and slowing its descent as it pierced the clouds. Closing in on a landing pad etched into the mountain's summit, it hovered briefly in billowing dust and smoke before the engines cut out, leaving the craft standing upright.

Two robots rolled boarding stairs toward the hull, and with a hiss, the hatch opened, revealing a man in a military flight suit. Straightening his hat, he surveyed the pad. Aside from several HWG-125 "Hog" transport aircraft lined up on the west side, a control tower looming on the edge, and the two maintenance robots, the pad was deserted.

Blast doors at the tower's base slid open, and a soldier emerged briskly, calling out, "Captain! You weren't supposed to return until tomorrow!"

Descending the boarding stairs, the Captain replied, "The slipstream drive is acting up, and Engine-3 was running hot. Have the service bots look it over. How is the hunt? Our benefactor's patience is running out."

The soldier fidgeted, nervously adjusting his glasses. "We're still searching, sir. No sign of JDE-82, but a local warlord claims to have found him. We have somebody investigating."

The Captain growled, passing the soldier without comment as he headed to the tower doors.

☣   ☢   ☣

Ashe woke to the glorious aroma of rendered fat and fried eggs, causing her mouth to water in anticipation. Rainwood worked at the wood-fired stove, frying something up. Bright sunlight filtered through the windows, revealing a clear sky after the night's void storm.

Even though Rainwood and Moonbeam seemed trustworthy, staying the night with two strangers still left Ashe feeling uncomfortable. It wasn't just because of the void storm hammering outside with enough noises and howls to make one's imagination go wild—she also didn't want to leave them alone with her new supplies.

So, instead, she'd kept her Arbiter at her side on a couch in the main room, where she could keep an eye on everyone. This wasn't the first time she'd slept with her rifle, but as she'd learned previously, it wasn't a great bedtime companion. That and the bone-rattling void storm made for a restless night—but what else could she do?

She pulled the blankets tight, relishing the pocket of soft, fuzzy warmth they created while wondering where Rainwood had gone in the early morning. He had slipped out while it was still dark, rousing her briefly, though she had resumed a restless sleep until his return hours later, and the sizzle of breakfast preparations woke her again.

It was hard to want to leave her nest of warmth, so she chose to remain curled on the couch. After some pestering from Moonbeam last night, she had relented, agreeing to help them out, but only as long as it was convenient for her. And with the condition that they help get her gear back from the raiders. Yet, the entire situation remained outside her comfort zone, and she considered changing her mind.

Rainwood, noticing Ashe stir, glanced her way before returning his attention to the food and adding in a quiet voice, "I scouted the raider's camp. Right where you figured. Are you still set on locating that backpack? They have themselves a decent-sized compound, and I spotted some mech repair frames."

She bristled at the thought of him backing out and growled, "Are you scared of a few raiders? Do you really think you're up for this? And did you actually lay eyes on anybody suited up in Mechanized Armor, or did you just see the maintenance frames for said armor?"

He ignored her response and pulled the pan from the stove, bringing it to the table. Ashe watched with hungry interest.

Moonbeam continued his light snoring from the lounge chair —apparently, he was a deep sleeper. Ashe pondered Moonbeam's AstroTec gear, curious about his origins. His shirt and jacket were similar to the uniforms everyone wore in Fenclave. The colors indicated your job and were always branded by AstroTec since they were the primary corporation behind building Fenclave. But Ashe had ditched all her Fenclave gear as soon as possible.

Yet his choice of clothing made her curious. He wasn't from Fenclave, of course, but was he from an enclave on Miratori? He certainly did have a lot of AstroTec-branded items.

Rainwood sat at the table, extracted a fork from his pocket, and polished it on a dishtowel before diving into the food. Between bites, he glanced her way. "Take my help or leave it, but cut out the nonsense. I simply asked if there's enough value in it to be worth retrieving. It's on you to decide."

She considered the mementos of her parents she had in the pack before answering, "Some things just don't have a price tag, you know? Like things from people I've lost."

He nodded, "I see. Very well."

Moonbeam suddenly lurched upright from his sleep while emitting a yelp. Then he froze and scanned the room with a slightly confused look. Observing Ashe, he paused while staring at her with a curious expression before approaching with his hand outstretched like they'd never met before. "Hi, I'm Moonbeam!"

Ashe scrunched herself deeper into the blankets, shooting him a puzzled look.

Rainwood growled and emphasized her name as he responded, "Boy, quit pestering *Ashe* and come eat."

Moonbeam tilted his head and studied her for a minute, then with a smile and a thumbs up, he declared, "Hey, Ashe!" before wandering over to the kitchen, where he started poking through the drawers, mumbling, "A fork, a fork, my kingdom for a fork!"

Ashe shook her head in bewilderment and muttered her Dad's favorite phrase under her breath, "Somewhere, there's a village missing its idiot."

Rainwood ignored her comment and offered. "Seeing as there's two entrances to the raider's compound, and you've mentioned your 'smooth prowess' slipping into a Warden's camp, perhaps the straightforward approach is best. We'll keep 'em occupied on one side while you slip in the other and fetch your pack."

"Gee, why didn't I think of that." Ashe let sarcasm salt her words.

Rainwood raised an eyebrow but said nothing.

She sighed, then continued, "I was hoping for more, you know? A clever plan, like the mythical Trojan horse, but maybe as a crate of food instead of a wooden horse. Then, after they took it into the middle of their camp, it'd release sleeping gas. We could just stroll in wearing gas masks and take what we want. But, you seem to prefer a frontal assault."

Locating a fork, Moonbeam turned to give Ashe a thumbs up. "Gas masks are tight. Let's do that!"

Rainwood asked, "Do you possess a timed or remote-controlled sleeping gas dispersal system?"

"Well, no."

"And even supposing you did, how are you aiming to deal with those suited in Mechanized Armor, with air filters?"

"So...that's a negatory on the gas masks?" Moonbeam asked, looking like a sad puppy while poking at the eggs in the skillet with his fork, then mumbling, "Plate," and standing again.

Making the tough decision, Ashe finally climbed from her blanket nest—which was difficult because they had finally accepted her as one of their own. Stepping over to the table, she picked up a handful of eggs with her bare hands before answering. "Hey, no need to get bent. I was just saying there's probably a better plan than 'I yell at them in front while you pick their back pocket.' No worries, though—I'm sure it'll be just fine."

Rainwood held out his fork, but Ashe waved it away, smirking to herself. *Silverware is optional when surviving on your own in the Fen badlands.*

Ignoring her display, Rainwood returned to the topic. "In my book, simplicity tends to be the best for success. Stick to the plan, and you'll manage just fine. The south end of the compound struck me as the most accessible, as I noticed a few gaps here and there in the outer wall. We'll draw their attention at the north gate, providing you an opportunity to slip in undetected."

She pondered and shrugged her shoulders, unable to think of anything better. "Very well. Any thoughts on the timing of this bold venture?"

"Now, if you can manage. Chances are they're sleeping in late. Raiders aren't exactly known for their discipline."

Excited at having help getting her stuff back—even if she had to do most of the work—Ashe declared, "Let's go for it!" before stuffing the last of the eggs into her mouth and stepping into a side room to get ready.

There, she checked over her chameleon body suit, a daily ritual fueled by concern over potential malfunctions—not that she even knew how it worked, especially with clothes over it, but it had saved her life a few times.

Satisfied the chameleon suit showed no wear and tear, Ashe dressed in the rugged Western attire she had discovered in the cabin—a functional and flattering ensemble consisting of jeans, a blouse, and a cowhide vest. To complete her preparations, she strapped on extra ammunition for her Arbiter and discreetly tucked away the commissioner's bullet hanging around her neck.

Upon her return, Ashe found Moonbeam still at the table, staring at the empty skillet while holding a fork in one hand and a plate in the other. He looked at her and asked, "Do we have more eggs?"

She grinned, tossing him a package from the food supplies. "Have an Atomic Cake. They never go bad!"

Reaching the door, Ashe paused and looked back. Her eyes scanned the comfortably worn interior and she hoped nobody would discover the cabin. With a final, lingering look, she turned and stepped outside.

The journey to the raiders' camp was uneventful. Rainwood had found an obscured road down the steep incline, after which they followed the hillside into a lightly forested area with rolling hills, mostly covered with evergreen pines and maple trees that had thus far avoided the encroaching Star Vines.

Ashe worked her way around the compound and crouched by a bush with a clear view of a potential access point in the outer barricade. She rankled at the delay and again checked the time on her AstroCom, wondering when the guys' signal would appear.

Moonbeam and Rainwood had old-fashioned watches, so Ashe had asked them to synchronize with her AstroCom. She preferred Solar Time, which changed daily so that 7:00 a.m. was always sunrise, no matter where you were on the planet. Spacers used this timekeeping method when on-world because their ships were always on universal time, regardless of the planet they orbited. A part of her still yearned to go to space, even knowing all of the other worlds were as desolate as Arcadia.

Exhaling a sigh, Ashe internally lamented the tedium.

Waiting is a drag. When will Moonbeam light his fireworks?

Her thoughts wandered, and she remembered her friend Talia from Fenclave before all the horrible things had happened. Talia could make any boring moment entertaining. With a vivid imagination, she tended to see everything as part of an action flick, even if only in her mind.

But no! That was then. I need to stay away from people now. They can't be near me, or—or—

Growling quietly, Ashe brought herself back to the moment. At the top of the barricade wall stood a disheveled raider woman, looking incredibly bored. A grim smile played on Ashe's lips as she sighted her rifle, focusing first on the sentry and then scanning around to consider her options.

Like most structures in the badlands, the compound was a mismatched assembly of salvaged materials, including the hull of an old rocket and what looked like an airship's observation deck on an upper floor.

Should I just go in? I can take her out now.

When did I become such a callous killer?

I won't kill her—just hit her in the shoulder, put her out of commission. Did Moonbeam forget to light the signal? Or perhaps the fireworks are duds?

Ashe's pulse throbbed in her forehead, and a thought struck her. *What if the raiders already split up my stuff? I can replace most of it...But the tape of my parents, I want that. And Mom's journals. Oh, and I need Kelly's bandana—it's all I have left of him.*

She swallowed a lump in her throat, reminding herself that Kelly was just a dog. After a deep breath, she realized something else bothered her, and it wasn't how long it was taking the guys or even if the raiders had split up her gear. It was the size of the compound.

If this really is Warthog's place, I wonder if I overpromised to all those folks at Mosstown. It's a big operation; I can't just sneak in and take out the leader like I had planned.

Calls of alarm interrupted her thoughts. Raiders shouted and ran about, then a firework hissed up through the trees, exploding overhead.

Finally!

The sentry remained vigilant.

Ashe pulled the trigger, having overcome any guilt about shooting raiders after her previous encounter with them. The shot hit the sentry's shoulder, spinning her before she dropped out of sight.

Taking a moment to quickly reload, Ashe bolted forward, glad to see Rainwood was right—much like everything else in the compound, the outer wall was a hodgepodge of assorted materials, including logs, corrugated steel, and old tires, offering plenty of openings. She sucked in her chest, squeezing through a gap.

The sentry groaned on the ground, writhing in pain, but Ashe ignored her and scanned for threats. Several ramshackle buildings sprawled up the hill. The larger structure on the lower side seemed more important, but she didn't know where to look.

The girl moaned at her feet, holding her bleeding shoulder, and Ashe poked her with a foot.

"I'll give you a Medipak if you tell me where you keep stolen gear."

The girl spat, laughing, "You think you can just waltz in here? You're already dead!"

Ashe didn't have time for a lengthy interrogation. She pulled the hood of her chameleon suit over her head and left the sentry, moving down the path to the lower structure. After carefully easing a door open, she stepped into a darkened interior, closed the door, and then froze. The chameleon suit made her invisible, but only when moving slowly.

The room was small and broad, perhaps ten by twenty feet. The only light filtered in through a door slightly ajar across from where she'd entered, leaving everything else in gloomy darkness. A table held a scattering of vacuum tubes, electronic parts, and an empty Pop-a-Cola bottle shaped like a rocket ship—no sign of her backpack.

She quickly crossed the room and peered through the opening. A bridge spanned to another building with corrugated tin sides. Most raiders ran to the other side of the compound, which was good. But the sprawl of buildings gave her a knot of worry; she didn't have time to search each one.

Just as she moved to leave, a faint child's whisper came from across the room, "Can–Can–Can you help me?"

Ashe glanced at her translucent arm to be sure the chameleon effect still worked, then looked around, wondering where the voice came from.

"Here," the voice whispered. Ashe finally noticed a small boy sitting in a cage, his brilliant green eyes fixed on her.

He must have heard me—He can't see me, right? I can just move on. He probably has family here and did something to get in trouble. It's like a raider timeout—

"I–I don't have a family. I need–I need–" he struggled with the words but finished with, "These are bad people."

Yeah, she thought, *well, I need to get my stuff and get out of here quickly!*

"I know where your stuff is. I can–can–I can show you. If you help–help me."

How does he know what I—? This is weird.

A surge in staccato gunfire across the compound urged her to move on. She focused on her needs, hardened her thoughts, and started across the bridge.

I don't have time for this, and the last thing I need is some kid adding to my problems. He'll have to figure things out on his own.

She had made it about halfway across when the thought struck her: *What if he really doesn't have a family?*

Ashe remembered how it felt being alone in the badlands after her parents died.

But...I can't keep anybody safe, she reminded herself with a twinge of pain before growling, "This is stupid," and returning to the room while reiterating to herself, *He can help me find my stuff. That's why I'm letting him out.*

"You came back!" the boy exclaimed, standing.

She pulled her hood off and whispered, "Where are the keys?"

He shrugged. "Warthog has them. He doesn't let any–any–anybody have them."

Biting back a curse, she knelt by the padlock on the cage and pulled out her lock picks.

Padlocks are easy, and this only has two tumblers.

Yet, it felt like an eternity passed while she worked through each tumbler, and her hands shook with adrenaline, making it even harder.

The lock popped open, and she took the boy's hand. "Come on, show me where my pack is!"

With a nod, he pulled her to the bridge. They crouched to avoid notice in case any raiders were nearby, but from the cries and gunfire, it seemed they had all rallied to fight on the other side.

The boy pointed at a reinforced door leading into a cave on the hillside. Somebody had painted "Warthog's Enclave" on a board over the door.

She sighed, figuring getting cornered in the cave would be madness. She needed to scout the camp better, perhaps try a diplomatic approach first. And if she was honest with herself, she now wondered if the quest to help Mosstown was really worth the effort.

Yet, if her gear was there…

"Are you certain that's where they took it?"

He nodded with wide eyes. Ashe considered how much she wanted her stuff back.

The gunfire slowed on the other side of the camp.

A shout came from around the corner of the path, "Hold them down. I need more ammo!" followed by the heavy machine tread of somebody arriving wearing a suit of Mechanized Armor.

She pulled her Arbiter and aimed at the edge of the shack where she expected the raider to appear, and the moment he rounded the corner, she stroked the trigger. The rifle kicked into her shoulder, barely making a puta-puta-put noise as it unleashed three bullets in suppressed rapid-fire.

Two ricocheted off his armored shoulder, but the third made it through, and he howled, reflexively bringing his minigun up and raising the alarm, "They're back here too!"

He pulled on the trigger, and they both could hear the impotent whine of an empty minigun.

She only had a moment to study his mech. They were powered suits of armor, enhancing a person's strength and adding layers of protection. But this mech was cobbled together from different models—including armored pieces that looked like they were from the first generation MA-15 Ogre, along with the later

MA-27 Griffin plus randomly welded bits of steel. Most importantly, this guy's mech was incomplete and didn't have a helmet.

Ashe stroked her Arbiter's trigger a second time—focusing on his exposed head.

Each bullet struck true—between his eyes. It was like shooting a watermelon, and he stumbled back, falling with a loud crunch.

A second firework hissed and crackled in the air overhead.

Ashe hissed in frustration. "That's the warning. Time to go!"

Her gaze lingered on the cave door while she clenched her fists, then growled, "You're on your own," before spinning around, retracing her path and slipping through the barricade. The boy scrambled behind her, doing his best to keep up. Shouts from the compound continued as they ran through the brush and up the flinty hillside.

Ashe didn't look back; she wanted distance from the camp before stopping.

Eventually, she slowed, catching her breath, and turned to face the boy who had managed to stay on her tail. With a glance around to be sure nobody followed, she leaned down, putting her hands on her knees.

"Alright, I got you out. Now you're free. Go wherever you please."

I don't want attachments, she told herself. *I'm a loner. And he…I just can't do it. But can I leave him alone? He's so tiny, probably not more than five years old. It's a liability.*

"I'm six," he said with a scowl, "and I wanna stay with you."

"I'm afraid not," she answered, wrinkling her brow at his unprompted statement.

"Why?"

"Well, you see, I go to dangerous places." The lie sat poorly with her—everywhere was dangerous.

He fixed his gaze on her, and she marveled at how the light pulled emerald highlights from his eyes, making them almost mesmerizing. His chin quivered, and tears welled up as he sniffled, "I don't have–I don't have–I don't have anybody."

Is he pulling puppy eyes on me? But...damn, it's working. I can't leave him out here alone.

Although the forest seemed quiet, she was anxious to move on and stood up.

"Fine, you little ankle-biter. But only until we sort out where your family is...or find a more fitting place for you to stay."

He smiled and held his arms out for her to carry him.

This sent a stab of fear through her, and she wanted to growl at him. Why did he think she'd carry him? She wasn't somebody who could take care of kids. But, her frustration came to a shuddering halt as she realized he wore no shoes. A trail of blood-red spots, clearly visible on the flinty stone, highlighted his path. He had run through the forest barefoot, ignoring sharp rocks and sticks that had lacerated his feet, all without complaint. And he was still able to keep up with her.

She sighed, let him climb on her back, and then started for the cabin.

"So, what do they call you?"

"Jade," he mumbled, sounding tired.

"Where are your parents?"

"Don' have any." His reply was almost unintelligible.

"That's silly. Everybody's got parents. Where are you from?"

He didn't answer, and she felt his grip relax. She shifted his weight so he wouldn't slip and glanced over her shoulder.

He'd fallen asleep.

She sighed, fighting the fear welling in her chest as she considered taking care of him, yet reluctantly admitted it had felt good to help him escape.

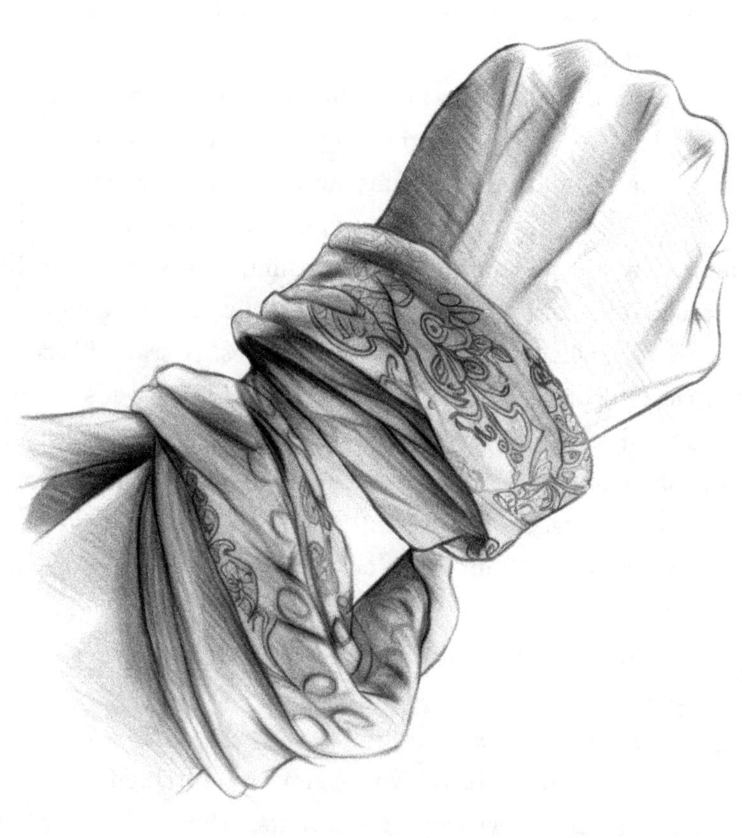

4.

It's All Over But the Crying

The return hike took longer than expected as Ashe strove to let Jade stay asleep on her back. Once she approached the cabin, she realized he had drooled on her shoulder.

The other two had returned before her. Rainwood stood on the porch, chewing on some jerky. As she walked past him, he lifted an eyebrow. "I thought you were aiming to fetch your gear."

Ashe bristled. "What's it to you?"

Once inside, she slid Jade onto the couch and pulled a blanket over him. He didn't even stir in his sleep.

Moonbeam tilted his head to the side and stared at the new arrival. After a moment, he asked, "You had a kid in your pack? Is he yours?"

She rolled her eyes. "Why in the world would he be in my backpack, and seriously, do I look old enough to have a six-year-old?"

The turrets chirped to attention as Rainwood flipped a switch and joined everybody. "Is he family?"

She shook her head. "Nope, he's a total stranger, never seen him before."

Rainwood asked, "Why'd you come back with him? Where is your gear?"

Meanwhile, Moonbeam retrieved a box of Frosted Sugar Bombs, pulled out a handful, and piled them on the couch in front of Jade before speculating with wide eyes. "Maybe he's a spy working for the Democratic Worlds Alliance communists."

Ashe snorted. "A six-year-old spy? Seriously?" She was tired and wanted to throw her hands in the air but resisted. "And isn't the DWA dead, just like the UOS? Either way, he sounded like someone from this world. He was locked up in a cage and asked for help, so I helped. Clearly, he's starved and worn out. Does anything else truly matter?"

She sank into a chair at the table, mumbling aloud, "I don't like this. It's another blasted mouth to take care of. I'd rather just worry about myself. I couldn't even keep my—" her voice caught. "Keep my–my dog safe," she ended in a strangled whisper, then stopped and buried her head in her arms.

Maybe they'll all just leave.

Moonbeam stepped next to her, wrapping his arm around her shoulders and giving a brief, gentle hug—for once, saying nothing.

She took a ragged breath. His embrace somehow made it feel like it was okay to let go of her emotions, and soon, hot tears rolled down her cheeks. She struggled to keep quiet, holding the sobs back but silently heaving.

I don't want these feelings. What does it matter if I lost my parents and my dog. What good does it do thinking about them now?

"What was your dog's name?" Moonbeam asked quietly.

" . . . Kelly"

"Was he fun?"

She smiled after a pause, although he couldn't see it as her head was buried in her arms. "We used to hang out in the enclave's central plaza. My parents always worried the Commissioner would blow a fuse. Said it wasn't proper for us—I mean, for me—to play there."

A comfortable fog began to settle over her memories, and she quickly stuffed them back into the dark corner where they belonged. *That is the past, and thinking about it is too hard.*

But what about her gear? She forced herself to be pragmatic and admit most of it could be replaced. But there were things she wanted back. Perhaps there was still a chance.

If they don't recognize me from our earlier visit, I could talk my way into getting it back . . .

Yet the whole situation suddenly seemed very complicated. She wiped her eyes and stood, angry at herself for letting things get out of control, and pushed Moonbeam's arm away, "Where's that treasure map of yours? Don't you need a hand finding something?"

Without waiting for a response, she stood and sifted through their bags to find the book, barely noticing Moonbeam as he reached out to give her another comforting hug only to be restrained by Rainwood, who answered, "We could use your help, I suppose, if it suits you."

Finding the book, she flipped through its pages. "There's no map here, just a bunch of writing. Is this someone's journal, or what?"

Moonbeam nodded. "Yeah, and it tells us where to go. Like a map, but with words!"

"Good grief, that's not a map!" She shook the journal at him, feeling a little betrayed. "There isn't even a treasure, is there?"

He responded with confusion. "There isn't a treasure? But it says it's where the greatest treasure of all is at!"

Rainwood shook his head. "I told him this is a fool's quest, yet here we are."

"Tell me, where did you pick this up?" she asked, holding up the journal.

Moonbeam took it while he explained, "Rainwood had it—he said it's from an old, dead friend. He didn't even realize it was a treasure map until I pointed it out."

Rainwood huffed.

Flipping through the pages, Moonbeam stopped and pointed. "See, it says here we just need to find Dayton's cabin."

"Seriously? Some square named Dayton had a cabin?! Have you flipped your lid? That narrows it down to just about *everywhere!*"

He ignored her response, adding, "Well, he does say it's by the pond springs, south of the Highway 95 interchange. And he said with all the void storm problems, he kept getting overrun by skulks, so he started to make a new house up in the trees. But the author left before they finished."

Ashe nodded. "Alright, I do know of a few tree houses in the Fen. Anything else?"

Moonbeam flipped through more pages, "Oh, he says Dayton scavenged a radio from a crashed rocketship at one of the ponds. Maybe it's still there?"

Ashe remembered a pond in that area with a crashed rocketship, and her curiosity rose again. "You may be in luck. I might know where that is, and I think I saw a treehouse nearby. But it's dangerous that way, with many frightening creatures. I've been a few times, but I try to avoid it. Most people do."

Moonbeam ignored her warning and gave a thumbs up. "Far out! I knew you could help us!"

"You know it'll take a solid week of walking to get there. And when I last checked, nobody was calling it home. This Dayton person is long gone." She paused, unsure if she should keep going, then decided to just go for it and gestured to the cabin. "Truth is, I stumbled on this place not long before you two. The former owner won't be coming back, so I'm thinking about making it my pad. But if I'm away for a few weeks, somebody else might stake a claim."

Rainwood nodded, "I'm aware of the risk. Could you give us directions, and we'll be on our way? We're good for some repairs today and will leave tomorrow."

She tried to keep her face clear of emotions, but inside her thoughts tumbled.

This is exactly what I want, right? To be left alone. So, why do I feel upset with how quickly he decided to just leave me?

After a moment, she replied, "Yeah, that could work. And I'd appreciate the help."

They searched the cabin and found tools in the basement, then started fixing what they could, such as broken shingles from fallen tree branches.

Jade woke and watched, saying nothing and eventually moving to a couch that looked out the broad picture window. But first, he did eat the pile of Frosted Sugar Bombs left by Moonbeam. Ashe also gave him a strip of fox jerky, then decided to leave him alone for the time being, figuring there would be plenty of time later to work out what to do with him.

As evening approached, they rustled up a meal. Ashe found some tubers in an overgrown garden outside the cabin to pair with the grilled skulk the guys offered. While she hated the creatures when alive, she did like how they tasted when properly cooked—do it wrong, however, and they turned very rubbery.

While Rainwood and Ashe prepared dinner, Moonbeam and Jade sat chatting—although Jade mostly just listened with wide eyes.

Ashe stifled a touch of ire. *Of course Moonbeam would get along with Jade.*

She carried the soup pot to the table, and all but Jade took a chair. He stayed on the couch, watching with uncertainty. Ashe pointed to an empty seat. "Hey there, want to join us?"

He nodded and slowly approached the table like a frightened dog. As everybody dug into their meal, he picked at his before diving in with a voracious appetite.

Ashe smiled. *I knew he was bone skinny after carrying him for miles. I wonder what they fed him, if at all.*

Finally deciding to prod, Ashe asked, "Jade, why did they have you locked up?"

He froze.

While waiting for a response, Ashe wondered. *Did they hold him hostage, trying to get ransom from somebody? Were they going to sell him? Or was he just in trouble, and it was his penance to be locked up?*

"I was in trouble. Or, they wanted to get ransom—" he stopped, scrunched up his brow, then continued eating.

Rainwood shook his head, a pleasant smile of approval breaking his usually stony countenance. "This world needs more folks like you, Ashe, willing to lend a hand to others."

She railed internally. *I don't want to help! How did this happen? I want to be alone.*

Moonbeam flashed one of his smiles. "After we find the treasure, we'll come back and visit, okay?"

She resigned herself to the situation and stood, wandering around to rustle up some paper and a pencil. Jade's gaze followed her around the room, which she found a little unsettling.

Perhaps I can find his family and go back to being a solo wanderer. I know he said he has nobody, but surely someone must be looking for him.

Pushing aside her bowl, she spread the paper on the table and started drawing a map, explaining what to avoid and which landmarks to watch for. "Just northeast of us down the hill is the old town of Ebley—you can even see it from the patio. But stay away, it's taken over by a variety of dangerous squatters and other void-tainted things. Cut across the Fen until you reach Highway 95. Just follow it north and then take a sharp bend to the west by the Hemlock Picnic area. If you reach the Rocket Ace truck stop, you've gone too far. Turn around. From there, you'll go into the forest to the east. I think I saw the rocketship here." She drew a circle on the map. "You should find Dale's cabin nearby."

"Dayton's cabin," Moonbeam clarified.

She ground her teeth, looking forward to the solitude of tomorrow while deciding it was good she was staying behind. If Moonbeam stuck around, she might end up punching him in the throat.

☣   ☢   ☣

The staccato rattle of the gun turrets lighting up startled Ashe awake. Adrenalized, she rolled from the warmth of the bed in the loft, grabbing her Arbiter on the way down, and then froze, looking for danger. Over the chatter of the turrets, she heard movement outside, and an unknown voice cursed.

It was still dark out, but they had visitors.

She crept over to Moonbeam on the top of a bunk bed and shook him awake. Then she turned to Jade on the bottom bunk. He rubbed his eyes, already awake, and Ashe whispered, "Get up, quick!"

Ashe was glad she decided to sleep in the new leathers she'd adjusted the night before, as she didn't have time to change into anything else now. She'd found a cache of cultist gear in the closet —the cult of the Kraal had taken over the area several years before.

While she didn't care for most of the garb she found, which was largely robes, she did find a pair of pants made from straps of supple leather and denim, with symbols and designs embossed upon the leather—stuff she didn't understand. Most importantly, the pants featured lots of pockets and places to attach supplies. She felt that, combined with her reliable flight jacket, the overall outfit made her look rather fierce, even without raider shoulder pads.

She had decided to sleep in the pants after she'd finished them, mainly to see how well they'd do for regular wear since she'd end up needing to sleep in them on the road at some point.

A rifle shot echoed, silencing the turrets, each in turn, making it clear they were under attack. Rainwood, already up and ready, carefully peered out the window on the main floor. "Looks like about a dozen or so raiders, maybe more. They've got the place surrounded, and they brought hounds."

Ashe speculated, "You think they followed us from Warthog's camp?"

From outside, a man hollered, "We have you surrounded. Just give us the boy, and we'll be on our way."

Ashe snorted, knowing the raiders had no intention of letting anybody go free.

Moonbeam crouched under a window, pistol in hand, and shouted, "Yeah, okay! He's tying his shoes, though."

Ashe hoped he wasn't serious.

After a moment the speaker responded, sounding a little confused, "Well, hurry it up. We don't have all day."

After supper yesterday, the first thing Ashe had done was find a pair of shoes for Jade, digging through the clothes for various ages that were throughout the cabinets. His old rags had gone outside over the cliff as quickly as possible.

Fortunately, she had put some of his newfound clothes in her pack last night.

Glancing out the back porch, she saw more people on the downward slope—there was no easy escape. Rainwood and Moonbeam joined her in the middle of the central room.

In his low, gravelly voice, Rainwood observed, "Looks like they've got somebody holding a lit flame thrower."

Ashe scowled and moved to a window at the front, carefully glancing out.

Where were the Star Rangers or even the Wardens when you needed them? Always there when you don't want them around, and never there when you need their help.

With a mental sigh, she resigned herself to letting the cabin go—it seemed the quest for a safe pad would continue.

If we get out of this alive, that is. She shook her head dejectedly and declared, "We're surrounded on all sides. I don't know how we can escape without a dangerous fight."

Moonbeam suggested, "Maybe we can sneak out through the mine in the basement?"

"What mine?" Rainwood and Ashe asked in unison.

He shrugged. "I don't know! It's behind some stuff. I looked in and saw some minecart things. You have a mine in your basement, Ashe. Isn't that the bomb?!"

Rainwood stated, "We'd be cornered—"

"But they'll have to come at us one at a time," Ashe added, feeling a bit of hope coming back.

"Time's up!" came from outside. "Get'em!"

Rainwood lifted Jade in his free arm and ran down the stairs to the basement. Ashe shouldered her newly assembled gear, glad for the habit of always keeping a go-bag packed, and followed him down, grabbing random things she thought they could use on her course to the basement.

Moonbeam pulled the boards away from the wall, revealing a dark passage.

Ashe flicked on the AstroCom's lamp, lighting the way as they entered. Above, windows shattered, and grenades shook the building as the raiders stormed the cabin. Moonbeam waited for everyone to pass, then put the boards and boxes back as best he could to hide the entrance. Ashe hoped they would be lucky and the raiders would think they escaped some other way.

The tunnel was cool and damp. The group passed a few side passages but stayed with the main rail line as it curved to the right. Jade kept tripping, struggling to keep up with everybody running down the tunnel. After the third time, Ashe pointed her lamp at him, only to notice his shoes were not tied. "Oh my gosh! Ankle-biter, tie your shoes!"

She knelt and quickly knotted each one while he watched with wide eyes, then she told him, "Come on, they're getting ahead!"

Ashe watched for good ambush points as they made their way further into the mountain. *If we're going down, we'll do it fighting.*

Rainwood carefully placed an anti-personnel explosive. "Even if it doesn't drop anybody, at least we'll know they're coming, and it's weak enough it won't bring the mountain down."

Weariness started to hit everybody after a while, and their pace slowed to a brisk jog. Ashe was about to push for another burst of speed when the passage opened to a large chamber. To everybody's surprise, a full-size camper trailer straddled the rails, and opened crates of supplies littered the ground.

Ashe stopped and leaned on the wall for a quick rest, but something teased at her thoughts.

"Neat!" said Moonbeam, trying the trailer door, which opened with ease, and shining his flashlight inside.

"Wonder if this was somebody's bomb shelter," mused Rainwood.

What's off about this? Ashe wondered.

She held back, pondering and listening while the others poked through the crates to see if anything useful remained. Their search turned up a few items of value, which they added to their supplies, including a ragged camp tent.

Looking at the trailer and trying to figure out what felt wrong, Ashe figured it out. "Hold on. How did it get in here? There is no way this trailer could have fit through the way we came in."

They all looked at Ashe, and their eyes lit up as they realized the same good news.

Moonbeam grinned. "There is another entrance to the mine!"

Jade ran along the rails through the large chamber and pointed. The rail line continued down another passage.

An explosion rattled the walls from the path behind them, shaking bits of gravel loose—the raiders were coming.

With renewed energy, they continued running, slowing only when approaching cross tunnels.

"We should stay with the main line," Rainwood reminded them at each crossing, his voice having an edge of urgency each time. "It's most likely to lead to the exit."

Occasionally echoes from their pursuers made it to them, but Ashe, Rainwood, Moonbeam, and Jade were confident in their lead and eventually slowed to a brisk walk, no longer able to keep up the faster pace.

"I hope the exit hasn't collapsed," Ashe mumbled at some point. Rainwood gave her a look and just nodded.

Jade started to lag behind, and Ashe fell back, staying with him. He walked funny, taking exaggerated steps, almost stomping, while staring straight down. Moonbeam had given him a flashlight, and Jade pointed it at his feet rather than in front of him.

"You'll trip if you're not careful," she observed. "What's with the way you're walking?"

He looked up with a giant grin. "I've—"

He paused as if he'd been interrupted and started again. "I've–I've," he curled his brow, frustrated. Ashe waited, trying not to be impatient with him. They hadn't talked much yet. He'd been pretty quiet—perhaps because of this challenge.

He finished with, "Shoes–Shoes are nice. Soft. I–I don't feel —" His voice got louder as he rushed to finish, "—I don't feel the rocks." His curious speech reminded her of someone trying to speak before anybody cut them off more than somebody stuttering.

Ashe swallowed a lump in her throat and asked, "Haven't you worn shoes before?"

The pleasant smile stayed on his face, yet he shook his head to the negative. The light even managed to bring out his green eyes, which shone with excitement.

"They help! See, I can run fast!"

He took off in a sprint.

She followed, wanting to both laugh and cry. *How was Jade raised that he never wore shoes?*

She caught up to find him holding Moonbeam's hand. "Jade," asked Ashe, "do you know why the raiders are so desperate to get their hands on you?"

He shook his head.

She suspected he knew more than he was willing to tell. His explanation yesterday made no sense.

"Lay it on us, anything you know might help . . . Are your parents with the raiders?"

"I don't know!" he shouted.

"Hey, little man, it's all good," Moonbeam said, giving Ashe a stink eye. "You don't have to tell us anything. We're here for you."

Ashe bit back a reply, which was fine because they had another problem. The air had become increasingly damp. The tunnel ahead was flooded—they either had to go through it or turn around.

Ashe sampled the water with her AstroCom. While it ran the analysis, Rainwood pointed his flashlight down the passage, trying to see how far the flooding extended.

"Blast!" Ashe cursed as the results came up. "This water, it's not just radioactive; it's loaded with toxic heavy metals."

Rainwood knelt at the edge. "How toxic is it? We can't turn back now—there haven't been any side passages for a while. I think we can reach the other side. It doesn't look overly deep."

She studied the results. "Well, we won't melt. But it won't be pleasant. Maybe like a sunburn. And don't drink it."

Moonbeam laughed, sitting down to take his shoes off. "So we grow a few extra toes; no problem. I've always wondered what it'd feel like."

Jade's eyes flared wide at the suggestion, worry spreading on his face, but he said nothing and pulled his shoes off, rolling up his pants like the others. Ashe helped tie the laces together and showed him how to hang them over his neck.

She started wading first because her AstroCom's lamp was the brightest. "It's not too bad. Bit cold. And the rocks—ah! Watch out for that one."

Unfortunately, what looked to be the end of the water was just a turn in the passage, and it continued to get deeper, eventually reaching Jade's elbows, and he walked with his arms held high, holding his shoes out of the water. Ashe stopped, shifting her pack to the front and let him climb onto her back.

They continued as quickly as possible, but moving fast in the water was hard. Soon it reached Ashe's waist, and she worried they would have to swim if it went any deeper.

"Was that a warm spot?" asked Rainwood incredulously from the back of the line.

"You don't want to think about it, Daegom, Just keep moving," answered Moonbeam with zero remorse and a grin in his voice.

Rainwood snorted, and Ashe bit back a laugh.

They couldn't help but make splashing noises pushing through the water, yet even over that, Ashe thought she heard something and held a finger up, hissing, "Shhh!"

Everybody froze.

Dog barks and howls echoed from the passage behind them —the raiders were closing in.

After a sobering glance at each other, the small group resumed their forward pace and tried to move more quickly through the water. Fortunately, the slope changed, and the level started to recede. They increased their pace and emerged a few minutes later, sparing only a moment to rinse the toxic water using their canteens. Ashe helped Jade dry his feet and tie his shoes. He took off at a run while she tied her own and jogged to catch up with the others, but they'd all stopped.

Boulders blocked the passage—it had collapsed. They were cornered.

Ashe exhaled, "Hell's bells."

Her inner thoughts darkened. *This is it—the end.*

Rainwood turned around. "Let's head back to the water. We can pick them off while they're wading, thin the ranks a little before they make it to us."

She nodded, dropping her pack and checking the Arbiter's action. Fortunately, it hadn't gotten wet.

Moonbeam checked his pistols, and she glared at him in the darkness—not that he could see her—and thought, *Seriously, who runs with a pair of handguns in the badlands? Any rifle's range is better than a pistol's. Relying on a pistol means waiting for your attackers to get close.*

Gloom settled over her. "After that first shot, they'll likely just turn around and wait us out."

She couldn't recall being in such a bad situation. *At least not since—not since that time . . .* She stuffed the thought away, not wanting to think of her family.

She shuffled after Rainwood to set up a firing position. *I may as well make it count, right? Take as many with me as I can?*

"It's raining," Jade stated clearly, stopping everybody in their tracks.

Ashe slowly turned around, listening, then nodded. "You can hear it! This is the exit."

She turned off her lamp, and the others followed suit. Dim spears of light filtered through cracks in the rocks. It almost made it worse, like the universe was rubbing in how close they were to freedom.

"No chance we can dig out," she observed, once again feeling hope drain away from her.

Everybody could hear the raiders moving through the water, and flickers of light from their lamps were becoming visible in the distance.

Then Jade disappeared, climbing over a boulder. "You—you can fit too!" he called out.

A glimmer of hope sparked in Ashe's chest. She grabbed her pack, climbed over the boulder to the hole he'd discovered. Looking at it closely, she gauged how tight it was. "It's small", she called out to the others. "I think we can make it out if we army crawl and push our gear in front of us."

She started through, squeezing on her belly and pushing her pack ahead.

Feeling the boulders scrape her back made it personal, and she couldn't help but think about the mountain's weight. The doom of their situation seemed to compound, and panic tightened around her thoughts.

What if the rocks shift?

She started to breathe quickly and froze in place.

Moonbeam's bag bumped against her feet. She realized she blocked their passage but couldn't move as paralysis gripped her thoughts. Doom crushed in on her, and her vision thinned to a tunnel as she huffed, unable to slow her breathing.

Just as she was about to lose it completely, the light ahead of her shifted, and she saw Jade peeking over the pack, his eyes crinkled in worry.

Worry for me? Ashe felt a warmth spread in her chest. His arrival helped calm the welling terror seizing her, and her pulse slowed.

She felt drawn by his focus as he spoke with a steady calm, "You are okay. It's okay." He pulled on the pack, encouraging her forward. "Come on!"

She choked back her fear and started inching forward, following as he pulled her gear.

Slowly, the light increased, and the tiny, constraining passage opened into a mess of vines and vegetation. Ashe quickly pushed past them, stumbling upright and taking a deep breath while relishing the open air and fresh rain on her face.

The looming pressure of the mountain faded, and she felt buoyant, almost floating. Giddiness bubbled up, and she grabbed Jade, spinning him around with a laughing shout, "Thank you!"

He giggled as they spun in a circle away from the entrance, and she lifted him higher with each turn. Feeling lightheaded and dizzy, she eventually stopped, and they both stumbled to the ground, ending up on their backs next to each other, still laughing.

She looked at him and smiled. *He has a cute laugh.*

The clouds stretched in the sky above them, and she relaxed, letting the rain wash over her and relishing in the relief of escaping. She hadn't realized how much stress she'd felt.

An explosion thundered, followed by a shockwave thumping over Jade and Ashe. Adrenaline took over, and she instinctively jumped up, grabbed the Arbiter, and pointed it in the direction of the noise, only to see Moonbeam running toward them with a grin. "It's okay! Rainwood put grenades in the tunnel. They aren't following us now!"

She dropped her gun and collapsed back on the ground, shouting with a grin, "Warn me next time!"

She wondered about that.

What did I mean by "next time?" Will I stay with these guys?

Maybe I can.

For a little while.

5.

Nobody's Fault but Mine

While everybody checked their gear, Ashe inspected the pile of rubble to be sure the raiders wouldn't follow them, then looked at the AstroCom's map to find their location. "We're a little north of Ebley now, and wow, it looks like we spent half the day in the mine!"

Rainwood approached, drinking from a canteen. "Sorry to say, but I'd advise you to steer clear of the cabin for a while."

Ashe worried at his comment. *Does he not want me to join them anymore? Or is he saying he does? Or is he just giving me advice?*

She gave a slight shrug, afraid to reveal her feelings, and declared, "Looks like we're teaming up after all."

He nodded, and her shoulders relaxed with relief.

Moonbeam opened his AstroTec-branded backpack and pulled out two cans. "I feel like lunch. Who wants canned ham?"

They shared food for a quick meal—Ashe was happy to have anything except canned ham, which she hated. *Mom would always slice it up and fry it, but nothing could help it. Just looking at the slab of meaty "stuff" as it glooped from the can, covered in gelatinous fat—Ugh.*

While times had been tough, they'd never been bad enough that she'd had to eat canned ham, and she held back the gag reflex just thinking about it and instead had some fox jerky.

As everybody relaxed and ate, she considered Moonbeam and shook her head, marveling at his gear. "Moonbeam, you're like a walking billboard for AstroTec. Is everything you have bright purple emblazoned with their logo? You look like their mascot!"

He smiled, a little embarrassed. "I just like their stuff. They used to make a lot of cool things!"

She thought about asking where he came from but stopped at the last moment—fearing that if she did, he'd then ask her about her family, and she didn't want to talk about that.

Jade shivered, leaning against her for warmth. Realizing the rain had soaked him to the core, she sifted through her pack, fighting against a mischievous grin as she pulled out the AstroTec University jacket she'd found at the cabin, and held it up to make sure Moonbeam could see it. "Jade, Put this on. It'll keep you warm."

Moonbeam's eyes lit up seeing the ATU logo, and she grinned, wondering how long it would take him to trade with Jade. The jacket was a bit oversized for the little guy, but it was better than nothing.

After everybody finished eating, Ashe dramatically gestured to the tangle-dense canopy of trees extending into the valley before them. "Welcome to the Fen, where everything wants to eat you."

They didn't seem impressed.

With a disappointed shrug, she set off, leading the way through the forest. The canopy quickly became so dense overhead that they couldn't see the sky anymore. Thick moss covered much of the trees and hung from the branches, giving the forest an otherworldly feel and adding a heavy, earthy scent to the air. Their path twisted and meandered around the thick gnarled roots.

She pulled up the AstroCom's map and debated the best course. It was probably a bad idea to backtrack, even if they could scavenge for supplies—she wanted to put as much distance between them and the raiders as she could.

By her reckoning, if they headed due east, they'd hit Highway 95, but that would take them past Mosstown—and she wanted to avoid that, at least until she figured out what to do with Warthog. Ashe wasn't sure how to steer their path, however—everything to the north was swampy, and some nasty creatures lurked there. She decided to backtrack south just a little—it wouldn't be too far out of the way, and the guys wouldn't know, right?

Ashe turned the AstroCom off, glancing at Jade walking next to her. He'd watched her the whole time, but she found it curious: his interest wasn't captivated by the AstroCom. Instead, he stared at her intently with wide eyes. Seeing her attention on him, Jade grinned and looked ahead.

What an odd kid.

She considered her interactions with him and started to wonder. He always seemed to know what she was thinking. Like he could read her mind.

But that's—she shook her head—*that's ridiculous. He's just really observant.*

It was hard to tell how much time had passed, and everybody seemed happy to hike in silence until Rainwood fell back and gestured at the trees, "What happened here?"

Hints of purple threaded along vines as thick as a tree trunk. They pushed out of the ground to twist around the trees, choking the canopy with their violet leaves.

"It's an infestation." Ashe patted one of the vines. "These are star vines. It all started sometime after the arrival. They came from Nova Dynamics up north. Some government experiment went wrong after the cleansing. It's supposedly a single, giant, void-mutated organism that came out of the labs. The vines grow during the void storms."

Jade seemed fixated, staring up into the trees, and she followed his gaze. A giant shadow detached, dropping to the ground.

"Watch out!" she yelled, bringing her Arbiter to bear.

Rainwood was even faster and launched himself forward, his gauntlet drawn back, ready to attack.

A mega sloth landed, shaking the ground with its impact. This wasn't a typical cute sloth. It was the size of a tank, with purple stripes covering its muscled back. These creatures had vicious claws and could shred you in moments.

Its deep rumble reverberated through the forest as it turned to face the team. Ashe sighted in on its head.

Jade jumped in front of her rifle, spreading his arms out and yelling, "Stop! Stop! Don't shoot it!"

Ashe froze, barely avoiding pulling the trigger.

She pushed him out of the way, but he held onto her arm, pulling. "It doesn't want to hurt us! It's nice!"

Rainwood must have heard Jade, for he pulled in his gauntlet mid-leap and instead shifted his momentum into a roll, pushing off the beast's side and coming up in a guarded stance just past it.

The sloth slowly turned its head, looking at Rainwood, then back to the other three. Ashe kept her gun trained on it, waiting for any sign of hostility.

A rattling rumble, deep enough to shake the ground under their feet, emanated from its chest as it watched them.

Jade folded his arms. "See, he's nice."

Rainwood backed away slowly, and Ashe shouldered her rifle. They gathered and watched it turn away, sifting through a pile of junk and debris collected in a heap.

Moonbeam punched Ashe in the shoulder. "Hah! Not everything wants to eat you here!"

She glared at him, renewing her dislike.

Rainwood asked, "Where'd these come from? Sloths aren't even from Arcadia, let alone this size."

"Heck if I know. Like anything else here, it's probably a failed government experiment. Or, just as likely, somebody had a few as pets, and after the void storms they just . . ." Ashe waved toward the giant creature, then gestured forward, letting the guys take the lead while she fell back with Jade. When the distance was good enough for a private conversation, she asked quietly, "How did you know it was nice?"

He said nothing, glanced at her, and started to run ahead, but she grabbed the hood of his coat.

"Hold on, speed racer."

She turned him around, and knelt, looking into his eyes. She doubted he'd be willing to admit it, yet forged forward, asking pointedly, "Can you hear thoughts?"

He swallowed and furtively glanced away, saying nothing.

Ashe made an effort to concentrate, feeling a little silly but hoping he'd hear her.

It's okay. I trust you. Can you trust me?

He glanced down, unwilling to look at her. She touched his chin, gently lifting it up. "I won't hurt you. In fact, I promise I will keep you sa—"

She froze. *I can't make that promise, can I? I can't keep anybody safe.*

"I—I mean—I promise . . . I will do anything I can to keep anybody from hurting you, alright?"

Tears welled up in his eyes, and he leaped forward, embracing her in a giant hug.

Ashe wrapped her arms around him, holding tight. It reminded her of holding—she swallowed, biting back her turmoil of memories, and whispered, "You can tell me whenever you want. Just . . . is that why the raiders want you?"

She felt him nod and stood up, still holding him with his arms wrapped around her, yet quailing at her unwanted thoughts and memories suddenly bubbling up from her past.

I couldn't keep my family safe. How can I keep Jade safe?

He squeezed tight and whispered, "I'm no them. I'm Jade."

She nodded, fighting back the tears in her eyes while trying to think of anything else—anything but that. Yet the thoughts still teased on the edges where a darkness of unbridled grief and guilt loomed.

Feeling like she was about to lose control, she focused her will and, little by little, forced her memories back into their locked box. With one leaden step after the other, she resumed hiking while holding Jade on her hip, forcing herself to think about the course they would take through the Fen and making a mental list of the possible dangers. It was a long list, but the process helped, and the ache in her chest faded.

The guys had noticed Ashe and Jade lag behind and waited for them. Moonbeam tipped his head, giving Ashe one of his trademark smiles. "You two okay?"

"Yeah, he's just tired."

Jade squeezed her, and she hugged back.

Rainwood turned on a flashlight. "I reckon we better find ourselves some shelter. It's getting dark. And I suspect not everything is as kind as that last fellow."

"There is an old pre-arrival picnic spot ahead," Ashe said. "We can stop there. It was a famous sinkhole or something and was safe last time I went through the area."

"Sinkholes are the bomb!" Moonbeam exclaimed, eagerly taking the lead.

After they got underway again, Jade whispered in her ear, "I can . . . I can hear what people think. And animals. Even when—when they die. That's—that's why I didn't want you to shoot it. I knew it was nice. I didn't want to hear—to hear—to hear it get hurt and die."

Ashe took a deep breath and held him tight as they continued. "I can't imagine how that'd be. Thank you for telling me."

She felt him nod again and wondered about the challenges he'd faced in his life.

A scream reverberated through the canopy ahead of them, and Moonbeam came running, waving his arms and shouting, "It's not safe! It's not safe!" A ball of fire arced over his shoulder, just barely missing him.

She dropped Jade and readied her Arbiter in a single motion. "Hide!"

Ashe ran and crested the hill to find three floating void-wisp abominations. Almost like jellyfish, they were foul, hostile balls of toxic gas with dangling tentacles and looked like a floating oil slick with an inner glow. Even without any visible face, they somehow still emanated a sense of hostility and danger.

Moonbeam brought up his pistols as Ashe arrived while Rainwood dashed past them and lifted his gauntlet, slashing downward at the first void-wisp.

"Take the one on the left," Ashe commanded while sighting in on the one to Rainwood's right, stroking the trigger and feeling calm take over as she heard the familiar *puta-puta-put* of her gun. She felt pleased to see each shot strike, but the void-wisp seemed unaffected and continued forward, spitting green globs of putrescence.

Not good. She unloaded an entire magazine into the creature, one stroke at a time, but it didn't appear to care.

Does nothing stop these things?

While swapping magazines, she glanced at Rainwood as he moved in a dangerous dance around the glowing wisp. It still floated, even if in tatters. Worse, Rainwood's movements seemed slower, and tendrils of smoke trailed behind him, lingering from the wisp's strikes.

Ashe's target closed in and spit, striking her shoulder with a glob of poisonous vitriol. She stumbled back, trying to lessen the impact and ignoring the stinging pain as it seeped through her clothes and ate at her skin. She slotted the magazine home and unleashed another series of bullets into the aberration.

It stopped, and Rainwood launched into it, stabbing his gauntlet into the sack that kept it afloat. The vicious claws pierced the wisp's tough skin, and it exploded in a cloud of caustic gas that engulfed him.

Only one wisp remained, and Moonbeam had it pinned, alternating between his revolver and semi-auto pistol. Ashe left him and ran to Rainwood, pulling his unconscious form out of the dispersing cloud, wiping the poison from his face, and checking for a pulse. It was faint. She pulled a Medipak from her waist and stabbed it into his chest.

His eyes flew open, and he gasped, sitting upright and growling, "Did we get 'em?"

Nothing like a government concoction of adrenaline and amphetamines to get you going, Ashe thought.

She glanced back—Moonbeam retreated with the last wisp still targeting him. She braced herself, kneeling by Rainwood's side, and used her Arbiter to finish it off. Once it shuddered and exploded, Moonbeam threw his hands in the air in a victory whoop.

He ran forward and helped Rainwood stand, but Rainwood pushed him away, scanning around. "Where's the kid?"

Ashe whistled and concentrated. *It's safe to come out.*

Jade popped up from his hiding spot behind a gnarled trunk, climbed over it, and joined the group.

Ashe followed the path to the sinkhole, watching for additional danger, and glanced down. The diffused glow of a wisp nest reflected across the still water at the bottom, and she caught the movement of a few wisps near the corner.

Gravel crunched behind her.

She spun, still on edge from the fight, only to see Moonbeam, and growled, "Get out of here! It's not safe. Looks like a nest of them below."

Moonbeam threw his hands up in surrender while he grinned. "You are one cool cat, Ashe. Scary, even. So did you see the shot I made? I hit the thing smack on."

He pulled his revolver, mimicking a shot, re-holstered it, then repeated this a few more times, saying, "Ka-pow, Ka-pow." Ashe smiled, letting him enjoy his moment, even though she'd made the final hit.

What a goofball.

Rainwood arrived, leaning on Jade and trying to hide a limp.

Ashe pointed at his leg. "You good to keep going?"

"Nothing I can't walk off."

Ashe knelt for a better look. His pants were shredded, and he had a blistered burn down his leg. "Jeez, man, you are hurt! You need to get that cleaned and stay off it for a while."

"Come on," he replied and continued on the path past the sinkhole. "Let's find a place for the night."

Knowing he needed help, she begrudgingly conceded that they should stop by Mosstown. She checked the map on her Astro-Com, then directed everybody northward—not that they could tell she'd shifted direction with the canopy hiding the sky.

They pushed as late as possible, but everybody grew weary of the hike. Rainwood struggled to keep a decent pace, and Ashe felt strung out from the long day. Jade kept wanting a ride, but she couldn't carry him—she could barely keep herself upright.

Ashe picked the camp spot more out of recognizing nobody could take another step than out of safety.

Moonbeam helped her set up the tent they had picked up from the mine and clear a perimeter as best as possible in the moonless night while Rainwood cleaned his wound from a worn first-aid kit he pulled out of his pack. Jade claimed a spot in the middle of the tent and fell asleep wrapped in a blanket before they'd even finished setting it up.

Once everything was settled, Ashe approached Moonbeam.

"We need to set up a watch, but I want Rainwood sleeping through the night."

He nodded. "Good luck getting him to agree to that."

Ashe rallied her will and found Rainwood wrangling to make space for more people in the small, ragged tent without waking Jade. She decided it was best not to give him a choice and whispered in a firm voice, "Moonbeam and I have the watches split. You stay in here with Jade."

Rainwood turned to look at her, and in the faint light, all she could see were the whites of his eyes. After a moment, he nodded. "This night only."

She was ready to argue more, and his sudden capitulation left her hanging—it didn't feel like a victory.

"Well, good," she said, feeling frustrated after building up for an argument that didn't happen, then turned and left the tent.

She joined Moonbeam, sitting across the small fire he'd set up.

"He's fine with it."

Moonbeam sounded a little surprised. "What?" Then he looked back at the tent with some worry. "The old man may be worse than he's letting on."

Ashe nodded, having considered the same thing, feeling the frustration in her thwarted anger fading.

Ashe watched the fire in silence for a minute, then realized it was just the two of them, and she suddenly felt awkward being alone with a guy her age.

She poked a stick into the flames, debating if she should offer to take the first watch, but her eyelids felt very heavy. When she looked up, Moonbeam stared right at her with a sheepish smile on his face.

She blushed at his attention and nervously broke the silence. "So, uhh—how about I—"

"—I'll take the first watch," he said before she could finish. "You go rest. You've done double duty, carrying Jade a lot too."

"—Oh."

The deep rumble of a rocketship echoed across the canopy, and Ashe wished they could see the sky. There was a spaceport nearby that was still used, and she could often hear the ships arriving and departing.

The rumble continued, getting louder until it abruptly cut off, and Ashe decided it must be an arriving rocket.

The uncomfortable silence resumed, almost compounded after the roar of the rocketship.

"Well. Thank you. I'll just go to bed then."

He nodded, flashing a quick smile. "Sleep well."

Ashe hung her coat outside the tent and found an available sleeping bag in the darkness. Rainwood was already snoring.

She looked at Jade for a moment, his arms akimbo, and the last thought she remembered was how quickly these three guys came into her life and—more interestingly—how it didn't bother her.

6.

In a Shanty in Old Shanty Town

*A*she woke to bird song and opened her sleep-crusted eyes to see dappled light on the tent. With a start, she floundered to turn on her AstroCom—it was just after 7:00 a.m., Solar Time. Her thoughts boiled. *Why didn't Moonbeam wake me? Did he fall asleep?*

She crawled from the bag, anger building up, expecting to find him asleep, and threw the flap open.

Moonbeam stood poking the fire with a stick, causing a shower of sparks to float up.

"Oh, hi!"

She froze, a little confused. The fire snapped and crackled, and the scent of smoke and burning maple wood permeated the area. She noticed he'd also spread everybody's wet gear around the fire to dry.

He just . . . let me sleep.

The act of kindness hit her hard. She wanted to stoke her anger, but it popped like a bubble. Feeling a knot in her throat, she turned and walked around the back of the tent for some privacy while mentally berating herself for the tears threatening to come out.

She clenched her fists. *I'm going soft. I am a survivor. I am a solo warrior. I don't need any help.*

Besides, what was he thinking? He must be exhausted. What if he'd fallen asleep?

She returned and told him with an edge in her voice, "Never do that again. Ever. You put us all in danger."

He shrugged. "Okay. You just looked really tired last night."

Ashe didn't comment on the bags under his eyes.

"Never again," she reiterated, her voice slightly softer. "And . . . thank you for letting me sleep."

He flashed one of his trademark smiles. "Anytime!"

She nodded and helped make breakfast for everybody before they broke camp, worrying about what to say to the folks at Mosstown. They hoped she'd pull a miracle out of her hat, and she had nothing.

After an hour, their path led to an escarpment overlooking a flooded valley. In the distance, shanty-style houses built into the trees poked through the canopy, the soft glow from their lamps lighting up the morning fog. The group followed the ridgeline north until they reached a path that descended to the water's edge.

As they arrived, Ashe felt relieved to see a raft moored in the reeds—she didn't want to wade through the swampy river bottoms to Mosstown.

Somebody fished at the water's edge, wearing a straw hat and holding a net full of fish.

Ashe recognized him and called out, "Glenn!"

Startled, he looked up and squinted while quickly retreating to his raft.

Ashe was surprised he'd survived this long—he was nearly blind, and she figured he didn't recognize her. The town didn't even let him have a gun because he couldn't shoot within a mile of any target. But he was a nice guy and was always willing to help.

Before he stumbled and hurt himself, she called out, "Glenn, it's me, Ashe!"

His face lit up, and he stopped, then eagerly waved. "Did you do it?"

"Well . . . there's been some complications."

"Oh. So no."

Ashe ignored his disappointed expression and tried to side-step the issue. "Glenn, this is Rainwood, Moonbeam, and Jade. If it's alright, we need a place to stop and recover for a few days."

He looked uncomfortable. "I don't know. That's up to Penny. You know food is scarce, with Warthog and all. A raider stopped by yesterday, wanting us to give them more." He hoisted his net. "That's why I'm out here."

Warthog's constant demands for supplies had left the residents of Mosstown starving, but they had to comply because he threatened to turn their haven into a blazing pyre. Guilt knotted Ashe's insides for failing them, but she pressed on. "We'll provide and help as we can. And . . . Warthog can't know we're here."

Glenn looked even more uneasy.

Ashe sighed, pointing to the raft. "Can you give us a lift?"

He agreed, and after helping them climb aboard, he poled the raft through the swamp. Jade's eyes grew wide in wonder as they closed in on the sprawling complex in the tree canopy, connected by bridges, some made of rope, others assembled from any number of objects, including the wing of an old prop plane. It was like a kid's dream. Ashe remembered playing in the maze of vents and engineering corridors in Fenclave. Something was exciting about man-made jungles—at least to a kid.

Glenn tied up the raft as they disembarked, then said, "You go up and make it right with Penny. These fish need to go on the rack."

Moonbeam gave Ashe an uneasy smile, Rainwood looked concerned, and Jade seemed eager to run through the maze of walkways. He glanced at her stern gaze as she thought, *Stay close.* He smiled and nodded.

"Let's go," Ashe gestured, mounting a rickety staircase. At the top, they stepped into a shack where a tired-looking woman busily chopped vegetables and a pot of water simmered over a wood-burning stove.

The woman's eyes lit up like Glenn's when she saw Ashe, who immediately lifted her hand in warning. "No, sorry, Sara. I haven't dealt with Warthog yet. Just need to talk to Penny."

Sara pointed up another flight of stairs and hammering started, coming down from above. Summiting those stairs, they found Penny fixing a loose railing. She wore her long brown hair in a series of braids and didn't look too old, maybe in her thirties. But, her skin had that weathered look of somebody who's been in the sun too much. Yet, even with that, her freckles stood out as she looked up at the new arrivals, and a smile spread on her face.

Before Penny could speak, Ashe declared, "I haven't dealt with Warthog yet. But we need some help. Could we stay for a few days?"

Penny brushed her hands on her hips and stood, taking in the guys behind Ashe while folding her arms. "I was hoping for better news. We're on rations now."

Rainwood asked, "When will they come next?"

"Usually on Fridays. You know, Ashe, as I told you before: we should find somebody older—" she stopped, noticing a scowl form on Ashe's face. "I mean, just—not that you can't handle it, but you know. You don't have to do it alone, maybe? Not to mention, the Sheriff stopped by not long ago. Wanted to know what you planned to do with Warthog. He's busy trying to keep Warthog happy, it seems. . . . Might be worried you'd rock the boat too much."

Ashe felt a growing knot of frustration. The Sheriff was a self-appointed constable of the area. Most people took it in stride, but he was nosy and never seemed to be around when people needed help. She always tried to avoid him.

Ashe tried not to growl. "So you asked him to take care of it, because you didn't think I could?"

"That's not true! I know you said you could handle things. And he had just stopped by—"

Trying to diffuse the tension, Rainwood interrupted, gesturing at his leg. "If you could be so kind, I could use a little help, and the rest of us will be out of your hair before too long. We can manage our own food and even help out. I presume the town isn't at a dangerous capacity?"

Penny nodded. "I know we shouldn't have more than 100 people, or the Kraal will come, and we even have rules for how to deal with that unfortunate population event. But people are leaving rather than going hungry, so at least there is one positive to the low rations. If y'all help around, that'll go a long way in everybody's minds."

Even with her assurances, Ashe felt uneasy. Everybody still alive knew the rules of the Kraal: they came from somewhere outside of time and space—nobody was quite sure where or why—and they were somehow attracted to large gatherings of people. Ashe didn't know why it was 100 people that mattered and felt it was a bit arbitrary. They also seemed to only come out of corners in rooms, which made no sense to Ashe. She'd never seen one and hoped she never would—surviving a Deathmark was itself notable, but surviving a Kraal, that was nearly unheard of.

Moonbeam gave a thumbs up. Ashe nodded and glanced around, suddenly realizing she'd lost Jade. She scanned the other buildings and walkways, trying not to feel alarmed.

His laugh filtered up from below, and she relaxed.

Penny perked up, her eyes glimmering in interest. "Did you bring children?"

She went downstairs with everybody else in tow. Sara sat with Jade at the table, holding a barbarian plushie in one hand and a blue Fuzzy Kat plushie in the other. In a squeaky Fuzzy Kat voice, she said, "If you do that, then I'll have to jump on you again!"

She made the Fuzzy Kat plushie jump on the barbarian, adding a *boop-boop-boop* noise with each pounce, bringing forth another stream of giggles from Jade.

"Oh, hey, boss," Sara said, seeing the group arrive. She handed the toys to Jade and told him, "You can play with these if you're careful. In fact," she pointed to the cat, "do you want to keep Mister Fuzzy Kat?"

Jade took the plushie, which looked like a fat potato of a cat with a monster grin, closed eyes, and a bean-bag base, then ran his fingers through its blue fur and nodded with a smile.

Penny watched Jade, then gave Ashe a curious look.

Ashe explained, "It's a long story . . . for later."

Penny sighed and gestured. "Come on. I'll find you some beds. Sara, see if Doc is still around. Somebody needs her skills before she heads out."

There were plenty of beds due to people leaving. Moonbeam and Ashe settled their gear, and a small, flat-faced woman arrived, stating in a no-nonsense manner, "Who needs my help? I need to be on the road again, but help needs help, as they say."

Ashe pointed to Rainwood, who sat on the bed, and he pointed to his leg. Doc sighed and set a bag on a table. "Looks like an acid burn. You're in luck. I have a pre-arrival burn kit, which should help you heal quickly. Take your pants off. Let's have a look."

Ashe quickly left, leaving Doc to do her thing.

Twenty people still lived in the village and busily started their day. Ashe helped Glenn repair the docks, which took most of the morning, leaving both of them covered in mud and slime. After Ashe washed up, Sara showed her some spare outfits.

Noticing Ashe's interest in the poodle skirt, which reminded Ashe of the good times before she was exiled, Sara suggested, "You should try it on! It's not my style anyway, but you'd look cute."

Ashe rolled her eyes. "This isn't something to wear now. It's from another time."

Sara laughed. "Pish posh, it's just for tonight, girl. You planning on going somewhere else?"

Perhaps it was the communal nature of the village affecting her, but Ashe threw caution to the wind and decided to go for it. She held back a slight grin while wondering what the guys would think. Taking the skirt from Sara, she had to admit they were nice threads—a light blue with a cute pink poodle. Her heart feeling a little lighter, she stepped into the bedroom to change.

Donned in her new attire, Ashe returned with Sara to the communal kitchen and assisted in preparing the evening meal. When Moonbeam saw Ashe, he froze, his eyes saucer-sized, and for the first time that Ashe could recall, he seemed at a loss for words. His hands were a nervous mess, and a pleased smile beamed on his face. "You. Uhh—you look . . ."

Ashe bit her lip, fighting back a grin.

Before he could say more, Penny approached, pointing up the stairs. "Do you have a minute, Ashe?"

Ashe glanced at Moonbeam, seeing him nervously running a hand through his hair, and gestured for him to follow.

Penny led them to a rec room with a pool table and a series of vintage Pop-a-Cola bottles on the shelf, much like back in the cabin. Except these bottles weren't empty. Penny retrieved a few and offered them, which caused Moonbeam to light up and gasp with a squeak of delight, "Unopened Pop-a-Cola!"

She chuckled and offered one to Ashe before leaning on the table.

Moonbeam opened his bottle, sighing when it emitted a hiss as the pressure released. He sipped it, enjoying the fizzy drink.

Ashe opened hers with a little reluctance. She'd avoided reminders of Fenclave, and there had been a soda fountain in their common area. But it'd be rude not to drink it.

Penny began, "You know I want Mosstown to be a safe place. I've hoped we could make it safe enough to have kids here. We just need to get rid of the raiders, of course."

Ashe jumped in, "I can get rid of Warthog. I was at his camp. The guys helped."

Moonbeam added, trying to be helpful, "Right, we were there to get your pack—"

Ashe cut him off before he could give too much detail, "—But I came across Jade when I entered their camp. They had him barefoot, in rags, in a cage. I couldn't leave him, so I broke him out instead of getting to Warthog."

Penny's eyes flared in anger when she heard about Jade being caged, and Ashe continued. "Unfortunately, they've been chasing us ever since. I do want to help you. I just need to figure things out. Take a few days to recover."

"Why did they have him?" Penny asked.

Ashe shrugged, putting on her best stony face. "I'm not sure."

Moonbeam grinned. "He's a good kid. Doesn't deserve anything like that. I mean, what a harsh 'timeout,' right?"

Ashe shook her head. "Jade has had a hard life. He—" she sighed, still bothered by what he'd told her. "He had never worn shoes until I gave him some. I think he'll open up when he's ready."

Penny held her hand to her mouth, her eyes watering. She was a very empathetic person, like a mother hen. From what Ashe knew of her, she always wanted to help people build a safe home.

The noise of conversation and silverware on plates increased below. Penny unfolded her arms and headed toward the stairs. "Let's finish talking about this later. It sounds like dinner is ready."

It was a lean meal, primarily of food the town members could scrape up from the swamp, but the atmosphere was still one of hope. After dinner was cleared, everybody migrated to an open platform, and a grizzled woman picked up a guitar, checking it was in tune. Three other people took instruments, and everyone else helped keep time by tapping and clapping.

The musicians came together in the familiar tune, "Don't Fence Me In." Soon enough, almost everybody was singing along. Ashe took a seat by Moonbeam and Rainwood, marveling at how the whole community joined in the song. It almost seemed like things were normal again.

Ashe felt herself relaxing when everybody started singing "Praise the Lord and Pass the Ammunition." She tapped her feet in rhythm and even joined in the chorus. Jade watched the social gathering, fascination on his face while remaining silent.

Ashe had a wide grin by the time the song ended, and somebody turned on a jukebox, giving the musicians a rest. "I Can't Dance, I Got Ants in My Pants" started up. People moved to the open center area, dancing, and Ashe felt a sudden scorn come upon her at the festive atmosphere.

Don't they see the harsh world we live in?

Moonbeam joined the crowd, dancing, having fun, and laughing. Then, seeing Ashe on the side, he came over and pulled on her hand. "Come on!"

She resisted, shaking her head, but he pulled harder. "You can't be gloomy all the time, Ashe. Just let it go sometimes. It's good for you!"

His smile won her over, and she reluctantly followed him to the center. Yet, it didn't take long before she found herself bobbing along with everybody else. Moonbeam took her hands, and she unwound a little further, having fun swinging back and forth with him like they were at a social in Fenclave.

She felt a twinge of sadness when the song ended and begrudgingly admitted it was fun.

"Earth Angel" started—a slower song. A few couples pulled together, swaying in time with the music. Ashe glanced at Moonbeam, realized they still held hands, and panicked. She let go and quickly moved to a seat on the side, glaring at nobody in particular.

Moonbeam didn't have difficulty finding another dance partner, which annoyed Ashe. Then, that annoyance made her even more frustrated.

I'm a solo wanderer. What am I doing?

As the song ended, somebody played a series of familiar slow notes on an accordion, introducing a favorite regional song: "Shenandoah."

Everybody cleared the floor, looking for drinks or an available chair.

Ashe nearly fell from her seat when Rainwood, standing at a side railing, started singing. His voice was a great fit—he had a deep bass and could carry a tune well.

It was moving and easy to tell that he sang it with heart. As he stood looking over the flooded river bottom, there was a yearning in his voice, and he struggled to finish the line "Farewell, my dearest." A few people wiped their eyes as they clapped in appreciation.

He gave an uncomfortable smile and then left, favoring his injured leg.

The guitars started up again, and Ashe realized Jade, now leaning against her, had fallen asleep. Penny appeared. "Aww, cute. Do you want me to take him to bed?"

Ashe felt protective of Jade but realized Penny just wanted to help. "Yeah, if you would like."

Penny lifted him into her arms, and as she left, it struck Ashe that Penny would be a great mother.

Moonbeam had sat with Sara when Rainwood took the stage and was still at her side, talking to her animatedly. Ashe glowered at them, feeling strangely jealous, then stopped herself. *Why should I care?*

She stood and left, deciding it was late. She didn't see Moonbeam coming to where she had sat, carrying an extra bottle of Pop-a-Cola, nor did she see him sigh, look around the room, and eventually take a seat alone.

The next morning, Ashe gave the skirt outfit back to Sara, stubbornly telling herself, *I need to think about surviving in the badlands. Besides, I like my usual outfit better. It's ragged, pieced together from scraps left behind, and durable—like me.*

The next few days passed in a blur. Everybody helped around town, leaving them exhausted by the end of the day. The community revival of the first night was a unique affair, and Ashe was glad when everybody quietly dispersed after dinner each night.

Just as the doctor assured, Rainwood's wound healed quickly with the burn pack wrapped on his leg, and he was able to take it off by Thursday, five days after they had arrived in Mosstown. That same evening, tension filled the air as everybody knew the raiders would visit the next day, resulting in virtually no conversation around the tables.

Ashe had grown so used to everybody doing their own thing that it took her a few minutes after dinner to realize Rainwood had been missing from the table.

She wondered if this was something Jade could help with and asked him, "Do you know where Rainwood is?"

After saying that aloud, she focused her mind, asking, *Can you hear him somewhere? Can you make out his thoughts?*

He wrinkled his brow and concentrated for a moment, his gaze focusing on the distance. She watched and was startled to see the green sparks in his eyes move. After a moment, they went still, and he shook his head.

"He's not around?"

Jade looked worried and shook his head again.

Ashe stood, looking for Penny, who noticed Ashe's scowl and quickly left the room. Ashe caught up to her on the walkway. "Where is Rainwood?"

Her face was a map of guilt, and Ashe knew she was hiding something.

"He—he said not to worry! He was going to take care of Warthog."

"What! How long ago did he leave?"

Penny looked scared, and Ashe realized she had yelled and squeezed Penny's hand in a tight grip. Ashe knew there was no way she could catch up with Rainwood in time. Anxiety ratcheted like a tight knot of pressure in her chest. She knew she couldn't leave Jade, but she wasn't good at waiting, so she let out a feral yell and then stomped off.

Rainwood wouldn't be back right away, and knowing that didn't help Ashe sleep.

Ring of Fire

Penny cornered Ashe in the morning. "You want to go find your friend, don't you?"

Ashe returned a cold stare, saying nothing.

"Well," Penny continued, glancing down at her feet, "maybe— if you wanted to—you could leave Jade here? I can keep watch on him. He'd be safe. Safer than wandering the badlands. You should go find your friend in case he needs help."

Ashe dialed her stare up to a glare, her thoughts in turmoil. *I want to help Rainwood. I want to protect Jade. I want to help Mosstown, like I promised. But I can't do all of these things.*

She looked at Penny and recognized concern in her eyes. Something inside her softened, and it almost hurt as she decided to leave Jade with Penny. She exhaled before nodding. "Okay. But just until I'm back."

A smile lit up Penny's face. "You are so nice, always wanting to help everybody."

Ashe hated it when people called her nice, but she ignored the slight.

Moonbeam and Jade sat together at breakfast. Ashe slipped by before they noticed, not seeing the irony in her actions being so similar to Rainwood's. She wondered how observant Jade would be, considering he could hear thoughts. Would he be able to notice she was thinking of leaving before she could get away?

She packed lightly, trying to think of nothing, and snuck out through the back of the compound, where it butted up against the cliffs.

This is the right thing to do, leaving Jade behind. Then a moment later, she muttered aloud, as if saying it would make it true, "He will understand."

She reached the top and looked back, wondering why it was so hard to leave. Then she started running south toward Warthog's Den.

It took her hours, but she pushed hard, stopping only when she could barely breathe. She remembered learning about people running endurance marathons before the arrival and did not understand the allure.

Shortly before noon, she recognized the terrain and knew Warthog's camp was close. Once the ramshackle complex came into view, she paused behind a tree to catch her breath and let the cramp in her side fade.

From inside the raiders' camp came the sound of gunfire, then somebody shouting, and her pulse quickened. Still gasping for air, she pulled her Arbiter and sighted in on the compound, hoping to get an idea about the situation and find Rainwood. But she couldn't see anybody, although a line of black smoke did rise from a structure on the side.

More gunfire.

Her side still hurt, but she needed to get closer, and she carefully slipped from tree to tree, hoping to stay out of sight but knowing she was moving too fast for her chameleon suit to work correctly.

The lower gate sat open, with nobody visible. Her anxiety rose, and she worried about being trapped. Seeing no other choice, she ran from cover, sped through the gate, and ducked to the side. Three bodies lay nearby, cut and maimed, obviously dead.

Ashe swallowed, and her thoughts wound in a knot of worry. *There's at least thirty or forty people in this compound.*

More shouts came from farther inside, and she followed them, moving slowly while pulling on her hood, engaging the chameleon suit, and keeping her Arbiter ready.

She passed more bodies until she arrived at the gate to the cave, Warthog's Bunker. This door also hung open, and the sound of fighting echoed out.

Lifting the Arbiter to her shoulder, she moved in, ready to fire in an instant, and followed the trail of bodies until she passed through an inner barrier just as somebody screamed, followed by a gurgle as they gasped out their last breath. The light was dim, coming from lamps placed in different corners of the cave. In the center, Rainwood stood, hunched over, surrounded by several more bodies.

Her foot dislodged a rock, and he snapped his head in her direction, straightening up in a fighting stance, the wicked bladed gauntlet lifted high, ready to strike. Something in his gaze shook her to the core, and every molecule in her wanted to flee. It was like the look a hungry lion might give a gazelle, but even worse. Feral, with some deeper anger underneath.

She backed up, wondering if she could outrun him, her pulse hammering in her forehead, the lizard brain part of her mind fighting for control. Fighting to get her to run away. But she ground her teeth, slapped the chameleon suit's switch on her thigh, pulled the hood off and gasped, "Rainwood, it's me."

His chest heaved, and he closed his eyes, his arms lowering. The gauntlet hung at his side, covered in gore. After a moment, he muttered in a low, gravelly voice with an undertone of anguish, "I wish you hadn't seen this. You should have stayed away."

She glanced around the chamber before asking, "Is this everybody? Did you—"

He shook his head. "Not everybody. About half of them left this morning, and I took the opportunity."

Her thoughts reeled.

He just killed them all in cold blood.

A feeling of guilt sliced through her when she remembered one of her plans had been to kill Warthog in his sleep. Was it really much different? The badlands changed everyone, and she had to do what she could to survive.

Still trying to comprehend it, she muttered, "You did this? All of them? What if some of them weren't here by choice?"

A haunted look shone from his eyes, and he growled, the last words sounding almost strangled, "I'm not a judge, just an executioner. I've resigned myself to this role. I've found that sometimes it's easier to kill them all and let God sort it out."

A cold chill went down Ashe's spine, and she wondered what he'd become, what the badlands had done to him.

What she was becoming.

She didn't like killing, she told herself. But she had become rather good at it. Bile rose in her throat.

Was this what she'd turn into someday?

Rainwood broke the quiet by rapidly swinging the gauntlet, leaving a stripe of blood along the floor and wall.

"Let's find your belongings and be on our way before the others return," he growled, his voice back under control.

"Warthog?"

He pointed to one of the bodies on the ground, and she nodded, staring at it for a moment while her feelings tumbled about.

He lay face down, with a mohawk painted red, and a pool of blood slowly spread from him.

As much as she wanted to get past it, seeing a dead person still shook her up. She forced herself to look away and bury the confusion she felt growing within her. This was what she wanted, wasn't it? Now Mosstown wouldn't be bothered anymore. After she'd initially declared to the residents of Mosstown that she would take care of Warthog, she had immediately regretted it. But she couldn't back down and continued telling them how she'd take him down, even in cold blood, if she had to. The hope in their eyes made her continue, despite Penny insisting she should let somebody else handle it.

So, why did seeing him like this now bother her? She had become good at ignoring things that bothered her—hiding from them rather than facing them. Instead, she wanted to cry, and she didn't know why. She started moving, walking away, trying to ignore the body so she didn't have to think about it anymore and soon found a room with a wide assortment of gear.

Remembering her original purpose, she sifted through the room's contents while Rainwood started hauling different bags and crates outside. Mostly it seemed like he found food, and she figured he was collecting supplies for Mosstown.

She found some of her gear mixed in with the other items and sighed, realizing the raiders had already dug through her pack. Starting a pile of her belongings to the side, she continued, worried if she'd have enough time to sift through everything.

All I want is some family things. The holo-tape of my parents and—

Ashe could recognize her backpack anywhere, as she'd spent so much time tailoring it to her needs. What started as a Pop-a-Cola-branded camping pack was now much more. Notably, it was hers.

At first, Ashe had drawn caricature pictures of her friends. But then she discovered that sometime before the arrival Pop-a-Cola had a promotional campaign with AstroTec, releasing a series of cute little two-inch-sized robots she couldn't get enough of. Since then, she'd made it a personal quest to find as many different ones as possible, and each was attached, either stitched in place or hanging from the corners.

"We should be going," Rainwood said when he returned next.

"But I need—" she started.

"Hurry," he growled.

Ashe quailed internally, then began tossing clothes and gear around until finally—seeing Kelly's bandana, she paused.

It's here.

She picked it up, drew it to her face, and breathed in slowly. His scent had long faded, but she could still tell it was his. He was always so proud to have it around his neck.

After tying it around her wrist, she glanced around, but the room had no holo-tapes. Anxiety driving her, she grabbed her pack and quickly checked the other rooms within the cave complex until she came upon a locked door. She had no time to pick a lock, so she kicked it with all her might. The flimsy sill shattered, and inside she found a desk with a stack of holo-tapes, some with a Fenclave sticker.

"Ashe?" Rainwood called from another chamber.

She swept all the tapes into her pack, hoping one of them was her parents', and jogged back to find Rainwood, who handed her a crate of canned goods. After they left the caves, she saw he'd found a brahman out in the corral and added their latest crates to the gear around its back before tying it tight.

With everything in order, he clicked his tongue and pulled on the lead rope around the brahman's neck. It moaned but started after him.

They left the compound without speaking.

She eventually interrupted the silence with a question. "Do you think the other raiders will follow us when they return?"

"Maybe. But probably not. There is a power vacuum now. They'll likely fight it out."

Ashe nodded.

An hour into the journey, she became frustrated. The brahman moved very slowly; by her estimation, their pace would put them back to the village well after dark. Now that something had finally gone right, she wanted to let everybody know. Her feet itched, and she needed to move faster.

She quickly walked past the brahman, then waited for it to pass her and repeated the process, hoping the dense beast would get the hint and pick up the pace. After a few iterations of this, Rainwood gave an exasperated growl. "Ashe, why don't you go on ahead?"

With a grin, she took off, gliding through the forest, her feet feeling light, and she made it back before dinner. She scaled the shortcut down the cliff, hoping to surprise Jade.

When she landed on the walkway, he stood a few steps away, his eyes bright with worry, fear, and maybe even some anger. "It's alright," she smiled. "Rainwood is fine. I'm back."

He turned and ran, disappearing into the complex.

That was not the welcome Ashe was expecting. She went to the dining room and gave everybody the good news, ignoring the sting Jade's reaction had left.

Everybody cheered, and the mood of the village immediately improved. The air filled with excited voices as people began making plans for the future.

Jade spent the evening with Penny and didn't want to talk to Ashe. He fought to stay awake, but it was a losing battle, and Penny took him to bed before Rainwood arrived.

Glenn and a few of the villagers waited for Rainwood by the water's edge. When he arrived, they left the brahman on the shore, with Glenn insisting he could get it onto the raft and bring it over later.

The townspeople congratulated Rainwood so much that it seemed to make him uncomfortable. Ashe sat on a railing, watching them unpack the food onto the docks below. Fireflies floated through the swamp, adding to the festive feel.

Moonbeam joined her, speaking quietly. "Jade was pretty upset when you left."

She nodded. "He seems fine now. He's a tough kid."

Awkward silence revisited the two as they watched the others.

Ashe finally spoke. "So, we can move on tomorrow then."

"Yeah, the old bear seems fine now."

Penny arrived, waiting to see if she was interrupting before saying, "Good job, Ashe."

"It was all Rainwood. I didn't do anything."

"So . . . I wanted to ask you about something. I—" Penny hesitated, struggling to find the right words, then finally mustered her thoughts. "—I wonder if Jade would be better off staying with us. We can keep him safe and take care of him. He likes it here."

Ashe swallowed back a lump that formed in her throat. Her hands curled into fists, but after a moment, she gave a strangled answer, "You might be right."

Moonbeam looked surprised.

Penny looked relieved.

Ashe spoke, feeling a little dead. "We'll go early in the morning before he wakes."

"Oh, that's not necessary. You can say goodbye to him."

Ashe whispered, "No. We'll leave early," and left the two of them. She wanted to be alone and went to pack her gear as quietly as possible, hoping not to wake Jade while staging everything outside the door of their room.

That night, she tossed and turned, unable to sleep, and finally, at 5:00 a.m., she quietly woke Rainwood and Moonbeam.

After they left the room, she gazed at Jade asleep on the bed, tightly clutching the Fuzzy Kat plushie Sara gave him, and tried to memorize how he looked.

She didn't want to forget.

Why are the right decisions so hard?

Glenn and Penny met the team at the docks. Glenn had volunteered to ferry them across the river bottoms.

Penny gave each of them a hug. "You are always welcome here in Mosstown."

They boarded the raft, and Glenn unfastened the rope, ready to push off.

A shout came from above. "Don't leave me!"

Still in his pajamas, Jade flew down the stairs. Penny reached out and caught him as he passed, holding him back.

Finding his progress thwarted, Jade instead hurled the Fuzzy Kat plushie onto the raft, perhaps hoping to somehow tie himself to the others, while shouting with an edge of fear coming through his voice, "I'm coming too!"

Penny tried to console him. "It's okay. It's better for you here."

"I–I–I don't want to be here!" he yelled at the top of his lungs.

A few heads poked out of the windows above.

Ashe bit her lip and looked away. Jade's Fuzzy Kat sat on the deck, where it landed at her feet.

"Ashe. You–You–You promised!"

"I promised to keep you safe. This is the best way to do that," she replied quietly, knowing he could hear her, even if nobody else could.

He stopped fighting Penny. Glenn held the raft's pole, unsure if he should push off.

Jade spoke in a subdued voice, taking time to frame each word, "You said nowhere is safe, and–and so–I want to be with you."

Ashe looked at Rainwood, his face stoic, expressing no opinion. Then she looked at Moonbeam, who offered, "Sometimes we can't choose the paths life gives us."

His statement jolted her thoughts. She didn't even know what he was trying to say, which frustrated her because she wanted somebody to tell her what to do, not give weird advice.

Ashe looked at Jade on the docks. Tears ran down his cheeks, but he stood firm, determined. His hands were balled in fists, not even taking Penny's. Ashe could see flecks of green in his eyes, even from a distance, and felt a connection that she didn't want to feel. *Am I just using him as a proxy for—*

"I am *Jade*."

Ashe nodded, smiling, even if the others looked confused.

"It's going to be hard. You'll have to hold your own. Carry a big pack. Be even tougher than Rainwood."

His face lit up, and he launched himself across the gap, landing on the raft and embracing her in a giant hug. She smiled, relief flooding through her and tears welling in her eyes as she returned the hug. *It may not be the best choice,* she decided, *but I think having him with us is the right one.*

Ol' Man Mose

The team returned to gather Jade's things. He eagerly stuffed his new belongings into the backpack they gave him, including making sure Fuzzy Kat was left sticking out the top—he didn't want the thing "to feel caged in." Ashe suspected it would take him some time to work through his past. But she couldn't help but laugh. *Anyone following Jade can enjoy a first-hand view of a creepy, grinning cat bobbing along.*

Penny had breakfast prepared by the time Jade was ready, and afterward, everybody in the town came out to see them off. Sara offered Jade another plushie from her collection—an alien "gray" dressed as a scientist in a lab coat—and he froze, shaking his head furiously. He seemed almost fearful. He shoved the scientist toy away when she offered it to him a second time, and then ran to the raft.

Ashe consoled her, trying to think of an explanation that would help Sara feel better. "Maybe he didn't want to take any more of your things?"

Sara gave a nervous smile and called out, "Hey, little guy, you take care, okay? Y'all come back whenever you can."

Then she turned back to Ashe, changing the topic. "Doc mentioned she met some traders on the road that came down through the United Chemicals factory, and it's overrun with hostile robots right now, for what it's worth."

"Thank you."

Ashe was the last to board the raft, and she sat next to Jade. As Glenn pushed off, she considered what she should say to Jade about how he treated Sara, even realizing it was silly to debate in her head what to say because he knew what she was thinking. She still said out loud, "Jade, you know it's not nice to turn away gifts. You should always accept a gift and say thank you, even if you don't like it."

He hunkered down and stared at the raft's deck.

Ashe sighed, then drew in a deep breath, noticing the mulchy scent of the swamp. The group was oddly quiet as Glenn pushed them through the boggy mire, which only highlighted the gentle sounds around them—the swish of the pole in the water, birds chirping from the canopy, and the croak of toads echoing across the river bottom. She hoped they were small toads and birds—you never knew what mutations the void storms would create.

As they approached the far shore, a church spire covered in vines appeared through the overgrowth.

"Ohh, neat. I like to look in churches," Moonbeam said to nobody at all. "It's always fun to go in and poke around. I wonder what people did in such a fancy place."

Rainwood gave an exasperated huff. "Kid, there is a lot you have to learn. I need to introduce you to the Good Book."

Ashe rolled her eyes, replying to Moonbeam. "Even I know why people went to church. Fenclave didn't have a chapel, but people met in the cafeteria to discuss the Good Book every Sunday. My parents never went, but I stopped by a few times to listen."

At the time, she had decided it sounded boring, if not silly—they spent most of the time reading from their book and talking about some dead guy who wanted everybody to be nice to each other.

She had since learned the world didn't work that way. *Most people want to kill you and take your stuff.*

Glenn spoke up. "That's the Fairmont Church. You don't want to visit there. It's infested with growlers, and some say it's haunted. At night, you can hear an organ playing inside the chapel. It's downright disturbing. If the air is right, you can even hear it all the way over in town."

Moonbeam grinned, and his eyes lit up. Ashe sighed, realizing that Glenn had only increased Moonbeam's interest.

Fortunately, Rainwood noticed and interjected, "Upriver it is, then. Moonbeam, no need to stop at every turn."

Jade grasped Ashe's hand, holding it tight. He looked worried and shook his head, pulling her close to whisper, "I don't like gr–growlers. They are not—they aren't dead. I can hear them, they yell and cry, and it s–s–scares me."

"Can you hear some right now?" she asked quietly.

He gave a firm nod, looking very afraid while staring intently at the chapel, its windows curiously unbroken in the gloom of the canopy. Yet clearly, it was in disrepair, with fallen siding and scattered shingles, let alone the overgrowth of vines.

Ashe spoke up, "Count me out too. Looks like you're outvoted, Moonbeam."

As they passed the church, she wondered about what Jade had said. She always thought growlers were some sort of undead zombies.

What did he mean they aren't dead? What are they, then?

After finding a landing spot near the crumbling Highway 95, they gathered their packs, and Glenn gave some final advice. "I'm sure you already know, but there are rumors of something dangerous in the woods up north."

"Everything is dangerous, Glenn," Ashe reminded him, "Are you talking folk tale-level things or something real?"

Moonbeam injected himself into the conversation with a grin. "I love folk tales! Have you heard about the lost towers of Nkuhlu? They're said to be from an ancient civilization on a long-forgotten world, and if . . . you . . ." His words trailed off as he noticed Ashe's piercing glare, prompting him to fall silent.

Glenn blinked, then continued with a nod, "This isn't a folk tale. I figure you've heard of the Deathmark?"

Ashe started to respond, but Moonbeam cut her off with an excited answer, "I have! And, it's supposed to be really frightening. But I've not met anybody who's seen one—or has seen one and is still alive, that is. Although I don't know, maybe I did meet somebody who met one but wasn't alive?"

Ashe carefully replied, "It's real, Moonbeam. It is terrifying. I've seen . . . just trust me. It doesn't kill for food. It's something else. It lives in pure rage. Compared to other nasty things—"

She couldn't explain the terror touching her even just thinking about it, so she whispered, "It's the scariest thing I've ever come across."

Fear continued to chase her thoughts. Jade took her hand and gave it a squeeze. She smiled at him while struggling to keep her voice steady. "Thanks for the warning, Glenn."

He asked, "So, you're heading up north? Anywhere in particular?"

"Yeah, taking these guys up by the pond springs area east of the Hemlock Picnic—" she stopped, wondering at his sudden interest, and her wariness kicked in. "Or, you know, just wandering, really. We could end up anywhere."

"Well, okay then. You guys plan on being out long? Think we'll see you come back this way any time soon?"

Moonbeam patted him on the back. "Hey, of course, we will! We had a blast with you guys! You betcha!"

Ashe was glad for Moonbeam's unending dialogue for once and quickly stepped away before Glenn could ask any more questions. The raft rocked in the water, bumping the rocks on the shore as they unloaded their gear.

Recognizing his opportunity was lost, Glenn tipped his straw hat and said, "You keep safe now, and I hope to see y'all again someday."

Ashe took a minute to check the map. "Considering what Sara said about the chemical plant, I think we should avoid the highway—it goes right through the whole facility. We can skip it by going east through the forest, although we'll have to head through the hills around Storm Mountain Lake."

Moonbeam gestured forward. "Lead on, oh great and indomitable leader."

She wanted to punch him. With reluctance, she held back. *He's lucky this time.*

☣   ☢   ☣

Glenn tied the raft to the docks and looked around Mosstown furtively, verifying everybody was occupied elsewhere before stopping by his room. He opened a hidden panel to retrieve a notebook, then slipped into the town's radio room. Squinting, he looked at the top page of the notebook, then dialed a frequency, picked up the microphone, and said, "E9FQ, E9FQ, this is VSF3 victor sierra fox-trot three standing by, using crypto pad seventeen."

After a moment of radio static, he repeated his call sign identification and waited.

Then a click signaled somebody else picking up the line. "VSF3, this is E9FQ listening with pad seventeen."

Glenn answered, "E9FQ, I have information on the target, but I want a different reward. Over."

"What reward do you want besides what is already on the table? Over."

Glenn clicked the button to speak but waited, let go, and took a few breaths before continuing. "E9FQ, this is VSF3. I want a Galaxy Express ticket. I can tell you where the target is. Waiting for confirmation. Over."

Silence.

"E9FQ, please hold. Wait for a reply."

Sweat rolled down Glenn's forehead, and he watched the door, hoping nobody would enter the radio room.

After another minute, the reply came in. "VSF3 answering E9FQ, that can be arranged. Over."

Glenn smiled, reassuring himself that getting on the Galaxy Express would be worth betraying his friends—he'd do anything to get out of the hellhole that Arcadia had become. He coordinated a meeting place using the cryptographic pad and signed off.

☣　　☢　　☣

The team forged into the forest, using Ashe's AstroCom to keep on track. Everyone watched for dangers, and after a couple of hours of nothing trying to eat them, they started to relax.

Moonbeam's comment about the churches stuck with Ashe, teasing her thoughts. *How can somebody not know what people do in church?*

She fell in step alongside him. "Can I ask you something?"

"You just did."

"Can I ask you something else?"

"You . . . just did."

She punched him in the arm—just enough to drive the point home.

He shot her a grin and a thumbs up. "Go for it, coolio!"

Ashe growled mentally, stuffing her growing frustration down with a deep breath, and asked, "Where are you from, and how did you meet Rainwood?"

He laughed. "I'm from AstroTec factory 23, part of their corporate outreach division, clone number MB-16."

"A clone? You want me to think you're a clone? That's science fiction! I'm serious!"

They walked for a minute without him saying anything. Ashe was about to prod him again when he said, "I came from a commune on Miratori . . . I think. My family lived 'off the grid' for a while. I don't remember much as a kid, actually. But I remember one time the raiders came and took all our crops, and things got worse for everybody. And then . . . something happened—" his eyebrows curled in thought before he continued, "—I can't remember, to be honest. But then Rainwood was there fierce as a bear. . . he helped me, and so I stayed with him. That's why I call him Daegom —he's a great bear. Then I found the treasure map, and now, here we are."

"Oh. I'm sorry."

Ashe felt a little bad for drawing this out of him, and they walked without talking for a minute until she couldn't help but ask, "You really don't remember what happened? Do you even know if your family is still around?"

He sighed, staring into the distance, and softly said, "No. I can't remember all sorts of things from time to time. But I do hope they're still around. Rainwood won't tell me. I figure it was a void thing."

Ashe gestured to the world at large. "Then why don't you care about all this devastation? Doesn't it make you angry that this all happened? That the void storms came, and your family . . . doesn't it even make you mad that raiders attacked and took your crops?"

"Will it change anything if I'm angry?"

"Yes! I mean . . . maybe?"

He looked up. "I think the world is beautiful. I know people talk about things from 'before,' but I don't know what that was like. This is all I've ever known. You grew up in a cozy underground enclave, but not me. We just had this," he threw his arms in the air, circling. "And it's so neat. I love it! There is always something new to find. What is there to be angry about?"

"You could be angry at the raiders that stole your crops! Or that the Kraal came and killed everybody! Or whatever happened to your family . . ."

"Would that make the hurt go away?"

She wasn't sure how to answer. "But getting revenge would help you feel better, maybe. Don't you think the raiders should be punished?"

"Will that bring my family's crops back? What if the raiders needed the crops more than we did?"

Ashe pointed at Jade, who intently watched their conversation with wide eyes. "What about how they treated Jade? Don't they deserve to be punished for that? It was wrong!"

"It was wrong . . . but now he's with us, and that's awesome. Right, little man?" He put up his hand for a high-five, and Jade jumped to slap it, smiling.

She bit back another response. *I just can't get through to him. Seriously, how can anybody live like that?*

"Ashe," he continued, "it feels to me like you're mad at everybody because you lost your family and everything you thought was good. But I want to ask you a question—don't answer it right now. Just think about it. Has anything gotten better because of your anger?"

She cinched up her pack and stomped ahead, pulling her headphones on and deciding it was up to them to keep up.

As she walked, she considered the bullet hanging around her neck. Ashe liked that she could feel its weight from time to time. It helped remind her of what she needed to do—the punishment she had to give to the Commissioner.

The woman deserves it and not because I'm angry—that's just silly—but because wrongs need to be addressed. It's all her fault this happened.

The trees thinned, and a broken building entangled by star vines came into view, with more appearing through the twisted trees beyond. Most of the structures were already pulled into the ground by the vines, and only their shattered rooftops were visible. It left a chilling feeling every time Ashe saw something like this.

"I see what you mean by the star vines being mighty voracious," mumbled Rainwood. Their path took them around the corner of the building, and they could see what remained of the small town. Ashe wondered what its name was. Its occupants were long gone, so she may never know. She could still see the hoods of cars peeking out of the dirt, and other buildings were in various forms of destruction, from only a scattering of bricks to a mostly intact church.

Moonbeam let his pack slip to the ground, stretched his shoulders, then stepped up to a window of a building to gaze in. "I think I can get inside. Looks like people left stuff behind."

Jade tugged on Ashe's arm, saying, "Something is hungry."

"Oh, sorry, that'd be me," said Moonbeam. "I should have eaten more for breakfast. Should we eat an early lunch?"

Ashe checked their progress on her AstroCom, deciding they could go farther before taking a lunch break. "No, we can go another hour or so. Come on."

She pressed forward through the depressing ruins of the small town. The ground had uplifted, splitting the asphalt and leaving heaps of soil, rocks, and debris, so much so that there was no road left. She pondered how fast this had all happened. Was it a slow process, or did it come all in one night? She shivered, thinking about how frightening it would've been if it had hit all at once.

After a moment, she realized that nobody followed her.

Rainwood stood in front of the church, studying the spire in quiet contemplation. Moonbeam was crawling into the window of another building, his bright purple shirt always a beacon, and Jade stood on his toes while holding the window's edge to see into the same building.

"Okay, let's take a break. Sound good?" Ashe declared to nobody in particular, scowling at being ignored. She shrugged off her heavy pack and rubbed her sore shoulders, thinking that perhaps a break was a good idea, but still kept her eye on the surrounding area, just in case.

She wondered what Jade had meant when he said something was hungry. But he'd followed Moonbeam and didn't seem concerned anymore.

Rainwood looked . . . she couldn't put her finger on it, but he looked tired, perhaps. His shoulders were slumped, and he slowly stepped into the church.

Curious, Ashe followed, moving carefully and engaging her chameleon body suit while creeping to the doorway and allowing her eyes to adjust to the darkness.

Rainwood sat at the front on a bench, looking up at the cross on the wall. He drew in a deep, slow breath and let it out in a ragged exhale. Ashe had the feeling she was intruding on something private.

A deep-throated croak reverberated through the area, then Jade screamed. Ashe bolted upright and scanned the broken street but couldn't see him. Adrenaline hit her, and she ran to her gear, snatching the Arbiter while dashing to where she last saw Jade.

A void toad had him tangled in its tongue. The beasts were the size of small cars and were willing to eat nearly anything. She aimed the rifle and tried to line up a good shot but hesitated. She didn't want to shoot over Jade, yet she needed to help him! He scrabbled at the ground, trying to find something to stop his progress into the toad's wide-open mouth while screaming in fear, "Help, Ashe, help!"

She ran faster than she could ever remember.

Not again!

She jumped over Jade, sighting her Arbiter onto the toad's head, and let it go on full auto, emptying the entire magazine while struggling against the recoil. Her muscle reflexes took over as she hit the ground and rolled with the movement, swapping the Arbiter's magazine mid-roll and instinctually pointing the gun at the monster once she came upright. She pulled the trigger again, not knowing if it was dead yet, but wanting it dead dead.

The bullets tore it to shreds.

She stopped.

It didn't move.

She ran to Jade, who growled, trying to pull his leg from the sticky tongue. Void toad toxins created a temporary numbing paralysis, and she wondered how much had made it into his system. He was small, and it might be worse for him.

Fear had her heart racing a hundred miles an hour. "Are you hurt?"

More *braaaaaaap* croaks echoed between the buildings—the toad had friends.

Ashe pulled another magazine to reload, but her fingers shook too much from the adrenaline, and she couldn't get it seated. Another toad appeared with its mouth screwing open to snap its tongue out, and Ashe stepped in front of Jade to take the hit. Barbs from the toad's tongue sliced her leg, knocking her to the ground. She rolled with the strike, avoiding becoming entangled, and came up to see Jade get free and hobble out of range, obviously hurt on one leg.

Moonbeam stumbled from the window, firing at the toads, while Ashe tried to reload again, finally setting the magazine in place. She snapped the Arbiter up to shoot at the toads, but a tongue struck her arm, throwing her aim off.

Tingling numbness seeped up to her shoulder, so she knelt, letting the Arbiter drop while drawing her Coyote from its holster with her left hand. Sparing time for a glance, she saw Jade limp around the corner, favoring his numb leg, and turned back towards the toads, hoping he was out of danger.

With a stroke of the trigger, the gun unleashed several rounds in a rain of crackling fire as each struck and exploded. Accuracy didn't matter much with this pistol because she had loaded it with explosive rounds. She called it Coyote because of a silly cartoon she watched as a kid about a coyote that always blew things up.

Fortunately for the others, the toads appeared to be focused on Ashe. Another tongue lashed, striking her knee, and she cursed aloud to help with the pain. "Blast it, those barbs hurt!"

Rainwood joined them, his gauntlet a blur as he sliced across the toad's back. Then Ashe heard Jade scream again, and he appeared around the corner pulling on his backpack—another toad had lashed onto it.

She struggled to stand, her leg numb and wobbly from the toxin. Fortunately, the toad attacking her had shifted its attention to Rainwood. She stumbled toward Jade, shouting, "Let it go!"

But he wouldn't release his pack!

The toad hopped closer to Jade with its maw wide open. She reached Jade and shoved him to the ground, aiming her pistol into the toad's opened mouth and unleashing another salvo of rounds. It was only a few feet away, so she took some backlash from the micro explosions and positioned her body to shelter Jade from the damage.

The toad had no chance—its cranium shattered as the rounds struck true, detonating on the soft inner flesh.

She turned and grabbed Jade, wanting to hold him tight and keep him safe—only to be hit by a memory of panic. Images of hiding in a cramped, dark box, with her dog Kelly. The smell of fearful sweat filling the air as something outside snuffled around. She knew it wanted to kill her, and she needed to keep quiet.

A wave of guilt rose up, threatening to drown her as the memory came back.

No! she mentally shouted, pushing Jade away while fighting her turmoil of thoughts and using the adrenaline to focus and scan for danger. She stood in front of him, her gun at the ready, and Jade had the sense to stay on the ground this time.

It was quiet.

She took a few more deep breaths, working to calm down and massaging her limbs, which tingled as they came out of the numbing toxins.

Jade sniffled.

Moonbeam arrived with Rainwood—they both looked worse for wear but otherwise okay.

Rainwood offered her the Arbiter. "You two alright?"

Barely holding it together and not sure she could speak without losing it, she took the rifle and nodded. *Why do these memories come back so randomly? I put that all behind me.*

Rainwood said, "You stay put. We'll check the area to make sure there's no more unexpected company."

Ashe's adrenaline faded a minute later, and she collapsed next to Jade. Dust covered him from head to toe, streaks from his tears drawing tracks down his face.

"Are you hurt?" she asked.

"My–My leg hurts."

She checked but saw no serious damage. "It's probably just bruised. You'll feel sore for a couple of days, but you should be alright." Fear caused her voice to rise. "You need to listen to me! It's just a bag! You should've let it go! Don't pull a stunt like that again!" She shook his shoulders to drive her point home.

Tears welled up in his eyes, his brow crinkled, and he flinched away from her.

His reaction was like a slap in the face. She quickly let him go and turned away while struggling to find words.

"I'm sorry. Just—let's not do the whole 'terrify Ashe' routine again. It's not my thing."

She didn't want him to be hurt and hoped he understood— that's why she was mad.

He sniffled. Then sniffled again. He was crying but trying to keep it quiet.

Ashe drew him close while leaning against the building and whispered, "You're fine. It's alright."

The guys returned a few minutes later.

Jade wiped his nose on the sleeve of his ATU jacket, then knuckled the tears from his eyes.

Rainwood suggested, "How 'bout we indulge in an early lunch."

Figuring some tunes might help lighten the mood, Ashe dialed the music library on her AstroCom, and *"Ol'* Man Mose" accompanied them while they patched each other up and shared a meal.

9.

Just a Fair Weather Friend

Moonbeam showed Jade how to dissect the toads, extracting succulent strips from the legs that he fried on an impromptu spit for lunch.

Afterward, Rainwood dug through his pack and pulled out a small .308 pocket pistol, then stepped over to Jade and held it out flat on his hand.

"Do you think you can handle this? It's a small caliber, so hopefully, it'll be okay for somebody your size. And it will help you if something like this happens again."

The idea of arming a six-year-old would have shocked Ashe to the core a year ago. But now it just made sense.

Jade stared at the gun for a moment, then reached to take it, but Rainwood pulled it back. "Easy there, Tiger. First things first, there are rules. Ready?"

Ashe perked up. Since leaving Fenclave, she had learned how to use a gun primarily by herself, so her curiosity was piqued.

Jade nodded, a serious look on his face.

Rainwood walked several paces away, placed a few cans onto a rock, then returned, kneeling by Jade's side and holding up the gun. "I'm trusting you not to use this without permission, but I also want you to have it in case we're not there to help. Promise to only use it if there's no other option?"

Jade nodded again.

Rainwood showed him all the parts of the gun, how it all came together, how to check if it had a bullet in the chamber, and how to load the bullet clip. He then offered the gun to Jade, moving with exaggeration to demonstrate that he was keeping the barrel pointed down, away from anybody.

"Now, pay close attention. Is there a bullet in the chamber?"

Jade furrowed his brow, studied Rainwood for a moment, then looked at Ashe.

Cheater, she thought. He looked back at Rainwood and shook his head with a grin.

"Here's the rule: you always assume the gun has a bullet in the chamber, okay? Now, even if you've checked and you're certain it's empty, is it okay to point it at Ashe, just for fun, like a game?"

Jade shrugged, looking confused.

Rainwood slid a bullet into the chamber, still pointing it down, and said, "Is it okay if I point this at Ashe now?"

He immediately responded, "No!"

"Good answer. This is the most important rule about guns: Never point a gun at anything unless you intend to kill it. It doesn't matter if there's a bullet in it or not. Always keep the barrel pointed away from anything you don't want to kill, even if you're just wandering around. Can you remember that?"

Jade nodded.

"Next up, always be aware of what's behind your target. So, what's behind those cans over there? What are you going to hit if you miss?"

Jade peered at the hillside behind the rock. "The dirt?"

Rainwood smiled and handed him the gun, taking extra care to keep it pointed away from anybody. "You catch on quick, kid. Now, take this, hold it like I showed you, and aim at a can. Let's see if you can hit one. And be ready for it to kick back."

Ashe stood behind Jade as he aimed the gun, preparing for what she figured would happen. He was tiny and light as a feather—any gun was probably too big for him, but she agreed with Rainwood; it would be good for Jade to be able to protect himself.

Crack! The gun fired, and he stumbled back from the recoil, throwing it in the air as he put his arms out for balance. Rainwood snatched the pistol before it hit the ground, and Ashe caught Jade as he stumbled back.

Rainwood kept his features flat, but Ashe could see a glint of humor in his eyes as he said, "Kicks a little harder than you expected, right? Want to do it again?"

Although Jade rubbed his hand—which likely smarted from the kick—his expression was of grim determination, unwilling to quit.

"This time, plant your feet and lean into it like this." Rainwood showed Jade the correct stance.

Jade mirrored Rainwood, and his fifth attempt nailed the can. Moonbeam whooped, "Great shot, my little dude!"

Jade reloaded and kept practicing, shooting a handful of rounds before he finally gave up, setting the gun down while shaking his hands yet sporting a wide grin.

"Hurts?" Ashe asked.

Jade nodded, and Ashe added, "Just keep practicing. You'll get used to it."

Rainwood worked up a strap and holster for the gun, making it more of a harness over Jade's shoulders because it was heavy and he was so skinny that it kept sliding down otherwise. Afterward, they packed up and set off.

Before they left, Jade made sure his pack was in order, including mounting Fuzzy Kat in his proper place. Then he took care to fasten the gun securely before straightening with a determined look on his face.

There was no way they could carry all of the meat from the toads, so they took what they could, and Jade kept a cooked strip in his hands, which he continued to eat as they hiked.

"If we push hard enough, we should make it to Storm Mountain Lake before night," Ashe said. "I'd like to be east of it in the hills before the sun sets."

A chorus of non-commital grunts was all she received as confirmation.

She directed them onto a side road, which turned up the hillside. As they approached the top, somebody called out from just over the hill in a prim, cultured female accent.

"I say! Hello! Goodness, I thought my sensors were on the fritz! It's people. Ordinary people, finally! You are ordinary, right? No mutations? Not gaunts?"

A unidroid robot rolled into sight.

It was not a humanoid robot, but rather had three all-terrain wheels, which connected to a central ring where many different types of appendages could be attached—in this case, it had three simple grappler arms, although one seemed damaged and was folded up by the chassis. Above that was the central body—an orb that held the main bulk of the robot's electronics. Two eye stalks poked out of each side.

Ashe liked this model, the unidroid. It was designed as a universal robot that could be easily reconfigured for a wide variety of purposes. Her robot teacher back in Fenclave, Emmett, was the same type.

This robot, however, looked agitated as it approached, waving its grappler arms. It was painted in an array of flashy pink and yellow colors that looked as if they were applied by a five-year-old, including a set of bright red lips painted on its front glass screen.

Ashe readied her Arbiter, worried this could be one of the rogue robots from the chemical factory.

A line on the glass screen moved while it spoke—the lips were correctly painted around the line. "Oh heavens, you gave my inner workings quite the start. I feared you were one of those nightmare creatures wandering about lately. But I certainly could use some help."

The robot seemed benign, but Ashe tried to stop any angle it might have with a quick statement. "We don't have any robot parts or fusion cores."

Its waving appendages froze before it answered, "Well, somebody could use a lesson in manners."

Jade laughed, still holding a chunk of fried void toad, and asked, "What's your name?"

It waved its arms in a vague bowing motion. "Victoria, at your service."

Jade walked toward her with an eager look of fascination on his face. "Why are you all colorful?"

The robot moaned, "My owner, Emelia, feels it's pretty. But that's not what I need help with—"

"Who is Emelia?"

"Augh," the robot threw its arms up in dramatic exasperation. "She's just the bane of my existence. A tyrant, I tell you."

Jade scrunched his eyebrows in confusion. "What's a tyrant?"

"Ah, well, she's a mean person who is out to terrorize my vacuum tubes, that's what. And you are?"

"I'm Jade."

"Master Jade, it's a pleasure."

It gave another bowing gesture.

Jade seemed unusually talkative, "What's a bane? Is a terror like a tyrant?" he asked while circling the robot, then immediately followed up with, "How do you turn around?" and pointed to the wheels.

"Well, I—that's many questions, Master Jade, and it's impolite to ask so many without waiting for a response. Let's see: first, my wheels can turn in any direction, giving me a great range of movement, although the rotator coupling on wheel two has been giving me problems. As for a bane—"

"How come your eyes are on tube sticks?"

Her eye stalks looked together, then back at Jade. "Why, I don't know. That's an excellent question. Another one of many which you have, it seems."

Ashe stared at Jade, surprised at how out of character he acted. Typically he didn't talk much, likely because of his stuttering. But now, he hadn't stuttered once and couldn't seem to stop with the questions. Ashe wondered if it had to do with his ability to read thoughts—or not read them, in the case of a robot.

He almost tap-danced as he circled the unidroid, intently studying each part with excitement, then stepped on one of its wheels and lifted himself up, asking with excitement, "Can I get a ride?"

Ashe put her hand on his shoulder, pulling him off the robot. "Okay, that's enough, Jade. We should let Victoria go on her way."

"Good gracious, are you not willing to help me?" the robot pined.

"Help with what?" Jade asked.

"Something has come upon my people. There is only one left, and he is letting out the most dreadful screeches. The noise terrified me out of my bolts, and I had to seek help as fast as possible. I fear the worst. Please say you will help?"

"I want to help!" Jade declared, jumping in excitement.

Ashe threw her hands in the air, deciding to give up—Jade was obviously going to do what he wanted. But she worried—did the robot's people become growlers? Were they locked away?

"Perhaps we should avoid looking for trouble," Ashe started.

Moonbeam leaned on Ashe's shoulder, a grin on his face, adding, "I don't know, sounds like it could be exciting. And the kid is interested. I think we should go! What do you think, Daegom?"

Rainwood gave an exasperated sigh, and Ashe realized he wasn't going to help one way or the other. With reluctance, she asked, "Is it close? And just one?"

Victoria bobbed her head. "Not far at all, just a few minutes that way. I'm surprised you can't hear the wailing from here. Such a dreadful noise! Quick, follow me!"

She spun on her wheels and moved down the hillside, shaking as she bumped over rocks, following a well-worn path.

Ashe sighed and started after the others. Moonbeam ended up in the lead and, a little while later, called out, "Hey, I love this song!"

The classic tune of "Country Roads" carried through the canopy. With caution, they approached the ramshackle complex where the music came from.

Somebody had assembled a hodge-podge building made from various scraps found around the badlands. Trailers, bricks, corrugated steel, and much more—all pretty typical for the times. What pushed it over the top for Ashe was the gaudy decorations, streamers, and giant sign that said, "Welcome, friends!"

From inside, somebody sang along with the song. Passionately off-key.

A swarthy guy stepped out, his wooly hair bright pink, wearing a gold-sequined tuxedo coat and red bug-eyed glasses while singing into an empty pop-a-cola bottle like a microphone. He struck a pose and belted out the line, "To the place I belooooong!"

"Isn't it simply dreadful?" Victoria asked. "Please, help him! Put him out of his misery if you must! I see you carry a rifle. Just make it quick!"

Ashe was horrified, not by Victoria's suggestion, nor the over-the-top decorations and the singer, but because she didn't need to meet him to know who it was.

She turned. "Quick, let's go before he sees us."

"What? Of course not!" said Moonbeam. "Anybody that chrome-plated has to be fun!"

"No! Not fun. I think it's something about the badlands, but a few people just go . . . not feral, but . . . trust me. They go . . . weird." She pulled his arm to leave.

Unfortunately for Ashe, the singer saw them and waved. "Hey! Come on in!"

Victoria declared, "You saved him! The wailing stopped!"

Jade giggled.

"I think I'll stay out here and, uh . . . and keep watch." Ashe declared to Rainwood as he passed.

Moonbeam, at max volume, replied to the guy. "This is an awesome pad you have!"

"Isn't it, though?" he enthusiastically answered.

Ashe scanned the forest, watching for danger while telling herself, *Ugh. This sort of camp will easily attract the wrong type of attention.*

"Ashley?"

She froze.

"Hey, I thought I recognized you!" The colorful guy approached her, arms out as if expecting a warm embrace.

Ashe knew exactly who this was. She ignored the offered hug and answered coolly, "Hello, Mason."

He drew up short, recognizing her coldness, and with a confused smile on his face, gestured to the compound. "Come check out this place my family put together."

Realizing there wasn't a choice, she followed the others.

The interior fared no better. It was a bright visual onslaught, with colored posters, comic memorabilia, Pop-a-Cola signs, and even a mirror ball.

The horror increased in Ashe's mind, and she reeled from the assault on her senses.

She overheard Mason telling Moonbeam, "Ashley and I were in the same class in Fenclave, and all the guys thought she was pretty cute."

Ashe wanted to fade into the ground and disappear with embarrassment.

"Hey, Muffintop, put a lid on it," she growled.

He laughed. "Everybody called me 'Muffintop' because I've always been big-boned."

He patted his belly, still a little tubby—a surprise, considering he had been living in the wilderness for a year.

"Then I decided, why not embrace it, right? So sure, call me Muffintop. I don't care."

Moonbeam waved Ashe over, gesturing at the couches, and said—emphasizing her full name—"AsheLEE, come on over!"

Mason beamed. "My folks and Emelia are out on a supply run to Pikeston, but I'm sure they'd love to see you again! I'm so glad they left me behind to protect the compound, or we would've missed each other! Can you stay a while? Mom would want to see you."

She grumbled, "Call me Ashe."

He paused, smiled, and declared, "Ashe, it is!" before looking beyond her, and asking, "How's the family?"

She glared at them all, thinking, *NOPE,* and made a beeline for the door.

☣　　☢　　☣

After Ashe left the room, Mason gave Moonbeam and Rainwood a confused look. Moonbeam sighed, stepped over to Mason, and patted his shoulder reassuringly before explaining, "Ashe lost her whole family."

Emotions warred on Mason's face, and after a moment, he sighed and, with a determined look, pulled off his gold-sequined tuxedo coat while declaring, "I'm going with you. She could use somebody she knew from before—"

"You don't know where we're going," Rainwood interjected.

"I don't care." He paused, unsure how to explain, then stepped over to the corner where a polished mech sat in a maintenance frame and considered it for a moment. Then he turned back to the others and nervously ran his fingers through his wooly pink hair before continuing, "I think—I just, I'm not sure. But I really think I should join you."

"Didn't you say you were staying here to protect the compound?"

Mason shook his head, saying, "My parents will understand. Victoria can explain everything. They'd want me to go, I'm sure of it."

Mason inserted an authorization key into the mech, powering it up, and Moonbeam shrugged at Rainwood.

☣　　☢　　☣

Ashe sat on a styrofoam rock and poked at the flaking concrete coating, wondering if Mason had carried it all the way from the Wobbly Walleye's water park up north of Highway 95.

Jade ran to her, scrambled up the boulder, and embraced her in a tight hug.

"Hey, everything alright? What's that for?" she asked him.

He mumbled, "Sometimes people need a hug."

She wrapped her arms around him and asked, "Do you need a hug?"

He sighed and eventually relaxed, shifting to sit by her side, his feet dangling over the edge.

The high-pitched *screeee, click-clack* of mechanized armor sealing up was loud enough to hear even from outside.

Rainwood arrived at Ashe's chosen rock. "Looks like your friend will be joining us for a while."

She straightened, her eyes flaring. "Wait, what? No, he can't!"

Rainwood shrugged and started westward.

"Isn't it neat?" asked Moonbeam. "Muffintop has a mech!"

The *ca-chunk* heavy tread of a mech arriving behind her made that clear. But she refused to turn around.

Through the mech's speaker, Mason's voice was tinny. "Look what I found, Ashe, a Banshee!"

He stomped in front of her.

Ashe shook her head, wondering how he found such a rare mech. It was a demo unit for Jet Atomics—the manufacturer behind the UOS Mechanized Armor. Made for the military, they normally were painted in camouflage. However, Mason had painted it with a lime green and bright purple paint scheme and polished it to a brilliant sheen. The Jet Atomics mascot adorned the chest—a curvy woman in a spacesuit giving a salute, with the slogan "Making the world a safer place" illustrated below.

The ostentation of it suited Mason, she decided, and told him, "Looks great," before stepping past. "Make sure to stay out of my way when the fighting starts."

"Geeze, Ashe, you have no faith!" he called at her retreating form. "I've learned a lot out here; don't underestimate the Muffintop!"

☢   ☢   ☢

Captain Wright pounded his fist on the console. "What do you mean the robots still won't do what you say? This morning one of them put hot sauce in my coffee! You've had a year to get this system in shape."

Lieutenant Simmons couldn't help but cringe in his seat at the terminal. The mainframe stretched behind him as a wall of blinking lights, and he nervously adjusted his thick-rimmed glasses before answering, "Just so, sir, the mainframe controls are very advanced. Somebody made many modifications—probably the enclave's occupants before we came. We'll have to do a full system reset at this point, but we don't have the original operating system tape reels. I put in a requisition three months ago for backups—"

Captain Wright held his hand in a warding-off gesture. "I don't need the details. If the robots are causing this big a problem, just shut 'em off. We can run things ourselves. Minimal systems, if need be."

"That will impact the repairs to the rocketship Goldstar-9, sir, and you said that was a priority. The repair bots are part of the same subsystem."

Captain Wright ground his teeth. "Lieutenant Simmons, I don't care if you have to do the repairs yourself. Just get the robots fixed—and the rocket as well. Use the locals if you have to. I'm holding you responsible!"

Simmons saluted. "Of course, Captain."

The captain held back his frustrated anger as he left the computer room and made his way through the empty halls of Fenclave, heading up to the control room that had a broad window looking over the enclave's underground plaza. At his arrival, two soldiers straightened and gave him a salute, which he recognized with a nod before asking, "Status update?"

"We just received confirmation—as you thought, Galaxy Express 3-9 is stopping at the station in a week, and the station's mainframe has dispensed a ticket. But, sir, everybody knows to avoid 3-9."

Captain Wright grinned. "The fool didn't ask which Galaxy Express he wanted on. Of course, we could never get tickets to the others, but I had hoped the system would give us a ticket to 3-9. Sounds like I was right. Just keep him isolated until we can send him to the station, and nobody mentions a word about 3-9!"

The two soldiers nodded, sharing a knowing glance.

10.

Run For Your Life

Ashe avoided Mason the rest of the afternoon and harbored frustration at the lost time. When the shadows stretched noticeably, indicating sunset approached, the team crested a hill and looked down on a new valley. The Fen's dense canopy stretched below, opening into a broad lake.

Ashe stopped and pointed. "That's Storm Mountain Lake. We're about halfway to your friend's place by the pond. You can just make out the chemical factory over there on the west side. We can stay on the shoreline and cut to the east."

Mason came up behind her, the treads of the Banshee easily detectable, and said, "There are hollows down by the lakeshore. I'm sure we can find one for shelter."

She ignored him. "Let's get closer to the shore and look for a quiet hollow."

Rainwood rolled his eyes and mumbled something about teenage drama.

As they descended the slope, their path crossed a small road, which helped them avoid all the brush that had built up near the lake, but soon they came upon a broken cargo trailer blocking the way. The pungent smell of rotting flesh wafted through the air—a foul, almost sweetly curdled stank.

"Hold on, let me check it out," Ashe said quietly. Rainwood warily scanned the trees for danger. Mason pulled the Banshee's minigun from its shoulder mount, making it ready, and Moonbeam drew his pistols.

Ashe nodded to Jade, who nervously pulled his pistol from the holster, checking the bullet in the chamber. A little pride welled up in her as she watched him handle it with exaggerated care.

With everybody ready, she crouched and moved ahead, tapping her hip to engage the chameleon effect.

Rounding the trailer, she found the torn and shredded body of a large furred creature which was once at least the size of a brahman, and froze in place, letting her chameleon effect fully engage while she scanned for danger, worried it was a trap.

Once she felt safe, she carefully stepped through the carnage, trying to understand what had happened.

Upon seeing the creature's head, she froze.

Her hands shook, and she fought the desire to run away. With care, she tugged on a long, needle-like spine embedded deeply in the flesh.

Terror gripped her thoughts, and in a flash, she remembered squeezing herself into a crate and her mom talking with panic, saying, "stay quiet," as she closed the lid.

She bit her lip until the taste of blood brought her back.

Ashe focused on the spine in her hand and quickly retreated. She rounded the cargo trailer to see Jade holding tight to Moonbeam's leg, his pistol forgotten on the ground—he'd heard the terror in her head.

She thrust the spine into Rainwood's hands, whispering, "We need to be very quiet and get as far from here as possible."

Rainwood considered the spine—at nearly a third of a meter long, it obviously wasn't from any normal creature.

Moonbeam looked at her curiously, and she gave him a cold stare before stating, "Deathmark."

Ashe gestured for everybody to follow and crouched to reinforce the need for caution.

As they passed the massacre site, everybody could see the aftermath of a Deathmark attack. The smell of rot turned their stomachs, and clotted blood covered everything in red from the brutal violence the void-spawned terror had unleashed on the poor beasts. Only shredded bits of the brahman remained, scattered across everything in the area.

By the looks in their eyes, Ashe figured everybody pondered what made the Deathmark so filled with hate and rage that it would do such a senseless thing. But she knew they just killed for the sake of killing, not because they wanted sustenance.

She couldn't help but wonder how long ago this attack had happened, and a chill ran down her spine.

Once past the scene, the team found an opening in the brush and left the road, making it to the shoreline a few minutes later.

The lake was still, and along the shore to the left, in the distance, they could see the distinguishable features of the chemical factory—various industrial buildings, massive pipes, and other machinery—which ran right to the shoreline.

Something caught Ashe's eye, and she pulled the Arbiter up, looking through the scope. Everybody drew weapons in response, and she added quietly, "Just getting a better look."

There was the movement of people or creatures or something, but the angle wasn't ideal, and with twilight coming, she couldn't make out who or what occupied the compound.

She sighed. "It does look like somebody is at the factory, so it's good we're taking the long way around the lake."

Rainwood looked up at the golden sky streaked with shadows from the clouds and declared, "We need a safe place for the night."

Ashe pulled up the AstroCom's map. "The idea of solid walls around us seems good, considering what we just came across. There is a warehouse in the direction we need to go."

Everybody agreed, so they retreated and followed the road eastward. The dark of night had reached them when the road opened to a parking lot. A tattered chain link fence circled the area, connecting to a small warehouse. Ashe held her hand up, whispering, "Let me check it out."

She didn't tell them about her last visit to this place, where she had to clear out a nest of hostile, gigantic void-gaunt squirrels that had developed an ability to spit radioactive fireballs—decidedly unpleasant. The void storms certainly were good at creating nightmarish terrors.

With slowly creeping steps, she followed the fenceline, leveraging her chameleon ability while listening for any indication of danger.

She crossed behind a rusted freight trailer, climbed the dock, and checked the door. It was locked. Somebody had visited since she last stopped by because she had left it unlocked. Picking the lock took only a minute, and she eased the door open. The gloomy interior was frightening, mainly because the pre-arrival business sold medical supplies, notably model skeletons, which were now scattered around the place.

After a quick circuit of the facility, she found no threats and returned to the docks, waving everybody forward.

Jade gave Ashe a grin. "I like when you sneak. Y–you disappear."

Ashe ruffled Jade's hair as she held the door open. A quiet squeak erupted from his mouth when he stepped inside, and his head snapped back and forth in fright as he looked at the items in the room. He nervously backed out, bumping into Ashe.

Are the skeletons really that scary? She wondered, holding his trembling shoulder, then explained, "Hey, it's alright. They are just for school. They aren't real. They can't hurt you."

He tore from her grip and ran pell-mell through the room. At each turn, his fright increased as he saw something he thought was terrifying. She gave chase, leaving the guys to work out sleeping arrangements, and finally caught up to him as he darted into a locker, slamming the door behind him.

She tried the latch, only to find it locked, and sighed.

"Hey, you alright?"

No response.

"Are you afraid of the skeletons? They can't hurt you."

"No," came a whisper.

Ashe thought, now confused. *What scared him, then?*

"Can you open the door?" she asked, reaching for her lockpicks.

A moment later, the handle jiggled, and he let the door open just a tiny bit—she could just make out his striking green eyes.

"Are you alright? You want to come out now?"

He shook his head negatively.

She directed her thoughts. *Are you sure you want to stay locked in that small locker?* She felt a little bad at manipulating him like that.

He looked away, then pushed the door open and buried his head in her chest.

She stroked his hair, repeating, "It's alright," until he relaxed.

After a minute, she asked, "You want to tell me about it?"

He answered in a muffled voice, still buried against her, "It reminds me–me of before."

"Before what?"

"Before I was–I was here."

Ashe considered his answer. "Do you mean the badlands?"

He nodded, and she realized the lab equipment bothered him, not the skeletons.

She gently pushed him back to give him her full attention. "How about you hang tight here, and I'll go clear out all those microscopes and medical things, alright? That work for you?"

Then she tugged Fuzzy Kat from Jade's backpack, and handed the plushie over. "Maybe he can keep you company?"

"Okay," he said, taking it from her..

The guys watched with concern on their faces. She approached them to speak quietly, "The medical equipment frightened him. Maybe he was in a laboratory at some point. Let's get it out of here."

Moonbeam shot Jade his trademark smile and thumbs-up before joining the others in clearing out what they could.

Rainwood wandered off while everybody else cleaned, and Moonbeam observed to Ashe, "You're good with him, you know. It's almost like you have some mental wavelength mojo going on between you two." He forced a laugh, letting it trail off when she didn't say anything.

After a moment, Mason interrupted the awkward silence, "So. A lab. Maybe that's why the raiders wanted the kid. What happened to him?"

Ashe glanced back at Jade, who watched their work from afar. "That's up to him to tell you."

The awkward silence started again.

"I'm going to see if Rainwood needs help," Mason said, leaving the two alone.

After a minute, Moonbeam asked in a soft voice, "Are you okay? You seemed rather bothered by the Deathmark spine."

Perhaps it was the fact that she'd asked Jade to open up, or maybe it was Moonbeam's gentle approach that swayed her decision, but she finally felt she could talk about it. With a sigh, she leaned against a table and ran her hands through her hair.

"Yeah. It's . . . well—a Deathmark killed my family."

"Ah."

"My mom . . . she hid me in a box. But I heard it—all of it. Everything, even when it—and my dad—and—and then it was sniffing around, trying to find us—me."

She stopped.

No, this isn't going to work.

Aloud she growled, "It doesn't matter. None of that would have happened if it wasn't for the Commissioner kicking us out. She's the one to blame. Who has to pay."

Moonbeam looked at her with a raised eyebrow, and she added, "Come on, let's figure out where to sleep."

He stepped over and embraced her with a hug, and she just stood there, arms hanging by her side. She thought it felt nice. She wanted to relax. She almost raised her arms and hugged him back, but fear seeped into her thoughts again—the fear of getting close to people.

If they die—she abruptly stopped her thought process, stating, "Thanks, but let's get this done. For Jade."

Moonbeam reached out and lifted the bullet hanging around her neck and asked, "What's this for?"

Ashe realized how close he was and felt confused. Part of her wanted him closer, hugging again, and part of her wanted him to leave. She looked down, answering, "It's a reminder. That I have unfinished business."

"Ohh, are you keeping this for when you face another Death-mark?"

She paused, unwilling to voice her thoughts, but they ran free inside her. *I've never faced another Deathmark. I've always run any time I've encountered one. It makes sense that that's why I'd keep the bullet, but . . . The Commissioner killed my family—the Deathmark was just the weapon.*

She took the bullet and gave him a quiet answer, "No."

Mason cleared his throat from across the room. The two jumped in surprise, and Ashe quickly stepped away, "We weren't —"

Mason looked surprised to see the two so close. Hammering noises reverberated from outside, and Mason paused. He worked his jaw a little before flatly stating, "Rainwood is trying to get the building's reactor going."

Ashe quickly walked outside, the other two following. Rain-wood tossed the hammer down as they arrived, grumbling, "It's not going to start. Somebody took the fusion regulator, but it's a lost cause, even with another. The parabolic matrix completely seized up. Something hit it hard."

Moonbeam pointed out, "You were just hitting it hard."

"I was trying to see if I could get it to break free and reset. I believe it was hit with gunfire." He pointed to bright spots on the outer frame. "Probably a plasma weapon."

A stack of cargo containers filled the area behind the build-ing, and he gestured to them. "Regardless. It might be better for us to stay in one of these tonight. The building has too many en-trances, and it'll likely be better for the boy anyway."

Ashe worked the latch on one, opening it with a loud metallic squeal—it was mostly empty.

They set up camp in the yard and made a small fire to heat a meal. Rainwood finished eating early and opened his bag, pulling out a black book. "Moonbeam, this is the Bible, the Good Book. Come here."

Ashe wondered why Rainwood carried a Bible and was a little curious to hear what he had to say but decided instead to take the chance to do some snooping. With everybody focused on Rainwood, she stepped away and slipped into the container, then quickly sifted through Moonbeam's pack, eventually finding the "treasure map" journal.

With the light of her AstroCom, she started reading, hoping to learn more about their treasure hunt, but frustration mounted as she scanned the contents. She flipped through more pages.

Looks like this person had a congregation? Like they were a pastor? In a church, even.

Ashe skipped past the bulk of the journal to the end, reading about the family cabin in the hills above Storm Mountain. She had just reached the part where the author had arrived at the cabin a few years after the cleansing when Rainwood stepped into the container.

She snapped the journal closed with a start, hoping he wouldn't notice. He knelt and put the Bible into his pack, then asked, "Find any new clues?"

Ashe blushed and abruptly handed over the journal, mumbling, "No," before exiting the container.

The team set up a four-way watch, with Ashe taking the first stretch. The others went to sleep while she found a good lookout position on top of the container stack. Fireflies bobbed around in the trees, and she smiled. She hadn't seen fireflies until she left Fenclave and had been fascinated with them ever since. She always felt they were magical.

After a couple of hours, tedium kicked in, and she retrieved her pack, finally having time to sift through the holo-tapes.

Was taking down Warthog's compound just yesterday? She felt the weariness sink into her.

She sifted through the tapes and was surprised to find two with Fenclave stickers. To her delight, one of them had the familiar, smudged writing of her mother, with only "birthday" still legible. She hadn't listened to it for a long time, she realized, holding it tightly. She yearned to hear the voices of her father, mother, and—

A cold ache seized her heart, and the wave of guilt threatened to rise.

Fearing the darkness, she stuffed the tape into her bag and focused on controlling her breathing.

She needed a distraction.

It struck her—why would another Fenclave tape be at Warthog's place?

She pulled it from the pile and slotted it into her AstroCom. There was silence, then a woman's voice spoke, *"What do you want, Warren?"*

Ashe's blood ran cold. She'd recognize the voice of the Commissioner anywhere.

A man laughed. *"Now, there's an old name I haven't heard for a while. Just call me Warthog."*

"I won't play these games. I came like you asked. Now tell me why I shouldn't just shoot you now. You betrayed us all by becoming a raider. How many of our people have you killed?"

He chuckled. *"You might shoot me, but you won't kill me, and you won't make it to the second shot."*

She sighed. *"What do you want from me?"*

"I know what happened back in Fenclave—you let somebody in, and the water systems failed. But they didn't just fail. It was

sabotage. I was the water systems engineer. I knew better. And I could have fixed it."

There was a long pause, and Ashe wondered if the recording had ended, but the Commissioner finally answered quietly, *"I didn't have a choice. He said he was from the Union and his credentials were valid. The mainframe approved his access. I knew something wasn't right and kicked him out the next day. But he returned and said his powerful military group had elevated access in the system, and if we didn't leave, he could tell it to kill us all while we slept. You see I'm out here, too, right? Do you think I want to be in this place? I did what I could to save everybody. I tried to put a positive spin on it and figured we had enough skills that we could help re-establish civilization."*

Ashe fingered the bullet around her neck, then hit the pause button as her thoughts raced. *I knew it! The whole "rebuild the planet" was obviously a ruse.* Ashe looked at the bullet, wondering if her anger was misplaced, like Moonbeam said. *No, The Commissioner was in charge. We should have fought for what was ours! We could have fixed the water system. She shouldn't have just given up. By giving up, everybody died anyway.*

Her finger hovered over the play button, but she couldn't continue. She wanted to listen to more, yet at the same time, it was frightening hearing the voice she'd reviled so much over the last year, so she ejected the holo-tape, quickly tossing it at the bottom of her bag, then repacked the other tapes on top. She wondered when it had been recorded but forced herself to stop thinking about it.

After pulling the ties tight, she put her pack aside, then scanned the forest from her vantage point on top of the cargo containers, trying to reclaim the pleasure she felt at watching the fireflies. But it wouldn't return.

Her determination to ignore the holo-tape was almost fully eroded when she heard a slight creak from the container's rusted hinges as the door swung open. Ashe checked her AstroCom—it was 1:00 a.m. She lifted her pack and jumped down to meet Rainwood.

She rubbed her eyes, looking forward to a sleeping bag.

Ashe decided whoever invented the soft felt liners deserved an award. Her sleeping bag even had a lovely smoky pine scent from being used next to many campfires. Despite the turmoil of her thoughts, she quickly drifted to sleep, only to have her dreams plagued with flitting fireflies arguing with each other in the voices of the Commissioner and Warthog.

Return to Sender

Ashe woke slowly, taking a minute to gather her thoughts and remember what dangers she had to worry about this day. She started to crawl out and join the guys when Rainwood's voice filtered into the container from outside, even though it seemed he was trying to keep quiet. She lifted her head to see him facing Moonbeam just beyond the door.

"—Ashe. And the boy is Jade. Her friend, Mason, has the mech. One of your bad mornings, I take it?"

Moonbeam nodded, his brow wrinkled in concentration.

Rainwood squeezed his shoulder, "you should tell her more."

He shook his head, glancing into the container.

Ashe closed her eyes, hoping they didn't realize she was awake, her curiosity piqued.

"I didn't forget *her*," Moonbeam growled, "Just her name. It happens sometimes, you know. I look at somebody and recognize them, they aren't a stranger, but I don't know who they are."

He exhaled and threaded his fingers through his hair in frustration.

Didn't forget me? Ashe wondered. She considered asking him about it as they broke camp, remembering he had said something about forgetting things but eventually she decided it was too personal. He'd tell her about it when he wanted to.

Besides, Jade seemed overly distracted. He barely touched his breakfast and dragged his feet when getting ready for the road. After several attempts to get him to pack his gear, Ashe finally took a moment when they were alone to ask, "You seem off. What's going on?"

"I—" He bit off his response, then shook his head.

She sat next to him, helping arrange his backpack and wondering why he had pulled everything out for just one night.

"Hey, you know you can tell me anything, right?"

"You–you will send–send–send me back to P–P–Penny."

"No, of course I won't. What's wrong?" He was obviously worked up about something.

"I—" He paused, taking another big breath.

After a moment, he continued. His voice squeaked and cracked as he fought back tears. "I got scared and ran last night. I can't be tougher than Rainwood."

Ashe swallowed a laugh.

This is what he was afraid of? I suppose I did say he had to be that way.

She took his chin, giving him a big smile. "You kidding me? You are totally tougher than Rainwood already."

Moonbeam arrived and, hearing what Ashe said, added, "Holy cow, little man, you are so tough!"

Jade's back straightened, and with a relieved grin, he finished stuffing his pack, taking extra time to ensure Fuzzy Kat was in his proper place.

They found a path back to the lake in the cool morning air, then started along the shoreline, walking east. Everything felt pristine—a light rain had swept through before dawn, and the clean smell of the forest was refreshing.

"Hey, what's that?" Moonbeam waded into the reeds without waiting for an answer, pulled a row boat to shore, and exclaimed, "It still floats!"

Ashe looked east, debating how far out of the way the land would take them. Going straight across the lake was appealing, but she had never learned to row a boat and didn't want to admit this. While they had a small "lake" in the underground atrium of Fenclave, she could wade across the entire length.

She eyed the boat with doubt.

Mason's voice crackled from the Banshee's speaker. "I doubt it'll hold my weight."

Ashe felt relief and was about to answer in the affirmative when Moonbeam responded, "Isn't that sealed up? Couldn't you just walk across the bottom?"

Rainwood ended the conversation. "No, he'll sink into the silt. We walk."

They continued along the shore, and Moonbeam reluctantly left the boat behind, bringing up the rear.

It took an hour, but eventually they passed around to the north side of the lake and turned back into the forest, heading up the hillside. After a while of hiking, they entered a small hollow only to find a cultist effigy at the bottom.

The cult had spread throughout Arcadia after the war, and people left effigies to the Kraal all over. Shrines to these new enigmatic horrors, as if worshiping them would placate their assault. They were assembled of wood and sticks and made to look like what people believed the Kraal appeared as—at least by those few survivor accounts that were shared around.

This effigy looked like a woman woven from sticks, which splayed out behind her. Above the woman was a large skull from some creature, and at the base were more bones and candles.

Rainwood stopped, set his pack down, and with silent determination, started dismantling the effigy. He tossed the bits of bone into the brush, then kicked over the tripod that held it up before ripping apart the structure that bound all the sticks together.

"Feel good?" Ashe asked him smartly, with a grin on her face.

He glared at her, and her smile faltered.

Grumbling, he answered, "It's wrong—these cultists. I can't tolerate it. The world needs better things to follow than this. The Good Word is almost forgotten, and—and now I have to deal with smart-assed kids."

With a strangled tone, he stopped talking and stomped off.

Moonbeam whistled, telling Mason in a sing-song voice, "Ashe got in trouble."

Ashe blushed and mumbled aloud, "Why does he care so much about that?"

Moonbeam shrugged before following Rainwood with Jade in tow.

She heard the click and mechanical whir of Mason's helmet opening, and she looked his way. He explained, "Rainwood likes the Good Book. Said last night we all should read it more. That it can help a lot of people."

Ashe couldn't help but answer with a barb. "So, you're now an expert about Rainwood after a night of conversation?" She wanted to be angry at Mason, and she didn't know why. He scrunched his eyes in reciprocal anger, and she could tell he wanted to respond. She always could get a rise out of him at school. But he didn't explode, and that surprised her.

Instead, he took a deep breath and said, "Ashe, I'm a friend. You don't need to be mean."

This only made her more angry, and she spun, stomping away while pulling her headphones on.

☣   ☢   ☣

They reached Highway 95, and Ashe checked her AstroCom before declaring, "We're getting closer. Probably will make it in a day or so. But it's late. Let's find a safe place to set up for the night."

They found a secluded spot just off the road and, after making a camp, gathered around the fire to share leftover fried void toad, swamp tofu, and some berries Moonbeam had found on the hike.

Ashe watched Moonbeam and "Muffintop" getting along just fine after the meal, carrying on an animated conversation. But her thoughts were drawn back to the holo-tape from Warthog with the Commissioner. *Should I tell Mason? Perhaps I should listen to the rest of it first—*

"Oh wow!" exclaimed Mason, cutting off his discussion and pointing to the sky. "Another rocketship."

They all turned, and sure enough, a rocket lifted off from the south, illuminating the sky as it arced up to space. The rumble of its departure arrived a few moments later, a deep roar rolling across the valley.

"I saw somebody made a launch pad by Fenclave," Mason added conversationally. "Boy, wouldn't it be great to ride a rocket someday?"

Moonbeam thought about it. "Where would you go?"

"Somewhere else. Anywhere not here," said Mason. "A planet without void-cursed badlands."

Rainwood rumbled, "There is no place. The Wardens made sure of that. All the worlds were nuked."

Everybody sat quietly until the rocket's light faded away, likely wondering what it'd be like to travel in space.

Mason broke the reverie. "I'm going to join the Rangers. My dad wants me to join the Wardens because he was in the corps. But I think the Rangers would be better. I haven't gone yet because my parents needed help securing the compound. But I've wanted to go ever since I found my mech."

Moonbeam asked, "What's the difference? I thought they both claimed to be the military of the old Union?"

Mason shook his head. "In a way. The Rangers were the exploration side of the UOS. The corps were the military. And when they nuked all the worlds, the Rangers separated themselves. Heck, the Rangers are behind the new Star Federation, and that sounds promising. Getting the worlds back together, even if not many people are left."

Rainwood stated, "Rangers, they're good folks. But, like the Wardens, they can be a bit much in their own way. If you do join, just remember to keep folks' interests in mind."

"*When* I join," Mason corrected.

Moonbeam grinned. "I hope they let you in!"

Mason smiled uncomfortably as the conversation trailed off. After a moment, he shot nervous glances at both Ashe and Moonbeam, probably wondering if there was anything between the two but was unwilling to ask.

He straightened, puffed out his chest, and blurted, "Ashe and I went on a date once."

Ashe flared her eyes at him, and Jade laughed.

"Stuff it, Mason! It was just a class function—Standards Night. We had assigned partners, and it was simply to teach us how to eat in a formal setting!"

Mason grinned, unrepentant and not relenting. "She had a nice red dress and looked very classy, a total knock-out. You all should have seen it."

Ashe stood with a huff and retreated into the tent. *How can I get him to leave?*

After a moment of simmering, she decided to instead listen to the rest of the holo-tape. *What do I care what those guys talk about?*

With angry tugs, she dug into her pack and pulled out the holo-tape, then retreated away from camp for privacy. Once she felt the distance was sufficient, she sat on a boulder, pulled her head-phones on, bolstered her courage, and pressed the play button.

Warthog's voice continued in the conversation from before, *"Well, there is a new player in the area: Ordyne. Seems they lost a lab experiment and will do anything to get it back. And you're going to help me get the reward."*

"*Why would I do that?*" asked the Commissioner.

"*Because you want back in just as much as I do. But more than that, you want to bring 'your people' back, and I can help you do that. How many of us are left? How much blood is on your hands?*"

There was a gasp, and a slap echoed off the recording.

Warthog laughed. "*Struck a nerve, did I? Well, either way, help me, and I can put you and your people back in Fenclave.*"

Ashe liked the idea of getting back in Fenclave. *Is that what the Commissioner was negotiating?*

"*What's in it for you?*" the Commissioner questioned.

"*We'll have a little arrangement. I'll rule things out here, and you can rule your little kingdom inside. I just want supplies and ac-cess from time to time.*"

"And you will get everybody back into Fenclave?" she asked, sounding incredulous.

"I have a good thing here. What do I care if you want to live in a hole in the mountain."

"What do you need me to do?"

"I already have what they want. We found their lost lab experiment, and I have it caged, ready for exchange. I just need a trustworthy middleman to work out the details and make sure Ordyne will return things to normal with Fenclave. And as I hear it, you can get back in the enclave any time you want, with this."

A pause.

"You searched my gear for my access card? You know, they won't let you in, even with it."

Warthog laughed again. *"I think I'll keep a hold of this for now. You can have it back once you've arranged what I need."*

"Even if I agree, how do you know I'll stick by my part of the bargain?"

"Because I've recorded our conversation on my AstroCom. It'd be awful if that fell into the wrong hands."

A sigh.

"I'll supply you for one year."

"Five."

"Fine, five."

In the background, people started shouting in alarm, followed by the distinct hiss of a firework launching and crackling.

"We're under attack, boss!" somebody called out.

The tape went silent.

Ashe trembled as it sank in that this was recorded just a few days before when she had infiltrated Warthog's camp to recover her pack. When she'd stopped looking for her pack and instead rescued Jade: the experiment.

The Commissioner had been right there.

Ashe's world reeled. She grabbed the bullet around her neck, feeling angry for missing the opportunity to finish things. But she shifted her thoughts instead to the lab experiment.

Did Warthog plan on trading Jade for access to Fenclave?

She remembered his reaction to the lab-coated plushie, and realized her conclusion was likely right—he had to have been raised in a lab, especially considering his special abilities.

But how did he get out here? His life was bad with the raiders, of course, but he hasn't said anything about how it was in the lab. His reaction to the plushie wasn't a good sign, but could it be any worse than out here?

For some time, she considered the scenario, both in part angry at whoever would raise a child in a lab but also remembering how much better her life was back in the enclave, rather than out in the badlands. *Maybe he'd be better off going back to Ordyne? At least then he'd be out of the badlands. This is no place for a little kid . . .*

While considering this, she slowly walked back to the fire and looked at Jade from the shadows, hoping to avoid drawing his attention.

He held a stick in the fire and laughed at something Moonbeam said.

I want back into Fenclave more than anything. Jade would be fine with those people, right? I could just hand him over—

Jade snapped around to look at her, his eyes widening with fear. He stood and started to back away. Moonbeam grabbed his arm. "Woah, little ranger! Watch out for the fire."

Jade's reaction cut her like a knife, and she fought back a wave of disgust at herself. Ashe took a deep breath, letting her hope of bargaining for Fenclave die, and wiped at tears that had come to her eyes, trying not to think about how bad of a person she was for considering betraying the kid.

She stepped towards Jade, but he retreated further, and she knelt, catching his gaze across the fire, thinking as clearly and emphatically as she could, *I'm sorry! I won't let them get you. I promise!*

Green sparks swirled in his eyes, but his stony expression and pinched lips remained. Ashe tried to open her mind and let him in—to show that she really meant it. She did care about him. And this surprised her now that she faced it—she wanted to protect him, and a desire grew in her to keep him safe.

Ashe held her arms open. Jade relaxed, nodded, and ran around the fire to hug her.

We Three (My Echo, My Shadow and Me)

Talia loved keeping watch. She was like *Tutu Pele*, the ancient goddess of volcanoes, looking down from on high, ready to reign fire upon those who would do evil. She hefted her heavy buzz-cannon—recently upgraded by some traveling tinkers—and scanned the area, ready for anything.

Due to her family's islander heritage, she was bigger than most other teenage girls her age, but she'd long gotten past letting that bother her. Her strength was an asset in her role as a protector, and she loved her silky black hair—although she would tie it in a bun when she went into the wild.

She didn't know much about her heritage, having grown up in Fenclave. Yet, with her father's help, she learned the different patterns her people would paint on their faces. She liked painting the red warrior spirals under her eyes, which she thought offset her olive skin very well and helped her overall image.

Her family had taken over the Black Pines mall as a base of operations, and with the others who stayed with them, they had a pretty good thing going. She could see quite a ways in both directions from the nest she had built on the sign near the highway. So when a caravan came into sight, she was ready as the land's protector.

It was a small caravan. Well, really, it was just two brahman and a wagon. She debated: stay where she was or go visit?

Her decision was made for her when a giant cockatrice leaped forth and started attacking one of the children. It was a mutated form of a chicken with vicious talons. She needed to act quickly before the poor kid was hurt.

With a howl, she launched from her perch, landed in a stunning roll, then charged the cockatrice with no fear in her at all. She was a warrior princess, sent to avenge the oppressed! She dropped her buzz-cannon, deciding she could do this single-handedly. The boy ran to his parents at the caravan, and she took the beast's blows so the boy would be safe.

It put up a brave fight. However, once she grabbed ahold of the cockatrice's neck, it was no match for her. She soon wrestled it to the ground, snapped its neck, and bowed to the family watching her in awe.

"No need to thank me; it's my duty to keep this area safe. Have no fear when passing through."

She holstered her buzz-cannon on her back, then took the corpse of the cockatrice by its neck and dragged it back to her home. They'd have a good meal tonight, and this would be a tale to regale everybody with.

As she departed, one of the men from the caravan said to a woman, "Did she just take our chicken?"

The woman replied, "Some things are best left alone, Leroy. Do you see where she's going? She must be crazy, considerin' all the growlers down there just milling around."

But Talia didn't hear their conversation and continued on her way.

Her dad had wrangled a special entrance outside the mall using the second-story fire escape so she could get into her family's area without dealing with all the others. Getting the cockatrice up would be the hardest part.

After some consideration, she decided the best approach was brute force. She tied the cockatrice on her back and crossed her dad's defensive bridge, glad she was such a strong woman compared to others she knew, and thought, *Big-boned, pshaw, that's what the jealous girls call it. Ashley never called me that. She knew I was a warrior.*

Talia reached the top and sighed, thinking about her bestie for the umpteenth time. Ashley was so tiny but ferocious. They were inseparable in the enclave, but Talia only saw Ashley once after they left—and she had just lost her family.

When they crossed paths outside Pikeston, Talia tried to get Ashley to stay with them, but she didn't want to. She shared a meal, asked Talia to keep track of her old gear from Fenclave, then left in the morning. Nothing Talia or her parents said would convince Ashley otherwise.

She wondered how Ashley was doing. Was she still alive? Had she seen any of the signs Talia had left out for her?

Talia grinned, remembering how Ashley was so fond of being hip and edgy in Fenclave. Speaking to her absent friend as if she were right there, Talia even added a dose of cringe-worthy slang to help summon the moment. "Holy cow, Ashley, what's buzzin' cuzzin? Did you see how I took down this cockatrice? I know it scared you. But it was nothing for somebody like me. We're doing so good now! We live in a mall—can you believe it? You should definitely stay, and we can make fun of the others that my dad allows to stay on the first floor. A bunch of boring old drips, if you ask me."

As much as Talia would have liked to find Ashley and wander the badlands together—two ferocious vixens taking on the world—she had a duty to her family. Talia's mother and father needed her help. But it didn't make it any easier. She was lonely. Plus, none of the others here were cute, let alone interesting.

She watched the sun slowly descend, stretching the shadows and casting all the clouds in golden highlights.

Then Talia whispered, "I wish you'd come back."

They woke to a cold, damp fog, bringing a chill to the air. While eating breakfast, Ashe admitted that she wasn't sure where to go next, just the direction, because the side roads were all over-grown or torn up by star vines. She only remembered they needed to go by the Hemlock Picnic site. But if they could find the right road, it'd lead to an old backwoods farmhouse with a red barn, and from there, she could orient herself to find the ponds.

They reached the broken National Forest sign for Hemlock in the morning, and Ashe selected a road while showing external con-fidence, even though internally, she was a mess of worry—and it wasn't just about finding the right location. While it didn't help that the fog reduced visibility and made everything creepier, her thoughts the night before had scared her. She'd quickly decided at the time that it was stupid to think she'd be able to trade Jade for access to Fenclave, but the thought kept coming back to her, and she worried Jade might pick up on that.

When Ashe heard Mason's mech's thumping treads coming closer as they hiked through the cool fog, she didn't slow—she needed more time alone, and made an obvious move to put her headphones on. But he kept following and opened his helmet. "Hey, Ashe, can we talk? You keep ignoring me and shutting me out. I'm sorry about your family. I—I shouldn't have asked about them. Just let me in—"

She sighed, realizing he wouldn't relent, and stated, "Look, I get it. We have an old connection. But it's a different world now."

"I know that."

"Do you? You seem to be having plenty of fun building a gaudy home and playing with comics and toys like nothing has changed. You're even planning on gallivanting off to the stars."

Mason didn't say anything for a moment, and Ashe hoped maybe he was done, but no.

"You were always intense, Ashe, but I liked that about you. You could do anything. You weren't afraid of anything either. I used to think you'd be the next Commissioner. And . . . you know, a guy like me . . . I didn't think you even knew I existed. I was thrilled about that dinner date, even if we were paired up randomly."

She clenched her fists. *Didn't he get it? I don't want to talk about things from before! Why is he still going on about it?*

Ashe forced herself to respond politely. "I'm glad you had fun. But weren't you into Sam?"

"Sort of? Off and on, I guess. Not then, though, and I was happy to be on a date with you. But forget that; I just wanted to say—"

She cut him off. "Let's worry about what we're doing now. It's dangerous and all."

"Okay, okay, I get it. But . . . I just wanted to say thanks. You didn't have to do that back then. And I was happy because I had a date with the cutest cat in Fenclave."

Ashe spun around, stopping, and growled, "Listen, it didn't mean anything, alright? I didn't see you any differently than I did anybody else. You were just the guy they partnered me up with. Got it? I didn't fancy you or anything."

Mason fell back to the end of the line, which was just fine to Ashe.

Why doesn't he understand that I don't want to think about the past anymore, let alone talk about it?!

Rainwood gave her a stink eye and looked to say something when he froze, holding up a hand.

"Did you hear that?"

Everybody paused, silence fell upon the group, and even the slightest sound seemed highlighted to their ears.

After a moment, Moonbeam opened his mouth to say something, but Rainwood hushed him, "Wait!"

They continued to listen, and it shifted the mood. Everybody started fidgeting with worry.

A faint howl cut through the stillness, almost like an atonal war horn, but from some other-worldly beast. Ashe's blood ran cold. She'd recognize that sound anywhere.

"Deathmark!" she whispered, her eyes rapidly scanning the area while her heart rate increased, and she felt herself wanting to run but didn't know where to go.

Flashes of darkness hit her mind—being cramped and the smell of sweaty fear.

Jade's grip tightened around her waist, grounding her in the moment.

"Should we go back?" Moonbeam whispered.

Rainwood muttered, "Hard to say where it came from, let alone how far away it is. Going back could lead us right to it."

They rallied themselves and decided to continue forward through the fog, although with a subdued mood. Nobody talked, and Ashe became aware of every sound—each pebble and *scrtch* noise of every footstep. She tried not to get annoyed at Mason's mech being so noisy.

A scream sounded. Ashe couldn't tell if it was human or animal.

"It seemed farther away, right?" Moonbeam asked, a thread of hope obvious in his voice.

"We can take shelter at the farmhouse, wait it out," Ashe suggested, and they continued, their pace hurried.

She worried too much time had passed without finding the house. That maybe they were on the wrong road or even going the wrong direction, when the barn's recognizable shape came into view through a break in the fog.

Ashe held up a hand. "Let me check it out first."

Rainwood stepped forward and spoke in his stern, deep voice, "You keep taking point. Let me scout this one."

She pulled the hood of her chameleon suit on and tapped its switch on the side of her pants. Then, as she blurred and faded into the surrounding terrain, she said, "Can you do this?"

He drew in a deep breath and sighed, "Just be careful."

Ashe stepped off the broken gravel road and walked on the grass. Something felt different. Even with the muted effect of the fog, the sounds of the forest still came as they hiked. But now, the silence was more profound. Like the usual creatures were hiding. Every sound made her heart skip a beat, and she was sure they were being watched, stalked by the creature that had haunted her nightmares for the last year.

The smell of fire teased her senses, and ahead the fog glowed. She left the barn behind, and the silhouette of the farm-house became visible, the glow surrounding it. Something burned beyond.

"Help! Help me!" somebody cried. It sounded like a child screaming in terror.

Still careful, she picked up her pace and worked around the farmhouse. A part of her mind noticed somebody had made repairs to the building. People lived here.

The smell of smoke was unmistakable now, and she rounded the corner of the farmhouse to see the entire back of the structure ablaze, the heat burning away the fog, and she could clearly see the area.

Bodies.

Torn, scattered, tossed about in the yard.

Terror rooted her in place. She felt torn. Finding out who needed help would mean leaving herself vulnerable. Her eyes darted about, trying to see if anybody moved. To see who had cried for help.

The flames grew, the heat pushing on her in waves.

Then the smell came to her—one she'd never forget—the foul rot of a Deathmark. Even masked by the smoke, it was there: a faint stank that came and went, like soured milk with a sweet fruity undertone. It turned her stomach, and she held back a gag, spinning around to see if it came from the fog behind her. Her thoughts raced so fast she couldn't help but see movement in every swirl and shadow.

With her heart hammering in her chest, she fought the urge to yell to her friends to run. A small part of her recognized that would draw its attention, and she didn't know if they'd even hear her. Instead, she managed to hold back, although she still let out a terror-fringed gasp. "Run!"

Ashe didn't know if she meant it for her friends or herself.

Whoever called for help was no longer crying out. She needed to return to her friends and struggled to calm her panicked breathing.

It's not here! She kept telling herself, over and over, until finally she could think straight again and remembered Jade. Not sure he was close enough to hear, she closed her eyes and focused her thoughts, trying to direct them to him.

Go! Run! Hide!

Taking extra careful steps, she backed away from the burning house, making her way around its side to the front and the barn—all the while trying to balance moving as fast as possible yet slow enough the chameleon suit would keep her hidden.

A guttural howl reverberated across the valley, sounding like it was drawn from the depths of hell, cloaked in blood, and blown by a horseman of the apocalypse. Its cry rattled the soul. The sound blasted any reason from Ashe's mind, replacing it with terror and panic. It was engraved in her memories, and recognition wasn't even a question.

She ran, no longer caring about being stealthy, crossing into the yard between the house and barn. The fog was still too dense, but she knew her friends had to be up the road ahead. With fear curdling her voice, she screamed, "Ruuuun!"

Five steps was how far she made it before the fog twisted in front of her, the gravel crunched, and a tall beastly form lurched into view, coming between her and her friends.

Standing upright with wickedly sharp claws and a muscled, hulking torso, the terror stood taller than two people. A ridge of spikes crowned its skull-like head and down its shoulders. Its arms bristled with a forest of spines, and its skin was a pallid, putrid green color, like that of rot. She'd never seen one this close before. Never looked it in the face. Its eyes, sunken in their sockets, were devoid of pupils, a dead-looking white with purple fringes. And worse, it wore bits of shredded clothing, like it tried to pretend to be human.

The Deathmark's lips curled, almost in a sneer as it towered over her, and then it spoke. Jarringly, in a terrifying juxtaposition, the meek voice of a child cried out from its lips, "Help me! Help!"

She froze, shock and horror pinning her in place, her legs feeling weak.

Then it huffed as if mocking her and drew in a deep breath to let out another howl with so much force spittle flew from its wide maw of jagged, needle-sharp teeth. It snapped its arm, sending a shower of spines toward her.

She scrambled back, unable to dodge all of them. A few lanced into her, hitting her left shoulder, arm, and thigh. She wanted to run, but she also recognized it might then turn to her friends.

Did they get away?

It stepped towards her, and the cold, sinking reality hit her that one of its strides was easily three of hers. Panic took over.

She ran, irrational fear giving flight to her feet as she dashed back to the farmhouse, hoping to get inside and a moment later remembering the back of it was on fire—but she was committed and had nowhere else to go.

The Deathmark's steps shook the ground, and she knew it was just behind her, but not how far. The back of her neck itched in fear and her adrenaline spiked even higher. She expected to feel the vicious swipe of its claws tear through her back. The spines twisted as she ran, still embedded in her.

At the base of the steps, she heard Rainwood's voice echo across the fog, calling out, "Jade! Come back!"

She didn't know if it was real or if the Deathmark had learned to mimic her friends.

Reaching the stairs of the farmhouse, she realized it no longer followed her. The Deathmark had turned away and now curiously stood still.

The wind picked up, helping clear the fog and revealing Jade in the roadway by the barn, facing the Deathmark. His fists clenched as he stood his ground and glared at the fell creature, their gazes locked in place.

What is he doing?!

"Run, Jade! Run!" she screamed.

The Deathmark shook its head, then huffed, almost like a bark. Whatever Jade had done to hold it in place had failed.

The guys appeared through the fog behind Jade, running with determination. Seeing his lock break on the Deathmark, Jade's eyes flared wide, and he stumbled back, then bolted to the barn.

The Deathmark ran after him, crying out, this time in Ashe's voice, "Run, Jade! Run!"

The barn had started to crumble years before, and the doors were propped open big enough for a person to walk through. Jade ducked inside. The Deathmark followed, ignoring the guys who had lifted their guns, but hadn't fired yet—Ashe realized that with the Deathmark between her and them, she was in their line of fire.

Without even slowing, the Deathmark shattered the barn doors, continuing inward after Jade.

A crack of gunfire came from inside the barn, and then another.

Ashe shook herself from the paralyzing shock that had taken over her, and ran to the barn, drawing her Arbiter, coming in behind Mason as they followed the Deathmark—Mason's GA5 minigun spun up, its rapid-fire growl rattling the hills, and a moment of panic hit Ashe as she worried that he might hit Jade.

The back of the roof had collapsed, and the entire structure leaned precariously, but the center of the barn was clear enough. The Deathmark turned around, and Ashe spotted Jade hiding between the rusted hulk of some broken farm equipment and the stall wall with his pistol held firmly in front of him. He was no longer in the line of fire.

She stroked the trigger of her Arbiter and unloaded an entire magazine into the Deathmark while fighting her terror. But it hunkered down, letting armored bone plates take the shots from the guns.

What's this thing made of? Where do we need to shoot it? Can anything stop it?

Despite the group unloading a ton of lead into the thing, it didn't seem to care and straightened up in a lull as Mason's minigun ran empty. If anything, the barrage only seemed to make it angrier. It sucked in a deep breath and started glowing with an inner demonic purple fire that flared through cracks and crevices in its hide—the gashes and holes of bullets closed up.

After healing, it stepped forward and slashed at Mason. Fortunately, the Banshee mech absorbed most of the blow, but he went to a knee to keep his balance.

Rainwood jumped in, slashed at it with his gauntlet, trying to find a vulnerable spot, then rolled away before it could react.

Ashe reloaded her Arbiter for the third time, wondering if anything would slow the beast. They had spread out, continuing their attacks. Moonbeam even cycled through his pistols as fast as he could.

It snapped its arms, sending another barrage of spines toward each of them.

Mason cursed—the drum had jammed on his minigun, and he couldn't cycle in a new one.

Ashe's thoughts spiraled out of control. The only thing that made sense was to flee. To try and outrun it. She glanced at Jade and mentally shouted, *We need to run! Flee!*

He nodded and crawled under the machinery, heading to the back of the barn. She hoped there was a hole he could escape through.

Rainwood dodged a slash of its claws and growled, "Can we somehow trap it in here?"

Mason released his minigun, letting it cycle into its storage position on the back of the mech as he planted his feet and shouted, "Get out of here. I'll hold it off!"

"No chance!" Ashe howled, this time aiming for its belly, hoping to find a weak spot.

It flinched as the bullets hit, spun to face her, then cried out in her voice as it stepped closer. "Run, Jade, Run!"

From the other side of Mason, Moonbeam howled, "Hey, you freak! Look at me!"

When it ignored him, he stepped closer, continuing his firing while Ashe cycled another magazine for her Arbiter.

In a blur of movement, the Deathmark turned and back-handed Moonbeam, who had gotten too close. The blow sent him flying against the far wall, where he fell in a heap.

Mason took the opportunity to launch himself forward, landing on the back of the Deathmark and grappling its arms in a vice-like grip amplified by the added strength of the mech. He pulled back, and the Deathmark howled as its arms strained, veins in the muscles flaring as it fought against him. Out of the corner of her eye, Ashe saw Rainwood checking on Moonbeam.

The Deathmark shoved backward, crashing through an outer wall into the yard beyond, and in the tumble, it landed on top of Mason, but Mason wouldn't let up and still held tight with one arm while punching it with the other. Ashe started to follow, but boards and debris were still falling from their destructive course through the wall, and she had to move with care.

The Deathmark bashed its head against Mason's helmet. At first, this seemed to have no effect, and Mason continued punching it. But the Deathmark did it again and again. Each time Mason seemed slower to respond. It hammered against the armor of his Banshee so hard, the front of the helmet bent under the onslaught, and a crack formed in the bone plates on the Deathmark's head.

Mason stopped moving, and the Deathmark straightened up, then stomped on his helmet, which flew off, and his mech shook like a boneless puppet.

It had all happened before Ashe and Rainwood could arrive and help him out. Ashe's heart felt lanced as she watched the final blow. She knew what it meant for Mason. And that left just her and Rainwood.

She hoped Jade had gotten away. She hoped that Jade would be able to live safely, even without her, that he could get free of his pursuers. But, she couldn't let up now.

The Deathmark turned to Ashe and gave another feral howl.

The bone plate in its forehead remained cracked, and something dark oozed out.

She sighted in, switching from full-auto to burst fire, and aimed between the Deathmark's eyes—which was easier now without everybody moving around.

When it stepped towards her, she stroked the trigger.

Only one shot landed on its face, glancing off an armored bone ridge near its eye. The rest either missed or did no damage.

It huffed and moved its head back and forth, looking in her direction, trying to focus better on where the shot came from, before It started toward her. Ashe glanced at Rainwood, frantically thinking of which way to run. She continued backing up while aiming and could feel the heat of the burning farmhouse on her back.

Blood loss made her lightheaded, and she wondered what toxins the spines injected. Her vision tunneled, and color seemed to fade.

Rainwood appeared as a blur behind the beast, slashing at the Deathmark's Achilles tendon, and it stumbled to its knee, showing the first sign of weakness—even as it twisted to hit him, barely missing, then snapped more spines in his direction.

Ashe ground her teeth, too afraid to call out and coordinate attacks, so with it now just meters away, she focused on the crack between the Deathmark's eyes and took a slow breath.

The Deathmark roared again, its rotten breath making her gag, but she felt calm settle into her. The memory of her dad's first instructions on using a rifle came to mind—she could almost feel his hands wrapping her, holding her arms balanced as she aimed.

She breathed out and pulled the trigger, focusing on the crack in the bone plate.

Each shot hit true. Black spots appeared on the Deathmark's forehead, puncturing the plate and sending an eruption of matter out the back of its head.

It crashed to the ground with a loud *carumph.*

Ash stood, almost in shock. The Arbiter slipped from her fingers, clattering to the ground. The house behind her crackled and roared as the fire consumed the entire structure.

She didn't know if this Deathmark was the one that killed her family or not, but it didn't matter. She had finally faced it and survived.

She fell to her knees, exhausted, wanting to cry but unable to even do that.

Rainwood stepped toward Mason but froze, then gave Ashe a slow shake of his head.

Ashe felt hollowed out. Staring at Mason on the ground, regret ran through her mind. Why was I mean to him? He was a nice guy.

Jade arrived and carefully pulled a spine out of Ashe as she stared numbly at the carnage before her. Then another spine. And another.

Even with Mason dead, all Ashe could feel was relief. Relief that she was still alive. And this crushed her. "I'm a mean person. I don't care about anybody," she whispered.

Jade finished pulling out spines, then hugged her.

Rainwood moved to the barn, and she figured he went to check on Moonbeam.

She wrapped her arms around Jade, who hadn't let go. But, she still felt hollow—burned out.

A minute later, Moonbeam stepped out of the barn while holding the back of his head. He came over to Ashe and asked softly, "You alright?"

She couldn't stop looking at the Deathmark's hulking remains on the ground, half expecting it to get back up.

To start killing again.

The memory of her mom closing the box overhead flashed in her mind.

"My mom," Ashe whispered, "she found a crate and put us in it when they heard it howl. Me and my—my dog."

She tried to control her breathing, wrestling with the vivid memories made real again by the fight, and untied the bandana from her wrist, clenching it in her hands and feeling its texture as if trying to remember how life used to be.

"But I could hear it. I heard my parents die. And it stayed. It was looking for us."

A tear rolled down her cheek, and her features hardened before she growled, "Forget it. Just—"

With panic welling in her chest, she fought the memories that threatened to burst forth, letting out a strangled "No! Not now!" and got to her feet, taking a step toward Mason while fighting a trembling lip. But Rainwood stepped in front of her, shaking his head. "I'll take care of him."

She stood, unmoving, her heart heavy—now with an added layer on top of the dreadful guilt in her chest that would never go away, no matter how hard she tried to hide from it.

In My Room

Glenn resisted waking up as he relished the feeling of clean sheets. His lingering dreams scattered with a stretch, and he wandered to the restroom, turned the faucet on, and shook his head with a giant smile, thinking, *Running water! It's the small things of civilization you miss the most!*

He dialed the shower to a pleasantly warm spray and enjoyed the experience. Bathing in Mosstown involved a bucket behind a shed. This was much better.

He rifled through the clothes left behind in the quarters he'd claimed and found something passable, again wondering who used to live here. Once dressed, he stepped to the exit and pressed the button, a smile on his face as he watched the door open automatically—sliding to the side with barely a hiss.

Just outside, a frightening-looking security bot stood where he'd parted ways with it last night. It was a sleek humanoid shape with glowing red eyes and virtually no personality.

Glenn grinned, refusing to let its intimidating stance ruin his mood. "Lovely day, M-7."

"I wouldn't know," it said laconically.

"Can you bring me something for breakfast?"

"I am not a service bot."

Glenn rolled his eyes, looking around with a squint. "Where is one?"

"They have been disabled."

"Why?"

"That information is classified 'need to know.'"

"Fine, when is breakfast served?"

"The morning meal finished two hours ago."

"Okay, looks like I'll wait for lunch."

He started down the passage, but M-7 blocked his way. "Where are you heading?"

"Just to the atrium, miss nanny. Join me if you want."

It moved aside and followed him as he ventured to the central plaza. Fenclave was mostly empty since Ordyne had taken it over, but they were allowing him to stay until his rocketship left.

At the plaza, he thought again what a shame it was that Ordyne had cut down some of the trees, making it a construction staging area. He walked around a squad of troops rallying in their black gear by the elevators and made his way to the atrium.

The atrium's glass doors slid open, and a wave of humidity hit him, loaded with the pleasant smell of vegetation and forest. Clean forest. The low rumble of a waterfall came from the far side of the chamber.

The lights cycled to full-day mode, and he wandered into the parkland trees, squinting to see details while marveling that such a large chamber existed underground. The ceiling had a mix of reinforced concrete and bare limestone, with bright grow lights spread around to simulate the sun. *There's even a small lake*, he thought in awe. Reaching the shoreline, he found a reclining chair and lay back, thinking, *A few more days until the rocket leaves.*

☣   ☢   ☣

Ashe woke to a light rain covering the valley, making a gentle tapping on the barn's tattered roof. They'd found a dry spot in its crumbling ruins the night before, yet even this didn't help—she felt exhausted.

Across the barn, Rainwood sat next to Moonbeam around a small fire, its warmth beckoning to her on the damp morning. Ashe glanced at Jade, still out cold, his arms splayed out, and figured he could stay asleep as they made breakfast. She'd tried to talk to him last night about what he'd done facing the Deathmark, but he'd stubbornly refused to explain his actions, and she'd given up.

Grabbing her flight jacket, she joined the guys at the fire, grumbling, "Of course, it's raining."

"Actually, it's letting up," Moonbeam clarified, "Was coming down real hard just a few minutes ago."

Ashe bristled. *Why is it he can just annoy the heck out of me sometimes?*

She bit back a snarky comment, instead asking, "How do you feel? That was a pretty tough blow yesterday."

Moonbeam shrugged, smiling, "I still feel dizzy, and my headache won't go away. Everything hurts to hear, you know, so talking quietly is nice."

After a moment of thought, Ashe internally sighed, then pulled her headphones from around her neck and held them out. "Will these help? They go over the ear and cut down on noise—even if not plugged into anything."

Moonbeam stood and took them with a smile, "Wow, thanks, Ashe!"

Then he opened his arms as if to embrace her in a hug, and she reflexively pushed him and backed away. "Just make sure not to break them! I want them back in one piece!"

Rainwood spoke in his quiet, deep drawl, changing the topic. "Might be a good time to say a few words for Mason, as I reckon the rain will come hard again soon."

Ashe glanced outside, noticed the lighter clouds overhead along with the darker ones on the horizon, and reluctantly agreed. They roused Jade and gathered around Mason's grave. Ashe was grateful that Moonbeam and Rainwood had taken time to bury him the night before. She knew she should mourn him more, but part of her felt like it was just how the badlands were: You either kept moving, or you were buried.

Rainwood said some words. Ashe thought they were lovely. He said they were from the Good Book.

She couldn't help but remember her time in the vault with Mason. They never were close, but she didn't dislike him or anything. He seemed kind of awkward but nice if anything. The memories drew her emotions into turmoil. Remembering the standards night when they had dinner together. He was funny and had made her laugh.

Despite trying to avoid it, she couldn't help but cry towards the end of the vigil and was glad for the light rain as she hoped it hid her vulnerability.

Why don't I want them to see me crying? She wondered, noting that Moonbeam didn't seem to have a problem with being seen crying. He'd already wiped his eyes several times, and not because of the rain.

All she wanted to do was forget the enclave but now, with Mason . . . she quailed, torn between wanting to remember him and wanting to move on. But just being with him had brought back many memories and rekindled her desire to go back to the good times before her exile. Thinking about how much she'd lost summoned something that almost felt like physical pain, and she struggled to keep the yearning in check. But she couldn't stop considering what she could do to get back into Fenclave.

I need to keep moving, she kept telling herself while preparing breakfast. *Just leave the past behind me. Think of the future. That's what's important.*

Rainwood stepped into the barn, brushing the rain from his trenchcoat and gesturing outside. "Ashe, if you're ready, we need to settle something."

They approached Mason's gaudy purple and red Banshee mech, now upright again. Rainwood slapped its metal hull, causing the pooled rain to streak and run down the side.

"I never could get the hang of using these, and Moonbeam hasn't had any proper training . . ."

He looked at Ashe, leaving the question open.

She stared at it, wondering, *Can I do it? They trained us on mechanized cargo frames in Fenclave, but—this was Mason's.*

"It's so noisy, I can't sneak—" she started, remembering Mason's family. *Somebody needs to take it back to them.*

She swallowed and nodded, dropping her pack on the wet grass. "I'll try, but just until we have time to stop by and leave it with his folks."

Moonbeam held out the authorization key. She took it, slotted it on the side, and then slapped the access button. The Banshee hissed and bent forward, its back scissoring open for easy pilot entry. She stepped in, sliding her feet into position and stretching into the arms, but she couldn't reach the handles.

Fighting frustration, she stepped out and retrieved the emergency toolkit from the Banshee's shoulder harness, dug out a tool, and poked it into the foot and arm adjustment slots until she was happy with the sizing. She took a moment to connect a cable to her AstroCom, then stepped in again. This time, it fit. With her feet in position, she grabbed the handholds and pulled up. The mech reacted, closing in around her and coming upright. She felt it making automatic adjustments, tightening around her body before it finally settled. The display flashed, "Identify pilot."

She looked around the inside of the helmet. *It's clean. I was worried I'd still see— It's good that somebody cleaned it out.*

The glass view plate was cracked, and she could feel a trickle of water drip down her neck, indicating it didn't fully seal. But that was understandable, all things considered. She brought up the heads-up display, which presented a better view of the outside than she could see through the shattered glass.

With the Banshee fully online, she keyed in "Ashe" and paused, briefly considering her real name as a nod to Mason, then decided against it—reminding herself she was no longer Ashley.

The mech's fusion core was already warming the interior, and she realized using this would be much better than walking in the wet, cold, muddy rain with the guys, even with a broken helmet. The suits were designed for many environments, from extreme winter temperatures to desert heat.

With a scan of the board to review the mech's status, she saw it registered damage to the helmet, of course, and also recorded severe damage to the shoulder plates and chest. But at least the lower frame seemed fine.

The damage was a problem for another day, she decided.

Hoping the skill of piloting a mech would return quickly, she leaned forward and lifted a leg. The Banshee's leg lifted in kind, and soon Ashe was stomping around, getting comfortable with its capabilities.

She marveled at the interface. It was top-of-the-line, far better than the cargo frames she used in Fenclave.

Everybody packed their gear and prepared to leave while Ashe got to know the Banshee. Moonbeam helped strap her gear into the cargo rack, and then they started up the hills in the drizzling rain.

Their path took them past Mason's cross, and she paused, thinking how callous it felt to just leave. *But—it's how things are now. Stopping means you die.*

Ashe noticed Jade watching her, probably listening to her thoughts, and whispered, "Sorry, Mason."

She added another notch to her mental tally of people lost because of the Commissioner's decision.

The rain continued through the morning, covering everything in a faint haze and muting sounds on their hike. Everybody struggled in the slippery mud and Ashe cursed the cumbersome mech interface a few times while trying to figure it out—it was like doing gymnastics while wearing a lead blanket. Her only solace was that her clothes mostly dried out, other than the drips that ran down her back.

Ashe expected Jade to struggle more, but he seemed built of energy and scrambled with ease up steeper slippery sections that gave her—if not Rainwood—some challenge. At one point, she noticed he'd tucked Fuzzy Kat inside his pack so it wouldn't get soaked, which brought a smile to her lips.

With a steady pace, they made it to the first pond by lunch, and the rain began to let up. A crashed rocketship lay in the middle of the water, exactly where Ashe remembered it would be, and she announced, "We're close. I think this is the rocket Dayton mentioned."

It looked to have come down hard, probably in an emergency descent, and then tipped over. It didn't explode since it was still in one piece, but its fuselage was bent, and the fins were crumpled. The passenger cabin was still attached, if not mostly submerged, and the cargo section had split open, spilling crates and containers which looters had since scattered around the area.

Ashe first came across it half a year ago and had spent some time climbing through its tattered remains, fascinated at the possibilities and debating what planet she'd fly to if she ever had the chance to leave Arcadia.

The ship's decay indicated it had rested here for years if not decades—most likely dating back to the arrival and cleansing. The paint on its side had faded over time. Still, Ashe could make out the livery of some corporation and, next to that, the flag of the old Union of Stars—the pre-war government which had collapsed after the arrival.

Although the Wardens claimed authority as the sovereign remnants of the Union, a new loosely organized government had since come about, called the Star Federation—a republic fostered by the Star Rangers, the separate branch of the Old Union's military that Mason had planned to join.

Ashe wondered what happened in the communist Democratic Worlds Alliance—did they end up with all their worlds broken and destroyed the same way? Her class debated it once, encouraged by their robotic teacher, Emmett. In the end, they decided that since the DWA never came and invaded, that alone was sign enough they had the same problems with the Kraal.

The travel pace had been aggressive thus far, so everybody took a moment for a break. Ashe exited the Banshee to stretch—although the mech assisted in walking and movement, Ashe still had to do a lot of work and was sore in new places.

Jade waded to the ship, and Ashe almost called out for him to take his shoes off, then realized he was already soaked to the bone from the rain. The pond looked very shallow, no higher than his knees. She watched him instead, glad for his caution while looking inside the wreck's cabin.

Moonbeam wandered around, poking at the various crates scattered about. If his head still bothered him, Ashe couldn't tell— he seemed just as recklessly curious as ever. She had already looked through the debris on her last visit, and knew everything was picked over, but didn't say anything.

He clambered into a large, orange cargo container half-sub-merged in the water. A moment later, his cry of excitement echoed from its interior—a drawn out sound that started low and ended in a high pitch. "Whaaaat!"

A few clunks came from the container, and he emerged lug-ging three mannequins, only to set them up on the pond's shore.

"What are you doing?" Ashe asked.

"This is better. Now they can keep each other company."

She wondered what went through Moonbeam's head at times, then laughed, feeling sorry for Jade, who likely would catch thoughts from that scatter-brained noggin. She grinned, wondering if she should be concerned at the impact it might cause.

Moonbeam took time to arrange the mannequin's clothes and left them as if they were mid-conversation and just froze in place when somebody stopped by. Ashe found it a little creepy, but he enjoyed setting it up.

Rainwood seemed on edge and eventually called an end to it, "Let's go."

Everybody reluctantly shouldered their gear. From the pond, the path turned east, and Rainwood took the lead. His behavior changed the closer they came to the treasure site. He was usually happy to stay in the background and let others take the lead, but now he seemed focused and set a brisk pace from the front. This piqued Ashe's curiosity because he had previously seemed disinterested in the treasure. Was there more to this "hunt" than they were telling her?

Fortunately, the sun finally broke through the clouds and the rain stopped. About half an hour later, they came upon another pond. The ruins of a cabin littered the southern edge, entangled by star vines.

Ashe exited the Banshee and pointed at a lofty tree in the middle of the still water. Scaffolding and a ladder were nailed to its trunk, providing a path to climb to the upper platforms in the high branches.

"There's your treehouse."

Rainwood continued to the cabin ruins alone. Ashe started to follow, but Moonbeam caught her elbow. "Let Daegom go. He'll need a minute."

She gave him a curious look, hoping he'd explain more.

Instead, he pulled the headphones from around his neck and handed them back. "Thank you for letting me use these. They did help. But I'm afraid I might break them . . ."

Ashe took them with a smile, shaking her head and figuring he was probably right, then asked, "So where is this treasure supposed to be?"

He grinned, obviously hiding something. "I don't know! Just here somewhere."

"Seriously?"

Ashe sat on a rock to rest in the sun and watched everybody wander about. Rainwood picked through the cabin. Jade threw stones into the water, disturbing its smooth surface, and Moonbeam meandered around the shoreline. She considered joining Moonbeam in exploring, and noticed how well his shoulders filled out his jacket as he strode away. And not just his shoulders. When he stretched to step over a boulder, she couldn't help but notice he had a nice—she stopped that line of thought with a growl, fighting a blush that she knew warmed her cheeks.

Glancing around to see if anybody noticed, she decided to focus on something else.

Her gaze ended at the treehouse up in the canopy, although her emotions still fluttered from the earlier line of thought..

"Jade, stay here. Don't go anywhere," she commanded, needing to do something.

❖   ☢   ❖

The water bubbled up from springs, making it frigid to her bare feet, but fortunately it was shallow as she waded across. Scaling up the rickety structure wasn't too hard, although it was nothing like Mosstown, where they at least had staircases and railings. For some sections of the ascent there was nothing more than a thin beam. Fortunately, Ashe had excellent balance thanks to gymnastic lessons in Fenclave. Back then, she was annoyed that her mom always made her practice, but the skills had come in handy many times since leaving the enclave.

She glanced back at Jade from time to time. He stood at the water's edge, watching her like a hawk.

I'll be fine, she thought with a grin.

At the top, she found the original owners—now just skeletons with a few crates and boxes. She rifled through the boxes to pass the time and found a journal.

Sitting on a folding chair, she started to skim the contents. The sun was pleasantly warm as it filtered through the leaves, which helped everybody dry out from the morning rain.

"Can–Can I come up?" Jade called.

"Not without help," Ashe replied. "Just wait a sec. I'll come down."

But she kept skimming the journal. Something had caught her attention, sending off a warning—the last entry said a skulk infestation had visited the ponds, led by a queen. They were vicious, void-mutated crustaceans with tentacles that nested in waterways.

She glanced down and saw Jade at the shoreside, watching with wide eyes—he likely heard her sudden worry—then she scanned the area, looking over the still water with renewed concern. Rainwood stood at the cabin, so where was Moonbeam?

A shower of water erupted from the far side of the springs, followed by a gurgling roar as a giant creature vaulted from the depths in anger. Moonbeam ran away from it with an excited grin, dashing through the shallow pools toward his friends as he carried a large speckled egg the size of a suitcase.

Skulk queens could grow to monstrous sizes, and this one was no different, looming at least two stories tall, covered in chitinous bits of exoskeleton, with a variety of tentacles coming from its base. Ashe always thought they looked like some weird hybrid of a crawdad and octopus.

What was he thinking, raiding a skulk nest right now?

Ashe didn't have it in her to fight again so soon, and she had stupidly left her weapons with the mech; all she had was Coyote on her hip. She wanted to get down quickly and considered the height of the platform and the depth of the pools beneath. The platform was high enough that the impact would be very painful, possibly deadly if the water wasn't deep enough for a plunge from the platform's height.

The queen chased after Moonbeam, tentacles reaching out and pushing trees and brush out of the way as she moved across the water.

"Put it back!" Ashe shouted at him, then looked at Jade, thinking, *Come up!*

He splashed through the water and started climbing. She met him halfway to help him across the treacherous parts.

Moonbeam had circled, turning back to the nest with the queen trailing behind, spitting acidic vitriol at him. Rainwood followed the two, hollering, "Drop it, you idiot!"

It was the first time Ashe had ever heard Rainwood berate Moonbeam.

After reaching the upper platform, Ashe commanded Jade, "Lie down. Stay quiet!"

With him settled, she descended as fast as possible, launching from a lower platform, rolling to soften the impact on the shoreside, and coming up next to her gear.

She snatched her Arbiter from the mech, deciding it would take too long to enter, and ran after the other two. Moonbeam circled and dropped the egg with a pile of others, barely slowing his sprint. He veered toward Ashe with a cheesy grin.

She took a bead on the queen—their carapace made them almost bulletproof—but she couldn't pull the trigger, her thoughts heavy, weighted down by the events of the last few days.

I'm tired of killing everything.

As Moonbeam closed, she shouldered her gun and joined his flight, keeping pace with him.

He grinned. "Isn't this fun?"

"You are crazy!" She shook her head as they ran but couldn't stop a smile from forming on her face. As Ashe expected, with the queen's egg returned, she quickly lost interest.

Ashe collapsed, catching her breath, the world spinning overhead. Moonbeam fell beside her, chuckling,

She punched him. He deserved it.

Ashe listened to the wind, watching the sky through the tree branches. For a brief moment, everything felt peaceful. Safe.

Moonbeam turned to her, then brushed at a bit of her hair.

His gestures sent her heart pounding. Feeling a flush rise in her cheeks, she sat up with a start before he noticed and declared, "Let's get back to the others!"

She took the lead and they jogged down to the water to find a quiet scene, with the distressed queen absent. Rainwood was halfway up the treehouse, and Jade remained on the platform high in the canopy, his fingers and the top of his head barely visible over the edge. Ashe waved, and he waved back.

They followed the others to the top. When Rainwood saw Moonbeam, he growled, "Boy, you need to start thinking before acting."

Ashe found the journal and handed it over. "Looks like the prior owners had new tenants arrive—as Moonbeam discovered—but there were so many, and they were pinned up here, with hardly any food or ammo. The rest . . ." she gestured at the skeletons.

Moonbeam lay facedown next to Jade, and they dropped twigs into the water.

Ashe felt the pulse on her forehead and growled at them, "Stop it! You never know what you might disturb again."

She sat on the folding chair and closed her eyes, taking a moment to calm herself. Rainwood sat in the chair next to her, causing it to creak.

Feeling more relaxed, she asked, "Well, where is the treasure?"

Rainwood sighed and started getting back up, knowing she'd want to get on right away once she knew where to go. He gestured to the shattered cabin at the shoreline. "Over there."

She descended quickly, getting the hang of the precarious path, and headed to the cabin to poke around, wondering if there was a marker or clue.

Rainwood arrived, with Moonbeam and Jade trailing behind, and he pointed along the ridge.

A rough cross of sticks stood about ten feet away, with a pile of fresh dirt around its base, making it look recently erected, which Ashe found curious.

They approached, saying nothing. Rainwood eventually explained, his voice breaking, "She was Rose. My wife. The treasure of my life."

Ashe stared at the cross, stunned. This entire time she thought they were coming for some gold, a secret pre-arrival archive, or something of trade value.

Rainwood's admission shook her so much that she felt tears threatening to come from her eyes. Up to now, she'd thought of him as some imposing force, like a mountain. Not only did this make her realize he had a family—of course, he did—but he had grief too.

Rainwood drew in a ragged breath, obviously struggling to control himself.

A knot built in Ashe's throat, and she fought it back, but a tear crept from her eye as she thought, *He considered his wife the treasure of his life, and she died. I am such an idiot, going on about my own problems. I bet Moonbeam even knew, the jerk.*

She wiped her eyes as Rainwood explained in a quiet rumble, "She was something special. But she had radiation sickness after the bombs. We made our way here—my cousin's cabin. Her last wish was that I just keep her in my heart, that I stay true, and not give up . . . But, I don't know if I did too well with all that. After she passed, I couldn't bear to stay anymore. Everything reminded me of her, so I took to wandering and lost myself for a spell."

He sniffed, then cleared his throat to cover it up.

"When this fool started on about the treasure hunt, I decided maybe I should return. Give her a visit. Let her know I haven't forgotten. I'm thankful you lent a hand, 'cause with the Star vines tearing up everything, I was downright lost."

Moonbeam grinned and winked when Ashe glanced his way.

He did know! She realized. *And that means the journal was Rainwood's! And Rainwood was a preacher? He must have lost so much if he was there during the arrival.*

The knot came back to her throat, and she remained silent, unwilling to speak or ask questions for fear of making it worse.

After a minute, she said, "I'm sorry. I can't imagine how it must feel."

He nodded, then looked around, cleared his throat, and said, "Is anybody hungry?"

They pulled out food for lunch, and after everybody ate, Rainwood took a moment to squeeze Moonbeam's shoulder, grumbling, "Thanks."

Moonbeam gave a thumbs up, his mouth full of fox jerky.

Rainwood sat by Ashe, sighed, and said, "Family is everything. And we'll always lose loved ones. Nobody gets out of this alive. Just . . . just don't forget them. Remembering is how you honor them."

She wondered about his unprompted advice but took a deep breath and thought about her family. *It doesn't hurt so bad anymore. But—I still don't want to think about it. Why?*

I killed the Deathmark.

I'm on top now, right?

Why is my lip trembling?

She cleared her throat and took another bite, struggling to get herself under control.

Rainwood waited another moment, then added, "When you're ready."

Jade stared at her. His eyes shone with deep understanding —he could hear the chaos in her head and seemed sad.

She stood and busied herself cleaning up lunch, wondering where to go next.

From the treehouse, Moonbeam hollered, "I think there is a treasure hunt up here!"

Ashe called back, "Don't you ever get tired of this?"

Jade perked up.

"No, I'm serious! Look here. Somebody scratched stuff in the tree. It says something about a circle? A circle that kept calling to him?"

"That's not a treasure hunt. It's the ramblings of a madman," Ashe replied

Moonbeam grinned. "There is more . . ."

Jade was already mounting the stairs, eager to see what Moonbeam had found. Ashe almost called out to stop him but instead stood, deciding to follow.

Rainwood shook his head, content to stay and clean up lunch.

Ashe reached the top with Jade to find Moonbeam taking notes. He pointed to the side of the tree where there were markings that looked several years old.

"What does—what does it say?" asked Jade.

Moonbeam spread his notes open and explained, "Let's see. It says, 'the circle is glowing, calling to me. I need to stop now, so they can't get me. I'll go to the circle.'"

Ashe glared at him. "Gee, that's an amazing treasure hunt. So full of clues. I think it's just some random person rambling about a circle. Big deal."

She turned to leave.

"I know–I know where it is," said Jade excitedly.

"You know where it is?" said Moonbeam.

He nodded and crept to the edge of the platform, pointing down.

A ring of glow mushrooms made a circle, illuminating the water from the depths.

"Far out," said Moonbeam, "they are mesmerizing, but I don't hear anything calling."

Ashe found her curiosity piqued and looked across the pond, wondering if the queen would wake again if they disturbed the water too much. Could they safely venture into this side?

"Come on, but you guys stay on the shore."

They followed her down, and she stepped into the water, approaching the mushrooms. The pond quickly deepened to her elbows, and she felt forward with her feet. As she disturbed the bottom, the silt quickly clouded the water, making it nearly impossible to see anything. Then there was a flash of white.

With an edge of caution, she looked back to where the queen had come from, then cinched up her resolve and dunked under the water, swimming to the bottom and waving her hand to clear the silt. The gaping maw of a skull appeared, and she jerked in fright, swimming back to the surface quickly.

The guys looked curious. She breathed to settle her frazzled nerves before explaining, "I think I found your guy. Literally, the circle called to him, and he's down there now. Obviously, he was deranged and probably jumped to his death."

Moonbeam's mouth made a round circle. "Ohhhh. I wonder who was after him."

Ashe emerged to the shore, shook the water off, and looked for a warm sunbeam. "It was years ago. Nothing to worry about now."

The water splashed, and she turned to see Moonbeam diving in. A moment later, he came back with something in tow. As he reached the shore, he clearly hauled the body.

"You couldn't just let him rest in peace?"

He shrugged. "We should do that. Yeah, we'll bury him for sure."

Up to this point, Jade was happy to watch from a few stairs up, but as the remains were drawn out, he became very interested and climbed down. The skeleton wore a silver jumpsuit, and he crouched at its side, wiping at a name patch to clear away the muck, exposing the name "Mei Tamura."

He stared at it for a moment, then whispered, "Mom."

Catch a Falling Star

"Ashe!" Rainwood called from the shore. "Get the mech, and everybody, find cover!"

Ashe shook her head, wondering if she heard Jade correctly. *Did he really say* mom?

The faint whine of an aircraft focused her thoughts, and she pulled Jade away from the remains, pushing him toward Moonbeam. "Hide!"

The guys veered to the cabin ruins, and Ashe jumped into the mech, powering it on while the turbine whine of an aircraft increased overhead and she mentally reviewed the possibilities.

It's just a random patrol of the Wardens. Nothing to worry about. It can't be the raiders, they don't have that kind of equipment. And, besides, nobody knows where we are, right? But her elevated pulse told her that she didn't really believe that.

The mech closed up and chirped in readiness. Ashe stomped

toward the ruins, ducking under a collapsed wall with the others just as a HWG-125 "Hog" transport appeared through the canopy. The stubby, tilt-thrust aircraft had been very popular with the Army Corps, and she recognized seeing them howl overhead from time to time, painted with the Warden's symbol—three vertical stripes almost making a "W."

Anxiety ratcheted in her chest as the Hog circled the area, its twin-engine pods on the end of each short wing tilted at an angle, nosing the aircraft forward in a slow hover. Then the jet engines rotated to vertical mode as the craft found an open clearing and descended to the ground.

The turbines spun down, and a squad of armed warriors in body armor exited and spread out.

Rainwood murmured, looking at the symbol on the tailfin, "They're not Wardens. They have to be on the hunt for us, though I don't know how they know we're here."

"G–Glenn wanted to tell somebody where we went," Jade said, trying to help.

Ashe felt a rising fury. She remembered Glenn asking about their destination, and growled, "What a square!"

The squad approached the pond. It wouldn't take long for them to reach the cabin. Ashe made a snap decision and crawled out the back of the ruins.

"Where are you going?" asked Moonbeam. She waved him off. "They don't know we have a mech. Maybe I can convince them I'm somebody else."

She dialed the AstroCom tunes up, letting it pick from her library at random, and the Beach Boys' *Wouldn't It Be Nice* started playing. Then she tried her best to act nonchalant and rounded the ruins, acting surprised as she saw the raised guns immediately point at her.

"Freeze!" shouted one of the goggled warriors.

She raised her arms and spoke over the music, "Just a badlands survivor here. I came over the ridge when I heard your Hog."

"What are you doing in this area?"

"Scavenging. I was . . ." Ashe tried thinking of a plausible story. ". . . poking through the ruins there looking for usable junk."

Ashe cursed to herself, realizing she had just conflicted her story.

"Did you come over the ridge, or from the ruins?" the soldier asked, but didn't wait for an answer, and called out commands, "Doughboy, stay with me. Everybody else, check out the cabin."

Ashe sighed to herself. *This is why I avoid people.*

But she still tried to recover. "Not much over there, besides old toothpaste, mold and stuff."

"We'll be the judge of that."

Blast! She scolded herself internally, then considered her options. There were six in the squad, very well-armed, and the stubby Hog also featured a multi-barrel minigun that looked bigger than the one on her Banshee mech. Her GA5 minigun could still shred as good as the Hog's, but she wasn't sure if anybody currently manned the Hog's gun.

Ashe's arms ached from holding them upright, but the two remaining soldiers kept their guns trained on her, while the rest of the squad approached her friends' hiding place.

Ashe wanted to curse like a sailor, but her mom's restraint held her back even now. She scanned the area, trying to think of anything that could distract the soldiers.

The treehouse? The water—that's right, the queen!

The song ended, and "I Don't Want To Set The World On Fire" from the Inkspots started inside her helmet.

Ashe grinned, her adrenaline rushing, and she hoped the guys would understand what she meant as she shouted, "The queen! Go see the queen!"

Doughboy glanced at the other soldier in confusion. "What queen?"

But Ashe already started moving. She snapped her helmet closed and launched toward them while drawing her Arbiter—hoping the Banshee could handle the shots.

Both men fired, and the Banshee shuddered from the impact, but she sucked it up and stroked the trigger, stitching a line up Doughboy and knocking him back.

The Hog's turbines started humming again.

Ashe couldn't let it take off.

Then something hit her and exploded. Everything went red. The force knocked her back, sending her thoughts into a painful daze. *Seriously? A grenade launcher?*

The guys, meanwhile, had run from the cabin, beelining for the other side of the swamp. The squad pursued, some fired, and somebody else yelled, "Don't hit the kid!"

The Banshee detected her wound and automatically injected a Medipak's cocktail of fun, helping her ignore the stabbing pain spiking in her hip. She rolled and came up, still taking more hits but glad the soldiers didn't fire another grenade.

With a twist of metal and a loud pop, the shoulder piece of armor flew off under their barrage.

She had dropped her Arbiter in the blast, but the minigun was on a hard mount, and she reached down to pull it online. The first soldier had recovered—his body armor had protected him from her Arbiter. Both he and Doughboy fired at her in full auto. Fortunately, her GA5 minigun would shred body armor at this range.

Ashe stroked the trigger as it swung into position, starting the rattling buzz of rapidly fired rounds and shaking the entire mech. At this range, she didn't have to worry about accuracy—anything in front of the barrels was fodder, and she sprayed her assailants. They didn't take it well, and both dropped, likely to never rise again.

She released the trigger and noted the ammo count—24 rounds left.

Yikes! This thing eats bullets like a 5-year-old eats a stolen bag of candy.

The Hog started to lift off.

Ashe let the minigun retract to its carrying position and charged the Hog, closing the distance and then using the Banshee's boosted shocks to launch eight feet in the air, aiming for the aircraft canopy.

As she closed in, she caught the pilot's surprised expression just before he pushed the stick down, making her overshoot. With a twist and a lunge, she grabbed hold of the chassis and slammed onto the roof. The jet turbines screamed ferociously on each side of her, reminding her how dangerously close they were. She wondered how well the Banshee would hold up if she was sucked into the engine.

"Catch a Falling Star" from Perry Como queued up on the speaker inside the mech. Ashe hoped it wasn't a bad sign.

Looking below, she watched Rainwood snatch Jade, tuck him under his arm, and put on an extra burst of speed. Moonbeam trailed the two in their escape, and as they reached the far end of the pond, the skulk queen burst from her submerged nest in a shower of water, coming up between them and the soldiers.

She stretched a tentacle out, snatching one of the soldiers and blocking their retreat from the water. The other warriors started firing, shifting from pursuit to fighting for their lives as they engaged the void-mutated terror.

Yes! Ashe thought. *Score one for the good guys!*

Rainwood continued running as he reached the shore and headed up the hillside, stopping at the top, where he set Jade down before looking up at Ashe. She could see him say something with a scowl, which caused her to grin, sure he'd just unleashed a string of curse words. Moonbeam scrambled up the hillside to join Rainwood in watching as the aircraft lifted her higher from the clearing.

Ashe held on with fierce determination as it banked from side to side, trying to shake her loose. Seeing few options remaining, she let go with one hand and punched through the aluminum ceiling of the Hog before pulling a grenade from the bandolier on her waist and dropping it into the cabin. Her mind raced as she considered how to escape the explosion, and she looked up only to notice how high the Hog had climbed above the tree canopy.

"Oh shh—"

The grenade exploded, shaking the entire chassis, and a moment later, the fuel tanks ignited in a flash. A fireball tore the craft apart. The turbines continued spinning, but, now unattached to the fuselage, they flew off in wild directions.

☣　　☢　　☣

Moonbeam's face turned white as a sheet as he watched. He lurched toward the tumbling debris, but Rainwood grabbed his arm. "Stay back, or the wreckage'll hit you."

"But Ashe—!"

Moonbeam struggled to break free of Rainwood, then fell to his knees, his eyes watering while he waited for the flames to die down.

Jade touched Moonbeam's shoulder and pointed.

The last engine crashed into the ground, and the flames billowed in a new fireball at the impact. But as they subsided, they could see a Banshee mech hunched on the ground in the center of it all, crouching as if it'd landed from a high jump.

With the flames reducing, the Banshee straightened up,

pushed a metal panel out of the way, and then limped out of the wreckage.

Moonbeam jumped up and yelped, "She's fine! We're good. We did it!"

"Perhaps not entirely," growled Rainwood, looking back to the queen still wrangling with their last pursuers, "but Ashe is walking, and that's a good sign."

Ashe made it clear of the wreckage, her mech trailing wisps of smoke. It clicked, bent forward, and unzipped with a hiss, letting Ashe stumble out, coughing.

Moonbeam ran to her, offering a hand while checking her bleeding side.

She accepted his help but said in a voice husky from smoke inhalation, "I'm fine."

"How? I thought you—" he gestured toward the flaming wreck, still poking at her side to check her wound.

She winced and slapped his hand. "I jumped free, barely in time. Mechs have shock absorbers. I could have leaped off a tower, and I'd have been fine. Just—" She coughed. "It wasn't sealed, so I inhaled a lot of smoke and fumes."

Moonbeam wiped his eyes and gave her a friendly punch on the arm. "You scared the jeebies out of me!"

He insisted on helping patch Ashe up, and she blushed almost as red as her hair as she lifted her shirt, even if just to show the gash on her hip.

Rainwood went to check out the queen's lair. Bubbles rose from the water, and he couldn't see any sign of their pursuers other than bits of scattered equipment here and there.

His lips formed a grim line as he informed the others, "I think we made it out this time, but there will be more. Some of that squad could have made it to the woods. We need to move on quickly, even though it's nearly sunset. Can you still move, Ashe?"

Ashe waved Moonbeam off, but he continued wrapping her waist with more bandages than was probably necessary. She replied to Rainwood. "I think so, just give me a Medipak."

Ashe returned to the Banshee and gave it a quick inspection. It occasionally emitted a slight *tink* noise as the metal cooled. Most of the paint was scorched off. Jade watched with fascination, but Ashe didn't have time to explain anything. Finding the mech operational, she climbed back in and motioned Jade to grab his gear as she looked for her Arbiter.

Before they left, Ashe took the Banshee back into the smoking debris and found the Hog's controls. She hammered on a console until it broke apart, then extracted a component.

Moonbeam stopped by Mei Tamura's remains, poked through her gear, then respectfully slid her into the water, letting her sink back to the depths. He joined the others and explained, "Perhaps we can come back another time to give her a proper burial, but I figured we shouldn't leave her out in the open."

Ashe held up the security key she'd dug out. "This could come in handy if we can find their base."

They retraced their original path, hoping backtracking would add confusion to any pursuers. As luck would have it, the rain started again, which was both a curse and a boon. It was cold, and everything became muddy, but it would hinder any pursuit.

Ashe realized she was still bleeding and had difficulty focusing, so she just put one foot in front of the other. The sun had long set when they reached the burned-out farmhouse and Mason's grave.

Unable to resist looking, she turned the lamp from the Banshee to where they'd left the corpse of the Deathmark.

It moved, sending a lance of fright through her, but then the shadows detached into humanoid forms—they were feeding on its remains.

"Growlers!" shouted Rainwood.

Rainwood directed the rest to cut to the north, leaving as fast as possible. Running in the dark was dangerous, and they moved so quickly that the ground became flashes of illuminated bushes and boulders, which they could barely recognize before it was too late. But even over the rain, they could hear the grunts and howls of growlers, seemingly devoid of their humanity and on the blood trail of live prey.

"We should find somewhere safe!" growled Rainwood.

As they ran, Ashe racked her brain, thinking of any hollows and places around, but coming up empty. Finally, she said, "There is a Rocket Ace truck stop. But that's out a ways."

"We can handle it. The question is, can you?"

"Do I have a choice?" she gasped out between strides. They were all exhausted. This would push their limits.

She looked back, noticing Jade lagging, and pointed to the cargo rack, asking, "Think you can hang on?"

He nodded, and they stopped long enough for Rainwood to help Jade find usable handholds, then they took off on a fast jog again.

Their pace was exhausting, but any time they slowed down, the cries of the predatory growlers gave them plenty of motivation to keep going.

An hour into the run, Moonbeam tried to lighten the mood. "Maybe we'll come across more void-toads, and they can distract our new friends."

Nobody had the energy to reply.

After what seemed like an entire night of running, they crested a ridge. While panting to catch her breath, Ashe pointed at the silhouette of a rocket that reached above the trees, which was all they could make out in the moonlight.

"That's it. Hopefully, nobody is there."

With a small breather, they resumed their hurried pace and soon made it to the open yard of the truck stop. Rusted and burned-out vehicle carcasses were barely visible through the rain and moonlight, surrounded by various buildings. She pointed to the nearest. "Let's try the repair bay. It has concrete walls."

Jade shouted, "More of the growl–the growl–them are here!"

And he was right. Shadows detached from the ground as growlers rose up from their rest scattered around the open parking lot. The team turned to the left, heading toward a convenience store, with new howls and grunts on their trail.

Rainwood smashed through the door, which somebody had chained shut, and commented on all the broken windows, "I'm not sure if we'll find much cover here."

Moonbeam whooped, "Ice cream!"

He pushed on Ashe, who blocked the door. She obliged but asked, "Seriously?"

"They have to have a cooler for all the ice cream, right? I've seen these stores before. They always have a walk-in freezer."

With even more growlers hot on their tails, they scrambled through the litter of debris on the floor to the stockroom. Rainwood made it first and held the freezer door open for the others, then jumped in and pulled it closed as growlers lunged after them.

Fists pounded on the door in thwarted anger.

Moonbeam found a pole, and they braced the latch as best they could.

Jade slid off the Banshee, and then it hissed, opening for Ashe to extract herself. She left it powered up so the lamp would illuminate the room. Rainwood stood by the door, his bladed gauntlet at the ready in case the growlers broke through.

Jade crouched on the floor, covering his ears.

Moonbeam knelt by him and asked, "You okay, little man? We made it. They can't get in here."

"It's noisy!" he shouted. "So many! They scream and cry!"

"It's not that bad," Moonbeam said. "Nobody is screaming, just some thumping now. The walls are thick here."

Jade shook his head and stayed crouched down, hands over his ears.

Ashe leaned against a wall and slid to the ground, watching Jade with concern, then checked her AstroCom—11:30 pm—and commented, "That felt like it took days, but it was only a few hours."

Her eyelids were heavy, and she mumbled to Jade, motioning to her side. "Come here," she said. He scooted close, and she leaned into him, closing her eyes.

Fortunately, growlers had a short memory, and soon they lost their fevered interest. The thumps diminished to an occasional bump to remind them they were cornered.

Jade relaxed, eventually pulling his hands from his ears.

Either from the blood loss or the crash of the meds, Ashe quickly faded into unconsciousness, with Jade not far behind.

Moonbeam sighed, staring at her.

Rainwood pulled a crate from under a shelf and sat on it, facing the door, grumbling, "Join them. I'll keep watch."

Moonbeam moved over to lean against Ashe, and soon all three of them were asleep.

Rainwood rolled his eyes, muttering, "I meant join as in get some sleep, not—gah!"

Just In Time

Sitting at the breakfast table, Talia decided it wasn't her fault that the cockatrice hadn't given much usable meat—they were stringy. The little bit that she and her father had eaten was great, even if it had only lasted a day.

"Good morning, *Penina*. How are you doing?" Talia's father asked.

Talia loved it when her dad called her that—he said it meant "precious pearl."

She embraced him in a big hug. "I'm doing fine, Daddy, just getting ready for the day."

He glared at her warpaint and combat gear. "You know I prefer that you stay in here. It's much safer."

"I want to meet people! Everybody here is so boring. You may enjoy hanging out here with the others, but I want to see the world."

"Penina, the world is a dangerous place. Just stick to the areas we talked about, okay? Don't go to the first level and always stay above the parking lot."

"Fine," she growled, knowing she had no intention of visiting the boring first-floorers anyway. She had already planned to go into Pikeston. Settlers were congregating in the town, and she knew of a gigantic insect problem building up there.

She kissed her dad on the cheek before leaving. "Say hi to Mom."

He nodded and smiled, though his smile turned into sadness as Talia headed out the door.

Before it closed, he called out, "You are an amazing girl. Don't ever forget that!"

☣   ☢   ☣

Rainwood held a mop like a staff, using it to help keep himself awake through the night. If he started to drift off, he'd let it go, and its falling would wake him up. Fortunately for the others, each time he began to nod off, he woke and caught it before it clattered to the ground. After the third time, he checked his watch and decided it was time for somebody else.

Standing reminded him how stiff his muscles were after such a run, and he even let himself groan as he stretched—nobody could hear him anyway.

He noticed both Moonbeam and Jade were drooling on Ashe and smiled, then nudged Moonbeam's leg.

Moonbeam woke slowly, wiped his mouth with his sleeve, and stood, yawning with a stretch.

"What time is it Daegom?"

"Almost four."

"Are you okay?"

Rainwood nodded, handed him the mop, and said, "Keep it upright, don't let it fall."

Moonbeam looked at it curiously, but Rainwood gave no further explanation and instead found himself a corner to curl up in.

Rainwood woke around eight, saw Moonbeam playing air drums as he sat on a crate, and asked quietly, "They still out there?"

A thump echoed on the door as if in answer.

Moonbeam held his finger up, then waited for another thump and continued drumming. Soon Rainwood realized he had made a game of it—bringing the growlers' noise into the orchestra in his head. An empty bag of NukaRancher candy and a scattered array of wrappers told Rainwood what was giving Moonbeam energy.

Moonbeam finished drumming with a flourish, then gave his virtual audience a bow before asking, "So, old man, what's next?"

"Did Ashe wake?"

"No sir."

Rainwood checked Ashe's forehead, then her bandage, and said softly, "She seems to be hanging in there. Girl's tough as nails. Let's let her sleep—although we should check that bandage soon, it looks to be still bleeding."

He straightened and looked around the room, realizing the confines and lack of facilities, let alone privacy.

Moonbeam pointed to the far corner, which featured a bucket. "I have already christened that corner as the potty."

Rainwood rolled his eyes. "Potty? Seriously kid, sometimes you seem younger than Jade."

Moonbeam smiled.

A growler pounded on the door again.

Jade knuckled his eyes and stood, and Ashe slumped to the floor without him holding her up, but she did not wake.

Jade started hopping, looking around. Moonbeam pointed to the bucket in the corner.

Once nature was taken care of, Jade looked at Ashe, who was now emitting a very inelegant snore, and asked, "Is Ashe–is–is she okay?"

"She'll be fine," assured Moonbeam. "Oh, hey, do you have any ideas on getting out of here?"

Jade got a serious look and started poking around the room, under boxes, and behind shelves. After his search, Jade informed them, "I don't–I don't know how to get out. But–but there are twenty-three growlers."

The other two turned to him. Moonbeam put his hand up for a high-five. "Little man can count? Totally cool."

Rainwood asked, "Why do you think there are twenty-three?"

Midway to his high-five, Jade turned to Rainwood, suddenly unsure. "T–there a–are t–t–" he stopped trying, scowled, and ran to sit by Ashe.

Moonbeam assured him. "Don't worry about Mr. Scary Rainwood. He's all growl and no bite. If you say there are twenty-three, then there are twenty-three. Oh, hey!" He reached into his pocket and pulled out a holo-tape. "This was in Mei's pocket. Figured you'd want it."

Jade rose and stepped forward, aware of Rainwood's silent gaze, and cautiously took the cartridge. He stared at it, unsure what to do.

"You'll need to get a player," Moonbeam said. "Maybe ask to borrow Ashe's AstroCom. The tape was all muddy, but I cleaned it while you guys got your z's on."

Jade nodded.

Rainwood said, using his best soft voice, "Jade, whenever you're ready to share more about yourself, we'd like to learn. It'll help us keep you safe."

❦ ☢ ❦

"What do you mean team three isn't responding?" Captain Wright growled at the radio operator.

"Just that, sir. I've tried raising them for the last hour, but there is no response. I fear something is wrong with their equipment, or . . . worse," she answered with a squeak.

"What was their last message?"

She queued up the tape and played it.

"We are circling the designated area but don't see any targets. . . . Doughboy thought he saw somebody from a distance, so we're landing to scout the area."

As the tape continued, the recording barely picked up the sound of somebody shouting, *"Freeze!"*

"Looks like a local has appeared. I will check in after. Squad leader Conner out."

The operator let it play silence a little longer.

Captain Wright pounded the console. "They were there, I know it. Glenn was right, the lucky sod." Then he spun, exited the radio room, and stormed down the hall.

Once in the plaza, he called, "Lieutenant Simmons! I want all squads mobilized. Send one to the same area as Squad-3 to search it and get back to us. Have the others start canvassing the whole region until they're out of fuel and then continue on foot. Coordinate with those already on the ground—I want JDE-82 found!"

❦ ☢ ❦

Ashe's snoring abruptly stopped with a snort. She gasped, then moaned, holding her head. "It's so noisy. Everybody's sooo noisy.?!"

"That's the crash from all the Medipaks you took. You have a stim hangover," Rainwood speculated.

Ashe sat up against the wall, pulled her knees in, and then, through bleary eyes, looked around the room while running her fingers through her hair.

The growlers thumped again, and she jerked in alarm, then grumbled, "So we're still stuck."

They all nodded.

Moonbeam pointed to the bucket.

"Not in a million years," she huffed, muttering, "guys."

Moonbeam shrugged, fighting back a smile, and gave Ashe a quick rundown of what they had talked about before she woke up, including Jade's reveal about the growlers.

Ashe dug food from her pack and, more importantly, a bottle of Pop-Up, the highly caffeinated version of Pop-a-Cola. Jade was suddenly at her side, curiously looking at the glowing green beverage.

"Hah! No. You'd be bouncing off the walls."

She shared the food but kept the energy drink for herself—she'd been saving it, and this seemed like a good occasion. The sugary beverage was terrific as it hit her tongue. She'd wanted to open it for a while, and it helped take the edge off her jitters. Once her mind settled to a more regular buzz, she processed Moonbeam's report.

"Twenty-three growlers, Jade?"

He nodded.

You can hear them? She thought.

He nodded again.

"Pretty cool cat for a six-year-old, right? Not many can count that high so young," suggested Moonbeam.

"I–I–I–," he stopped, unsure how to explain.

Would you like me to tell them? Ashe thought.

He sighed and nodded.

"Jade has a special ability," Ashe said. "He can hear thoughts. But he has learned that when people find out, it goes badly, so he doesn't want anybody to know."

"So you can hear what everybody's thinking? That's the bomb!" Moonbeam offered another high-five, and Jade slapped his hand with a grin.

Rainwood rubbed his goatee but said nothing.

Ashe shifted the subject to what Jade had said the day before. "Jade, do you know who Mei was?"

He nodded. "She–she took us from the lab. We were tiny, long ago. I don't–I don't remember much."

"We?" asked Moonbeam.

"Me and—and my sister Ember."

"I take it you lost track of each other?" Moonbeam asked.

Jade nodded.

"Do you remember anything else?" Ashe questioned.

He scrunched his brow in thought, "We–we crashed. People helped—took us. Then others. Nobody was nice."

"You don't know when or where?"

He shook his head, "I–I was just a kid."

Moonbeam chuckled, raising an eyebrow while making an exaggerated measurement of Jade's short height with his hand.

"A baby kid," Jade clarified with an exasperated tone.

Rainwood fought back a smile and asked, "So, you can tell we're surrounded by twenty-three growlers then?"

Jade shook his head. "Now only f–fifteen. And some people."

They realized the thumps on the door had stopped, and everybody held their breath, listening carefully.

A crack of gunfire echoed from outside.

Rainwood unblocked the door and looked out.

"Looks clear."

They grabbed their gear, and Ashe entered the Banshee. Once ready, they crept out as a team, with Rainwood in the lead and Jade taking up the rear.

Gunfire rang clearly with the door open. Every few moments, a rifle shot cracked and echoed across the area, but it was hard to pinpoint where the shots came from.

Rainwood held up a hand and crept across the broken glass, peeking out the window.

Growlers darted across the highway. Another gunshot cracked, and one spun in a circle, falling to the ground. Rainwood scanned the hillside but couldn't see anybody.

He waved the others off. "Try the back door."

Ashe opened the rear exit and stepped out, crouching. Automatic gunfire chattered, and bullets struck the curb near her, the ricochet sounding like a series of zings. She dove back into the building.

"I think we're pinned down," Ashe said.

"At least we're out of the *bucket* room," suggested Moonbeam.

Jade giggled, and Rainwood snapped his hand, gesturing for silence. He crouched below the window and listened.

The gunshots were less frequent, and he whispered to Jade, "How many now?"

Jade looked off into the distance. After a moment, he pointed. "Two, over there."

Another crack of gunfire echoed.

"One."

A moment later, another shot rang out, and Jade held up his fingers in a "zero" sign.

They waited, unsure if they should step outside again.

Ashe worried. *Are these the people looking for Jade? Or are they raiders?*

"I wonder what ice cream tastes like," Moonbeam mused.

"Can you pay attention to one thing at a time, boy?" grumbled Rainwood as he looked around. "We need something to make a flag out of."

Jade scampered across the floor to retrieve a cafeteria tray and took it to Rainwood, who waved it in front of the window.

"We are peaceful!" he shouted.

"Toss your guns and fusion cores out. Leave your mech inside."

Moonbeam drew one of his pistols and made to toss it out.

Rainwood growled, "Put that back!"

Unsure what to do, Moonbeam froze and mumbled, "But they said—"

"Regrettably, we can't do that," shouted Rainwood. "How about I step out, but the rest stay put?"

"Fine. Keep your hands high."

Rainwood dropped his rifle and gauntlet, then stood and stepped into the yard raising his hands. Before going farther, Rainwood growled to his friends, "Stay in there for now."

It wasn't easy to pinpoint the assailants—they were all undercover behind cars and buildings.

"Rev? Is that you?" Somebody stepped out. "I'd recognize that top hat anywhere. Hey all, it's the Rev! Put your guns down."

Rainwood squinted and said, "Henry Mullins? You old dog, how are you still kickin'?" Then he walked toward the newcomers, his arms lowered slightly, and shouted, "Last I heard, you were heading down south, something about the Rangers."

Six people approached him, their guns lowered but at the ready.

Ashe exited the mech, leaving it out of sight, and crawled to Jade, whispering, "When we go out, I want you to keep quiet and don't look at anybody. If anybody asks, you're my little brother from over by Harrisburg. And here," she pulled out her sunglasses and put them on him, "keep those on. And you are not Jade. You need another name. How about Ke—"

She stopped, berating herself. *Not Kelly. Of course not. Stupid.*

"No, how about—"

Moonbeam joined in. "Jace. He can be Jace."

She glared at him, wondering if he was serious or not. "We need something that doesn't sound the same as Jade."

They all glanced around the store, looking for ideas.

All Ashe could see was Rocket Ace memorabilia. Everywhere. She asked, "Jade, what do you want?"

He smiled and pointed at the sign. "Ace."

She ruffled his hair. "Okay, Ace, it is."

Outside, Rainwood kept his arms up, facing a tall, olive-skinned woman with her dark hair pulled back into a ponytail under a cowboy hat. She nodded, drawling. "That's right, Henry is a Star Ranger now. You vouch for this guy then, Henry?"

"Yeah, he's good folk. Glad we could help you out—looks like you had a right old party going on here."

The woman returned her rifle to its shoulder holster. "I'm Athina, judge of this troop. You know Henry." She gestured to the others. "That skinny kid is Dex. Nia has the M-150 shoulder cannon—she saved your behinds. That's Max, my lieutenant, and then the Sheriff."

After the introductions, she held out her hand. "And you are?"

He took it and shook. "Rainwood is what folks know me by these days."

"Your friends?" She waved to the building.

He looked back but didn't signal them to appear and instead asked, "What are the Star Rangers doing here?"

The Sheriff approached, dropping a toothpick he'd been chewing on. He looked as grizzled as Rainwood, almost a mirror image of him. He even had a trench coat—but brown rather than black. Both looked like dangerous badland warriors.

"I invited them. We're hunting a Deathmark," declared the Sheriff, his gaze studying Rainwood. It seemed like he had more to say but chose to hold back for the moment.

"Dangerous beasts," Rainwood responded, returning the knowing look.

Athina interjected, "Perhaps you two could measure your respective lengths another time, and invite your friends out here?"

Rainwood nodded and called, "Come on out."

Moonbeam jumped up, bouncing out the door and giving a thumbs up. "Hey, sorry I missed the introductions. I'm Moonbeam!"

Ashe followed, and behind her trailed Jade.

"Oh, and that's Ashe, and there is the little man, J—uhrm," he cleared his throat, "that is my little dude, Ace, of course. We helped him from a tight spot—"

Rainwood gave him a cold stare, and he stopped talking.

"You sure that's all?" Athina said, "Dex claimed he saw somebody in a mech."

Ashe nodded. "It's mine. Inside."

"Well, we planned to set up a base camp here if you want to join us for breakfast before we keep scouting," offered Athina.

"No need—we already took care of the Deathmark," said Ashe, waving to the forest. "After a few miles of hiking, you'll find its remains over that way."

Athina paused, considering the group with a bit of skepticism while noting the bandages on Ashe, and said, "Well, if that's so, then we owe you our thanks. Please, join us for a celebration. We've been scouting all night, and the team needs a rest."

Henry stepped up and slapped Rainwood on the back. "I'd love to catch up with the Rev. Come on, guys. The restaurant has some tables we can use."

They rustled up a warm breakfast, shared their food, and got to know everybody. Henry tried to regale the group with stories of "the Rev" but soon realized Rainwood didn't want to discuss it and let it drop. After the initial banter subsided, Nia said she thought the repair bay had a mech repair frame, and Ashe took the opportunity to extract herself from the others, making sure Jade was in tow. Before walking the Banshee to the bay, she scouted it out, checking each nook, corner, and crevice for surprise dangers.

Jade sat on a table, swinging his legs while watching Ashe lock the mech into the frame and start tinkering.

The Sheriff stepped into the doorway a few minutes later, silhouetted by the bright day outside. "There you are. Wanted to talk."

Ashe poked her head up from inside the Banshee. "I'm busy. We don't need to talk."

He gave a pleasant smile, saying, "All good, all good. No worry," before stepping into the room and approaching Jade. "Hey, Ace, is it?"

Jade nodded while fighting back an excited grin.

Ashe hopped down and stepped in front of the Sheriff, blocking his approach. "Listen, we're alright. I've heard of you; I know you're the helpful type, but we're good without your help."

He smiled, nodding. "Good, good," then turned and started poking at a parts shelf, "So you and the kid here—you guard him like a lioness. He family?"

Ashe wasn't sure why he was so interested but figured it couldn't be for any good purpose.

"Yeah, he's my br—" she couldn't even say it for some reason. A pinch in her chest kept tangling her tongue.

"Brother," she finally finished.

"Oh, that's good. Family is good, real good."

He tossed a piston from the shelf, and she ducked instinctively. While she was distracted, the Sheriff lunged at Jade, snatching the sunglasses.

Ashe snapped Coyote from its holster and aimed it at him. He just stood there, grinning with his hands in the air. She kept Coyote pointed at him and gestured to the door. "I think you should leave."

He slowly returned the sunglasses to Jade. "Your secret is safe with me. But may I suggest it's best to keep him out of sight? It's better not to be seen at all than to be seen with a disguise."

Jade took the sunglasses and put them back on.

Ashe lowered her gun slightly. "What are you talking about?"

"I think you know what I'm talking about. There are a lot of dangerous people looking for him. I don't think anywhere planetside is safe. You should get off-world if you can. But of course, that's difficult, so maybe head westward, leave the area."

"Why do they want him?"

He paused with a distant look before adding, "It's best if you never know. But I promise I'm not with them. I'm doing everything I can to throw wrenches in their work. In fact, I had a hand in helping him and his sister escape."

"Escape what?"

The mumble of voices outside interrupted their conversation. Ashe quickly holstered the pistol just before Dex and Nia stepped into the repair bay.

Nia said, "Hey, you found it! My boy Dex here is a certified mechanic if you need help with anything."

As Dex and Nia passed the Sheriff, he lifted two fingers to his lips, making a zipper motion to Ashe, then backed out of the room.

Dex asked with enthusiasm, "Is that really a Banshee!?"

He seemed as excited as a kid in a candy store and crawled all over it. "I've never seen one before. This is so cool. Mostly you see the Griffins and Ogres. I don't think many of the Banshees were even made. Although I heard the Wardens had a lead on a vault with a bunch of them hidden away somewhere."

Ashe decided he seemed to know his stuff and reluctantly agreed to let him help. He found a diagnostic system in the repair bay's back corner and plugged it into the mech. After a minute of reviewing the information, they started into what field repairs could be made with their limited resources, and she was fine letting him do most of the work, as she was distracted considering the Sheriff's words.

The guy was an authority figure in the area, and drove her nuts. She'd seen him before, at Mosstown, a few months back, although she had stayed out of sight at the time. *How is he involved in all of this? And why wouldn't he tell me more? He can't just tell me to go away! I need to know what's going on!*

It was apparent the people after Jade weren't going to stop, and completely leaving the area like the Sheriff directed made complete sense, but she didn't know anywhere else to go. And now that she knew Jade had a sister, leaving without her didn't seem right, either.

Ashe mulled the options to find Ember while helping with the repairs. Asking around would probably paint a target on them, but she didn't know what else to do.

She decided to corner the Sheriff and get answers, put her tools on the bench, and was about to tell Dex she'd be right back, when Athina joined them in the repair bay, explaining, "the others just headed out to find the Deathmark's remains, so we wondered if y'all needed any help here?"

Ashe clenched her teeth to keep from yelling, and carefully picked up the spanner wrench. *They'll be back later, and I can ask him then.*

With her frustration dwindling, she pointed to Dex and said, "Ask him," before retreating to check her bandage while racking her brain for contingency plans.

Her bandage was soaked with blood, and she gasped as the layers of wrapping pulled at the edges of the wound, then stared at the ragged gash, easily a few centimeters long.

I need stitches. This is too big for a Medipak.

She remembered seeing a first-aid kit, rooted it out, and was glad to find it had a suture stapler, although no numbing spray. She sighed and proceeded anyway, first cleaning her wound, then twisting while trying to get the right angle when Athina offered, "Need help?"

Ashe paused. Her first instinct was to say no, but she could use help, so she held up the stapler.

"Yeah, if you could. I need two or three."

Athina pinched the wound, lining up the stapler, and said, "Hold on, this will sting."

Ka-chink.

Ashe pounded the table with her hand, gasping, "Yaaaaaah! That is more than a sting!"

Jade's face screwed up in a wince, sharing her pain.

"One more should do it."

Ka-chink.

Ashe pounded the table several more times, unable to even say anything, then gasped slowly.

After a few more deep breaths, she looked up to see Jade curled over on the table, his eyes closed tightly, tears squeezing out of the corners. A glance around the room confirmed nobody had paid much attention to Jade's reaction, and she directed a thought, *Sorry, tough guy. You good?*

He nodded and straightened up, wiping his eyes.

Athina cleaned the suture stapler and put it back in the first-aid kit before saying, "So, the Sheriff says you and your brother could use a ride off-world."

Ashe applied a new bandage, hiding her frustration at the Sheriff being all nosy, and nodded. "Yeah, that."

"Well, if you really did take down a Deathmark then that says a lot about your capabilities. We could use somebody like you. If you sign up with the Star Rangers, you can catch a transport to any number of worlds after your training. And we help take care of family," she pointed to Jade.

Ashe wasn't expecting to be recruited, and she immediately thought of Mason—if only he was here. Unable to form any other response, she mumbled, "Oh."

Athina tapped the brim of her hat. "Well, think about it. Feel free to stop by our Arcadian headquarters just north of the spaceport by Saratoga. And here," she pulled a package from a bag, "these antibiotics should help you recover."

The unexpectedly kind gesture struck Ashe, bringing a lump to her throat, and she struggled to keep her face stern while carefully accepting the offered medicine and expressing her thanks. After Athina left, Ashe wondered how long it'd be until the guys would return—she wanted to hit the road again, even if she wasn't sure where to go, but also wanted to get the Sheriff somewhere private where she could dig more information out of him.

Around 2:00 p.m., Rainwood and Moonbeam returned with Henry, reporting the others would be back before the night and were taking care of the carcass, but worse, at least as far as Ashe was concerned: the Sheriff had already headed south somewhere.

"How long ago?" she growled at Henry as he gave Athina his report.

"How long what?" Henry asked in surprise.

"How long ago did the Sheriff leave?" she clarified, hoping she had time to catch him.

"Oh, he headed out early. It's been at least what, an hour or two?" he answered, glancing at Rainwood, who nodded.

Ashe needed answers, and wasn't going to get them.

They needed a plan, and just running wasn't going to cut it. She returned to her gear and started gathering it, again doing mental gymnastics as she struggled to think of options. It took a few minutes, until she remembered something on the tape recording, and pulled it out, rewinding it until she found the point she wanted, with the Commissioner speaking.

"You searched my gear for my access card? You know, they won't let you in, even with it."

Warthog laughed again. *"I think I'll keep a hold of this for now—"*

Ashe hit the pause button, a glimmer of hope growing in her chest. *If they had the Commissioner's access card, and it worked like he said, then I can just sneak in and find Ember, then we can leave the area.*

Her emotions calmed, and she grinned, suddenly anxious to get back on the road. She wanted to run, but instead kept herself reserved as she stepped into the repair bay, where Dex was in the process of putting tools away and cleaning the shop.

"She's as good as I can make her, considering what we have here. At a regular repair bay we can do more."

"I'm sure it's great," she offered, "Thanks!"

Ashe found Rainwood and Moonbeam sifting through the cafe for supplies and informed them as firmly as she could, "We need to go! I have a plan, but let's hit the road soon!"

Moonbeam complained, as he'd spent the day hiking, but Ashe wouldn't hear it. With the occasional muttered complaint they gathered their gear and headed to the highway, Athina following them, before trying one more time.

"Ashe, think about it, okay? It's a good gig. We could use people like you."

With a nod, Ashe started toward the brush on the west side of the road. Rainwood and Moonbeam looked ready to hike south but veered around and followed her instead.

After they were far enough away, Rainwood asked, "So what's this way?"

"I don't know."

"Well, as long as you're sure," Moonbeam said smartly.

"I just don't want them to know where we're heading."

Poor Little Fool

A she stopped in the shade of a tree once she felt they were far enough away and exited the Banshee. While everybody else rested, she retrieved a box of Bazooka Bars she had found hidden in a toolbox at the truck stop, offering one to each of them. "Sorry for making you go right back on the road. I needed to get away." She sat on a log before continuing, "Did the Sheriff ask any odd questions?"

Moonbeam joined her, stuffing the chewy marshmallow treat in his mouth—still fresh even 25 years after its expiration—and said, "Nah, he just wanted to know how well we knew you. Aaand, where you came from. Said he saw you had a totally amazing AstroCom. Wondered which enclave you were from. Thought you were a pretty cool cat and all. You know, nothing weird, at least."

"What?! What did you tell him?"

Rainwood growled, "He didn't pry much, just wanted to know how well we know you."

Moonbeam grinned, chuckling silently and causing the log to wobble.

She lunged sideways, bumping her shoulder into his. "You doof, don't do that to me."

Jade laughed, his legs flying up as he tried to keep balance on the wobbling log while holding a half-eaten Bazooka Bar in each hand. Then he doubled forward to avoid toppling backward, still giggling.

Ashe thought he reacted to humor well and wondered if it was because he could hear both sides of the joke. She jabbed him, eliciting another string of giggles, and smiled, thinking it maybe wasn't all bad for him.

"We didn't tell him anything other than we've known you for a while," clarified Rainwood.

Ashe noticed he had no Bazooka Bar, and realized how Jade acquired the second one.

She explained her curious interaction with the Sheriff and the offer Athina gave her, finishing with, "I'm not sure where to go next. Jade, I want to help you find Ember. Do you know where she might be?"

He sobered up quickly, shook his head, and then stuffed the last of both bars into his mouth, looking like a chipmunk.

"Well, as I see it, our options aren't great. We could chase down Glenn in Mosstown and see if he's the one who put that Hog on our tail. But that might show them where we are."

Rainwood nodded, and Ashe continued, "Other than that, there is the tape I found at Warthog's Den—" she stopped, realizing she had yet to share it with anybody else. After quickly explaining how she found the tape and what she'd learned from it, she said, "Perhaps we could go back to Warthog's and see if we can find the Commissioner's access card to Fenclave? Or anything else that might help? Maybe the remaining raiders have all left?"

Rainwood shook his head. "It's too nice a compound to abandon—although they're likely a bit disorganized. Best I know, nobody caught sight of us, so we could aim to approach as traders."

"Okay, so that's an option."

Jade unseated FuzzyKat from his backpack and dug through his things, retrieving the holo-tape Moonbeam found on Mei and offering it up, "M—m—maybe she says something."

Ashe carefully took it from his sticky fingers and inserted it into her AstroCom.

The recording sounded garbled—probably damaged from the years in the water and silt—but not so far gone you couldn't hear what was said.

It began with some labored breathing, then a woman started, *"This is Mei Tamura. The rocket is damaged, and this landing is going to be hard. I wanted to get to Lostar-5, but we won't make it. Arcadia is the closest world I could plot."*

She gasped, *"And I've been shot. The kids—they seem fine, at least.*

"I'm recording this in case I don't make it; hopefully, somebody can pass this info on to them as they grow up.

"I was a Space Dynamics scientist, and I received an invitation into a project for a partner company called Ordyne—I didn't realize they were so horrific. They sent me to a space station called the Citadel.

"Ordyne—they've been around since before the arrival, and they're a dark, corrupt organization. I was horrified when I learned Ordyne is actually Ordo Deus Irae, *or 'the Order of the God of Wrath' in some ancient language. It's an old cult, almost, run by somebody called Suzerain—"*

She breathed heavily for a moment, then said, *"Hell's bells, what am I going on about? You two won't understand this.*

"The worst was being at the Citadel. Anybody who is brought in, well, it was a one-way trip—a prison. But when I escaped, I made sure nobody could repeat their research. I wish I had known what was expected of these kids.

"They were conducting genetic experiments. I freed JDE-82 and EBR-19—both are iterations of some unusual non-human DNA that we spliced into them. None of us knew where it came from. They just called it 'the contributor.' They even made us provide our genetic material for different 'iterations of biological material,' as they put it, but let's call it what it was—forced eugenics. So few were viable, let alone healthy. If the iterations didn't exhibit what Ordyne was looking for, then they—they forced us to terminate the failures, regardless of how old they had become. With the success of these two, they terminated all of the others, and I couldn't take it anymore.

"They are four, and Jade can speak, although Ember still hasn't. The kids rely on each other quite a bit, like a yin and yang thing.

"The kids," she sighed. "I'm making this tape for you two. You were both successes. I wasn't sure what Ordyne planned next once everybody was happy with your progress, so I put a destructive data-worm into the mainframe and left a bomb in the labs before fleeing with you—Jade and Ember now. Never think of their horrible designations for you. You are individuals. You should choose your own destiny in life.

"I think—I think maybe Jade might be from my—from the eggs they made me donate. I never dared run a DNA test, but the timing is right, and with his curly dark hair, he looks—"

Her voice broke, then she continued, *"—even if not, you're my babies. I will get you somewhere safe. I just wish I could help more. . .*

"Jade, say hello to the recorder."

"Hello reh-score-der?"

Ashe felt her heart race. It was clearly Jade's voice—just more squeaky sounding.

She glanced at him to see a frown drawing his face long, with tears wallowing in his eyes, and paused the tape then held him tight.

He sniffled, burying his face in her chest.

"Do you remember this?"

He nodded.

"We don't have to listen now—you can wait if you want."

He shook his head.

She pulled him away and tweaked his nose. He knuckled the tears from his eyes and pinched his mouth in determination.

Moonbeam mussed his hair. "You are one tough cat."

Ashe held out her AstroCom and let him push the play button.

Mei continued, *"Jade—if we ever get separated, I want you to keep track of Ember, okay?"*

"Kay"

"I want both of you to be very careful with who you trust, okay? Ember, listen to your brother. He knows who to trust. If he doesn't like somebody, leave. Don't try to do anything with them."

"If you ever get a chance, try to get to Lostar-5. I heard they have a safe colony. Can you say it for me? Lostar-5?"

"I–I–I can do, umm, say loster fieeeve?! And, a–a–and I need a-go pee."

Mei sighed.

"And E. B. R. want—uhh—Emmmburrr wants a snack—"

The tape had a clicking sound, then a moment later, Mei's voice started again.

"You are both settled now, right? Okay, listen to me."

"I want you to remember to stay away from Ordyne, or any-body asking about your abilities. See this symbol on your clothes? A

circle with a diamond in the middle? This means they're from Or-dyne. You stay away from anybody with this. I think Ordyne has something to do with the Kraal, and you're somehow involved. But, just—stay away from them. They're dangerous! Do you understand? Stay away from Ordyne!"

"Kay."

"On a good note, I had a friend help get you two out. He ar-rived as an inspector on the project, but I didn't get his name. He just said he's the Sheriff. He's a bit gruff, but I think he's a good person. I hope he was able to escape before the explosion. I hope ev-erybody could—"

The recording warbled and crackled for a moment, then Mei continued with a note of panic in her voice, *"That was a rough landing. It knocked me out . . . I don't know how long I've been un-conscious, but the kids are gone! I found a lot of tracks outside, so somebody was here."*

"I hope you're all right. I'm coming, kids—"

She continued after another series of clicks and static, but her voice sounded much more hoarse, *"I've looked for you for months. Now I'm just talking to myself. I hope you survived. I think Ordyne has found me, and I've been running ever since. They expect you to do something with the Kraal, so I hope they have as little luck finding you as I have. I don't know how much time I have left. I'm sick, and I have no more food or water."*

And then static.

After listening a bit more, but finding nothing else on the tape, Ashe stopped the recording.

Nobody spoke. Instead, they just watched Jade, wondering how he processed all the information. His face was stony, then he looked at them and said, "I c–c–can handle it."

Moonbeam gave him a gentle punch on the shoulder. "Of course, you can."

Ashe checked the timestamp on the tape. "Looks like this was recorded almost two years ago. Do you remember what happened?"

"Not lots. I—it was scary when we crashed. Then she wouldn't wake up. And some people came to help. T–took us to their home. But then we were attacked, and mean people t–took us. I–I–I couldn't stop them from taking Ember. She was asleep. Sick. And then m–more people wanted me to tell what people were thinking. A lot of people owned me. They traded me. Not n–nice people. Then you let me out."

Ashe said, "Well, I'm glad I found you. I think we all feel that way. And we're here to help you find Ember. You up for that?"

He nodded.

She handed the holo-tape back and said, "You hang onto that. Mei seemed like a nice person, maybe even your real mom. I'm sorry she got hurt, and, you know... when you're ready, I'm here if you wanna chat, alright? Do you need a minute before we head out?"

He shook his head, shouldered his backpack, then started walking away, eventually coming to a stop, facing away from everybody while waiting for them to join.

Ashe watched him, then focused her thoughts, hoping he'd hear. *Jade, It's okay to grieve. I know I said it's best to keep moving in the badlands . . . And that is good. But don't forget we care about you, okay?*

He nodded but didn't turn around, although he wiped at his eyes with his sleeve. Ashe's heart hurt watching his pain, and she wanted to hug him again. While gathering their belongings, Rainwood noticed her movement towards Jade and touched her shoulder, advising, "He may be six years old, but he's inwardly far older —life hasn't given him a choice. Pressing him now could make him bury his feelings. Give him time to digest this and talk to him later."

"Yeah," she sighed. "Well, let's find Ember. For that, I think Ordyne is in Fenclave, and that means Warthog's is a good next step. We can find Highway 95 shortly enough and retrace our steps. Although we should stick with the highway this time and try to sneak past the chemical factory; it'll be faster."

Rainwood nodded, Moonbeam offered a thumbs up, and they were shortly underway.

☣   ☢   ☣

The small ebony-skinned girl with black, wooly hair stared at the man in a lab coat. Deep in her eyes, rose sparks swirled. The scientist sweated, his gaze focused on his hand, which slowly moved toward a bag of NukaRancher candy—fighting a battle against himself to hold his hand still. He gasped, grabbed the candy, then said, "Okay, fine. But you need to do what we ask after *this* piece. Can you do that, EBR?"

She smiled, her cheeks dimpled, and then she nodded. The man gave her another piece of candy and, with a strain of exhaustion in his voice—as if he's said this many times—asked, "I need you to think really hard. Can you tell us where you last saw JDE-82? Perhaps just draw a picture?"

He tapped a clipboard with blank paper.

She shrugged, sucking on the sugary blue treat.

The scientist sighed and turned to the chamber door. It slid open with a hiss, and he stepped out into a laboratory where others watched through a one-way window. A short, lanky alien with gray skin wearing a lab coat stepped over—a "gray." Its eyes were wide and black. At least half the techs were grays rather than humans.

It made a series of noises, almost like hiccups, but Frank knew that was how they laughed. This gray spoke, "Good idea, Frank. She's apt to talk at some point, right? How much candy did you give the cute little monster?"

"Stuff it, Vraux," Frank growled, setting down the bag of NukaRancher candy and collecting his clipboard before storming away from the restricted area. His coworkers didn't worry him. No, his concern was his meeting with Suzerain. A year had passed since Ordyne recovered EBR, but they still could not find JDE-82.

Since Mei went rogue two years ago, the entire program had come to a standstill, and their benefactor Suzerain did not appreciate the delay. Frank worried the question would arise again about just "making more." But Mei had made that impossible, at least not without repeating another 25 years of research.

After passing through several pristine halls, Frank approached a wood-paneled door featuring a gold-inlaid circle with a flared diamond in the center. He straightened his coat, then pressed the button.

The door slid open, and Frank bowed before entering.

☣   ☢   ☣

Lieutenant Simmons was a spaceman, born and raised in climate-controlled environments. He hated going into the open, let alone into destroyed towns like Pikeston. At least in a city, the tall towers helped him feel less exposed, but here the buildings were only a few stories tall at best. And the smell! He adjusted the scarf over his mouth, trying to avoid breathing.

How can the locals stand it? It's like sour milk and raw sewage.

Just thinking about it made him nearly gag. When he had first arrived in the town, he tried breathing through his mouth, but that was worse—like tasting it while also smelling it.

Public utilities didn't work anymore, and it alarmed him how many people were together in one place. While the city was not crowded, Simmons had crossed paths with dozens of people in his investigation. Didn't they realize the danger it posed? Why didn't the Wardens make these people spread out?

He watched every corner, expecting the Kraal to appear at any moment. Strangely, the extra-dimensional horrors could only emerge from corners, which made him only feel comfortable in rounded rooms, of which there were none in Pikeston.

Simmons stopped to study a building. The weathered sign overhead used to say "Hardware—electronics and other sundries." The windows were all boarded up, and somebody had roughly painted over them "Cooperative Mercantile."

It had taken all of his barter skills to get this far. Fortunately, canned goods did well in this society, and after the directions of a few people, he found his way here.

He needed somebody to help repair the base's pre-arrival mainframe, and everybody seemed to think "The Commissioner" could help him. She used to run the enclave, of all things, and now coordinated a community supply kitchen.

If anybody can straighten up the robots and mainframe, it should be her, right?

He adjusted his pack, still half-full with cans, nodded to himself, then stepped inside.

☣   ☢   ☣

Ashe decided she needed to teach Moonbeam or Rainwood how to use the mech. It was really nice to have, but she liked to walk on her own two feet. After many days of hiking in the Banshee, her body ached in new places, not to mention the blisters.

The team had started south on the highway but soon heard another Hog tilt-engine aircraft howling in the distance, which drove them to the trees for cover. Hog transports continued to appear from time to time, searching the area, so Ashe and Rainwood had agreed that they remain in the forest instead—relying on the canopy of the Fen for cover.

Jade was glad they would find Ember but didn't want to talk about her or listen to the tape again—much to Ashe's frustration. She wanted to drag information out of him, and Rainwood kept reminding her it was better to wait.

They reached the chemical factory in two days, this time from the west, and when they broke for lunch behind cover, Ashe took a moment to look across the valley and scan the industrial yard using her Arbiter's scope. She pointed to one side and handed the gun to Rainwood. "Looks like the Wardens, not robots. See that ATV personnel carrier; it wasn't there when I last passed through here."

Rainwood peered through the scope and said, "I believe there's somebody on the upper catwalk behind the barricade. Might be in a Union Corps uniform—the Wardens keep using that style, thinking it makes them look legitimate."

"Do you think the Wardens are behind all this with Jade? They have taken over back east. I know they have Hogs as well as airships."

Rainwood handed the Arbiter back to Ashe. "Could be. But those who attacked us at the lake wore black and blue. Union field colors are green, and dress colors are green, blue, or white for Army, Sky, or Fleet Corps."

Unable to get any other information from their distance, they wrapped up lunch and were able to pass the area without detection by the Wardens. Ashe smiled, her hopes rising at their success. Soon they were back at a steady pace southward.

It took another day to reach Mosstown's river bottoms region, their journey finally coming full circle. They stood on the shore and could smell the cook fires from Mosstown in the distance, even though trees obscured the buildings.

"Should we swim?" asked Moonbeam.

"No. You don't want to see the size of the leeches in there. Regardless, I'm afraid to visit right now," said Ashe.

Rainwood suggested, "We might stay by the shore. How long does it last like this?"

"A ways. About a mile or two south is an accidental dam. The highway collapsed where it crossed the river. But, that will take us by the Fairmont Church." She didn't need to explain the risk, as everybody remembered passing the church earlier.

"We'll just keep our distance," Moonbeam suggested, but Ashe thought she detected a hint of mischievousness in his voice.

She pointed at him. "Fine, but you stay with us. No wandering off!"

They followed the boggy shoreline, and when the church came into view, they tried to push their way into the briars, but it was impassable. Even with Rainwood's machete, it'd take them a day just to pass the church.

Ashe remembered the chainsaw mount for mechs she saw once and wished she had it now. Unable to think of a better option, she asked, "Jade, what do you think? Can we go closer?"

He looked scared, glanced at the church through the haze, and shrugged his shoulders. "None have s–seen us yet."

"Good. Follow me, and be quiet."

They walked along the church's fence line. In the back was an old playground with a swing set and a spinning platform. Jade stared at the equipment curiously, probably wondering what it was for. Some internal wiring recognized the equipment was for kids his age, and he instinctively started toward the swing set. Ashe had to act quickly and reel him in.

After they crossed the yard, she looked back and swore she saw somebody holding curtains open in the church window, watching them.

That is not normal—if they had seen us, why didn't they swarm out?

A cold chill ran down her spine, and she buried the thought, thankful they had avoided another problem.

☣   ☢   ☣

The Commissioner pushed away from the enclave's mainframe console. Her silver hair added an air of authority that Simmons couldn't help but defer to. She offered a shrug before explaining, "It was worth a try, but something more is going on here. Like I told you, I'm not a programmer. But I can bring in somebody who knows how to deal with this."

Simmons glanced around nervously—the security chief was out on patrol with the others, so he hadn't even completed the proper authorization paperwork to let the Commissioner in. But Captain Wright had said he had to fix this.

With reluctance, he answered, "I suppose. Just one more?"

"My chief mainframe programmer was Enoha. This is all likely her work. She probably set up a failsafe to cause problems if anybody else came back. However, she and her husband were inseparable, and they programmed this together. I think we should ask them both to come."

Simmons took off his cap and nervously ran his fingers through his hair. "Fine. I'll give them access passes. How long will it take you to get back?"

"Can't you fly me around with one of your Hogs?"

"No, they're all out on patrol."

"Well, to find them, maybe a few days—assuming they're in the area I think they are—then the walk back. Perhaps half a week to a week? And I'll need more supplies for their payment."

All he could think about was how to avoid Captain Wright for five days. At least he'd have time to prepare the captain about how more people would be entering the base.

"Okay. Just hurry."

The Commissioner smiled, gathered her things, and departed.

17.

Civilization (Bongo, Bongo, Bongo)

Talia found a place to sit on the second floor's balcony, dangled her legs over the edge, then dialed "Lonely Teenager" from Dion to play on her AstroCom.

Accompanied by the very apropos song that spoke to her soul about how hard it was to be alone, she tried to have fun people-watching. The others below were annoyingly boring drips, yet she still tried her best to make a game of it—finding those similar to her friends from Fenclave.

Like that one there she always thought looked like Mason—at least an old guy version of him.

Boredom settled in, however, and she dramatically flopped back.

Her father approached and sat next to her. "Okay, *La'u Penina*, tell me about it."

"I need to meet new people. Go see the galaxy! I should be out finding my destiny!"

He chuckled. "I love that you set your sights high. Never let go of that. But you know we aren't in Fenclave anymore. The world is dangerous. I want you to be safe, and it's safe here."

"Safe and boring, maybe."

He changed the subject, "Have you checked on Mom lately? Do you think she'd like you to read to her again?"

Talia reluctantly stood up and left, saying, "I'll go ask her."

Talia's father watched her go, shaking his head. He worried about Talia—she still refused to see the truth before her. He lifted a gnarled hand covered in scars and wiped at the tear that ran down his gaunt cheeks, looking almost like a burn victim. *She's still hiding from the truth. Hopefully, she will be able to face it before it's too late.*

☣　　☢　　☣

Keeping under cover from the regular Hog patrols, it took two days to reach Warthog's old raider camp, and Ashe had a lot of time to think. As their hike ended, she tried to reconcile her thoughts between her self-definition as a solo wanderer and her growing attachment to the people now surrounding her.

Her wandering mind noticed Moonbeam as he walked in front of her, having a one-way animated conversation with Jade. *He is so easy to be around. Annoying too, but maybe not in a bad way.* Catching herself, she shook her head and focused on their mission to find Ember.

Rainwood held up a hand and crouched, pointing to the sky. Everybody ducked for cover, part of the routine they'd become used to, but he shook his head and said, "Not a Hog, but I think I see a skyship over the trees about where Warthog's camp is."

Ashe used the Banshee's optics to inspect and decided he was right. She could see silver glints from the rounded top of a floating, rigid-hulled airship. She popped the mech's helmet open and asked quietly, "The Wardens?"

Rainwood stared at the airship over the trees. "More than likely. Did you notice we haven't seen any Hogs or ground troops this morning? I wonder if they're keeping clear of the Wardens."

"If the Wardens are at the old raider camp, maybe we could just say the raiders took our stuff, and we want it back?" suggested Moonbeam.

Ashe didn't like that idea—she'd learned to avoid the Wardens by principle, mainly because they liked to be bossy. But she didn't have any other plan. "By *we*, I think you mean only one or two of us. We can't take Jade in there now."

Moonbeam put an elbow on Jade's head, leaned on him, and asked in an oblivious tone, "Who?"

Jade grinned and poked Moonbeam.

She rolled her eyes at Rainwood, who nodded and declared, "Moonbeam and Jade, you two stay hidden, and Ashe and I will go in. Wardens look at themselves as peacekeepers, so I think we'll be fine. Let's pick a rallying point to meet at in an hour or so."

Moonbeam replied, "The only places I remember around here are the raider camp and Ashe's cabin. Isn't it like an hour away?"

"That'll work. Back away and watch for us, but be willing to bug out if anything happens, then we'll catch up to you at the cabin."

Jade scowled. Ashe thought she knew what he was upset about—he didn't want to split from her, so she told him, "It's better this way. Can you keep Moonbeam in line?"

Jade looked at Moonbeam, and a slow smile spread on his face, before he answered, "No."

Rainwood grunted, "Ain't that the truth."

They split ways, with Moonbeam dramatically holding his chest as he followed Jade into the brush, acting wounded.

Ashe and Rainwood followed a well-worn road toward the camp. The airship loomed overhead as they approached. Two Wardens in bulky MA-15 Ogre mechs stood sentry on the road. They were similar to her Banshee, but looked less refined, with thick armored plates that didn't quite seem to fit well and a stumpy helmet that had three mismatched lenses, making the overall armored suit look more like a clunky robot than a mech.

They casually pointed their guns toward the two, and Rainwood held up his hands. "We come in peace. Just curious; if you've dealt with the raiders, reckon there's a chance we could reclaim our belongings?"

"Stay here," said one, "and leave your weapons holstered."

The Warden guards stood still—presumably talking over their radios.

"General Nicanor said to proceed, but remove any magazines, clips, or power cores from your weapons and let us secure them," he offered up a ball of twine.

Rainwood popped his magazine free, stuffed it in his long coat, and offered his gun to the soldier, who tied the twine through the slot. It wasn't any serious security measure, but it would mean he would have to waste a few precious moments removing the twine before he could rearm the weapon.

Ashe decided it wasn't that unreasonable a request and pulled the magazine from her Arbiter, then detached the drum's ammo belt from the minigun, letting them "secure" both.

"Any other weapons?" they asked.

She thought about Coyote, holstered on her leg—well out of sight inside the mech. They couldn't know she had it, and the idea of having something for protection seemed solid. With her heart racing, Ashe said, "Nope."

They waved up the road. "Somebody will be waiting for you."

After making it far enough away, Rainwood mumbled quietly, "I hope they haven't already found the Commissioner's badge."

Worry started to gnaw at her once he suggested it, almost taking over the fear of being caught hiding Coyote.

What else can we do but forge forward and hope for the best? Besides, they won't find Coyote if I stay in the Banshee.

Three sentries stood at the north gate to the raider's compound, with two also in the older MA-15 Ogre mechs.

It's probably what they let the grunts use, with it being the least desirable model available.

The soldier not wearing a mech held up her hand, approached, checked their weapons, and then told Ashe, "I need you to exit your mech. You can leave it parked here."

Ashe noted the name on her uniform. "I'd rather stay in it, Lieutenant Donavan, thanks."

"It's not a request. General's orders—if you want to go in, you must leave heavy armor and weaponry here. Your choice. You know which way to go if you want to leave."

Blast. Her mind raced with worry over what they'd do if they discovered her hidden pistol.

"Alright. Where should I put it?" she asked, thinking of how to keep Coyote hidden as she exited and hoping they wouldn't notice.

Donovan pointed, and Ashe moved her Banshee into position but turned it around to face them so she could climb out in cover. When it scissored open, she reached down before stepping out while casually drawing Coyote from its holster and slipping it into her jacket's pocket.

Donovan approached, and Ashe shifted, hoping the woman wouldn't notice a bulge. Fortunately, the lieutenant's focus was on the MA-35 Banshee, and she barely spared a glance at Ashe.

"Nice mech. I have only seen a few Banshees. Looks pretty burned up, though. Did you have a problem with it?"

Ashe smiled blandly while pulling the Banshee's authorization key. "Nothing we couldn't handle."

She scanned her gear then shouldered the Arbiter—even with the "safety" twine, Ashe hated being separated from it.

Lieutenant Donovan pointed to the entrance. "You can step into the compound over there. The general would like an accounting of what these raiders did to you. Part of our documentation. Then we'll see about finding what you claim is yours."

Rainwood cooly watched everything with his calculating gaze, putting Ashe on edge and reminding her to be cautious as it sank in that they wouldn't have free reign to search the compound.

Donovan left them in a room with a clerk, who wrote down the story Rainwood fabricated—a similar story to what happened at Mosstown, with some details changed for their protection.

With that done, the clerk switched to a new form and asked for a list of all the supplies they had lost, aside from any food, which had to be requisitioned through the normal outreach program.

Ashe and Rainwood shared a glance, realizing it would have been a good idea to get their stories straight. She took the lead. "Well, we did have a lot of food, actually. But they also took ammo and personal effects. And a friend was taken here against her will, goes by The Commissioner, who left something behind when she escaped, and she wants us to get it."

Even calling her a friend stuck in Ashe's throat. She couldn't forget the bullet that hung around her neck.

"As I said, no food," the clerk replied. "But, what type of ammo?"

".45 and," she glanced at Rainwood, trying to recall what else everybody used, ".308 and .38."

The clerk finished his report, put it on a pile with others, and then stood. "I'll get this sent over for review. All ammunition requisitions must be approved. You can check back in 48 hours. Meanwhile, I can take you to a room to review personal effects right now."

"Wait, two days?" Ashe hadn't expected that.

She felt Rainwood's heavy hand on her shoulder and bit back her frustration.

They followed the clerk into a room with sorted piles of clothing, pots, books, and other items. The clerk gestured. "Feel free to scan for your and your friend's belongings, but know we'll record each item you claim, and if somebody else asks for it, we'll want you to return for adjudication."

Rainwood poked through the piles, even if just for show. But Ashe hadn't found all her things on her last visit and started searching eagerly—completely forgetting her original goal of finding the Commissioner's access badge.

Another soldier entered the room and spoke quietly with the clerk, who approached Ashe and asked, "What was the name of the friend?"

"The Commissioner."

With sudden interest, the new soldier nodded and replied, "We're aware of her. Last we heard, she was in Pikeston. Do you know what she'd be doing with the raiders?"

"She wasn't *with* the raiders. Like I said, she was taken here against her will."

"Others have mentioned they saw her here, but it was voluntary. What's your relationship with the Commissioner?" The soldier noted her AstroCom and added, "Are you from Fenclave?"

Ashe's back stiffened, and she felt frustration building as her heart pounded in her chest. "I don't have a relationship with her. And it's none of your business."

Rainwood stepped over. "Ashe, have you found any of your personal effects? If not, perhaps we should go. Now."

She took a deep breath, then glanced around the room, finally remembering her original goal.

There is no way they'll let us search for the badge if they haven't found it already.

Deciding she'd already found what personal effects were important to her and she could replace anything else, she shook her head, and they retreated quickly.

As they entered the clearing where Ashe had left the Banshee, alarm bells went off in her head, and she froze.

Ten soldiers in mechs stood between her and Mason's Banshee. They were a mix of MA-15 Ogres and MA-27 Griffins. A grizzled soldier stood in front of them with an array of medals on his uniform. "We appreciate you returning this MA-35 unit. We will, of course, compensate you for your effort and time."

Then he pointed to a pile on the path. "We've already removed your gear."

"What?! That's mine!"

He forced a smile, but it wasn't genuine. It was condescending—like she was nobody, wasting his precious time.

"Of course it's not. Civilians cannot own heavy weaponry."

She unconsciously grabbed her Arbiter and stepped toward him, growling, "Get bent! Of course, I can. You aren't going to bogart my mech!"

The soldiers all stiffened, and a look of weary patience crossed the man's face.

"I see. First, I am Brigadier General Nicanor, and second, I had hoped we could handle this peacefully. Please remove your hands from your weapon before we requisition it as well."

She wanted to jump and punch him in the face. He was only a few feet away. She moved forward on the balls of her feet, readying herself and wondering how dangerous it'd be to dash between everybody. If she could get into the Banshee before—

The general held up a fusion core and flashed a genuine grin this time. He knew he had both check and mate.

"It won't power up without this."

She almost went cross-eyed with fury. Who was he to do this?

Rainwood held her shoulder, saying, "Another time, Ashe."

She huffed, raging internally.

But that was Mason's mech! I need to get it back to his folks!

Rainwood's hand clamped tighter, probably feeling her tense up as she wanted to launch herself in a fury.

Then she remembered she still had the authorization key—and decided maybe they could sneak back later and take it at night. "Fine," she snapped, spun, and stormed down the path to her gear.

As she pulled her pack on, the general asked, "Don't you want to discuss compensation?"

Her vision tunneled with anger, and she could feel her pulse on her forehead. She was on the edge of going full berserk, so she did the best thing she could think of and offered a rude hand gesture, even knowing her mother would be in shock. But it felt stupidly good. Then she turned and left.

As they passed the outer sentries, she swore she heard them laughing. One blocked their way. "The general requests that you provide the authorization key. It's just a courtesy, as the engineers can re-key it in less than a day. But you can stop by Fort Nelson for compensation if you provide it."

It was too much. They were taking Mason's mech!

She thought of Jade and tried to calm down—she should be responsible. The pressure of the authorization key weighed in her pocket, and she took a few breaths, debating what to do.

"Tell your general if he's going to steal people's equipment, then he's no better than the raiders! You guys aren't the military! You're a pompous bunch of pretentious thieves pretending the Union still exists! Now get the hell out of my way."

She pushed past him and stormed ahead, trying to get her anger under control. About five minutes after they left the compound, she stopped and dropped to the ground.

Rainwood offered, "I'm sorry. I should have figured they'd want the mech."

"Yeah, you should have! It's all your fault!"

She wanted to be mad at somebody, and Rainwood was convenient. Why didn't he see this coming? It felt good to point the angry finger of blame.

She reviewed the events that had just happened and realized it was all a theater setup by the Wardens. Securing their weapons and getting her separated from the Banshee was to help them identify what they could steal, and she had to admit, begrudgingly, that she should have realized it.

Rainwood interrupted her thoughts. "I suggest we head back. South, of course."

"But we need to go north to meet—"

"South," he reiterated firmly, cutting her off.

She scanned the trees and saw a flash of color, quickly picking up on Rainwood's unspoken point.

"Oh, right. South!"

They cut into the forest, heading southward in the opposite direction from the cabin. The new threat helped clear her mind, and after her adrenaline cooled, she felt rather stupid and apologized to Rainwood.

He grumbled acknowledgment, "Don't worry about it. Any thoughts on how to ditch our tail?"

She brought up the map on her AstroCom and considered her notes of the area.

"I suspect they will wait until we rest to do anything, so if we keep moving we can push it," she looked up at the sky, realizing she'd skipped lunch, before returning to look through the map. Something drew her attention, "Oh!"

It was hard, but she held back a grin. "A cultist compound. I stumbled across them a few months back. They like to gather each night and celebrate in a meadow. They're a little weird, but seemed nice enough. Maybe we can join their gathering at dusk and possibly lose our tail in the crowd." She waited for the reaction she knew was coming.

Rainwood gave her the stink eye, and she grinned.

☣ ☢ ☣

"Suzerain said to proceed with the experiment. The chamber is ready," one of the lab techs informed Frank while they watched EBR through the one-way mirror. "This system was already tested elsewhere, and we know it'll summon the Kraal. You can't stall anymore, or he'll take it out on all of us."

The girl played with toys, unaware of the horror soon to come on the other side of her room.

"I don't think she's ready for it," Frank tried to form an excuse again, his pulse speeding up in fear at the idea of intentionally summoning the Kraal.

Would the containment really work? Am I stalling for her sake or my own?

The short, lanky gray, Vraux, stepped up next to him and asked, "Would you prefer I take charge of this experiment?"

Frank shook his head to clear his fearful thoughts and cleared his throat. "Proceed with the summoning."

Somebody called over a public address speaker, "Attention, attention, this is not a drill. We're starting a category-1 summoning. All nonessential personnel should enter their safety spheres."

The wall on the opposite side of Ember's room slid up, revealing a blast-proof glass window into a spherical dark room.

Ember looked up, curious at the new development.

Frank took a deep breath and flipped the switch.

A rumble shook the floor from the machinery of the inner chamber, and a hum increased in tempo. Everybody readied themselves, holding onto solid furniture or closing their eyes and looking away.

A thunderous report emanated from within the dark room, something so beyond comprehension nobody could identify how it sounded; the deafening peal had a cataclysmic tone and seemed to rend even the walls themselves. With it came a pallid sense of nausea and vertigo, sending some to collapse and vomit.

Within the outer sphere came flickers of light rooted in a spectrum so alien it hurt the mind to see them, and those trying to explain it later could find no words other than how it tasted.

Ember, able to see within the chamber, shook as fear raked her body, and she screamed, her voice lined with an edge of hopeless terror and fright as if she looked upon death.

The otherworldly light flickered, highlighting her face. She hurriedly scooted back, screaming all the while, her movements driven by instinctual panic based in primal fear as she tried to escape but knew all doors were locked. She curled into a fetal position and covered her ears. Her eyes screwed tight as she continued to wail in horror.

Faint ethereal tendrils of light, almost purple in their otherworldly, intensely alien color, touched the glass, glowing where they made contact from the acherontic darkness.

Frank hammered the abort button, his movements driven by no logic other than an instinct of self-preservation.

☣   ☢   ☣

Jade sat on a rock, worried.

He peeled bits of grass apart and flicked them onto Moonbeam, who lay on the ground. With a start, Jade jumped up and shouted, "Ashe is pissed!"

Moonbeam sat up, brushing off the stray bits of grass, and asked, "You heard her? And don't say pissed—it's not nice—wait, are they in trouble?"

Jade's face scrunched up in concentration, and after a moment, he said, "I don't think so. B–but they're going away."

"Going away?"

He nodded. "She was mad. They t–took the mech. But they are far."

Moonbeam stood and looked down the hill, hoping to see his friends returning. "You sure they don't need help?"

"They wanted to go away from us on p–purpose."

Jade paced back and forth, then plopped on a boulder, looking decidedly unhappy.

Moonbeam knelt before him. "They'll be fine. I think between Ashe and Rainwood, they could take on the whole Warden fleet if they wanted to and would still come away without a scratch."

The look of worry on Jade's face said it all. Plus, the folded arms. After a moment, Jade turned and looked away, saying nothing.

Moonbeam decided to focus his thoughts. *They will be fine. Trust me. We should go to the cabin. That's where we are supposed to meet them, right?*

Jade drew in a deep, shuddering breath, and Moonbeam wished he could read the kid's mind or know what he was feeling. After a moment, Jade picked up his pack and followed Moonbeam.

They walked up the hillside for a while before Jade asked, "Will you always be nice to Ashe?"

"What?" responded Moonbeam, a little surprised by the question.

"You like her."

Moonbeam blushed, which was something Jade had never seen him do before. "Well, sure, don't you like her too?"

"I like her, but you really like her. Do you L–L–" started Jade, but Moonbeam cut in before Jade could finish, afraid of where he was going with the question.

"Hey, what's that up in the tree?" he pointed, trying to change the topic.

But Jade was determined. He gathered his thoughts for a moment and then said clearly, "I've seen guys be mean to girls. Hurt them, even if they were n–n–nice at first. Tell me you won't. Ever."

Moonbeam stopped walking, turned around, sat in the grass, and asked Jade, "So, I like her? You understand my thoughts more than I do, then. All I know is the thought of her getting hurt—it makes . . . It makes . . ."

He shook his head and then dramatically tried to flop on his back while throwing his arms wide, but his bulky pack thwarted the melodrama.

Jade grinned, patted him on the head, and resumed hiking up the hill.

A minute later, Moonbeam hopped up and hollered, "Hey, wait up! What does she think about me?"

Ordyne

18

I'm a Believer

Ashe and Rainwood did their best not to push too fast and alert their tail while also not going too slow and missing the cultist gathering. From what they could ascertain, only one person tailed them, but calling for backup was easy enough, considering the Wardens had an airship in the area.

A fading twilight covered the land, and every minute they wasted on this side trek was more time away from the soft bed Ashe remembered in the cabin. She wanted to get back as soon as possible.

The warm glow of flickering fires seen through the trees was the first sign they were getting close, and they picked up their pace until they broke into a clearing.

A large gathering of people milled about in a meadow, with torches on poles scattered here and there. Ashe wasn't sure what the cultists actually did in their celebrations, to be honest. Most wore loose white clothes. Some had more involved leather garb, with decorations, runes, and shoulder harnesses.

In the center of the clearing sat a giant effigy made of woven sticks and straw in strands, mimicking the Kraal. It all came together in the form of a man two stories tall, his arms raised to the sky.

One of the cultists on the edge of the clearing sat in rapt fascination while studying a leaf he held up to the torchlight. As Rainwood and Ashe arrived, he looked up and asked, "Hey man, have you ever noticed how leaves have veins just like people? Does that mean trees are people?"

"Umm, I don't think so," Ashe said, trying to step around him.

He pointed to their gear. "You brought a lot of donations to the family. Father Scrivner will be proud."

Rainwood pushed him aside and proceeded deeper into the crowd without comment.

Ashe shrugged at the cultist, offering, "We're taking it to him right now."

She started to follow Rainwood, then had a thought and turned around.

"We have a friend who is joining us soon. But he doesn't know anything about the teachings of Father Scrivner. Can you take some time to teach him?"

The guy beamed and said, "Oh yeah, of course. Hey, Shelly," he called out to somebody else. "we have a new member coming. Call the others!"

Ashe hurried to catch up with Rainwood, who had made it to the effigy in the center. He glared at it, and she knew he wanted to tear it down.

He turned, gave her a cold look, then grumbled, "Too many people are here. At least a hundred or more. Aren't they afraid of the Kraal?"

Looking at the effigy behind him, she suggested, "I think that might be their hope? But it's outside—there aren't any corners here for the Kraal to come through."

Ashe looked back and saw a knot of people forming where they had arrived and hoped it was about their tail.

Drums began rumbling across the clearing, and everybody cheered.

"Let's scoot. I think they're starting soon."

Rainwood glanced back at the effigy, then nodded. They made a beeline for the opposite side, trying to stay inconspicuously low to avoid detection.

Just as they reached the edge of the clearing, a woman stepped in front of Rainwood and asked, "Hey, where are you going? It's about to start."

"I forgot my robe," he growled.

Ashe grinned. "We're off to fetch it right now."

"Ohh, if that's all, we have extras just over here."

When the woman turned, the two bolted for the brush.

Rainwood took the lead, and they jogged through the forest, doing their best to escape through the darkness of night. Ashe couldn't help but remark, "They seemed like nice enough people."

He said nothing. Not even a grunt.

Ashe felt disappointed but let it go, deciding it probably wasn't a good idea to poke the old man too much.

The risk of detection by the Warden's airship was too great if they used lamps, so they chose to travel by moonlight instead. With occasional checks on her AstroCom to guide their course, they made it back to the cabin in three hours.

She hoped Moonbeam and Jade had arrived without problem and looked forward to the warm glow of the cabin that should appear at any moment.

Instead, they came to a dark clearing that held only the burned shell of the building—a brick chimney standing amidst the debris as a lone testament to what was once a cabin. The raiders had made true on their promise to burn it down.

While staring at the charred remains, Rainwood slowly continued forward. Jade and Moonbeam stepped out from the trees.

Ashe clenched her fists, feeling a conflict of anger and sadness.

Could just one thing go right? The Wardens took my mech, and now this?

She looked at the others—noticed similar emotions—then sighed and joined them in considering the ruins. "Well, I guess that option is off the table."

Moonbeam stepped next to her. "Sorry, Ashe, I know you were looking forward to the cabin."

"It's not your fault, doof."

He tried to take her hand, and she jumped in surprise, pulling it away. She couldn't see his expression in the dark but figured he was being goofy or annoying. "Let's find a safe place for the night," she suggested.

Moonbeam paused, seeming a little subdued, then pointed toward the cliffside. "We set up a small fire out of the way over there."

By small fire, he wasn't kidding. It was tiny, directly against the cliff. But it was out of the wind and was well secluded.

They cleared an area for the tent and prepared a meal of canned stew while Ashe explained their encounter with the Wardens. Once everybody settled into their meal, she added, "This just proves that the Wardens are to be avoided at all costs. At least the Star Rangers are out here trying to do some good, you know? I think the Wardens are just a bunch of thugs grasping for power.

They take all the military toys and get off bossing everybody around with their big sticks."

"So, how do we get Mason's mech back?" asked Moonbeam. "I assume you already have a plan to sneak into their compound tonight?"

She had considered this during the long walk back from the cultist's meadow and answered, "Maybe not tonight—I expect they'll have a live guard on it all night. But that doesn't mean we can't get it back later. Right now, we need to think about how to keep Jade safe from Ordyne and figure out where Ember is."

As if to highlight the danger, a Hog howled into view overhead, coming from over the cliffs.

Before it registered with anybody else, Rainwood jumped up and kicked the fire, tossing dirt on it and quickly extinguishing its light.

Everybody froze, hoping he'd been quick enough. The red and white tail lights of the Hog continued east in the darkness, before turning back around.

"Hold on, hold on," murmured Rainwood as the others jumped for their gear, "maybe it's just flying a search pattern—their first approach angle couldn't have seen the fire."

It passed by a second time and appeared again a few minutes later, but farther northward.

They all relaxed, and Moonbeam offered, "Well, at least we got our food heated for dinner."

After setting up watches, they settled into the night, unsure what to do next. Ashe had the last watch and, with some melancholy, enjoyed the sunrise, deciding this really was a great place for a cabin if only it hadn't burned down.

While debating what to do, she listened to the holo-tape between Warthog and the Commissioner, hoping to hear something she may have missed.

Once everybody was up, she played the tape again, musing aloud, "It's obvious Ordyne took over Fenclave. But how and why?"

Rainwood rolled up his sleeping bag and answered after a moment of consideration, "The Ordyne folks seem well connected. It makes sense that they had people in the old Union government too. Probably used that for access. As for why, I don't know."

Ashe wasn't sure this helped much, however. Fenclave was locked up tight. She'd spent days at the external controls trying to break in, all to no avail. At least if they'd recovered the Commissioner's badge, it would have let them in.

"Didn't Mason say somebody had added a launch pad to Fenclave?" asked Moonbeam.

"I'm sure Ordyne secured any new doors just as tight as the original enclave door," she said with a note of despair.

Rainwood added, "The Wardens mentioned the Commissioner was in Pikeston. Perhaps it's time to give her a visit. She may have made contact with Ordyne since that tape was recorded."

Ashe tugged on the bullet around her neck. She already had her plan for the Commissioner. But if the woman could help, then that would have to wait.

She sighed and added, "I tried to break in with my old Fenclave gear and couldn't. So I dumped all of it with a friend, Talia. But maybe the old access cards will still work once inside? We'd just need to find a way in."

"I collected the ID cards from those soldiers off the downed Hog, and you pulled the bird's authorization key which could also help," Rainwood offered.

"It might work—It just might." She slapped her hands on her knees and stood. "Okay, let's go to Pikeston. But I reserve my right to deal with the Commissioner as I see fit after this is all done."

Rainwood glared at her, rubbing his goatee, then just grunted, leaving her thinking he wanted to talk about it more at another time.

Once all their gear was packed, they returned to the burned ruins of the cabin and poked through it, trying to find anything of value. After a half hour, Ashe stomped out of the mess, brushing her sooty hands on some wet grass, and declared, "It's a complete loss—everything is either melted or warped."

Moonbeam found a pile of cans that hadn't burst and added them to his pack.

"The labels are all burned. You don't know what's in them," observed Ashe.

He waggled his eyebrows. "And that's part of the fun!"

Later that day, as they ventured toward Pikeston, a rocketship lifted off in the south. Ashe estimated it was from the vicinity of Fenclave, and turned to Jade. "We'll get Ember out, I promise."

Glenn couldn't help but grin while holding a glossy ticket as he sat on the rocketship. The roar and hiss of the system during takeoff surrounded him, and a faint chemical smell permeated the air. It didn't surprise him that nobody else was in the passenger section of the rocket; very few civilians could travel anymore.

The g-forces pressed him back in his seat. Somebody wearing a space suit with a helmet had helped him strap into the five-point harness without saying a word.

The guys from Ordyne had stuck with their agreement! He was on his way to meet with Galaxy Express 3-9. He couldn't believe his luck; finally, he'd be out of this mud-grubbing existence and into something more relaxing.

He was only a kid when the bombs first fell and had survived on his own ever since. But he knew what good looked like because his parents had taken vacations on Galaxy Express each year, touring different planets and rubbing shoulders with the elite of the elite.

The same elite had kept Galaxy Express running through all these years, and it became their home—a safe place that never stopped moving lest the Kraal find them. As long as the ships were moving fast, the Kraal wouldn't appear, so the elite didn't worry about population density. From what Glenn had heard, the Galaxy Express luxury ships still worked like before civilization fell, with robot waiters taking care of every need.

Glenn squinted, holding back excitement as he tried to read the signs in the rocket's passenger chamber. It seemed each gave instructions on what to do in various emergency scenarios, and he felt a moment of concern that he didn't have a space suit. He clenched his hands on the armrest, stuffing the fear away and instead thinking of his future.

They told him that Galaxy Express 3-9 would be swinging by this area soon, and he'd need to spend just a little bit of time at the station before it arrived.

The engines cut out, and his chest lurched as they entered zero-g. He looked out of a viewport, wondering if he could see the space station while holding tight to his embossed ticket. His heart soared as it started to feel real: he was returning to the stars.

19.

Into Each Life Some Rain Must Fall

After two more days of hiking to the outskirts of Pikeston, Ashe decided the Banshee had been nice for one reason in particular: it helped with the heavy pack. She was ready to take a few weeks' break from all the travel.

The sky had darkened ominously, and violet-tinted clouds twisted within a storm front on the horizon—a clear sign that a void storm brewed.

"It's too bad none of the cars work anymore," Moonbeam mused as they passed another rusted caddy abandoned on the side of the road. Its rocket fin fenders a classic sign of a time long past.

Ashe groaned, her patience frayed. "We got it the first twenty times, Moonbeam. Are you going to say that for every single car we pass?"

He grinned. "Maybe."

"I've seen folks hitch old trucks to brahman, making them into a wagon," offered Rainwood.

"Again, not much help," Ashe sighed. She reached into her pockets, digging for some jerky or anything to help her flagging energy.

"Neat! Ashe, you painted your name. And you love to . . . hang?" asked Moonbeam.

She looked up. "I what?"

Moonbeam pointed. Somebody had painted graffiti on the side of an abandoned cargo trailer: "Ashley luv 2 hang -T."

She stared at it dumbly. "I didn't paint that."

"Somebody thought it was important. It's also on the sign ahead," Rainwood noticed.

"And a car," said Jade.

Ashe stood perplexed. Down the road, the same message was painted over and over. She hadn't been to Pikeston since she'd last visited with Talia ten or so months ago, just after—

Not now. She fought the darkness that came every time thoughts of the past bubbled up. She boxed them in with a concerted effort, shook her head and smiled. "I think I know who did it —an old friend. She always was a bit over-the-top."

"What does it mean?" Moonbeam asked, his curiosity piqued.

"It means I can find her at the mall," she said with a happy grin.

Ashe knew because it was one of the big topics she and Talia would discuss in Fenclave before the exile. They wondered what the old pre-arrival malls were like and why so many people had liked them. Ashe had always wanted to visit one, so they could "hang out."

She didn't bother explaining this to the group but just said, "If we hurry, we can make it to the mall before the void storm starts."

The impending storm added urgency to their pace. They stayed on Highway 25 instead of turning into Pikeston, arriving at the mall a few minutes later accompanied by light rain and gusty winds. Stopping on a rise to look down into the complex, everybody immediately ducked.

"I don't think we want to go there," observed Moonbeam, glancing at the horde of growlers milling in the parking lot.

A light rain picked up before the full storm arrived, and they each pulled on jackets and rain gear. Luminous violet clouds boiled in the distance, quickly coming closer. Lightning flashed, its color an extra-cosmic purple, leaving Ashe feeling the hairs on her neck rise and highlighting the sheets of rain around them. Her Astro-Com clicked ominously.

"We passed a trailer not too long ago, it might provide enough shelter," Rainwood suggested, answering the question on everybody's mind.

The wind and soft roar from the rain hitting the ground made it hard to hear anybody approaching, and their focus was on the horde of growlers. So when somebody squealed behind them, it came as a surprise, causing everybody to jump. They snapped around, bringing up their weapons—or in Jade's case, fumbling with his pistol, trying to pull it from the holster.

A tall, stocky girl stood before them armed to the gills. Hands covering her mouth in surprise, she shouted at full volume, "Ashley! It's you!"

Then she barreled forward and tackled Ashe in a giant hug, lifting her off the ground.

"I thought I recognized you as you approached. Your red hair and skinny frame stand out anywhere! I had to come closer and see, and here you are!"

Talia set her down and stepped back, continuing, "It's so nice to see you again!"

Rainwood ignored the teenage whirlwind and asked, pointing at the purple clouds. "Do you have shelter?"

Violet lightning skittered through the clouds, followed by booming thunder a few seconds later.

"Oh yeah! Friends of Ashley are friends of mine."

She proceeded toward the mall.

"Uhh, Talia, are you sure?" asked Ashe, holding Jade back.

"Oh, don't worry, my dad won't mind."

Ashe grabbed Talia's arm, bringing her to a halt, and pointed. "What about all the growlers?!"

"What? Oh, the others down there? They're not growlers, silly. They guard the place."

Ashe studied the milling mass of growlers, which only seemed to get more animated as the storm started. "They are definitely growlers."

Talia rolled her eyes and tugged on Ashe's arm. "Come on. Dad made a bridge to get to our second-floor pad."

They followed her across the ridge overlooking the parking lot cut into a hillside forming a wall at the back of the mall. Below, the growlers wandered.

A rope bridge crossed the gap to a fire escape. Talia started across, making the bridge sway frighteningly.

Jade grabbed Ashe's coat, his fingers clenched so tight the knuckles were white. "Let's g–go away," he said.

"I don't think we have a choice. We need to get into cover. I trust Talia. She probably has something safe inside. I know it'll be tough for you, though. Can you handle it?"

He winced, covered his ears, and nodded.

Ashe took a moment to tie a rope from Jade to Rainwood— she would have tied it to herself but worried if Jade slipped, she might be unable to hold on.

Everybody worked their way across in the deepening gloom lit by increasing violet flashes. Only a few frights came from the slippery rope bridge.

Talia held the door open on the far side. "Don't you see the storm? Hurry up!"

They entered a maintenance hallway, and Talia led them to another door, gesturing. "Welcome to my humble abode."

It looked comfortable. She'd spent time working to make it like home. It had a nice entry with couches, tables, and other mundane domestic furniture. A kitchen opened around the corner. Most notably, she had electric lights, and it was dry.

As they dropped their gear, Talia said, "Oh, let me get Mom and Dad. They'll be so happy to see you!"

She ducked around the corner, and everybody stood mutely, trying to understand this energetic, enigmatic giant of a girl.

Thunder shook the rafters. Over the storm, they could hear the occasional moan and grunt of growlers somewhere outside the room. Ashe hoped she wasn't wrong and that this was safe. Jade still had his face screwed tight with his hands over his ears—there were a lot of growlers.

After a minute, Ashe couldn't suppress her curiosity anymore and started wandering about, nosy as it might have been. Off the first room, the kitchen opened into a department store. The home was in what used to be a back stock room, perhaps.

A boarded-up barricade with a door in it filled in the front of the store. The door opened, and Talia appeared, saying, "I don't know where my parents went. Maybe Dad is taking care of something, but he'll be by later. I'm sure he'll be super happy to see you!"

She dragged Ashe back into the room with the others and declared, "I'm Talia, and this is Ashley, as you know."

Then she looked pointedly at Rainwood, who brushed the water off his top hat as he offered, "It's a pleasure to make your acquaintance. Call me Rainwood."

Talia nodded and then shimmied close to Moonbeam, bumping her hip against his. "And who's this dreamboat?"

Ashe was surprised to see him blush and to feel her own ears start to burn.

He responded with a cheesy grin. "I'm Moonbeam, you lovely goddess."

"Ohh, what a nice guy. Definitely a keeper. I'll call you Moony."

She missed Ashe's glare and knelt before Jade. "You alright, little guy?"

He opened his eyes, still keeping his hands on his ears, and Ashe explained, "That's Jade. He has a headache."

"Aww, poor kid. I know, I have just the thing."

Talia left, returning a moment later with two Atomic Cakes still in their plastic wrapping. His eyes widened, and he let go of his ears, took them and carefully tore the packages from the cakes while a smile spread on his face.

With introductions finished, Talia guided Ashe to a couch and sat across from her, relaxing while folding her legs. "I'm so happy you're here!"

That much was obvious—she almost vibrated with excitement. Ashe felt her confusion and wariness soften.

"I'm glad to see you too, Talia. Looks like you're doing well. Your parents, are they okay?"

"Oh yeah, my dad found this place a month after you left, and we've been making it better ever since."

They continued their discussion, and Jade offered Atomic Cakes to everybody. Talia was saddened to hear about Mason. Every time Ashe tried to ask about the growlers, however, Talia would laugh it off and talk about something else. This worried Ashe. *What happened to her family? Did she lose them as well? Are they growlers?*

The door leading into the mall rattled, and everybody tensed up.

Talia stood, unconcerned. "Daddy? Is that you? Guess who stopped by!"

They followed her into the larger store area, but nobody was there—the inner door slowly closed, rattling against the frame.

"Hey, Dad!" she hollered, then told the others, "Just a minute," before stepping out to the balcony, pulling the door closed behind her.

"Are you sure she's all there?" asked Moonbeam.

Ashe found the question very ironic coming from him but said nothing.

The door opened a crack, and Talia poked her head in. "Dad wants to talk to you, Ashe, but he's being silly and wants you to come out here. Alone."

Rainwood tensed up.

Ashe considered her friend, then asked, "Are you sure everything is alright, Talia?"

"Of course it is. He's just being shy, I think."

Ashe turned to Jade, his attention still focused on consuming the Atomic Cakes, one half-eaten in each hand. "Jade, Talia wants me to go out and meet her dad just outside the door. Is that going to be alright?"

Recognition of what she asked dawned on Jade, and he stared toward the door with white frosting on his mouth. Sparks swirled in his eyes, but then he looked confused and shrugged before putting his wrists against his ears so he wouldn't have to let go of the treats.

She sighed. "Okay, Talia, I'm coming."

As she stepped past him, Rainwood murmured, "Just holler."

The lights were off in the main hall, and Ashe paused, letting her eyes adjust to the darkness.

Talia gasped in frustration. "Now, where did he go? Oh, there he is!"

She pointed down the balcony, and Ashe saw a shape move into one of the stores. She couldn't help but grip her Arbiter, bringing it around but keeping it lowered. Talia was already halfway there, and Ashe rushed to catch up. *This is not what I had in mind when we dreamed about hanging out in a mall.*

The store was even darker, and Ashe hovered at the entrance, her pulse racing in counterpoint to the rumbling thunder of the storm outside. She pulled up her AstroCom to turn on the lamp when she heard, "No lights yet."

It was the familiar deep rumbly voice of Talia's father. Ashe's shoulders relaxed a touch, and she asked, "Mr. Weilani? Are you alright?"

"As good as I can be, considering."

She began to step into the room, and he interrupted her, "Stay there. Before you come closer, I want to warn you. Don't be alarmed."

"Why would I be alarmed? Are you hurt?"

"Could you put your gun on the ground?"

She glanced at Talia, who shrugged.

Ashe set the gun down.

Mr. Weilani stepped forward into the dim, purple light coming from the skylights outside the door, and despite all of the preparation, Ashe still jumped—instinctively feeling her fight or flight impulse kick in. He once was a mountain of a man. Now he seemed withered, his flesh gaunt, looking almost burned.

He looked ghoulish, like a growler. Talia pushed past Ashe and hugged him.

Ashe couldn't help but stare, only managing to mumble, "What—why? What happened?"

"Earlier in the year," he explained, "we were caught in a void storm. The only shelter was the trunk of a car. I put Talia in it, but her mother and I—we were exposed."

"Is Mrs. Weilani alright?"

"Of course she is, Ashe," said Talia.

Mr. Weilani glanced at Talia, looked a little sad, and said, "She's not doing as well as I am, unfortunately."

Ashe's world tumbled in circles, and the thought kept repeating like a broken record in her mind: *Growlers who aren't feral killing machines?*

Primal fear teased her thoughts, urging her to flee. She took her friend's arm, pulling her away. "Talia, come here. Let's go."

Talia released her father and stepped past Ashe, heading back to her living quarters. "Yeah, come on, Dad, and meet Ashe's new friends."

"I'll be right there," Mr. Weilani replied.

Ashe slowly bent and retrieved her Arbiter, keeping an eye on Mr. Weilani. He stood patiently, then gave her a smile, which didn't help much because it made his face look more skeletal. Then she gazed into his eyes. Looking past his twisted form, in his eyes she saw the same kind, giant man who was always happy to have her around.

She wanted to cry for him but held it back and asked, "Are you a growler?"

"I don't know. . . . Enoha, unfortunately, is. I figure I'll eventually become one as well."

Ashe gestured in Talias direction. "Why doesn't Talia recognize this?"

He grimaced. "She's had a hard time coping with what happened. I've tried to let her recognize it on her own, but she seems determined to pretend everything is just fine."

Ashe leaned against the door frame, working to come to grips with this new information. "Are there more like you? Do the growlers ignore you?"

"That's what is most interesting. They ignore me like any other growler, and I can hear them in my head sometimes. I think there are others like me, but I haven't found any yet. I'm calling myself *charred*, not a growler—at least not yet."

Ashe remembered Fairmont Church by Mosstown and thought this could explain a few things. Then she realized the swarm of "others" below suddenly made sense—Mr. Weilani had them as a shield.

"Talia can't stay here," she said with determination.

"I agree."

Talia shouted from the balcony, "Are you two coming?"

Ashe drew a deep breath, then said to him, "Give me a minute to explain things."

He nodded.

In the end, she first introduced Rainwood to Mr. Weilani on the balcony, and he took it in quiet stride. Moonbeam was happy and curious about the whole situation.

Jade was her biggest concern—he just wanted to leave. He said it was like being in a crowd with everybody shouting and crying in pain.

They welcomed Mr. Weilani into the room, and Ashe asked Jade, "Does he sound different to you?"

He looked up and stared at him, then said loudly, "A little? It's n–noisy."

Moonbeam arrived with a tin foil hat he'd put together in the kitchen and offered it to Jade, "See if this helps, Ace man."

Jade put it on his head and visibly relaxed. Ashe couldn't believe the foil worked and wondered if it was psychosomatic. Either way, Jade seemed better with the silly hat.

She asked Moonbeam, "How did you know that'd help?"

He shrugged. "I remembered this funny guy in the Capital on Miratori with a tinfoil hat and a whole tinfoil outfit. He said it was to keep the government's mind-control powers from influencing him. I figured it would also help Jade if it helped that guy."

Ashe marveled. It was oddly logical, considering the source. She doubted she'd ever have come up with such a solution.

With everybody past the fright of Mr. Weilani, they settled in and explained most of the challenges before them, including Ordyne wanting to capture Jade—although Ashe left out that Jade could hear people's thoughts. Moonbeam had lost interest early on and started wandering the mall—at least the upper level.

The unearthly lightning and thunder of the void storm faded, which helped people relax—sometimes, the storms could last for days.

"And that's why we're here now—I'm hoping to get my old Fenclave ID card and things," Ashe finished.

"I'll show you where that stuff is," Talia offered, before leading her to a store section piled with boxes. While Talia shuffled through them, Ashe distractedly poked at things as she considered how to broach the subject of her friend's dad being a charred growler.

Talia should recognize what happened, not hide from it. At least her parents are still alive—sort of.

Talia exclaimed, "Aha!" and pulled out a crate, setting it on a table.

Ashe stared at it, feeling an internal resistance—the idea of opening it scared her. She had boxed it away on purpose, a physical manifestation of how she boxed away her painful memories.

With dread weighing her hand down, she opened the crate and quickly dug out her ID card, ignoring the rest of her belongings—like her forest-green Fenclave jumper. The same jumper she was wearing on that day—

She snapped the lid closed and said, "This is all I need. Talia, maybe you should come with us?"

Talia perked up. "You think so? Oh—but I don't know if my parents want me to leave."

Ashe pinched her lips, a strange frustration building at Talia's obliviousness. "Look around you. Your dad is sick, and you live with growlers!"

Talia looked down, mumbling, "No, he's fine."

Ashe took Talia's hand, dragged her out to the balcony, and pointed down to the growlers. "What do you see down there?"

Talia wouldn't look at them and said, "It's just the others."

"Holy cow, girl, are you daft? Face reality already! You can't pretend the truth is something else! Your parents are growlers!"

Talia's face crumpled, and she bit her lip, still avoiding looking down.

Ashe suddenly felt horrible. "I–I'm sorry. I didn't mean it."

"No, you're right. Maybe I am daft. But—" Talia stopped herself, glaring at Ashe, then hurriedly added, "—but maybe I'm just doing the same thing as you. It's easier to pretend, right?"

Ashe blinked, confused for a moment. *Doing the same thing as me? I'm not pretending my parents aren't dead. My family—*

Her line of thinking froze as a crack splintered through her carefully constructed facade of reality. Flashes of memories spun in her mind of the Deathmark. Its huffing so close to her hiding place as it sniffed, trying to find her and her dog, Kelly, hiding in the box. She struggled to ignore the barrage. Darkness started to overwhelm her, and a wave of nausea threatened to rise as she felt anger at herself. An avalanche of guilt pulled her down, but she fought it back, stuffing it away and rebuilding the walls in her mind.

With her pulse racing, she scowled, fighting her thoughts, and redirected her anger at her friend, hissing angrily, "You don't know anything about me!"

Talia stepped back, her eyes widening.

As Ashe closed the dark box in her mind, she felt a detached curiosity come over her at Talia's response. She concluded that she had pushed Talia too far. *This was a mistake. She should face it when she's ready.*

Ashe sighed, her pulse racing though she could not remember why, and she smiled at Talia. "Just come with us when we leave in the morning, alright?"

Talia warily returned the smile with confusion and worry showing on her face.

Moonbeam's voice interjected, "Lovely talk you girls are having, but could one of you help me?"

They looked around, unable to see him.

"Down here."

Moonbeam hung onto a store sign from the first floor—an AstroTec store sign, to be precise—and he appeared stuck. The growlers watched him intently from below as if waiting for a tasty morsel to drop from the sky.

"Dang it, Moonbeam, what are you doing?" Ashe growled.

He tried to chuckle, but she could hear the strain in his voice. "Oh, just 'hanging out,' I think."

"Were you trying to get into the AstroTec store?" she asked him.

"Are you going to yell at me if I say yes?"

Ashe rolled her eyes, retrieved a rope to make a harness, then had Rainwood and Mr. Weilani pull him up to the balcony.

They filed back into the living quarters. Once everybody was happy he was okay, Ashe pulled Moonbeam aside. He looked embarrassed and said, "Sorry . . ."

She stiffly handed him a folded jacket in a wine colored purple, with an original package tag still hanging from its lapel.

Unsure why she gave him a gift, he opened it to find a bomber-style jacket with pockets on the sleeves. His eyes lit up when he saw the AstroTec logo, and he flipped it over—unconsciously holding his breath—to see the AstroTec logo stitched on the back.

Ashe explained, "Talia raided the store for supplies a few months ago, and I saw this in with the other things. I figured, maybe . . . you might, umm—"

He looked at her, a grin spreading, and said, "It's awesome! Thank you, Ashe." Then he spread his arms wide to hug her.

Her cheeks heated up, and she darted into the Weilani's quarters, leaving him alone on the balcony with a smile.

Everybody discussed what to make for dinner, and Ashe continued to avoid Moonbeam when a bell rang.

"You have a doorbell?" Moonbeam asked with surprise.

Talia jumped up from her seat and stepped to the outside door with everybody except Mr. Weilani following her. She looked through a peephole and then exclaimed, "Holy cow, what a day! First Ashe shows up, and now the Commissioner!"

☣   ☢   ☣

Glenn restlessly waited at the shuttle's staging area, his meager belongings in a bag floating next to him. The space station had barely functioned for the few days he'd spent on it. At least it had gravity controls, except in the boarding areas. The hydroponics were barely operational, and most occupants were robots.

The station seemed ghostly, and he thought it was interesting that more people didn't live on it. But it also had a lot of corners, which he tried not to think about. He figured that was why nobody was around. He'd only seen two other people his entire time on the concourse, and they had turned away from him when he approached.

It was just a sad commentary on how far civilization had fallen, and he wondered how long it'd be before the stations stopped working and fell back to Arcadia.

Then the ship arrived, and now was the time—excitement nearly drove him bonkers.

Through the window, the white hull of Galaxy Express 3-9 slid into place, and the gantry passage extended, connecting the two ships.

The seal opened, and pleasantly-themed music emanated out. A gold-plated robot attendant waited for him.

"All passengers must present valid tickets," it declared in a stiffly cultured male voice.

Glenn pushed off and floated over, offering his ticket.

The robot took it and slotted it into an automatic computer console in its chest. Glenn waited anxiously while it clicked and clattered.

Then the light went green.

"This way, please."

He kicked off and floated down the bright passage, giddy about his new life.

20.

Wouldn't It Be Nice?

Talia threw the door open, and the woman Ashe had cursed for the last year stood before them. She had more silver hair than Ashe remembered, but otherwise, she was the same chiseled woman who ruled Fenclave with an iron fist. The same one who exiled her family and friends to their deaths in the badlands.

Ashe immediately reached for the bullet around her neck, her pulse suddenly racing. After months of wanting this moment, here stood the Commissioner. Ashe clenched her fist around the bullet and glanced around, wondering what options she had. Could she get to her Arbiter and back quickly enough? Would everybody step aside and let her mete out justice, or would they try to stop her? What if she just punched the horrible woman?

Then Jade's green eyes caught her attention, wide with surprise at her thoughts, and her heart lurched in frustration, anger, despair, and a little bit of embarrassment that he'd noticed.

I should act now! But—

With a growl, she turned and fled to the back of the Weilani's home, found a corner in the department store, and curled into a ball while fighting back tears. Anger, frustration, and grief spun into a giant knot that wouldn't stop ratcheting in her chest. She couldn't even properly cry at this point; as much as she now wanted to let go, even tears wouldn't come.

The Commissioner caused my family to die! It's her fault!

She felt the giant arms of Mr. Weilani gently drawing her close while holding her in a tight embrace. He said nothing but just hugged her. It reminded her of her father—the father she'd never see again.

Then she gave up fighting and quietly cried.

It's not fair! It's just not fair!

Mr. Weilani hummed a nonsensical lilting tune, and she eventually brought her breathing under control and leaned into him—knowing he wasn't her father but pretending for just a minute that he was.

Ashe realized he was whispering *la'u afafine malosi* and asked, "What's that?"

He stepped back while holding her shoulders in his giant hands. "It means you're strong and amazing. But I know you well, and you always take too much on your shoulders. Just don't forget you can let other people help as well."

She nodded, smiled at him, and straightened up so nobody else would notice her weakness. Mr. Weilani gave her shoulder a final squeeze, leaving her a moment alone. After bringing herself under control, she returned to the others.

It seemed introductions had been made, though Mr. Weilani was not there. The Commissioner saw Ashe and said, "Hello, Ashley. I'm glad to see you're doing well."

Ashe intentionally turned away and sat next to Jade, who was adjusting the shape of his tinfoil hat. She knew ignoring the Commissioner's welcome was rude, but rationalized, *At least I'm not punching her in the neck.*

Jade looked at Ashe suddenly, his eyes wide at her thought. She patted his knee, then pulled the bullet from around her neck and made a point of holding it while glaring at the Commissioner.

Jade stuck the hat back on his head.

The Commissioner gave Ashe a sad smile, then turned to Talia. "Could you go get them then? I need to speak to both of your parents."

Talia said, "Of course, let me go see where they're at," and stepped out.

Rainwood rumbled, "Mrs. Commissioner, you should know the Weilanis are not . . . well. Mr. Weilani is dealing with a sickness, and I fear his wife has fully succumbed to being a growler. We haven't met her."

Moonbeam added, "Yeah, it's pretty far out. Who would've thought you could have a growler who was normal like a person?"

The Commissioner looked alarmed and confused. "Is he sick or is he a growler?"

Moonbeam replied, "I don't know. That's what makes it so interesting, right? It makes you wonder: can any growler be this way? Can they get better? Who knows!" Moonbeam hopped up in excitement, his arms waving wildly about.

"But, didn't Talia indicate they were fine?" the Commissioner asked.

Moonbeam noticed the glares from Ashe and Rainwood and lost his energy. "Well, yeah, I think they—oh hey, did you hear that? I think somebody called me. Tootles." He made a beeline out of the room.

The Commissioner watched him leave with a bewildered look.

Rainwood clarified, "It's certainly curious. Mr. Weilani seems fully self-aware yet looks like a growler."

Her eyes widened.

Talia stepped into the room. "My dad is being silly again. He wants you to come out here."

Rainwood called out, "It'll be fine, Mr. Weilani. You can join us."

Mr. Weilani stepped in and waited for the Commissioner to take in his appearance. To her credit, she stayed calm, showing little reaction—Ashe figured it was from all the years of being a backstabbing soulless politician.

"Hello, Kane. They explained your condition. How is Enoha?"

Mr. Weilani shook his head and answered with a catch in his voice, "She is no better than any of the others around here."

"I'm sorry for your loss," the Commissioner responded, her tone sincere.

"Laura," he rumbled, "Why are you here?"

She waved her hand. "Pay it no mind. It doesn't matter."

Moonbeam returned, stepped in front of Jade, and failed at being inconspicuous as he offered a partially eaten Atomic Cake behind his back. Jade snatched it.

Mr. Weilani repeated, "Laura, why did you come here?"

"It doesn't matter now. Some people at Fenclave need help with the mainframe. I remember Enoha said she'd left some tricks in the system. I figured she could help fix it back up."

Ashe straightened and spat an accusation, "You work for Ordyne."

The Commissioner curled an eyebrow in muted surprise. "Of course not! I'm just helping. They can give us supplies, medicines—things people need."

Ashe pinched her lips and growled, "That's what you always do! You keep rationalizing your actions while the world crumbles around you, and you don't care what effect it has on anybody but yourself."

The Commissioner shook her head. "I don't understand what has made you so upset. I'm doing what I can to help."

Ashe felt her anger building and waved her arm at the world around her. "Of course you don't. You can't see what's really going on."

Rainwood interjected, gesturing to Jade. "What she's trying to say is that Ordyne is a disturbing bunch. They have conducted illegal genetic experiments and have kidnapped this boy's sister."

"Ah, I see," she said, her gaze fixed on Jade as she carefully considered the information.

Ashe finally realized something and froze, then asked, "Were you *in* Fenclave? Did you see any labs? Did you see where they're holding Ember?"

"I didn't get the run of the place, unfortunately. They just took me to the mainframe and back out. But they had a lot of construction equipment—it looked like they expanded or remodeled."

Ashe's brows pinched together as she considered a plan. "Ember's there. They took her. And we need to get her out. You're going to help us do that."

Mr. Weilani's eyebrows lifted in surprise, and the group looked at each other with curiosity about where Ashe was heading.

Laura said, "I am?"

"Yes. You came here to get the Weilani's help with the mainframe, which means you can get back in—presumably with the Weilanis."

"This is true, but not in their current condition."

The plan was coming together in Ashe's mind. She could pose as Enoha and get in with the Commissioner. She asked, "They don't know what the Weilanis look like, right? Or how old they are?"

Laura nodded. "Ahh, I see. Yes, perhaps that could work. But they want help with the mainframe. Our subterfuge would rapidly become apparent if we couldn't do the work."

Everybody else seemed content to watch the conversation go back and forth between them. Ashe's excitement grew, and she asked, "What's the problem they need fixed?"

"The robots were acting odd, so they had to shut them down, but that left a lot of systems non-functional."

Mr. Weilani gave a deep laugh and explained, "Enoha set them up to distrust anybody but a few of us. And, if they were pressed into service, to occasionally rotate their orders and do something different. The Ordyne were dealing with a robot insurrection."

Moonbeam's eyes lit up, and he grinned at the thought.

"How hard is it to fix?" asked Ashe.

"It shouldn't be too hard for me," Mr. Weilani said, "However, Ashe, I don't remember you taking my COMTRAN programming courses."

"I'm sure it's not that hard. I hack robot commands and automated systems all the time. You tell me what it is, and I'll do it," Ashe declared confidently.

He looked skeptical. "Do you know programming for robots? Or are you just good at getting around in the menus?"

"I can do it," suggested Talia. "I know COMTRAN."

Ashe nodded, and she straightened up, getting more excited. "That's right, you can take care of the mainframe, and I'll slip out to find Ember."

The Commissioner looked doubtful. "I'm sorry, Ashley; I told them Enoha was Islander and had a husband. That's who they're expecting. Although she's young, I think I can convince them Talia is Enoha, but," she waved at Mr. Weilani, "I already told them he was coming too."

Talia sauntered next to Moonbeam. "Did you tell them a giant islander was her husband, or just 'Kane'?"

Ashe didn't like the direction this had taken.

The Commissioner looked at Talia and Moonbeam and said, "Well, I suppose it might work. Son, can you hold still and take direction long enough to act the part of her husband?"

He straightened up and saluted. "Sir, yes, sir—ma'am."

The Commissioner's eyes thinned. "These people are dangerous. But, if we can get the necessary medicines and supplies while also helping rescue this boy's sister, perhaps we should try it."

Ashe worried Moonbeam couldn't sneak around the enclave on his own, and she also wanted to be in Fenclave again. "Maybe you two could open the enclave's door and let me in. Moonbeam won't know how to get around inside like I do."

Mr. Weilani nodded. "I can provide a subprogram to do that. But what about all the people who are occupying the place?"

Jade offered, with a little gleam in his eye, "Turn on the robots!"

"That's a great idea, Ace!" said Moonbeam. "We can have a robot army as a distraction."

Ashe realized, "They probably know the remodeled facility too! Send one to meet me, and I'll ask it where Ember is. That could save a lot of time."

They all considered the plan. It was coming together and seemed sound.

"Wouldn't they notice if the front door opened?" asked Rainwood.

The Commissioner smiled. "Actually, they have added a launch pad above the enclave that you could enter through. I didn't see how it connected to things, but they extended the elevator up. Although, I expect it isn't as fortified as the main, nuclear blast-proof door."

While the others talked through the details, Ashe glanced at Jade, wondering if he would be safer staying at the mall.

He saw her attention and smiled, asking, "What?"

She poked at the hat. "This actually helps?"

He nodded. "It's noisy here. This makes it quieter."

"Just a thought—how about you stay a night or two here with Mr. Weilani? We'll be back before you know it."

He grabbed at the tinfoil hat, holding it tight, then shook his head, giving her a sad look. His face dialed up the cuteness, his eyes becoming wider. The idea crumbled before the force of his kitten eyes, and Ashe ruffled his hair. "Alright, alright, but you need to do what we say."

They decided to stay the night to make preparations, with the plan to head out first thing in the morning. Talia, Mr. Weilani, and Moonbeam wandered off to the mall's computer room so Mr. Weilani could give the other two instructions and prepare the subprogram tapes. Rainwood started working on a meal for everybody, leaving Ashe, Jade, and Laura, the Commissioner, alone.

Ashe folded her arms and glared at the Commissioner. She finally faced the woman, and her fury boiled. This woman was the reason Ashe's family died. The Commissioner was why so many horrible events had happened in Ashe's life. Ashe stoked the fires, relishing how good it felt to finally face her enemy, even if she couldn't do anything about it. For now.

Laura cleared her throat, recognizing the awkwardness of the room, and asked Jade, "So, that's a neat hat you have."

Ashe's pulse throbbed in her forehead.

He smiled. "Moonbeam made it for me. It'll help keep the government from controlling my brainwaves."

Ashe realized it was probably good Jade couldn't hear her thoughts. Just sitting across from this woman—all Ashe could think about was punching her, grabbing her by the throat . . . Ashe's anger screamed through her veins. And curiously, she also felt like crying.

She focused on her rage instead.

Laura glanced at Ashe, looking a little uncertain, then started, "Ashley—"

"Ashe," interjected Jade. "She's Ashe. Not Ashley."

Laura smiled and continued, "Ashe it is, then. Are you sure we can trust Moonbeam? He seems a little . . . unreliable."

Ashe took a deep breath and tried to clear her thoughts, suddenly feeling defensive of Moonbeam. She responded in short, terse words, "Yes. He's very reliable. I know I can trust him to—to—" she froze. She had almost said she could trust him to have her back. Could she? She remembered how often he tried to help, even if it wasn't executed well. A warmth spread through her as she thought about it, then she noticed the Commissioner waiting for her to finish and wrapped up with an angry, "Yeah, I trust him. And you should too. He's my friend."

"Well, that's good then."

Ashe's pulse roared again. She could hear it in her ears, and knew she was barely holding it together.

The awkwardness continued.

Ashe stoked the fire inside her, relishing how good it felt to finally face the Commissioner, happy to let her anger off its leash. If only she could do something about it! She had to remind herself there were more important matters.

The Commissioner cleared her throat and started, "One more thing, Ashe. I'm—I'm sorry about your family. They told me about what happened. About your—your, uhh, your dog—"

Red.

Ashe snapped. It was that or cry, and she wasn't going to cry.

She launched from the couch, her arm raised—she needed to punch the smug woman so badly—but Jade grabbed her leg, and that threw off her trajectory. She hit the coffee table instead, knocking dishes across the room in a loud clatter of noise, with Jade holding tight to her ankle.

Laura pressed back in her chair. Her eyes flared wide to show the whites all around.

Rainwood appeared—ready for danger—to see Ashe towering over the Commissioner, her arm raised, with Jade holding her back.

Ashe glanced at Rainwood, and her rage disappeared like a balloon popping as she realized how ridiculous this must look. She felt her lip tremble and bit it back, growling to the Commissioner, "Never speak about them."

Once Jade let go, she straightened up and quietly left.

☣ ☢ ☣

It took the group a day and a half to reach Fenclave. They split directions before getting too close, and now Rainwood, Jade, and Ashe were hiking up to the summit of the mountain where they could see the launch pad—easily identified by the silver rocket towering above the trees.

They had stashed their gear when the team split, taking just the minimum required. Rainwood was never a talker, and Ashe was happy to stay with her internal thoughts as Jade trailed behind the two. Ashe pondered Talia's behavior when they had left her parents' place—Talia had spent time talking to her father in the morning, and Ashe saw her tracing the scars on his hand at one point. She hoped this meant Talia was able to accept his condition.

And why was she so frustrated that Talia went with Moonbeam into Fenclave? It annoyed her, but she didn't like how Talia flirted with him.

Jade—still wearing his tinfoil hat—interrupted the quiet of their hike with a question. "Does Moonbeam have to lift something really heavy?"

"Why would you think that?" she asked.

"You think about how strong he looks a lot. Are you worried about how much he can lift?"

Her face felt hot and flushed, and she fiercely denied, "I do no such thing!"

Rainwood snorted.

"Well, I think he is strong enough. He can pick me up. I bet he could even lift you!"

Ashe sputtered. His statement made her unable to form a coherent reply.

Jade added, "And, Moonbeam's arms aren't guns. I don't know why you keep thinking they are nice guns."

She growled, "That's enough, Jade!" Then she sped up, so he couldn't see her reddening face.

Jade grinned.

Once Rainwood stopped shaking with quiet laughter, he told Jade. "While I appreciate the humor, I suggest that you refrain from discussing other folks' thoughts."

"Why?"

"Privacy. Everybody thinks differently from what they might say or do. You have the privilege of hearing other people's inside thoughts, but bringing their thoughts up in front of others takes their choice away."

"What if I have a question because I'm confused?"

"Well, perhaps you just wait for them to work it out on their own. Or, if you must, ask in private."

Jade remained quiet, but his contemplative look indicated he considered the advice. When they reached the top of the hill, Ashe looked through her Arbiter's scope, considering the space pad's visible details.

"I see a few automated turrets. One rocket looks to be ready on standby. All the Hogs are gone, though, probably trying to find us. When they load the intrusion program, we should see the turrets deactivate, and that will be my signal to head in." Ashe put the Arbiter down and dug the Hog's authorization key from her pocket. "Perhaps we can just go in with this?"

Rainwood scowled, finding a seat on a rock near her before answering. "Stick to the plan, Ashe."

Jade asked, "Will they take long?"

Ashe reluctantly put the authorization key back in her pocket and then poked the hat on his head. "With it so quiet, now you're bored?"

He shrugged. "I'm not bored. I just don't have anything to do."

"How far can you hear somebody?"

"I don't know?"

Ashe lifted the hat from his head, still thinking about the access key, and asked, "Can you hear anybody else? I don't see any guards. Could we try and sneak in?"

Jade concentrated, staring at the landing pad, before eventually shrugging. "Nobody."

"That either means he can't hear that far, or there is nobody. Hopefully, the latter," said Rainwood.

Jade took the hat and stared at it for a moment, before looking around at the canopy, smiling as he noticed the birds and other creatures, then folding the hat and putting it in his pocket.

Ain't That A Kick In The Head

Laura couldn't get rid of the heavy sense of anxiety that settled upon her. She wasn't wired for this sort of thing—sneaking around places.

Lieutenant Simmons answered the enclave entrance's comm, which surprised her—she had expected some lower-level soldier to answer it like last time. He seemed glad they had arrived, however, and a few minutes later, the enclave's blast-door slowly cycled open.

A sleek military robot accompanied Simmons. It was a model none of the three had seen before. Seeing their attention on the robot, Simmons smiled. "It's a Covenant series—he is here to help keep things in order."

Laura thought Simmons seemed nervous, but she couldn't decide why. Something was definitely off.

"These are your programmers?" he asked with a skeptical look, considering Talia and Moonbeam, then said, "M-7, please register them for security access."

The robot stepped up and scanned Talia, then said, "Enoha's records indicate she is forty-five years old, which does not match the scan for this specimen."

Talia smiled, touching her cheeks. "Aww, how nice of a robot to say I look young! I think it's something to do with the radiation out here, makes some look old, helps others look younger."

Moonbeam looked up. "Did you hear that? Is a void storm coming?"

Simmons glanced up in a panic and said, "Hurry it up, M-7, just let them in already."

M-7 paused, then declared, "As acting commander, you can override my protocols and allow these people into the compound. Otherwise, I must continue with them as programmed."

"Yes, I command it—just let us in already. I'll fill out the paperwork later."

It stepped aside. "You may proceed."

They passed through the long blast corridor into the intake chamber, which featured a glass window overlooking the central plaza of the enclave.

M-7 gestured to a series of lockers. "Please deposit all firearms and other weapons into a locker. You can retrieve them when you depart."

They reluctantly shed their weapons. Moonbeam looked incredibly excited and kept darting his eyes around in wide-eyed fascination at all the new sights. When he started toward the window, Laura feared he'd blow their cover before they even began. She walked to Moonbeam and called back to Simmons, "I don't see any robots."

"I had to shut all of them down except M-7 here—and others like him, too," he awkwardly added.

Once their weapons were properly stowed, Simmons led them down a staircase that opened onto the main floor, then gestured forward. Moonbeam had eagerly moved to the front of the group but didn't know where to go. He smiled at Simmons, then proceeded confidently to the left while gawking at the vaulted roof.

Laura's heart raced, and she tugged his elbow, guiding him in a different direction, saying, "Yes, Kane. It looks like your lighting project is still functional. But we have work to do."

Moonbeam got the hint and followed her direction, tailed by Simmons, Talia, and then M-7.

Arriving at the mainframe data center, Talia handed Moonbeam a tape. "Spool that one up over there, honey, and I'll get started with things over here."

"You brought a program?" asked Simmons, stepping forward to look at the tape she handed Moonbeam.

"Of course, silly, I know how to fix what I did."

He looked at her warily and asked, "How long will this take?"

"Well, it depends on how much damage your people did."

Moonbeam stared at the panel of blinking lights, trying to remember what Mr. Weilani had told him. There were too many tape slots, and he started to sweat, struggling to recall which was the right one to plug the tape into. Then he remembered the mnemonic he'd chosen—it was the third one because it was like Ashe's red hair, and red was three letters long.

He slotted the tape in place and pressed the button. The system spun up and started unwinding the tape from its container, spooling it onto a larger reel. He wiped the sweat from his brow.

Talia approached and beamed, then pushed a flashing green light and gave him a peck on the cheek.

He smiled. *This might only be the second mainframe I've ever seen, but it doesn't seem so hard.*

She whispered, "Don't forget: When the light changes to blue, type 'RUN PROGRAM 3' on the terminal. I'm going to program the uprising now."

He nodded, suddenly stressed again, and sat at the terminal. *It's just a small green screen.* He struggled to focus, worried about remembering the instructions, and surreptitiously looked at his palm where he'd written the steps down. His hopes faded as he realized all of his hard work was for naught: the ink had smeared in his sweaty palms.

It'll be fine, I can remember what to do. Just ignore all the other blinking lights. Watch the screen.

Worried he'd forget, he repeated in his head the command he needed to type while waiting for the tape to finish loading.

Run program 3.

Program 3.

Program.

What is a program?

Pro-gram.

Is gram like grain? A pro-grain?

I like grain. It makes good bread.

Why do we want the grain to run?

He laughed, imagining grain stalks running.

The light on the tape drive flashed blue.

His mind blanked as he stared at the cursor incessantly blinking at him—almost like it was angry.

He drummed his fingers and then noticed Simmons watching him sternly.

Moonbeam smiled at him, cracked his knuckles, and, one key at a time, punched in: RUNNING GRAIN

It beeped and printed: NO RUNNING PROCESS 'GRAIN,' VIEW PROCESS TABLES? Y/N

"Look at tables?" he mumbled, glancing around.

He stepped over to the table and wondered what it wanted him to look at. There were manuals on it, but that didn't seem right.

Laura noticed Moonbeam poking through papers, stepped over to him, and whispered, "What. Are. You. Doing?"

Simmons stared at them. Laura's pulse increased.

"Come here," she snapped, tapped the "N" on the keyboard, and sat him back at the terminal. "Type what she told you to type."

Moonbeam typed: WHAT SHE TOLD YOU TO TYPE

The system responded with: 'WHAT' NOT FOUND

Laura's pulse throbbed in her forehead, and she wondered if he was intentionally trying her patience. She couldn't remember anybody more frustrating than Moonbeam, and she barely knew him.

He stared intently at the screen, looking confused, then whispered, "I don't know what it can't find. What is not found?"

She grabbed him by the elbow, steered him to Talia, and snarled, "Enoha, it seems the other program isn't loading. Perhaps you could help?"

Simmons approached the terminal they had vacated.

Laura nodded her head toward the same terminal, shoved Moonbeam in a chair, hissed, "Don't touch *anything*," then made a beeline to Simmons to stop him before he saw the screen.

Talia moved to Moonbeam's terminal, read the screen, held back a laugh, and then entered: CLEAR; RUN PROGRAM 3.

The tape spun, and the computer lights began flashing.

☣   ☢   ☣

When the turrets stopped scanning the area, Ashe felt her adrenaline spike. "Time to go!"

They ran through the brush, onto the tarmac, and to the tower. Nobody appeared to stop them, which made her feel a little on edge. When they reached the tower, the door slid open. A unidroid robot sat inside the small chamber on its three wheels, with a body painted white and gold.

Ashe grinned. "Emmett!"

"Why, hello, Ashley, what a pleasure to see you after so long. I'm sorry there has been no class recently. We've had some very odd visitors, and things have been rather confusing if you ask me. It's all very improper, and I am ashamed to say I've even disobeyed orders."

Jade hopped in place with a giant grin, tugging on Ashe's shirt.

She introduced him, "Jade, this is Emmett. He was my teacher in school, and I loved his classes."

"Master Jade, pleased to meet you. Will you be joining my class?"

"Yes!" he jumped, throwing his hands in the air.

"Sorry, not right now," Ashe said. "We have a mission."

"Of course. I do have an order to help you find somebody in Fenclave."

"Jade's sister. But first—"

She stepped to a control panel in the antechamber, plugged her AstroCom into a maintenance port, and then loaded a program from her holo-tape. "Okay, Rainwood, the panel now has a connection through the enclave into my AstroCom, so you can contact me if there are any problems."

She turned to Jade. "You stay with Rainwood. I need you two to keep watch up here."

He scowled.

"We talked about this, Jade!"

He growled.

Rainwood touched his shoulder. "Kid, it's safer up here."

Emmett joined Ashe in the elevator, and she spoke to him while it descended. "Have you seen a small girl anywhere?"

"I can't say I have—not since all of you left. But they shut us off for a few months. They also did a lot of construction, and I am unfamiliar with the new section."

"Sounds like a great place to start."

Talia decided she needed to dial things up a notch, and rather than correcting the problems with the robots, she added a little more chaos. She knew it'd ruin the Commissioner's plan, but she figured Ashe would applaud.

A minute later, the door to the data center slid open, and a blue security bot rolled in, waving thick articulated hands and announcing in a gruff male voice, "Illegal access detected. Move away from your stations and line up on the wall!"

Simmons spun. "What are you doing activated? Stand down!"

"I am authorized to act with force; do as I say!"

"You are not!" Simmons drew a laser carbine.

M-7 moved with catlike grace and wicked speed, igniting a plasma lance and, in a fluid motion, stabbing it into the security bot, which sputtered and fell forward to the ground.

Simmons turned to the others. "What have you done?"

"Nothing!" Laura answered. "It must be a side effect of the . . . the scrubbing to fix the systems."

After a quick glance into the hall, he growled, "There are robots everywhere!"

Before they could act he waved his carbine at them. "You three, over there."

Talia hit Enter and quickly typed CLEAR to hide her activity before backing away.

☣   ☢   ☣

The elevator descended into the main plaza, the last few floors visible through glass panels, and Ashe felt her heart lurch at what she saw. What was once a beautiful area with groomed bushes and paths was now flattened, covered in debris, construction equipment, and storage crates.

They reached the main level, and when the doors opened, she hid behind a stack of crates while she assessed the area. Several utility bots awkwardly stomped around, and more were arriving from the hallways, but she didn't see any people.

A sense of unease settled into her—she wasn't sure if it was the lack of people, the changes, or something else. It just felt off, and she worried. The doors closed, and the elevator moved upwards, leaving the two on the main floor.

She whispered, "Emmett, where is everybody?"

Ashe's AstroCom chirped, a familiar sound she hadn't heard for a year, indicating a new message:

"The people are gone; just robots left. One guy and a combat bot here. I called a security bot to see if we can take control."

Ashe assumed it came from Talia at the mainframe. As she read this, a second message arrived:

"HELP"

"Emmett, change of plans. Let's hit the data center first."

She raised her Arbiter and carefully stepped down the engineering hallway, hoping Talia was right and all the people were gone. Perhaps that's what made her feel uneasy.

After a winding path, she peeked around a corner. In the hall ahead, a Covenant series security bot stood, scanning both directions, its plasma lance ignited and ready to slice any threat. She had never seen this model outside of the RoboTek catalogs.

Two utility bots stomped by, but the Covenant ignored them.

She pulled back, considering her options. The Covenants were said to be very dangerous and well-armored. But if she could surprise it, she might have a chance.

"Emmett, I need you to distract the Covenant bot."

"This is highly unusual. I'm a teacher, not a warrior," he said.

"You don't need to fight it. Just do it, please!"

His lower appendage ring twisted in agitation. He bobbed and then rolled around the corner. A moment later, she heard, "Excuse me, are you aware the ancient Assyrian warriors would carry lances into battle much like what you hold?"

Ashe leaned around the corner and lined up her sights, focusing on the Covenant bot's head, then stroked the trigger. Her gun fired with a quiet pop.

She missed, if only barely.

Blast! She mentally cursed as her pulse increased.

The Covenant heard the shot, even silenced, and looked down the hall in her direction. Ashe ducked out of sight.

Emmett called, "I say, do you know where the students have all gone? How rude. Why would you walk away from me when I'm talking to you?"

Ashe glanced around and saw a door a few feet away. She slapped the access panel with her badge and slipped inside the opening door, her heart racing as it slid closed behind her.

Lights flickered on to reveal an office with a maze of desks and cabinets covered in a layer of dust. She tapped the light panel, cycling it to nighttime mode, then crouched and ducked under a desk, considering her options.

They had scoured the Weilani's supplies, and she had a handful of pulse grenades. They were mostly useless against biologicals but could immobilize a robot if detonated close enough.

She reached to her waist and pulled a grenade. A moment later, the door opened, and from under the desk, she saw the Covenant's feet as it stepped into the room, the hum of its plasma lance putting Ashe on edge—she knew it could cut through nearly anything.

"Surely you can provide information on your employers," Emmett continued from outside, "I need to know if they have any students I should register for my class."

It brought a smile to Ashe's lips that Emmett was still trying to help, and she hoped he'd keep his distance. Things were about to get ugly. She pulled the pin out of the pulse grenade and rolled it under the desk toward the Covenant bot.

A flash illuminated the room, her eardrums popped, and her hair stood on end. The crash of something falling was a good sign.

Leading with her Arbiter, she came up from under the desk. The Covenant bot knelt on the ground, leaning on the lance while struggling to come upright.

Out in the hall, Emmett spun in a circle, bumping the wall with each rotation—he had no shielding for this.

Flipping the Arbiter to semi-auto, she stroked the trigger— the shots hit the Covenant, leaving streaks on the metal where they impacted but did not penetrate.

With a slight wobble, the Covenant struggled to its knees.

Ashe pulled a second pulse grenade and tossed it right at its feet. It looked down just as the grenade flashed. This time, the explosive kinetic force pushed the Covenant back, and it stumbled, releasing the lance, which clattered into the hall.

With it on its back and partially immobilized, she stepped forward, aimed at a gap between its head and torso, and pulled the trigger. The shots hit and shattered through its inner workings. The robot shuttered, its lights fading. To be sure it was done for, she added a few more shots, then glanced in the hall. Emmett wasn't in view.

She peeked around the corner and saw him holding the lance aloft, rolling away while howling, "¡Soy el gran Don Quijote!"

A blur of purple came from the right as Moonbeam appeared, tackling Emmett.

The two spun to the ground, the lance flying free—this time planting itself into the wall before shutting off. Moonbeam landed on top of Emmet, pinning the robot's appendages with his knees and hammering on its central sphere with a degaussing tool.

"Moonbeam! Stop! He's friendly."

Moonbeam held the tool up, huffing.

"¡La culpa es de la mafia, que exige tonterías!" Emmett announced.

"I don't know what he's saying," Moonbeam grumbled peevishly, "and he was about to attack you."

Ashe smiled, a little at the humor and a little at the noble gesture—even if it didn't need to happen. She pulled his shoulder. "Let him up. I need to run a diagnostic."

Moonbeam backed away, and Ashe asked, "Are the others alright?"

Moonbeam gasped in response to her question. "Oh—I don't know! I left them with Lieutenant Simmons."

He took off toward the data center with Ashe on his heels.

They found Talia looking at the Commissioner's shoulder. "—It should be fine, but you'll want a suture later."

The Commissioner saw Ashe and explained, "After the Covenant bot left, Talia rushed Lieutenant Simmons, and he fired at me and ran. He's probably heading to central operations."

Talia added, "Before he left, he yelled that the teams are due back soon."

Ashe considered their options, then asked, "Talia, can you lock out central ops from here?"

Talia was already heading to the console. "I think so. Give me some time."

"We need to get out of here quickly," said Laura.

"Or, we can take them all on and claim Fenclave for our-selves!" Ashe declared with growing excitement, her mind racing at the possibilities. She was finally back in the enclave. And yet, her uneasiness ratcheted up another notch.

Emmett arrived, holding the re-ignited lance upright, ask-ing, "¿Quién sabe dónde está la locura?"

"Turn the lance off and come here!" Ashe commanded.

He complied. The lance went cold, and she plugged her As-troCom into his maintenance port. After a moment without finding any errors, she sent the Reset command.

Emmett's lights blinked, and he relaxed, looking down as his system began a full diagnostic scan.

Laura looked at him. "I think he was quoting an ancient story. He always loved history."

Ashe returned the Arbiter to her holster, ignoring the com-ment. "Any ideas on what we can do about all the soldiers coming? I don't think we'll stand a chance in face-to-face combat."

Moonbeam suggested, "Oh, I know! That idea you had before, Ashe. The horse with a gas mask."

It took her a moment. Then she remembered their conversa-tion about the Trojan horse.

Laura was thoroughly confused, and Ashe grinned. "I suggested gassing Warthog's camp earlier, sneaking something in like the Trojan horse. Unfortunately, just like a few weeks ago, we don't have the supplies."

Talia interrupted, "Actually, I found an equipment inventory, and it has Riot Control gas canisters listed as 'Oneirogen.'"

Laura nodded, explaining, "Oneirogenic anesthesia is used to induce sleep."

"Good enough for me," Ashe said.

22.

The Man Comes Around

Talia finished locking down central ops so Simmons couldn't get out and then resumed adjusting the robot instructions, reversing her mother's program.

Moonbeam took the elevator to retrieve Rainwood and Jade while Ashe and Laura gathered the canisters and gas masks, hoping to finish before any Ordyne soldiers returned.

They gathered in the central plaza. Emmett joined them, still holding the lance but apologizing for his behavior.

After talking with the group about how they would dispense the gas, Ashe announced, "I'm going to find Ember. Jade, can you tell where she's at?"

He wrinkled his brow, got a distant look, and his eyes swirled with green sparks. After a minute, he shook his head with worry.

"It might be all the dense rock," suggested Ashe. "Come on, let's go find her."

"I'll join you," said the Commissioner.

Ashe froze, her fists slowly clenching. Everybody paused, wondering which direction this would go.

Ashe drew a deep breath and said, "Do whatever you want—Emmett, take me to the new construction."

He spun and waved the plasma lance, calling out, "¡No has visto nada todavía!"

Ashe raised her eyebrow in concern. "Emmett, are you sure you're fine?"

"Of course, why would you ask?"

She stepped over to him and pulled the fusion core from the lance, mumbling, "I think this is best for all of us if you insist on carrying this."

He happily took the now cold lance as she offered it back, and followed her through the corridors, trailed by Jade and the Commissioner.

After a few turns, the Commissioner stepped next to Ashe and said, "Ashe, the others told me what happened . . . what you've been saying about your time in the enclave. . . and your, uhh, about Kelly—"

Ashe stopped and curled her fists, drawing a few careful breaths before hissing, "No. I'm not talking about it."

"But, you know Kelly was—"

"NO!" she shouted before storming off, glad for the sprawling maze of corridors to get lost in while she struggled to control her boiling emotions.

Fenclave was a sprawling complex. It was initially designed for a population of 2000, but after the arrival of the Kraal, everybody feared such a large gathering. The Wardens had launched the nukes so quickly that the Fenclave's population ended up being only around sixty people, primarily the original operations crew preparing Fenclave for future residents.

The adults used to say Fenclave felt lonely with so few people, but Ashe liked being able to explore. And she grew up with plenty of friends. By the time they were evicted, their population had reached eighty-two.

Wandering the empty halls evoked a sad melancholy in Ashe as memories of before came back, and she was glad when they entered a roughly hewn section—it was something different. *Is this what's making me feel uneasy?*

Ashe noticed the passage was cylindrical rather than rectangular, a new design to avoid the Kraal. She asked again, "Jade, do you sense Ember?"

He shook his head.

"Don't worry, Master Jade, we'll find your sister yet," Emmett told him.

The long passage curved, eventually ending at a bulkhead hatch without any signage. Ashe's wariness increased as they reached the heavy door.

Not sure what else to do, Ashe slowly reached for the button to cycle it open.

Emmett asked, "Are you sure you want to open that?"

She paused. "Well, I was until you asked."

"Sorry, my apologies. Proceed."

Ashe glanced at the Commissioner, then at Jade.

Do you sense anybody or anything inside?

Jade shook his head.

Laura said, "I can't imagine it's anything too horrifying. It's probably a specialized lab of some sort."

Ashe pressed the button, and the door slid open to reveal a large, vaulted cylindrical chamber extending toward the far end. All corners were rounded, and machinery of an unknown purpose sat on rails that spanned the chamber. An elevated gantry walkway followed the entire length of each side, and held up by the machinery was a series of metal beams shaped in angles, which sent a warning off in Ashe's mind.

Laura stepped in, looking around curiously. "Somebody has been very busy."

Ashe pushed past Laura and into the chamber. She walked along the gantry, her feet making the steel walkway rattle with each step. Jade followed.

Ashe stopped at the machinery on the far end of the chamber. The beams were attached at their base to a series of gears and looked to be articulated. But she couldn't fathom their purpose.

She sighed. "I don't see anywhere else we could look. Jade, you can't sense her?"

He shook his head.

☣   ☢   ☣

Talia watched from a closed-circuit video camera as a military squad exited their Hog onto the launch pad and split up, sending five soldiers into the elevator while the others waited—with all of their gear, it was too crowded for everybody to fit in one run.

As the elevator descended, the five soldiers muttered about the expected lecture from the captain, not relishing the thought. The panel at the top of the elevator popped open, and Moonbeam stuck his head down with a grin, declaring, "Hello, soldier guys and gals!"

Before any of them could respond to the oddity, Moonbeam pulled a gas mask over his face and dropped a canister which immediately popped with a flash, filling the small chamber with gas.

The soldiers shouted and pounded on the walls, and Moonbeam counted five thumps before the elevator reached the main floor, and he hopped down as the doors opened.

Rainwood stood before him, clenching a radio which he shook as he growled, "Boy, I said drop the canister and keep that jaw shut! You aiming to get yourself shot?!"

Moonbeam grinned and shrugged. The two quickly removed all of the soldiers, holding the door open as it buzzed impatiently at them. Moonbeam was about to climb to the top again when a klaxon siren started, and a voice declared over the MA, "Category-1 Kraal summoning proceeding in 60 seconds. All nonessential personnel should enter their safety spheres."

They froze, and Moonbeam's eyes flared wide, "Daegom, did that mean what I think it meant?"

Rainwood gestured. "Go! I'll deal with the rest."

Moonbeam ran down the halls, driven with fear.

☣　　☢　　☣

The klaxon blared, making Ashe jump, and she looked around in fear.

Warning lights flashed, and an announcement echoed through the halls, "Category-1 Kraal summoning proceeding in 60 seconds. All nonessential personnel should enter their safety spheres."

The chamber's exit door slid closed, sealing them inside.

Ashe bolted to the door, followed by Laura, Jade, and Emmet. She pounded on the access button, but it ignored her and continued flashing a red light. "Door Sealed."

"Blast it!" shouted Ashe.

"Are they doing what it sounds like?" the Commissioner asked.

Ashe didn't want to think about it. Kraal were monsters of legends. Few survived crossing paths with them.

Adrenaline and terror gave her focus, and she pulled a small tool from her essentials pocket and then started opening the access panel. Jade backed against the door, crouching down.

"15 seconds," the emotionless voice announced.

"This is all very exciting, but does anybody know what it means?" asked Emmett, waving the lance and looking agitated.

"I don't think we want to be here when it happens," the Commissioner declared. "What are you doing, Ashe?"

The access panel popped open, and Ashe reached in, pulling a tangle of wires and rooting around for the maintenance port. "I'm getting us out of here. What does it look like?"

Ashe plugged her AstroCom into the port and made a connection, finding the right comm rate and pulling up a diagnostic menu.

"Summoning beginning in five, four, three, two, one," the announcement notified.

The machinery shifted into motion, sending a rumble through the room and rattling the gantry.

The beams twisted around, weaving within each other in a hypnotizing pattern, each cycle creating a square, then shifting away only to come back again as a square. They moved slowly at first but soon were fast enough they became a blur, and the noise became a high-pitched whine.

The ground shuddered unnaturally, reminding them of the weight of the mountain overhead. Within the cycling beams, a glimmer of light appeared, oscillating in colors beyond comprehension. A shattering peal burst from within, sending a deafening silence across the chamber, which pulled at their very essences, leaving them feeling torn at the atomic level.

Jade retched at the stench that followed, losing his lunch.

The Commissioner gagged, biting back bile that rose in her throat, and whispered, "Oh dear Lord, for all that is holy, please save us."

Everything looked brighter, yet somehow not real. Colors no longer made sense, and Ashe felt she could taste them. She didn't dare turn to look but stayed focused on her task.

Jade closed his eyes and curled up, covering his ears.

The klaxons stopped, and the spinning slowed, yet a watery rift of intense color remained, suspended in the middle of the slowing machinery. The chamber became quieter except for the breathing of those trapped inside, the sounds of which seemed amplified to their ears.

Ashe remained focused on her task, although the notion of turning to look pulled at her thoughts.

A tendril of the aberrant light teased at the rift's edge, reaching out.

"No, no, no, no, not this way," moaned the Commissioner. "Hurry, Ashe!"

"Just a second!" Ashe responded, working her way through the system's menus.

Emmett looked at the others, his frame shaking from the vibrations, but his robotic optics were unable to process a Kraal's presence, and he asked, "What is it? What do you see?"

A form drawn from outside infinity crawled from the rift, casting off tendrils of vaporous light, its shape beyond comprehension to anybody gazing upon it. The human mind struggled to make sense of the extra-cosmic being, seeing anything from maddening tentacles with eyes lined by teeth-driven suckers to bilious, dysmorphic, scaly arms holding mouths that vented unnatural sounds.

The form advanced. In response, the Commissioner took a step toward the thing, her face pale as milk. "I'm sorry, Ashe. About everything. Your family. Kelly . . . Ashe, this is important! Lookup Fenclave rule 15.3.2."

Laura's steps resonated through the walkway as she strode toward the horror.

Ashe couldn't think about what the Commissioner said, however, as she had just found the diagnostic menu and selected the override option.

In the blink of an eye, the Kraal moved as a blur of unnatural light to the Commissioner—Laura—who stood boldly on the walkway, protecting the others while Ashe worked.

The Kraal's form changed as it encountered Laura, and it shuttered, then coalesced into a shape that seemed like light cast by a cathode tube. Faint beams trailed behind it, connecting to nearby corners, if not the rift itself. The form it made looked like a glowing woman, almost a mirror of Laura as she held her ground.

The door slid up.

Ashe glanced sideways, grabbed Jade, and lunged through the doorway, pulling him along. Turning, she saw Laura on the gantry, facing down the Kraal, its unnatural light painful to look upon.

It seemed content to stay before Laura, who yelled back, "Run!"

Pins of light lanced from the Kraal, stabbing through her and tearing a guttural scream of pain from her throat.

Ashe hammered the close button on the door, and its descent seemed to take forever. Laura screamed the entire time.

☣   ☢   ☣

They hadn't let Ember out of her room for some time, but today the man who had given her candy took her to a new room with soft couches. On the far wall was a large glass window looking out into the deep blackness of space; small, glimmering spots of light were scattered across the broadly black tapestry.

She wanted to step closer, but it frightened her, and she leaned against the candy man's leg.

He pushed her into the room, and she reluctantly entered, still staring at the starfield. It was fascinating and terrifying, reminding her of a few days before when something else had appeared in her bedroom window. Thinking of that memory, she started shaking.

Ember noticed somebody else in the room. A man sat on a chair, looking at her with eyes dark as coal. His features were chiseled, his eyebrows looked mean, and his hair was as black as the space outside. She shrunk away from him.

"Master," the candy man asked, "are you sure? Alone?"

The black-eyed man smiled, and it looked unnatural on his face. Forced, like it was something he wasn't used to doing. It didn't fit him at all.

"Child, do you understand me?"

She nodded.

He turned to the lab man and said, "Leave us, Frank. Don't interrupt unless it's a report from Arcadia."

As Frank started to go, Ember grabbed his pants, not wanting to stay with this man and his window into the void of space. Frank turned, wanting to push her away, but felt the mental touch of Ember and found himself physically compelled to pick her up instead.

His eyes were panicked, and the white shone around the edges.

"Frank, I said leave her."

He managed to gasp, "I know. I can't—"

The man barked, "EBR, look at me."

Reluctantly, she turned to him.

He locked eyes with her, and a cold fear slammed into her, a fright so instant and primal that she wet herself—terror being the only response she could feel as she connected with his mind.

23.

These Boots Are Made for Walking

With the bulkhead door finally closed, Ashe leaned her head against it and huffed, trying to calm her racing heart. Her hair stood on end, she felt chilled, and every part of her wanted to run. But she was stunned by the Commissioner's actions. Was there any chance they could have saved her?

Emmett sounded upset and asked, "Not to be a bother, but my optics were unable to detect anything unusual, and yet, obviously, something happened. Can somebody explain what just transpired?"

Like a bubble popping, the abnormal sensation that curdled Ashe's guts suddenly disappeared. The hairs on her neck relaxed, and she breathed deeply, hoping the release of tension meant the Kraal had left.

Ashe turned, leaned against the door, and slid to the ground. Her voice trembled, but she managed to answer Emmett, "A Kraal appeared."

Emmett bobbed, saying nothing as he considered the situation while his lights blinked and little clicking noises came from him.

"Well. It seems I must trust your biological senses, then. But can't they go through walls?"

Jade coughed, then spit to the side, wiped his mouth on his sleeve, and whispered, "It's gone."

Ashe took deep breaths, still struggling to understand what just happened, and her eyebrows curled in frustration. *Why did Laura have to do that!?*

"Are you certain?" Emmett asked Jade, unaware of Ashe's inner struggle.

He nodded. "I felt it leave. I could feel it. Not anymore."

"Interesting. I didn't know you could do that. Well, then, should we retrieve the Commissioner?" Emmett asked.

Jade looked at Ashe, and she shook her head to clear it. With her pulse calm again, she stood and stared at the door.

She waited. They looked at the door, but nobody wanted to open it.

"What if she needs help?" Emmett asked.

Ashe nodded and curled one hand into a fist as she built up her resolve before pushing the button.

Within, the chamber was quiet. Where Laura had stood was a splash of glowing orange matter that almost looked like fungal growth, but it dripped from the railing, through the grates of the walkway, and to the floor.

The orange matter's glow pulsed with a slowing beat, and it started to decay at the edges. Fascinated, they watched as the curling extremities blackened and floated away, breaking apart into a vaporous mist that quickly faded, leaving nothing to show that Laura was once there other than a pile of clothes and gear.

Ashe now understood why there were so few bodies around the badlands, despite the many varied buildings and structures that showed evidence that large populations used to live there.

Jade gave a long sigh, and Ashe put her hand on his shoulder, thinking of all her interactions with Laura, even those from before when they lived in Fenclave.

She wanted to stay angry but could not. Instead, her thoughts led her back to the Commissioner's last words. *Why, of all things, was the last thing she talked about . . . rules?*

A wry smile touched her lips. *It fits. The woman bled by the rulebook to the end.*

Moonbeam arrived, running down the hall, looking alarmed, and asked, "What's going on?"

Ashe swallowed, unsure how to explain, and started with, "The chamber—somebody summoned a Kraal. It took the Commissioner—Laura."

Moonbeam glanced around, then pulled Ashe. "We need to run!"

She held her ground. "No, it's gone."

Her knees felt weak, and she sat in the middle of the doorway, curling forward to hug her knees. Jade sat next to her.

Ashe whispered, "Why did she do that?" She felt hollow again, her emotions frayed. "We could have gotten out together."

Jade shook his head. "She stopped it."

Moonbeam joined them on the floor and asked with trepidatious curiosity, "Ashe, why did you summon a Kraal?"

She gave an exasperated gasp. "I didn't!"

"Who did?"

Her world came into focus, and she remembered everything else going on at the moment. Were her friends okay?

"It had to be the lieutenant," she decided.

"Isn't he locked up?"

She stood. "Let's find out."

Their course took them to the plaza, where they could see the control room up a few stories. Simmons stood at the windows, looking down on them with his arms folded.

Ashe growled, "Let's take care of him."

Jade, Moonbeam, and Emmett followed Ashe, while Rainwood and Talia stayed at the elevator to deal with any new arrivals.

They made their way up the stairs to the third floor. A glowing sign stating "Operations Center" sat above a glass-paneled door. Just inside, Simmons stood, smugly holding a device with a button. He'd scribbled a sign which read, "Release me, or I summon hundreds more."

Ashe drew her Arbiter and pointed it at him, her expression grim as she considered the options. *The glass isn't bulletproof. One shot. All it'll take is just one shot.*

His eyes widened, and he backed up, then yelled through the door, "It's a dead man's switch! Shoot me, and it automatically starts!"

She followed his movements with the muzzle. Her hands trembled, and she wondered if he was bluffing.

If he summoned more, how many people would the Kraal kill? All of her friends? She never wanted to live through that again.

She sighted onto his forehead, thinking about how fast it would end for him. She'd become a cold-blooded killer. This was just another person to add to her tally.

He tried to look confident while brazenly holding the device up, and growled, "I'm not bluffing!"

"Jade—" she started, thinking to ask him if Simmons was telling the truth, then realized what she was about to do in front of him.

The haunted look she had seen in Rainwood's eyes when she found him at Warthog's place came back to her. Did she want to become that?

Or worse, did she want Jade to see her like that?

He looked at her with worried eyes but said nothing.

With a growl, she snapped, "This guy just killed Laura!"

A few heartbeats passed, then she exhaled and lowered her gun.

Simmons' smirk returned.

Her movement was almost instinctual. She lifted the gun in a quick motion, and with one pull on the trigger, the device in his hand shattered.

He yelped and jumped back, favoring his hand.

Cracks quickly spread through the glass pane where the bullet had pierced it, and then it fell apart in a crash of small pieces. Moonbeam dashed through the broken door into the room and tackled him, with Ashe following quickly behind, and they tied him up before finally relaxing.

Ashe's doodles

24

Keep Me In Your Heart

With Simmons subdued, Moonbeam jumped up and energetically paced around the Ops center, "Woah, guys, can you believe it! We did it! We just took over an entire enclave!"

Standing at the window overlooking the plaza, he waved at Talia and Rainwood below, then gave a thumbs up. Jade bounced at his side and grabbed the window sill, hoisting himself up to see out, leaving his legs dangling above the ground.

Ashe collapsed into a chair. She knew she should feel as elated as the other two, but something kept her feelings tied in a knot, teasing at the fringes of her mind.

"Well then," Emmett rolled to her side, "Perhaps now things can get back to normal? I'm ready to resume classes whenever you are."

At the window, Moonbeam leaned over and listened as Jade whispered in his ear, then he straightened up and said, "Of course, little dude! Let's do it!"

Jade ran out of the room while Moonbeam walked over to Ashe and Emmett, smiling.

"Emmett, could we speak with you in the hall?"

Ashe glared.

"Why, of course." Emmett followed Moonbeam out of the Ops center.

Ashe knew she should join them. She knew something was going on that they didn't want her to see. But she couldn't stop thinking about the commissioner. Why had she sacrificed herself?

"Why I suppose it would be all right," Emmett's voice echoed from outside, "Although it is unusual, and I don't know about the safety of such—"

Both the boys gave shushing sounds, and Ashe growled, then reluctantly stood and stepped into the hallway to find Moonbeam helping Jade climb onto the back of Emmett's frame.

"What do you think you're doing!?"

Jade jumped in fright, slipped and fell on his butt, then folded his arms and scowled.

Moonbeam grinned, stepping between her and the other two while nervously running his fingers through his hair, "Hah, just a little fun. Nothing for you to worry about!"

Ashe put her hands on her hips and declared. "Jade! You can't ride Emmett! You can't ride robots!"

"Sorry, Ashley, I didn't realize you had forbidden such behavior!" Emmett apologized, somehow managing to look embarrassed.

Finding themselves well-berated, they returned to help Rainwood and Talia. The group eventually subdued all five search teams and the base commander, who arrived later on a skiff.

With the soldiers tied up in the gym, Ashe declared, "Now, let's find Ember!"

"I bet the mainframe has information about where she might be held if she's here," Talia suggested.

They followed Talia back to the Ops Center, and Moonbeam became riveted with rapt fascination as she typed away at one of the green-glowing terminals.

Ashe felt wiped out and eased herself into a chair next to another terminal, staring at the others as they watched Talia work.

A cold calm descended upon Ashe as she nervously fingered the fabric of Kelly's bandana around her wrist. She leaned forward, resting her head in her hands. Kelly's bandana touched her cheek, and she closed her eyes, relaxing and remembering playing fetch with him in the plaza.

There had been so few people in the enclave. It was an open area, even more so than the atrium, which had too many trees. She'd throw the ball, and he'd fetch . . . no, he'd run . . . he'd catch it?

Her thoughts came to a jumbled, confused halt, and a looming guilt built up in her chest—a heaviness she didn't want to face. Her body went cold and she swallowed the lump in her throat, thinking instead about what the Commissioner had said.

What was it she meant about rules?

Ashe's pulse increased, and she looked up, staring at the glowing green screen of the terminal embedded into the desk.

She licked her lips, wondering why she felt so worried. The anxiety coming upon her was palpable, like that panicked feeling that came when she slipped, except this wouldn't go away.

"This is stupid," she growled, hitting the power button on the terminal and watching the blinking cursor fade as the cathode ray turned off.

She drew in a deep breath, wondering what rule 15.3.2 was all about, yet also worried about what it might say. Not even sure why it bothered her, she glanced around. With a heavy hand, she pushed the power button again, turning the terminal back on. Using slow, methodical movements, she swiped her access card and tapped the keys, bringing up the Fenclave rules and scrolling until she found the section Laura had mentioned. One line long.

15.3.2. Pets are not allowed in the enclave.

Ashe had to read it a few times before it sank in. A fracture tore through the carefully constructed walls in her mind. Her heart beat slow and heavy, a throbbing in her forehead. Her vision tunneled. She couldn't make out the words on the screen and realized her eyes had filled with tears, blurring everything.

Swallowing an aborted sob, she shoved away from the console while blinking to clear her eyes and whispering, "No, no, no . . ."

"Are you okay?" asked Rainwood, but she ignored him, biting her lip to keep it from trembling.

She untied Kelly's bandana with shaking hands, her thoughts reeling as she muttered, "Of course, we had pets. It doesn't make sense. We had to have pets, right? Kelly was my . . . dog. My dog!"

Moonbeam stepped over and looked at the console. His features softened, and he turned toward Ashe.

Jade barreled into her, grabbing tightly, his lower lip trembling, giant tears streaming down his cheeks, and he growled, "You didn't mean to."

She mutely shook her head, staring at nothing.

"We couldn't have pets," she whispered, then drew in a deep, shuddering breath, feeling herself on the edge of a cliff. She looked down, reeling, vertigo pulling her forward, and a dark wave of grief rolled upwards, engulfing her.

The full, unedited memory of playing catch in Fenclave's plaza hit her—not with her dog, but with her brother, Kelly. Laura had chewed them out after they broke a lamp. *But, he's only five!* Ashe had argued. *It wasn't his fault!*

Ashe struggled for breath and managed to mutter through a stifled groan, "Kelly was my brother! He had the cutest cherub face. Why did I think he was my dog?"

Like the roar of a rocket's engine, all the memories she'd carefully bottled up flooded back, crashing upon her and taking her breath away. And finally came the last memory she had with him.

In the crate with Kelly, holding him tight. He smelled sweaty, the stink of fear on both of them. He didn't want to stay in the cramped box and struggled against her. She held him close in her lap. But the Deathmark snuffled outside, looking for them. Calling for them in their mother's voice. She had almost climbed out, thinking it was her mother, but it wasn't quite right, and the smell—the stench. Something had warned her, and instead she stayed.

Ashe gasped, "I kept trying to keep him quiet. 'Shhh, just a little more. Don't worry. It'll go away. Just shhh.'"

Sobs overcame her as waves of guilt and sorrow racked her body. She wanted to push away from everybody, to run away and hide, but she felt her friend's arms circle her, holding her tight, not letting go.

She needed to get away. It wasn't fair!

Her friends held her firmly.

Facing what she had done cut her to the bone and ripped her heart out. She stuttered, "H-he didn't understand. He wouldn't stay quiet. And I covered his mouth. Even while he struggled. And the Deathmark, it was so close. I could smell its breath."

She swallowed.

"And then he was quiet." A sob broke out of her.

She never had a dog.

Memories of Kelly bubbled up, uncontrolled, but she didn't hide from them anymore.

His laugh never failed to bring a smile to her lips. He was always happy. His giggle was infectious.

His chubby cheeks and red curly hair.

Playing with army figures on the steps of the enclave's plaza.

Looking up at her with a grin, asking her to play a game with him.

Ashe had loved him so much.

She couldn't stop sobbing. Hot tears ran down her cheeks.

He had laughed at everything and jumped when excited, constantly moving.

He was never angry, and his happiness could always lift her spirits.

The pain tore her apart, and she howled.

They played, with her chasing him through the halls until she caught him and lifted him up in a shower of giggles.

She just wanted him back. She wanted to hear his laugh one more time.

She clenched the bandana, remembering him wearing it while playing cowboys with her.

Holding his still, lifeless body in her arms as she hid in the crate, and the Deathmark wouldn't leave.

Then, after, trying to wake him up.

Being alone in the badlands, her parents dead.

And he wouldn't wake up, no matter how hard she'd tried.

She was alone.

The memory lay engraved on her soul—she'd just hidden from it all this time.

"I killed my brother," she gasped. "I killed him."

She tried to push away from her friends again, but they wouldn't let go, and she clung tightly to them instead, fearing she'd drown in the pain that engulfed her.

And she finally let the grief burn through her.

25

Jump In Line

They searched the entire complex for the rest of the day but could find no evidence of Ember ever having been there. After finally facing the truth about her brother and the frustrating search for Ember, Ashe felt completely spent when they gathered for dinner.

"We'll find her," Moonbeam said to Jade, shaking a spoonful of pork-n-beans. "I promise. Even if we have to cross the entire galaxy, we'll find her." Ashe nodded and hugged Jade as he sat next to her on the bench.

Talia offered a thumbs up. "Me too! We'll all help!"

Jade smiled.

Once finished with their meal, Rainwood went to the communications room and worked on contacting the Star Rangers—hopefully, they would have an idea of what to do with the Ordyne teams locked up in the gymnasium. He also contacted Mr. Weilani on the radio, suggesting Mr. Weilani help guide the future of Fenclave and any invitations for others to return.

Ashe and Talia took Moonbeam to the Atrium. It had started as a natural cave but had been hollowed out further by the enclave designers, creating a soaring space with bright illumination to support natural plant growth. Much of it was thickly forested except for a small lake with a waterfall on the far side.

Moonbeam found it fascinating that a forest could grow underground, let alone be so lush and healthy. "And you would swim in it?" he asked, marveling at the lake.

"The water is in a closed loop with our hydroponics. It's totally safe," Ashe explained. "And the system even keeps the air warm enough to help the flora."

"Well, let's go!" Moonbeam declared, sliding out of his jacket while fumbling with his belt.

Both girls shouted, "You need a swimsuit!"

He shot them a grin and waggled his eyebrows. "Hah, gotcha!"

Ashe punched him in the shoulder.

Movement caught her eye—a glass wall separated the Atrium and Plaza, making it easy to see beyond.

Emmett rolled into view, shaking his lance dramatically with an arm. Jade crouched on top of Emmett's dome, holding tightly to the robot's eye stalks while pointing forward like he was ordering the cavalry and yelling commands, bouncing to hurry his mount.

Ashe's first impulse was to run and stop Jade before he got hurt, but then she just laughed, deciding Jade deserved some fun.

She looked around the Atrium and breathed in deeply, relishing the clean earthy forest smell. She fell back into the soft grass—Moonbeam followed her on one side, Talia on the other.

Above, the tree branches moved in an unseen breeze, causing the leaves to shudder gently.

"What are we looking at?" Moonbeam asked.

Ashe took his and Talia's hands, closed her eyes, and relaxed with a soft smile teasing her lips.

Appendix

This Appendix is a subset of the expanded setting details available on https://RidersOfTheStars.com.

In the vast tapestry of the multiverse, a reflection of the familiar emerges—a realm where the golden age of the atom takes center stage, and the stars themselves become the canvas for humanity's aspirations. As happens, powerful notions reverberate across realities, mirroring the mid-twentieth-century ethos, styles, and ideas onto an interstellar canvas.

Riders of the Stars recounts tales not of our earthly past or future but of a unique universe, a world both familiar and markedly different.

Within this cosmic expanse, humanity embarks on its journey alongside other species, notably the grays. Before the arrival, a society filled with hope thrived—the Union of Stars (UOS)—locked in a struggle against the encroaching menace of the Democratic Worlds Alliance (DWA), an imminent communist threat. Yet, profound darkness loomed—an ancient, seemingly immortal people desired to reshape the fabric of reality. But they pushed too hard, opening a door that should have remained closed, and the Kraal arrived, driven by an insatiable quest.

The galaxy was never the same.

Power Groups

Democratic Worlds Alliance (DWA) — [defunct] A foreign power opposing the Union of Stars (UOS). While sharing cultural similarities, the DWA boasts a communist government. Tensions escalated over time, leading to fears of a looming conflict. The People's Liberators stand as remnants of the dissolved DWA government.

Galaxy Express — This prestigious pre-arrival fleet comprises luxury ships that maintain a continuous moving circuit through the stars to avoid Kraal attacks. Each ship has become a distinct sovereign entity. These ships are highly automated, featuring robot services categorized as 1-9, 2-9, 3-9, 4-9, and so forth. Securing access to these ships is extremely challenging, usually limited to those with blood relation to an existing relation. However, on rare occasions, individuals may obtain tickets through specific connections. Visiting a Galaxy Express as a non-citizen is possible but requires an invitation from a ship resident. Prominent vessels in the fleet include 6-9 and 3-9. Six-Nine hosts the Calloway Academy—an institution for exceptional children, imparting military and leadership skills to groom them as future leaders. Three-Nine has ceased communication but continues its circuit as a ghost ship.

Ordyne — Before the war, Ordyne operated as a prominent corporation with extensive connections to various other corporate entities, frequently playing a central role in military-industrial complex research projects. However, beneath its public facade lies a clandestine history dating back to the Ordus Deus Irae—a secretive organization shrouded in mystery that predates the cleansing. Led by the enigmatic figure known as Suzerain, few are aware of the organization's true origins.

Raiders and Pirates — A diverse array of land-based and space-based factions. Whether acting as opportunistic groups or under the command of ruthless warlords, these marauders have inflicted havoc on both terrestrial settlements and the space lanes. Raiders instill fear in planetary settlements, looting resources, and enslaving populations. Pirates use agile and heavily armed spacecraft to engage in theft, extortion, and illegal trade as they target trade lanes or assert dominance over regions of space.

Star Rangers — Initially the exploration arm of the UOS, the Star Rangers played a pivotal role post-collapse in uniting a new government known as the Star Federation. Often in conflict with the Wardens and Liberators, the Rangers function as pragmatic troops rather than heavily militarized forces. Troop leaders also serve as official traveling judges. Their equipment prioritizes survival, with their mech frames excelling in space capabilities, maneuverability, and shielding but lagging in ballistic capabilities compared to corps mech units.

Star Federation — A distinct entity from the UOS, the Star Federation strives to shape a new societal structure. Operating as a loosely interconnected network, they embrace a federated republic style of governance. The Star Rangers hold a seat on the senate and serve as a loosely affiliated military force. Crossing both the defunct DWA and UOS, the Star Federation does not recognize the authority of the Wardens and Liberators, viewing them on par with raiders and warlords. Each world within the Star Federation functions as an independent state. Communication within worlds relies on shortwave radios at on-world settlements and a network of couriers for interstellar connectivity.

Union of Stars (UOS) — [defunct] The original government of over three-quarters of the known star systems, now colloquially known as "the old Union." Apprehension of a conflict with the DWA triggered the widespread construction of nuclear shelters and enclaves on both sides. The Wardens, remnants of the UOS military, adamantly assert their legitimacy and reject the term "Old Union."

Wardens — Originating from a collective of generals spanning the original Army, Sky, and Fleet Corps of the UOS to combat the Kraal menace, they ultimately resorted to nuclear strikes on the worlds they sought to protect. Driven by the belief that dispersing populations will ultimately force the Kraal to retreat and vanish, the Wardens display fervent dedication, zealously obliterating settlements or gatherings perceived as overly substantial. While rejecting the authority of the Star Federation, they reluctantly acknowledge the authority of the Star Rangers, even forming treaties to demarcate separate territories of control.

Arcadia (world) — A UOS planet where the Atom Bomb Baby saga unfolds, Arcadia was originally among the larger worlds of the Union of Stars.

Bunkers, Enclaves, Vaults — Fearing escalating nuclear tensions between the UOS and DWA, underground shelters proliferated. Enclaves are town-sized shelters with completely closed-loop ecosystems, usually created by local municipalities. In contrast, Bunkers generally refer to smaller complexes suited for only a handful of people. Vaults are shelters specifically oriented to storing critical information, technology, or other items (such as notable people placed into cryosleep to avoid attracting the Kraal). Despite their size, they usually don't have enough life-support systems for more than a handful of people. Vaults are sought after by many as a trove of valuable supplies. SAINT works hard to keep the government vaults hidden.

Fenclave — Situated in Arcadia, Fenclave refers to the Fen Enclave established by the local county government (a common word suffix, "-clave," denotes enclaves). Managed by the Commissioner, appointed before the arrival, it played a crucial role in the region's survival strategy.

Miratori (world) — The world where Rainwood and Moonbeam came from before visiting Arcadia.

AM-25 Rifle — The workhorse of the UOS military, this is a semi-automatic to automatic rifle that supports many configurations.

Arbiter (Rifle) — An elite version of the AM-25 specifically designed for special forces.

Autocannon, Chaingun — Large-caliber cannons featuring fixed barrels (as opposed to the rotating barrels of a Minigun). These are too hefty for Mech armor frames but are deployed on larger vehicles like the HWG-125 transport and Airships.

Mechanized Armor (Mechs) — Along with robots come many human-type mechanized vehicles for exploration and warfare, including mechanized suits of armor (aka Mechs). Mechs are suits of articulated, mechanized armor, which often will include environmental seals, allowing soldiers to be in many extreme conditions—although not all units can support the vacuum of space.

Within the UOS, there were three generations of mech frames:

> **First Gen** — Ogre (MA-15)
> **Second Gen** — Griffin (MA-27)
> **Third Gen** — Banshee (MA-35)

The first-generation Ogre frames are the most prevalent, with the Griffin reasonably being less common, while the Banshees remain rare—being only in early development during the arrival. Designations for mech frames with vacuum/space capabilities conclude with an S, such as MA-35S. Rangers use an MR-xx frame naming system instead. Ranger frames are always space-worthy, boasting agility and jet packs while sacrificing some ballistic armament.

HWG-125 "Hog" Transport — A common military transport aircraft with tilt-thrust jet pods mounted on the ends of stubby wings to support vertical and horizontal flight modes.

M-150 Rifle — A sniper's long-range rifle.

Minigun - GA5 and GA7 — A rotary barrel Gatling-style machine gun common throughout all three branches of the Union Corps. It must be fixed to a hard-mount (such as on a mech), as it's too powerful to be used by an individual. The GA5 fires a smaller caliber bullet (5mm) vs the 7mm used by the GA7.

Chapter Titles

Perceptive readers may have noticed that the chapter titles serve multiple purposes—they are Song Titles but also hold a thematic connection (even if only in name) to the contents of the respective chapter. The songs featured are contemporary with the time of the arrival—they aren't nostalgic "oldies," regardless of whether they are old-time songs in our world. Visit our community chat service at https://RidersOfTheStars.com to discuss other easter eggs and see if you found them all.

Pistol Packin' Mama — Bing Crosby

Crazy He Calls Me — Billie Holiday

Straighten Up and Fly Right — Nat King Cole

It's All Over But the Crying — The Ink Spots

Nobody's Fault but Mine — Blind Willie Johnson

In a Shanty in Old Shanty Town — (Various) / Johnny Long

Ring of Fire — Johnny Cash

Ol' Man Mose — Eddy Duchin and Patricia Norman

Just a Fair Weather Friend — Henry King

Run For Your Life — The Beatles

Return to Sender — Elvis Presley

We Three (My Echo, My Shadow and Me) — The Ink Spots

In My Room — The Beach Boys

Catch a Falling Star — Perry Como

Just In Time — Frank Sinatra

Poor Little Fool — Ricky Nelson

Civilization (Bongo, Bongo, Bongo) — Andrews Sisters & Danny Kaye

I'm a Believer — The Monkees

Into Each Life Some Rain Must Fall — The Ink Spots

Wouldn't It Be Nice? — The Beach Boys

Ain't That A Kick In The Head — Dean Martin

The Man Comes Around — Johnny Cash

These Boots Are Made for Walking — Nancy Sinatra

Keep Me In Your Heart — Warren Zevon

Jump In Line — Harry Belafonte

Epilogue

Glenn waited patiently as the Galaxy Express 3-9 airlock cycled, his feet planted on the deck while he anxiously held his bag with clammy hands. He hoped they would give him a decent room, but he'd accept an interior closet at this point.

The signal light switched from red to green, the inner door opened, and a yawning darkness greeted him.

Glenn hesitated, his boots anchored to the cold deck as if some primal instinct warned him of the shadows lurking beyond.

With a reluctant step, he entered the ship but stayed within the beam cast by the airlock's lights, squinting to see beyond, his vision less than stellar to begin with.

The airlock door closed, and his sliver of light shrunk to nothing, leaving him in pitch darkness.

Dread built in his chest as he waited, the palpable silence broken only by the erratic cadence of his breaths.

His imagination conjured images in the dark, attempting to make sense of the void—contorted shapes, an eye, a hand reaching for him.

The air grew dense with impending terror.

An unseen presence brushed against Glenn's skin, accompanied by skittering sounds.

The shapes took on form.

Faces.

Teeth.

On a world far, far away, Suzerain descended a series of archaic stone stairs. His sole companion, a mere flashlight, struggled to push back the ancient shadows, its light occasionally revealing glimpses of the alien architecture and chiseled glyphs surrounding him.

Upon reaching the terminus of the stairs, Suzerain entered a chamber so immense the impenetrable darkness defied his feeble illumination. Even the scratch of his feet dissipated into the vast emptiness as he approached the edge of a yawning abyss.

A noxious, rotten breeze stirred the otherwise still air.

What initially appeared as a 10-foot wide pillar on the ledge's side shifted, unveiling its true nature as a link in a colossal chain.

Suzerain cast his gaze downward where a dim, otherworldly light flickered, revealing ominous shadows and glimpses of a titanic horror within the stygian depths. A tentacled head emerged through the deepening gloom, its face a mass of feelers adorned with spider-like eyes—each glimmering with an inner, malevolent fire that spun with an unnatural violet intensity.

The magnitude of the eldritch god's size defied estimation. The colossal chains descended to wrap prodigious clawed hands as if they were simple bindings, hinting at the awe-inspiring scale of the entity bound in the shadows below.

Suzerain felt, more than heard, the grumble of abhorrent discontent.

About the Author

During the day, Brandon serves as a VP of Engineering. He is a video game and open-source pioneer, avid programmer (language of choice: Elixir), technology architect, serial entrepreneur, game designer, writer, and artist. His diverse expertise includes building numerous startups and companies.

Although initially pursuing English and Graphic Arts with an interest in Film, Brandon unexpectedly found his way into Computer Science. It was during this time that he met his lovely and patient wife. Throughout his career, Brandon has achieved numerous accomplishments, such as his team receiving the Innovator of the Year award from Redhat, and in his capacity as an executive consultant, he provided counsel to the CIO of a three-letter federal agency known for collecting foreign intelligence.

Residing with his family in the Rocky Mountains, Brandon takes pleasure in outdoor activities. Above all, he harbors a deep passion for sci-fi and fantasy and has crafted many captivating stories, games, and settings.

Author's Note

Thank you for taking the time to read this story; I hope you enjoyed it as much as I did writing it. If you could kindly leave a review on Amazon or your favorite social reading sites and share it with your friends, it would mean the world to me as an independent author. A star rating or your thoughts as a review, even a simple note, is invaluable. Reviews and ratings help authors like me tremendously, and word of mouth is the most powerful form of support. Thank you for your kindness!

To receive notices on new book releases, short stories, and other content, visit the website: `https://RidersOfTheStars.com`

www.ingramcontent.com/pod-product-compliance
Lightning Source LLC
Chambersburg PA
CBHW061011120726
47910CB00006B/1872